THE LOVE TRAP

BOOK THREE OF THE QUICKSILVER TRILOGY

NICOLE FRENCH

To Eric. Wherever you are, you are missed.

PRELUDE

1996

Eric turned the book upside down, then back over. He had been looking at the thing for days, and he couldn't understand why his father was so obsessed with it. As far as he could tell, it was just a book. An old, moth-eaten, chewed-up hunk of pages that smelled like mothballs and stale coffee. You couldn't even read the thing—it was all in Latin.

And yet, just the other week, when his mother had threatened to toss it out, his father had gotten angry. And Jacob de Vries never got angry. Irritated, sure. Melancholy at times, maybe. But mostly, Eric's father was affable and easygoing, the kind of man who could make anyone smile. He was never angry.

Except about this book.

"He's a bully, Jake. He's dangerous."

Eric shrank into the love seat at the sound of his parents jogging down the stairs of the townhouse. His mother entered the living room first in a huff, followed by his dad carrying his monogrammed Vuitton overnight bag.

"Johnny just wants what he can't have, hen. He always has. And he'll get over it, just like he always does."

Heather turned around in front of the big bay window that looked out onto East Sixty-Seventh Street. "You say that like he didn't try to—"

"John's bark has always been worse than his bite, sunshine."

Eric remained stone-still, listening to one of his parents' rare arguments unfold. He had learned long ago that silence was sometimes a better tactic than speaking up, especially in this family. It was like one of Grandmother's favorite quotes: "Speak softly and carry a big stick." Teddy Roosevelt said that. Eric hadn't found a big enough stick yet (he wouldn't have been allowed one in the apartment anyway), but he had definitely learned the benefits of quiet.

"That's because you've never given him anything to chew on!" Heather swept around, making her paisley skirt twirl.

"And I'm not going to start now," Jacob cut back.

Then Eric's father paused, and as he looked at Heather, his face transformed. Gone was the haloed, carefree man Eric generally knew. Jacob was the golden heir of the de Vries family. Its fatted calf, he liked to joke. His purpose in life was to be its symbol of youth until his mother, Celeste, passed her fortune to him, and he generally took that to mean he should offer comic relief whenever possible. But when he looked at his wife, Jacob de Vries's boyish charm evaporated. He resembled a Viking more than an indulgent heir.

"Is that what you want?" he asked almost dangerously. "Is it the fight you want to see? Maybe you want him to win after all. Is that it?"

If his father had looked at him that way, Eric would have escaped immediately up the stairs. Yet Heather seemed almost drawn to her husband. She remained perfectly still as he stalked toward her. Their faces nearly touched. She lifted her chin and met her husband's glare straight-on.

"I never did," she said. "And I never will."

Jacob took his wife's chin between two fingers and tipped her face left, then right, like he was examining a piece of fruit, checking for bruises.

"Good," he said finally. "Because that would be a damn waste, and you know it."

Was it Eric, or did his mother glow at the brooding words?

"Jake, please," she whispered, her jaw tight between Jacob's fingers. "Don't go. *Please.* Just stay home."

For a moment, Eric dared to hope that his father would obey. Neither of them liked it when he went on these trips—sailing excursions without clear destinations. Some lasted days. Others weeks. "His one rebellion," Eric's grandmother called them. But Dad was an excellent sailor, Eric reminded himself. He always came home to his family.

And so, instead of answering his wife's pleas, Jacob kissed her. Eric observed with a sort of morbid curiosity the way his mother's bone structure seemed to dissolve in his father's arms. Jacob held her up with a broad hand around her waist, the other at her neck. He kissed Heather for a long time, until they were both out of breath, and the sun cast slightly longer shadows through the drawing room.

When he released her, Jacob was smiling again, one of his eyebrows raised like a villain's.

Heather giggled. Eric made a face. She sounded like the girls at school—the ones who always seemed to have endless questions and comments for him these days. Like Nina's friend, Caitlyn, the one Aunt Violet had let stay the summer with them. She always liked to pretend she and Eric were married. He didn't understand why all the girls seemed to want Prince Charming to save them. Why couldn't they learn to save themselves? What was wrong with that?

So, when his parents started to kiss again, Eric wasn't curious at all anymore. Just grossed out.

"Ahem."

At the sound of their son, his parents sprang apart, both of their faces flushed.

Jacob coughed. "Eric. Kid. You, ah, been there long?"

Eric shrugged. "Just reading."

Heather's face turned even pinker as she adjusted her blouse and reset her pearl necklace.

"When I get home, you had better be waiting for me, sunshine," Jacob said to her with a wink. "In that piece I bought last week, if you know what's good for you."

"Dad!" Eric had had enough. "Do I need to leave the room?"

Jacob chuckled, pinched Heather's waist, then danced away from her swat as he crossed the room to Eric. His normal corona—the one that seemed to draw everyone to him—was back in place. Eric relaxed. This was the dad he knew.

"Sorry about that, kid," Jacob said as he squatted next to Eric's chair. "You'll understand one day."

Eric shrugged. "Mom likes it when you kiss her. I can deal with it. To a point."

His father laughed, a broad, booming clap that filled the room. "You watch, kid. One day, you're going to find a girl you can't stop kissing either."

Eric made another face. "I don't think so."

Jacob's laugh boomed again. "It gets worse, too. Soon you'll do anything to make her smile. Make a complete fool of yourself just for an extra glance." He looked at Heather, who was patting her hair in the mirror above the console. "Right, hen?"

Heather's smiled, but it wasn't bright and warm. It was almost sad. "Only if he's very lucky."

They looked at each other for a long time, and once again, it was like they had forgotten Eric was in the room despite the fact that he was no more than a foot from his father.

He cleared his throat again.

Jacob jerked, and Heather turned back to the mirror.

"What's that you're reading?" Jacob asked, pointing to the book.

Eric held up the ancient volume. "It's yours. I saw it in the living room."

"*The Aeneid*? Really?" Jacob looked surprised. "I would have thought that a bit above your paygrade, kid. It's all in Latin."

"Mrs. Hendrix made us learn some last year," Eric said. "But I don't really understand it."

"Well, twenty grand is a lot for school, but I wasn't expecting fluency in a dead language before at least fourteen." Jacob took the book and thumbed through it with familiarity. "You have to be careful with this, you know."

"I don't know why you like it so much if it's this hard to read," Eric remarked.

His father shrugged good-naturedly—a family trait. "It's a classic."

"Just because it's a classic doesn't mean it's good."

"Some parts of it are good. Others are just important."

"What's it about?"

Jacob flipped through the pages again, zooming past yellow- and pink-highlighted passages with yards of scribble in the margins—also in Latin. "It's about a Trojan traveler. Aeneas. He starts a journey after the sacking of Troy."

"Troy? Like my friend at school?"

"Troy as in Helen of," Jacob replied with another wink at Heather, who was watching them through the mirror. "A woman almost as pretty as your mom. For whom a giant battle was waged."

"Oh, please," Heather said, though she was clearly unbothered by the comparison.

"Troy was a city?" Eric asked.

"Yes," Jacob agreed. "And in the story, after the Greeks take it over, Aeneas escapes with his merry men, wanders for a while, and eventually ends up in Italy, where he fights Turnus and becomes an ancestor of the founders of Rome. It's an origin story of sorts."

"Is that why Grandmother calls Mom 'Helen' sometimes?" Eric asked. He flipped through the pages of *The Aeneid* until he came to a part where he had seen the familiar name: Helena. "Who fought over her, then?"

"No one," Heather put in too quickly.

"And it doesn't matter anyway," Jacob added. "Grandma just likes to stir up trouble."

Eric narrowed his eyes. "She doesn't like being called Grandma, Dad."

But his father's eyes just twinkled with mischief. "Which is exactly why I do, kid. Someone has to give old Grams a run for her piles of money, don't you think? If everyone does exactly what she wants, she'll start thinking she's better than us."

Eric snorted. Grandmother already thought that.

Jacob ruffled Eric's hair, then returned to Heather. Eric watched him wrap his hands around her waist, and yet again, it was like they were alone. Jacob set his chin on his wife's shoulder, and together they gazed into the mirror.

"My Helen of Troy," Jacob said, so low Eric almost couldn't hear him. "I'd fight a million wars for you."

For a moment, Eric wished he had a camera. His parents looked at each other's reflections with such naked adoration. He wondered if every marriage was like theirs. Aunt Violet and Uncle Christian seemed to hate each other most of the time. Come to think of it, he didn't know anyone in his family who actually seemed to enjoy their spouse's company.

"Come here, hen."

Jacob turned Heather around and gave her one last kiss that made the console bump against the wall behind them. This time, Eric didn't clear his throat. He didn't make a sound. A warm feeling glowed in his belly, and he didn't want it to stop.

When Jacob finished, Heather's cheeks were bright red again, her patted hair out of place once more. But her eyes shone like the stars in the sky, the ones Eric could only see on Long Island when they went to the summer house, far from the city. Jacob murmured something in her ear that made her gasp.

"Jake!" She batted his shoulder, but that only earned her one last kiss before she was released.

Jacob grabbed his bag off the floor. "That book. It's important, Eric."

"I'll take care of it, Dad."

Father and son traded meaningful looks. Then, Jacob nodded. "I'm off, then. Take care of your mother too, will you?"

Eric nodded back. "I will, Dad. I promise."

———

Present

Eric woke to his father's voice echoing through the jail cell.

Aeneas.

Helena.

Heather's eyes.

"Take care of your mother."

Was that really the last thing his father had ever said to him? It was nearly twenty-three years since Jacob had left that day and never come back. Twenty-three years since his mother had smiled like that. Twenty-three years since he had a real, full family.

A guard's baton clanged on the cell door. "De Vries. Visitor."

Eric frowned. He wasn't expecting Jane today. His hearing was imminent, so he had told her on Monday not to bother. He didn't like the idea of her or their child-to-be in this disgusting place. The conditions at Rikers were notorious for mistreating visitors nearly as poorly as inmates. Eric himself had little to worry about. Bribery was easy enough, and being one of New York's most prominent citizens helped too. But Jane was a different story. All he wanted to do was keep her safe.

Not, of course, that she would ever listen to him.

Eric followed the guard through the same routine he'd been following for close to two weeks now. Search, wait. Change, wait. Hustle across the compound to the big converted gym they used as a communal visitors' area for his particular cell block.

But instead of Jane, or even Nina (who had visited once over the last miserable twelve days), he found his mother sitting at the far end of the room, hands clasped primly over her deep brown Birkin bag, the rest of her covered with a conservative knit thing Jane had once called a poncho.

"*Little known fact,*" *Jane said one evening while she paged through a back issue of* Vogue. "*Every time a designer renders a culturally appropriated artifact in beige, a star at the far end of the universe dies a terrible, colorless death. Case in point: this poncho.*"

God, he missed her. It didn't matter that like clockwork, she had been here every other day during visiting hours to see him. It wasn't enough. Not even close.

He had gone to sleep every night in that godforsaken cell, broken springs poking his back while he plotted all the ways to find John Carson and wring his fucking neck. It was only imagining Jane—her soft skin, her wry smile, her dancing eyes—that kept his fury at bay. He needed her like he needed water. Air. It was a dangerous thing, this kind of love—an obsession. He was beginning to understand how it drove the poets crazy. How it started wars.

"Mom." Eric accepted an aerated kiss on the cheek from Heather, who seemed almost scared to touch him.

"Eric." She sat back in her chair, looking like she deeply regretted wearing such light-colored clothes.

Eric sat too and pushed a hand through his hair. It was still wet—today he'd been allowed to shower before coming out. He took every opportunity for hygiene he could in this place.

"So, this is a surprise," he said.

"They said...they said I could bring you some reading material." She held up a book and set it on the table. A guard, no doubt paid off handsomely, gave her the privilege of bringing something inside without submitting it for inspection. "I don't know what you did to anger John Carson, but, Eric, I must urge you—leave it alone."

Eric eyed the small black volume, then his mother. "You have to know it's too late for that."

Heather sighed. "Are you absolutely sure?"

"This is Jane, Mom. *My* wife. No one on this planet has a claim to her other than me. But maybe you wouldn't understand."

"You don't think I—" She cut herself off with a sigh. "I did love your father, you know."

"Is that why you remarried less than a year after he died?"

Heather's primrose mouth dropped. "I—" She shook her head. "Honestly, Eric, I wouldn't expect you to grasp the intricacies of that situation. All I can say is that I did love Jacob. I loved him very much."

Eric folded his mouth tightly. If jumping straight into another marriage was love, then Heather only confirmed all his suspicions about his tundra of a family. None of them ever comprehended what love was at all.

All the more reason he needed Jane.

"You're so like him," Heather murmured.

Eric glanced up sharply. "Who, Carson?"

"No, your father."

Eric shifted uncomfortably under the sudden intensity of his mother's gaze. He wasn't used to this kind of directness from her.

"For a time, I mused how you were even mine, for how much the two of you resembled one another." She swallowed visibly. "It wasn't easy, you know. You were a constant reminder of him after he was gone."

Eric wasn't sure how to respond to that. Was it an apology for all the years of neglect and distance? When his father was alive, at least he could remember times they had spent as a family. His childhood had still been regimented, as any de Vries's childhood would be. Facilitated mostly by hired help. But he did remember that his parents had been happy. And in those moments, *he* had been happy.

Until a sailing accident ruined everything.

After that, he hardly remembered Heather's presence. She had remarried, and Eric had ended up living in Grandmother's fusty old penthouse until he could escape to Dartmouth. At least at Grandmother's he didn't sit alone in his room listening to his mother cry or entertain strangers. At least there someone cared enough to talk to him, even if it was to criticize and dictate.

And Heather hadn't fought the decision. She hadn't fought it one bit.

"Okay," Eric said, unwilling to fight her now. "And anyway, it's fine. I'm not alone in this. Jane and the Sterlings are working with the legal team. I'll be out of here in no time."

"But—oh, dear, you really don't know, do you?" Heather asked. "Eric, Jane's gone."

Suddenly his skin felt pricked by a thousand needles. "Come again?"

He had just seen her two days ago, sitting in the middle of this very room in a pair of black leather pants, a bright magenta sweater, and her favorite combat boots like she owned the joint.

"I have to wear them while I can," she'd said about the pants. *"My tits are already the size of Honeycrisp apples, dude, so you know my ass is next. This baby is barely bigger than a peanut, and it's already eating us out of house and home."*

It had been all he could do not to leap over the cheap plastic table and kiss her. Fuck the rules. Fuck the jail. He and Jane weren't supposed to be separated. It was unnatural.

"I'm so sorry. But that's what I'm here to tell you. That, and to give you the book."

"What the fuck do you mean she's gone?" His voice was sharp enough to catch the attention of the guard patrolling the scattered visitors.

Heather sighed. "She—oh, darling, Nina should have come instead. It was all very sudden..." She drifted off, clearly ashamed. "Jane departed for Seoul early this morning."

"She's in *Seoul?*" Eric's heart turned to ice. "Jesus fucking Christ, Mom. She went to South Korea?"

There was only one reason Jane would have left for Korea just a few days before his court date. She, or the investigator she'd hired, had found something about the whereabouts of Yu-na, Jane's mother, who had recently gone missing, likely abducted by John Carson. Something bad. Something that would have taken Jane, pregnant and vulnerable, to another fucking hemisphere while Eric was wasting away.

But instead of exploding the way he wanted, Eric swallowed back his emotions. Heather looked more than a little scared of him, and the guard behind her was ready to pounce.

"I assume she left contact information," Eric said at last.

"Of course. And Nina gave her the plane to use. She took your security team too. All of them. She said you wouldn't forgive her otherwise."

The fact that Jane had left with four of the largest men in New York only made him feel marginally better. Fuck. *Fuck.* She couldn't have just waited a few more days? Despite the fact that Carson had managed to keep Eric locked up for almost two weeks, the legal team seemed to think it would be no problem to have the suit tossed now that they had finagled a change in judges. After all, there was no evidence to stand on. The whole thing was a farce.

Eric sucked in another breath, then picked up the book again and flipped through the pages. "Is this—this is Dad's journal, isn't it?"

It was a black Moleskine, the same kind Eric had used since he was eleven or so. One more way he had unconsciously paid homage to his father over the years. It started in 1983 and continued through 1996, stopping a week or so before Jacob's death.

Eric opened one of the early sections.

May 14, 1983

All hail the conquering graduates! Or should I say just Heather? Back to Princeton for her ceremony. So many old memories.
Portas was open this week as well, and the vote is in. Johnny was disappointed, but could he really have been that

surprised? The DV have been making Caesar salads since the early 1800s, longer than his family has even been here. Pop made a great one; Grandad too. Shouldn't I have a go at it? The party was fun. Mom made the trip too. Everyone getting along famously, even Johnny. Heather has really charmed her way in, angel girl.

I plan to take her rowing tomorrow on Carnegie Lake. I'll propose with mom's ring. After all, it's where we first met.

Eric looked up. "Why haven't I seen this before? You gave me all the others."

"I—it will tell you a story better than I can," Heather said. "Perhaps you'll understand why I think you should let this go with John Carson. I know you love her, Eric, but she's gone now. Maybe it's better that you let her be."

"She went to get her mother, Mom. She didn't leave *me*. She's—" He started to say Jane was pregnant, but stopped. Jane told Skylar, but they had otherwise decided to keep it to themselves for the time being. To keep everyone safe.

Heather looked like she wanted to say something else, but before she could, Eric pushed back from his chair. He needed to figure some shit out, and hopefully get a call to his attorney. Above all, he needed to get the fuck out of here and find his wife.

"Eric?"

He turned around. Heather was standing now, hands clasped in front of the beige wool.

"I'm sorry," she said. "Really, I am."

Eric blinked. Sorry for what? For her absence? Her lack of mothering? For what John Carson was doing to his life, or for the fact that she wanted him to let him do it?

"It's fine," he said, not knowing *what*, exactly, was fine.

And then he turned, gripping the journal with white-knuckled fingers as he left the crowded room.

PART ONE

SINGLET

I woke with light in my eyes,
The sun seeped at a slant,
And I sat up straight, though my head
Nearly crashed on the cement.
She flew away, a cudgeled bird,
A dove without her peace,
And left me here with rents her loss
Had torn from my chest.
I mourned and cried, but in the end,
I can't forget her face.
It's how I learned much more than love,
My marriage needed grace.

"Grace"
—from the journal of Eric de Vries

ONE

Present

There was no way around it. The man was dead.

He was dead when I arrived in Korea after an almost fifteen-hour flight.

He was dead after the hour car ride to Suwon from the Incheon airport outside of Seoul.

He was dead when I identified the body at the morgue and began the very long process of sending it back to Lawrence Kim's second cousin in San Francisco, who, along with the Suwon police, was very curious to know *why* the private investigator had been found face-down in a fallow melon field.

Sudden heart failure, said the coroner. At the ripe old age of thirty-six.

Dead, dead, dead.

"Shit," Skylar said when I told her.

From the hotel penthouse's sixteenth-floor picture window, the Suwon skyline glimmered in the night, then faded to a sudden black where the city's busy neighborhoods gave way to a massive park, then eons of rice paddies, farms, and nurseries. I pressed my forehead against the glass, eager to feel the chill counteracting the heat that seemed to course through my body all the time now. Being approximately eight weeks pregnant apparently turned me into a furnace. It also made me miss my husband. A lot.

"That's one word for it," I muttered. "Fucking hell."

"You sound like Eric."

I winced. I *did* sound like Eric, who was probably going to use the same exact phrase when he discovered where I was. "I just don't know what to do next."

"Did you talk to your cousins?" Skylar asked, referring to Suejean and her mother, Ji-yeon, some of the few Korean relatives we had a close relationship with in Chicago.

"I did. Suejean said we have some extended family in the area, but I don't know them. My mom didn't keep in touch with anyone after she left, you know? What am I going to do, show up and say, 'Hey, it's me, the half-breed daughter of the whore cousin who shamed the entire family! Want to help me find her?'"

"I think that's unfair, Janey. And honestly, kind of selfish."

I sighed, letting the condensation from my breath cloud the glass. I drew a heart through the fading smudge, then the letter E before the whole thing disappeared.

Skylar was right, of course. I couldn't let a little thing like family estrangement stop me from finding my mother. And the truth was, I had no clue what my mother's relationship had been like with her family—only that her mom died when she was little, and her father a few years after she left. Some cousins had moved to Chicago when I was growing up (Ji-yeon, for instance). But I had never seen my mother call anyone in Korea. Never seen a single birthday or Christmas gift with *hangul* on the packaging. Not a card, a photo. Nothing. As far as I knew, her relationship with her birth country had been completely severed the moment she met my father—whichever one of them.

"The detective at the station was nice," I said lamely. "He said if I came back tomorrow, he would help."

"He spoke English?"

"He did, thank God. A lot of people here seem to speak English pretty well, so maybe I don't need a translator after all." I considered Jae-ho, the translator that Eric's assistant hired while I was en route from New York. Jae-ho was a diminutive graduate student of linguistics at one of the Seoul universities. His glasses were even thicker than mine. After discovering that the detective assigned to Lawrence Kim's body didn't require an interpreter, he had just loitered awkwardly behind us for a solid hour until I had asked him politely to take a car back to the hotel. I'd see him the next morning.

To do what, I still wasn't sure.

"Well, that's something," Skylar said. "I'm sure the detective will help."

"Yeah," I said. "I'm sure."

"How are you feeling? Traveling almost twenty-four hours straight while pregnant? I can't even imagine it."

"That's because you were puking your guts out by this point. No one likes being sick on a plane."

"No one likes being sick, period." She didn't even bother to disguise the loathing in her voice. Skylar had been sick as a dog throughout most of her pregnancy, and I did wonder if she hoped a little too eagerly that I would suffer the same fate. Misery does love company.

"I'm fine," I replied. "Tired, but I don't know if that's because I'm knocked up or because I've barely slept since Monday."

"Not even a little?"

"Sorry, dude. I wish I could commiserate, but the bun seems pretty happy in the oven so far."

Skylar heaved an irritable sigh. "Some people get all the luck. What about your sonogram? Aren't you supposed to have a scan at eight weeks?"

"Well, yeah. But I'll have to do it here," I replied. "Suejean gave me the names of a few good doctors in Suwon. I have an appointment."

"Was it awful...seeing the body?"

"You are really determined to make me feel terrible, aren't you?" I backed away from the picture window and sat on the bed, fatigue sinking into my bones. "It wasn't...I don't know. It was just a body."

Prior to last week, when I'd received the phone call from the Korean police about Kim's death, the P.I. had only been a name to me. Hired by Brandon, not Eric or me, in order to get around John Carson's potential suspicions. Kim was terse, to the point, but more importantly, trustworthy after coming highly recommended by Matthew Zola. Since he was also a Korean, he had happily continued the lucrative work to collect information about my mother's where-abouts, but beyond that, he was a stranger.

He had found Carson almost immediately in Suwon, the larger city on the eastern side of the Hwaseong area. It hadn't taken long, he said. There were limited four-star accommodations here, not to mention a tall, rich white man with curly hair, piercing hazel eyes, and a hooked nose was fairly conspicuous in this part of the world.

Unfortunately, Kim hadn't been stealthy enough. The coroner said his death was of natural causes, but even after identifying the markless body, I didn't buy it for a second.

Found in a melon field. Found in a melon field.

I didn't know why, but something about that statement sounded very familiar.

"And you have the security with you, right?" Skylar used her mothering voice, like she was asking her daughter whether she had remembered her raincoat.

"The gorilla squad? Why, yes, but I might be running out of bananas for them."

"Jane..."

"I know, I know. Yes, Tony and the others are shadowing me everywhere, I promise. You can tell that to Eric too when you see him, okay? Tell him I *know* it's important. And that I won't go anywhere by myself." I rubbed my forehead. "I don't even want to think about what he's going to say when he finds out I'm gone."

"Actually, I think he already knows."

I straightened. "*What?*"

"Nina was going to meet with him and his lawyer tomorrow before the trial starts, but his mom offered to do it today when she went to visit."

"His *mom*? Sky, are you kidding me?"

There was an awkward silence. "No...why?"

"Skylar, Eric barely has a relationship with Heather. You really think the best person to inform him that I had to leave the country two days before his trial was her?"

"She said she had something to give him anyway," Skylar said weakly. "A book, I think. Nina and I both thought it was the right thing to do." Behind her, I heard a vague murmuring male voice that sounded like it was saying, "I told you so, Red." Brandon, no doubt, chiming in on my side.

"Shit," I said. "Oh my God, I bet he freaked, didn't he?"

"Eric doesn't really freak."

"Says who?"

Skylar thought she knew him, but she didn't even scratch the surface. Eric was better than almost anyone at masking his true emotions. He would put on a calm, implacable face that hid whatever turmoil he might be experiencing, but I knew the truth. A whole host of passions simmered under that stoic surface, and I had been on the receiving end of them from time to time—usually when I pressed his buttons. If he wasn't careful, if he was pushed too hard, I was genuinely worried that one day, Eric would burst beyond repair.

"Just...Sky, be careful with him, okay?"

"Careful?" My friend was genuinely surprised. "You want me to be careful with Eric?"

My heart expanded in my chest. "You're surprised." Of course she was. Most people knew Eric and me as antagonizers of one another. Was it my fault they didn't know what we truly were? Even my best friend?

"I—you know what, no. I'm not," Skylar said.

I sighed, relieved. At least someone knew.

"I love him so much, Sky," I said softly, fighting not to hide my face, even thought I was the only one who could see it in the window reflection. "I wish I were there. I hate, hate, *hate* that he has to stand up in that court without me."

My friend paused, like she was feeling everything with me. "Oh, Janey. He knows you love him."

"Does he?"

We both knew the truth. It's not like I had made it easy for him over the years. Or even the past several months. I was many things, but an easy person to love wasn't one of them.

I was torn in half. On the one hand, my husband, the father of my child, love of my utter fucking life, was about to be put on trial for a crime he didn't commit, a crime that my megalomaniacal biological father had framed him for as a repercussion for marrying *me*. I should be there. I was the entire reason for this bullshit, and now I had deserted him.

But on the other hand, my mother had been abducted by said bio-dad not two weeks before. Eric, Skylar, and Brandon had all been convinced that I should absolutely *not* go in search of her. She was bait, they said. Me leaving was exactly what Carson wanted. To lure me away. Separate the unit Eric and I had become.

Well, now he had gotten his wish. Because the only link I had to my mother was sleeping with the fishes, so to speak, and now she had no one else in the world who could find her. I wasn't abandoning her in this country now. But apparently that meant abandoning my husband instead.

Rock, meet hard place. And then crush me hopelessly between the two of you.

Skylar's pause was as pregnant as I was.

"Well, I won't let him forget it," she said at last. "We'll get him out of there in no time. Brandon is even consulting with his lawyer, and they got a new judge too."

I shook my head. "Really?"

"Just last night. The lawyer motioned for an extension on account of bias—to no one's surprise and shock, the previous judge and Jude Letour are members of the same Princeton society and have a weekly squash date."

"Of course they are." I was only just beginning to realize how deeply the nepotistic ties of the Janus society really ran.

"Anyway, there will be a new hearing tomorrow about the case. Brandon thinks there is a good chance the new judge will throw the whole thing out. If I know Eric, he'll probably be on a plane the second the judge bangs the gavel."

I cringed. I was in big trouble for being here. But I had to come, and Eric would be the first to tell me. My mother was missing. A madman had abducted her. And the only person we had sent into the fray had been found dead.

I couldn't risk another person's life for my family drama. And I couldn't just leave my mother alone either.

I fell back onto the bed again. It was the kind of bed Eric would have liked, big enough for his long limbs to splay, and wide enough he could toss me around however he wanted. Right now, though, I wouldn't have been the slightest bit interested. Fatigue was drawing over me like a thick cloak, and this time, I couldn't fight it off, even as nerves warred within my stomach.

I turned onto my side to where the contents of Kim's files were spread across the bed. I had intended to go through them all tonight before meeting with the detective, but now I wasn't sure I could keep my eyes open long enough to read the first page of notes. I needed to read them, though. I needed to determine everything I could about this case so I could hopefully solve it myself and go home.

"Tomorrow," I murmured to myself, promising a future I couldn't quite see.

Skylar continued to chatter about what she thought would happen in Eric's hearing. But before long, her words blended. I fell asleep with my face plastered against four newsprint clippings from 1987.

TWO

2009

"Someone get me a whiskey."

I grinned at my new roommate. We were both sweaty messes after spending the day running around Harvard Law School orientation events like a couple of frantic hamsters, but Skylar, with her bright red hair and freckled skin, was more flustered than most. HLS didn't mess around. Today alone we had listened to a supreme court justice, followed by a couple of deans, section leaders, and then we had attended the LAWn party for the entire five-hundred-student entering class.

We were beat. And thirsty.

Cleo's, the dank, unofficially official bar for HLS students a few blocks off Harvard Square, offered just the thing. I ordered Skylar a whiskey soda—I'd learned the girl's drink preferences within minutes of meeting her—and myself an ice cold PBR. It was late August in Boston. I would have thrown myself naked into the bar's ice bin if that were socially acceptable.

Skylar grabbed the stool next to me and pulled a list of internships already accepting applications for the next summer from her orientation packet.

"Sky, are you serious?" I said, trying to bat the thing away. "We're done for the day. Put that away."

"That's easy for you to say," she said, dodging my reach. "Your dad already has you set up with an internship with the state's attorney's office, right? Not everyone has those kinds of connections."

"Christ on a cracker, Ms. Crosby. We haven't even started classes yet. And my dad's a VA employee, not the Illinois governor. He hasn't set me up—he dropped my name at the office." I didn't mention that the current SA had also been my dad's college roommate at Urbana. Skylar was a little bitter about the nepotism at Harvard.

"I'm still behind the curve." She took a sip of her drink and made a couple of emphatic check marks on the list.

"I thought you said your mom was helping you with law school," I said. "Why are you so stressed about this?"

"Financially, yes. But we don't really talk much. And my dad doesn't really meet a whole lot of movers and shakers while emptying their garbage." She pointed at a few of the bottom listings. "This one is promising. Sterling Grove is one of the top ten firms on the East Coast."

I made a face. "If you want to work for a corporate bloodsucker, they seem like a good choice."

"Well, I'm coming from a corporate bloodsucking background. It would make sense to capitalize on it."

I took a long swig of my PBR. "Aren't you trying to get away from that, though?" All I knew about Skylar's time in the finance sector was that she hated it. "Or is Patrick trying to talk you back into it?"

The new pink in her already flushed face told me I was spot-on. Skylar's boyfriend still worked on Wall Street. Not for the first time since meeting her, I wondered just how supportive he really was of his girlfriend moving four hours away for law school.

"We've been together a long time," was all she said. "You didn't leave a special someone behind in Chicago?"

Would it be embarrassing to say the only special someone I'd ever had was my dad? If I was being perfectly honest, I'd say that the hardest part about leaving Chicago was leaving him. My mother drove me absolutely bonkers, but Dad was my biggest cheerleader. His dog whistle sounded across the entire graduation when I finished at Northwestern. When I received my Harvard acceptance, there was no way I could say no to his chubby, proud face.

"With great power comes great responsibility, kiddo," he said *before I got on the plane. "This degree is going to give you the power to change the world."*

"That's from Spiderman, you goon," I joked back.

"Hey, Stan Lee is a modern prophet, Jane Brain."

Now I looked down at my t-shirt, which had Spiderman plastered across the front. I'd found it at Newbury Comics just after arriving in Boston and had deemed it a sign. My talisman, a way of carrying Dad's good wishes with me into this life I still wasn't sure I wanted. But it mostly reminded me of the fact that Dad loved me in a way no one else ever had or ever would. Why even bother trying to replace it?

"No," I said finally. "No one special. I had a few boyfriends here and there in college, but the truth is, I don't think I'm relationship material. No one else really walks to this drumbeat, if you know what I mean." I bent over the internship list, suddenly wanting to change the subject. "So, are you going to apply for it?"

"No, they only want second years." Skylar sounded deflated. "Maybe next year."

"Are you talking about the Sterling Grove internship?"

We turned to find a tall blond kid signaling for the bartender.

"We are." Skylar's tone was immediately guarded.

I smirked. I had only known my roommate for a few days, but I already knew she wasn't an easy nut to crack.

The kid shrugged, like Skylar's chill didn't bother him in the slightest. He nodded at the bartender, a cute young girl who sprinted over the second he smiled. For a moment, I was also transfixed. At first, the guy looked like any other twenty-something student from Connecticut or wherever. Fair, blond, kind of lanky, with a face that was handsome, but nothing remarkable. But then he smiled, and personality flashed across those otherwise nondescript features like a lightning bolt. As he leaned forward to flirt openly with the bartender, his mouth tugged to one side like it had been caught with a hook. I had a hard time swallowing.

The bartender squealed. She actually squealed, like a mouse ready to run straight into the jaws of a trap. I watched curiously as the blond guy's gaze darkened, like a cat identifying its prey. I was suddenly turned on, but annoyed at the same time. Awkward.

He paid for his drink—two fingers of top-shelf vodka on the rocks—and turned away, features smoothed back into bland curiosity. Until they sharpened all over again. On me.

"So." He set his drink on the bar with purpose. "Are you HLS too?"

I felt like I was stuck in place. Did this guy have superpowers? How could someone go from being eight percent unremarkable to the most charismatic person in the room on a dime?

Even so, I knew the look I was currently receiving. I'd been getting that look my whole life. I was the weird girl at a suburban school. The one who busted out vintage jeans and spiked bracelets when everyone else was sporting Abercrombie and Fitch. The one who went through at least two short-lived Avril Lavigne lookalike phases between the ages of ten and seventeen until I could sew well enough to make my own ideas come to life. Boys like him were fascinated with girls like me long enough to get their rocks off. They fucked us or bullied us. Sometimes both.

Okay, so I lost my virginity in the back of rugby-shirt-wearing Decker Carlson's 4Runner only so he could announce to our entire high school that he scored with the slutty goth girl. And yeah, I might have had a hard time with it. But that was more than five years ago. My prejudice had nothing to do with that. Nothing. I swear.

It was just a matter of difference. Blondie here was a CW show. I was an indie film festival short. Total opposites, plain and simple.

But the kid just peered at me that much more intensely and continued his questioning. "How old are you, anyway? You look about fourteen."

I cleared my throat. "That's really too bad. I work damn hard to conceal my youth with unhealthy doses of eyeliner."

I didn't say I was actually twenty-one, a minimum year younger than the rest of the incoming class. I also didn't say that I was horribly intimidated by the other students at Harvard. I had already met two conferred PhDs and another kid who had finished a tour with the Peace Corps. Their accomplishments made my degree from North-western seem downright commonplace.

"Since we're making snap judgments," I said, "if I'm a baby-faced Asian girl who snuck in despite being a model minority, then what are you? The trust-funded son of a senator? Or is it a governor? Where are you from anyway? Newton? Maybe somewhere in Connecticut?"

He barely looked uncomfortable. "No," he said after a measured sip of his vodka. "I'm from New York, originally." He held out a hand. "I'm Eric."

"Eric what?" I asked. His name was probably Clinton or Bush. I'd bet ten dollars this kid was part of a political dynasty, or one of those families who only reproduced with others like them to corral all the wealth and natural magnetism in their own gene pool. No one could work charm that way without generations of breeding.

His gray eyes narrowed and glinted like steel. "Ah, Stallsmith. And you are?"

I searched for any signs of condescension or mendacity in that strangely penetrating expression, but found none. Just sharp curiosity. So I shook his hand, ignoring the way his touch, which was strong and gentle at the same time, sent tingles up my wrist.

"Lefferts," I replied. "Jane Lefferts."

"That's not an Asian name."

"I'm only half. My mom is Korean."

He nodded. I tucked my hand away and sipped on my beer. Skylar was ignoring us completely, reabsorbed in her internship list.

"I saw you at the orientation meeting," he said. "Section six, right?"

"You saw me?" I said. "What kind of come-on line is that?"

But instead of shuttering like so many men do when challenged, Eric just tilted his head, looking amused. "Well, you're kind of hard to miss. I think you were the only one in the hall with bright blue hair."

I picked up a lock of my hair and examined it. "Actually, this is aqua. Like the sea." I chuckled to myself. "New school, new color."

"Like a siren," Eric murmured.

"Well, my dad did say it reminded him of the Little Mermaid. I guess that makes him King Triton, huh?"

Eric started, like he'd been shocked, but didn't move his gaze. For a moment, I couldn't move myself.

"Yo! Eric!"

We both turned to where a group of other students in a booth called our new friend, shattering the oddly intense moment. They waved at Eric, beckoning him.

Eric turned back to me with a lopsided smile. The intensity was gone, but the charm offensive was back. I wasn't sure which was more deadly.

"Listen," he said. "I'd love to get another drink with you sometime. Maybe before classes start?"

"I..." I watched, unusually dumbfounded as the beautiful boy scribbled his number on one of the bar coasters. I was unaccountably shy—under normal circumstances, I'd tell him that the drinks could hang. We could leave right now, get what we both clearly wanted, and go our merry ways. No more lingering stares or electric touches that left me feeling distinctly unsettled.

But instead, I said nothing.

Eric pushed the coaster across the bar to me and winked. "See you, Jane."

I remained silent, watching him go until Skylar pulled me out of my odd little trance.

"Who's Ariel?" she asked, reading the coaster.

I finally looked down at the note.

Ariel—

When you're ready for that drink, let me know. We'll take a swim together.

Eric
(212) 555-4982

I chuckled. "The Little Mermaid, of course," I said with a quick tug at my hair.

For good measure, I stole one last glance across the bar and found Eric smiling at me. He knew exactly what I'd discovered. I almost fell off my stool.

"What did he say his name was again?" Skylar asked as she looked between us.

"Eric Stallsmith," I said, still unable to break eye contact with this increasingly attractive kid. Eric. Just like the prince in the movie. Oh, he was a smooth one, all right. I was going to have to be careful.

"That's weird," Skylar said. "I heard him tell the registration people his last name was de Vries."

Her comment was the rock that shattered the illusion. I turned away from Eric, frowning. A fake name? Really? What was he going to do next, put a false number in my phone and forget to call me?

I had known it from the start. Guys like him were really only good for one thing, but they were so damn self-absorbed they assumed every girl they met was already half in love with them. They never once considered the idea that the weird girl with the piercings and the crazy hair might want to use them as much as they wanted to use her.

Well, I wasn't ashamed of who I was, nor did I expect every penis on the planet to fall in love with me. But I wasn't about to be played for a fool either. That, I couldn't handle.

I examined the coaster with renewed suspicion, then tossed it aside. "Goodbye, Eric Stallsmith de Vries, or whoever you are. You can try running your game on some other unsuspecting coed."

THREE

Present

I burst from the water of the hotel's pool, echoes of the dreams I'd had the night before still dancing behind my vision. I rarely dreamed of my past. Usually mine were more of the Salvador Dali persuasion—surreal unicorns erupting from the sky before they morphed into my mother yelling at me. Lots of ticking clocks, reminding me of how very brief this life was. You know, the normal stuff.

But lately, it was like my subconscious was reminding me of something, and in these scant free moments, I brooded on those memories from so long ago.

Eric and I had had several other chances together over the years. Every time we'd completely fucked them up. Now I wondered if he'd been trying to tell me something, even back then.

When we first met, Eric had been fighting his own battles. At that point, he would have been just over a year or so out from Penny's death. That boy, as cocky as he'd seemed, had really been full of bravado. Just like me.

Was he still Triton then too, or had he already walked away from the society? Had it been strange to him when I'd brought up the reference at all?

I took another lap in the pool. The water was the same bright blue shade that my hair had been when I'd started school. Vaguely, I wondered if I should do it again. It had been almost a year since the rainbow job.

Skylar recommended swimming to help with my energy while I was pregnant. Stress wasn't good for the baby, she said, and swimming was about as safe an exercise as you could get. Exercise and I generally got along like oil and water, but I had to say, she was right. Although my friend, with her aquatic habits and red hair, more closely resembled the mermaid of my dreams. Somehow being in the water brought me back to those first moments. Maybe that's why I was enjoying it. Over the last few weeks, when the realities of Eric in the slammer and my mother abducted to God-knows-where were too much for me, a dip did my mental state some good.

Or maybe I was just putting off the inevitable.

"Ms. Lefferts?"

Tony, my head security guard, approached the edge of the pool from where he and another guard had been sitting dutifully by the door, keeping out anyone else who wanted to swim while I took a few morning laps. The team of four had been alternating shifts while we were in Korea, standing like sentries outside of my hotel room while I slept, shadowing me everywhere else I ventured. It was a little much, but considering who else was at large here, they made me feel safe. And I knew Eric would never forgive me if I was careless enough to make myself vulnerable.

I swam to the side and looked up at him, pulling awkwardly on my swim cap. "What's up, Tony?"

He averted his eyes—the big man was oddly conservative, probably out of deference to Eric. He generally avoided looking at me directly whenever he could and absolutely refused to use my first name. When I announced I was going swimming this morning, the dread on his face—apparently at having to watch me in a bathing suit —was practically a Halloween mask.

"I just thought you would like to know that your appointment with Detective Cho is in approximately two hours. We need to leave in about forty-five minutes, ma'am, to reach the station on time."

I let myself sink back into the water, touch my feet to the bottom, then reemerge before answering. "Okay."

I accepted Tony's offer to help me out of the pool, trying not to wince when he stepped away quickly. I understood why he did it. It's not like it would be the slightest bit appropriate for the big man to touch me more than was strictly necessary. No hugs, no stroke of the back—nothing like that was even remotely acceptable.

But it's not like I wanted it from him anyway. The truth was, there was another touch I ached for. One I had come to depend on to keep me sane.

I closed my eyes as I wrapped a big towel around my dripping body, imagining that moment at New Year's when Eric had pulled me to him. I'd been a mess, crying and shaking, as the news that I was pregnant burst from my lips. He had held me to his chest, half laughing, half crying, his joy radiating through us both like heat from the sun.

Now, even under the fluff of the towel, the cold air made my skin break into goose bumps, dying for that warm touch. Dying for him.

Well, there was only one way I would be able to get it back. And that meant forging on alone.

"Okay," I said again to Tony, who was waiting by the pool's entrance. "Let's go."

FOUR

Detective Cho was a man on a mission. What mission that was, I didn't really know, considering I understood next to none of the Korean ricocheting around the Hwaseong-Seobu police station. But I knew from the minute I met the relatively young detective that he meant business. His manner was curt and professional. His eyes, however, met mine directly with every question I asked, and beneath his abrupt exterior flickered genuine concern.

"This is not my beat," he said as he escorted me through the halls of the large station. "Missing persons is downstairs. I work in homicide."

I glanced back at the elevator we had just left. Tony and another detail followed with suspicious eyes on Cho. Downstairs was the opposite of where we were headed.

"Just as well. When I was here before, they didn't seem to care much about a missing Korean-American woman," I remarked, ignoring the suggestion implied by his use of the word "homicide."

"What do you say?" Cho replied over his suited shoulder. "Not our jurisdiction? She is an American now, isn't she?"

"Well, the embassy didn't seem to care much either," I said. I had spent a solid two hours this morning on the phone with the U.S. Consulate, and no one there had been a damn bit interested in my mother's whereabouts, despite the fact that she was an American citizen. More of John Carson's insidious influence, no doubt. Despite Zola's contacts, the CIA thus far had also been no help.

With the case against Eric still in progress, Zola wasn't reachable either. Well, maybe it was time to start throwing the weight of my new last name around. I wasn't just some random person. It was time to act like it. My mother's life depended on it.

"Look, Detective Cho. I want to make something clear."

Cho turned outside a conference room and waited patiently.

"I only just got here," I said, "but I'm not exactly one woman. I am part of a very powerful family back home, and we can be very... loud...if we don't receive the help we need."

Was that clear enough? Too clear? It was honestly hard to tell, and I was new at this innuendo thing.

Cho raised his eyebrow. "I am very aware of your husband's family, Mrs. de V-vries." He stumbled slightly over the compounded V-R sound of Eric's last name.

I folded my arms. The subtext was clear—the de Vries family weren't necessarily *my* family. At least he wasn't an idiot.

"Am I talking to the wrong person, then?" I asked. Fuck innuendo. I was better direct.

Cho shrugged. "Your husband's company operates several large ports in South Korea. The Korean government will not wish to upset him."

"Good," I said. "Then hopefully we'll have an understanding. And perhaps you can convey the importance of that to them in a way I haven't managed." I had yet to get any major Korean official to call me back—maybe Detective Cho could grease the wheels.

"But," he continued, "Chariot Industries also has many contracts important to South Korea."

Shit. So basically, South Korea itself was stuck between a rock and a hard place and was choosing to pretend the conflict didn't exist at all.

As I followed Cho into the conference room, I decided to pursue a different tack.

"So, if you're in homicide," I said after he closed the door, "does that mean you think Lawrence Kim's death didn't occur from natural causes?"

The detective didn't answer right away, instead moving to a counter in the corner bearing an electric kettle. He calmly fixed us both tea, and we waited the few awkward minutes for the water to boil. This was obviously not a man to be rushed.

I accepted a cup of tea from the detective before he took his seat.

"I think the death of Lawrence Kim is very suspicious," Cho replied at last. "Mrs. de Vries—"

"Jane," I interrupted. I needed the detective on my side. "Please call me Jane."

His gaze levelled on me. "Jane. Okay. I will be clear. You should be very careful who you talk to about Jonathan Carson. Or even about Lawrence Kim. As I believe we have established, not everyone is on your side."

"Are you?" My palms were damp. *Please say yes*, I pleaded inwardly.

Again, Detective Cho took a very long time to answer. "I am not on anyone's payroll other than this station's."

I exhaled.

"But you should still be careful. Lawrence Kim's death, it reminded me of something. Have you ever heard of the Hwaseong serial murders, Mrs. de Vr—Jane?"

I shook my head. "No...should I have?"

"They are very famous here. There are two movies, I think, and many TV shows about them. An unsolved case even now, but the subject of much curiosity from the public." Cho tapped his mouth. "I don't know. My colleagues think I am crazy, but I think maybe there is something here. Maybe yes, maybe no."

"What happened?" I asked.

Cho leaned back in his chair with the ease of a practiced story-teller as he cradled his teacup. "They started in 1986, and ended in 1991. Ten murders. All women. All of them raped. All strangled with their own clothes. Pantyhose, brassieres, things like that. All but one of the bodies abandoned in rural areas around Hwaseong— rice paddies, melon fields, canals. Four in eighty-six, two in eighty-seven, two more in eighty-eight. And the last in 1990 and ninety-one."

Rice paddies. I couldn't imagine that was an uncommon place to leave a dead body in the history of this country. After all, rice paddies were ubiquitous all over Korea, not to mention most of Asia.

Still, the dates struck home.

"John Carson was here in 1987."

Cho nodded. "And eighty-six and eighty-eight. Lawrence Kim had his travel records in his notes."

I put my teacup down. "You have the rest of Kim's notes? Can I see them?" I wondered if they contained anything different from the ones the station had given me with his other belongings.

Cho shook his head. "They are part of the evidence of the case. I cannot have tampering."

"Because you think John Carson killed those women?"

"No," Cho said quickly. "I do not. It was not that simple. He has too many alibis for all the incidents. John Carson was not here when they were found. He did not kill those women."

I gulped. I wasn't sure if I felt fear or relief. I didn't want my biological father to be a serial mass murderer, but a part of me did wonder if he was capable of it after what he had done to Eric. And what he might be doing to my mother.

"But then I think about," Cho continued, "there were ten murders. Seven of them were similar. Young girls. Fourteen, fifteen, twenty-one, twenty-five, twenty-nine. All raped, then strangled with their clothes, and abandoned. Then three others were older. Fifty-four, sixty-nine, seventy-one. One had DNA of a local boy on her, someone witnesses say they saw on a bus." He shook his head. "It didn't go anywhere."

"Do you think that some of them might have been copycat crimes?" I chimed in, now following his train of thought.

"Some, yes. To confuse investigators," Cho agreed. "Killed in the same way as the original. Maybe to lead them away from the real criminal. Maybe just to mask someone else's crimes." He sat back up and leaned across the table. "Does the name Park Seo-hyeon mean anything to you?"

I started to shake my head, but then I stopped when I realized that it *did* mean something to me. "That's the name of my mother's friend. The one who worked with her on the airline. The one who—"

"Organized a prostitution ring, yes?" Cho pointed to the table, like he was gesturing to evidence that was actually there. "It was in Kim's notes. She was also one of the victims—found in a melon field."

Found in a melon field.

Just like Kim.

I blinked, trying not to shake. I hadn't read through all of the notes yet. Obviously there were some critical things I had missed.

The pieces were starting to come together now. Carson had been involved with a prostitution ring gone awry. For whatever reason, Carson wanted these women taken care of, but he was smart. He didn't do it himself. He likely sent someone and had them camouflage the crime with the rash of others that had happened in the area.

"But there was nothing—nothing at all—to condemn him or... whoever he sent?" I asked. It was hard to believe.

He shook his head. "The technology was so bad back then. They did not even take samples from the bodies until the last two, and even then, they only show it was maybe not the same person. It is the reason the cases were never solved."

He was being delicate, but I understood what he meant. If the victims were raped and strangled, "samples" meant semen. Blood. Looking under fingernails for skin or other bits of the killer scraped during a fight for the woman's life. The last two, then, pointed to the possibility that there were multiple killers. Maybe one was actually committing the crimes of the original.

Which pointed to a new question: who was the original murderer?

"The only witness we ever had was a victim of attempted rape in 1991 who gave the police a description of a young man, no double eyelids, maybe in his twenties, who was on a bus with her." Cho continued like he was telling a fireside tale, not updating me on a homicide case.

"God," I muttered. "That could have been anyone."

"That is the statement that was in the papers. It was the strongest evidence we had, along with one hair found on another body. You can see why we had a hard time solving it."

"I do, yeah. But what does this have to do with my mother? Or Lawrence Kim? He's not a woman, and he wasn't strangled. Was he raped too? The coroner would have noted that."

Cho shook his head. "No, he was not violated that way. But..." He tipped his head to one side, like he was trying to divine the answer to this mystery from me. "When I saw who he was looking for, I wondered if there was more of a connection."

"Why?"

Cho stretched his arms lazily over the chairs on either side of him. "Another rape victim was treated at the Hwaseong hospital in early 1987, but she would not give a statement to the police." He looked at me meaningfully. "When they tried to contact her a few months later, she had left the country. Her name was Lee Yu-na."

He pronounced it in Korean, without the Americanized accent he had been affecting since greeting me outside the station. I recognized it nonetheless. Yu-na. My mother.

Someone had raped her, possibly tried to kill her, just like her friend after all. Her fears, apparently, were founded in her own experience. And so, heeding the warning John Carson had given her back then, she stayed quiet. Until she fled.

"Oh, *Eomma*," I murmured, my hand closing over my mouth.

Was that why Carson had brought her back here? Some demented attempt to finish the job he had started thirty years ago?

"I think Lawrence Kim was killed because he was too close to finding something that linked John Carson to these crimes," Cho said. "The statute of limitations on murder is only fifteen years in Korea, so it would not matter now. But it *would* ruin the contracts he has in the country, no?"

"It would ruin a lot of things for him," I murmured.

"Your mother was last seen in Jinan-dong."

I looked up. "What? Kim said—"

"I asked more," Cho interrupted gently. "People here, they didn't forget what happened all those years ago. They hear of strange people, they keep watch. She came back, and she was recognized."

I swallowed. "Where—where is that?"

"It's a neighborhood east of here. South of Suwon, on the other side of the river." He tipped his head, like he was surprised I didn't know. "It's where your family is from, Mrs. de Vries."

I swallowed down the rest of my tea, now lukewarm from sitting on the table. "Why—why would he take her there?"

Unfortunately, Detective Cho was all out of answers. "I would like to know everything you know about John Carson," he said mildly. "I think it will help me to answer your questions. And find your mother."

I looked up. "So you—you're going to help?"

He smiled then, and for a moment, he looked almost familiar. "Why, yes, cousin," he said, dropping one last revelation in my lap. "Family has to help family, after all."

FIVE

I remained at the police station for another two hours sorting through the evidence with Cho, who, yes, turned out to be a distant cousin—the son of a son of my great-grandfather. He still would not show me Kim's notes, though. However, he did tell me everything he could remember about them, then dragged out the four boxes of files left over from the other murders, and together we pored over documents and photographs. Many of them were quite gruesome, detailed accounts of each of the murders. After looking at them, I tended to agree with Cho—it seemed unlikely that *all* of these crimes were committed by the same person, despite the clear *modus operandi*. There were too many key differences.

"I think the place is important," I said again as Cho escorted me and the security detail to the parking lot. "Especially if we are trying to link any of these to John Carson."

Cho did not agree. His opinion was that too much of the previous investigations had focused on place.

But I wasn't willing to let it go. "Cousin," I begged. "Please. Help me look again. John Carson was here during those years for a reason. We should check if he had dealings in any of the towns where the bodies were found. It's worth a look. Ask about the prostitution ring too."

My mother wouldn't thank me for reminding any members of her family, distant or not, about *that* side of her life, but it couldn't be helped. It was part of the case.

Cho rubbed his chin. "Go back to your hotel," he said after a moment's thought. "You will be safe there while I go to Jinan. You said you have a doctor's appointment, right?"

I nodded. "Yes, the day after tomorrow in Suwon. I'm pregnant, you see."

Cho nodded, like he was unsurprised. My cousin was even more unreadable than Eric. Why hadn't *I* inherited that particular family trait?

"I will call you," he said. "But this is dangerous, so please stay in your hotel otherwise. I think we are close. We will find your mother, Jane."

My chest tightened. I wanted to say thank you, but couldn't get out the words. As the real stakes of what I was doing here caught up with me, it was very hard to breathe.

"Please be careful," I managed finally.

Cho tipped his head. "I am always careful. It's my job."

And with that, we said good night.

But instead of directing Tony back to the hotel, I had another destination in mind. I wasn't *quite* willing to sit around my tower like a princess and wait for the world to do my bidding.

"Tony, I want to go to Jinan. Can you take me there?"

Tony frowned at me through the rearview mirror, as did the other detail sitting beside him. "Mrs. de Vries, the detective—"

"I know what he said, Tony," I cut him off. "But I want to see it for myself. You guys will be with me. I'll be fine."

JINAN WAS BARELY visible from the car when we arrived about

an hour later. The middle of the town was a ramshackle mix of apartments, new construction, and the Korean versions of strip malls, which eventually gave way to wide swaths of farmland. Thirty years ago, it had been a tiny village, but recent growth had upgraded it to a municipality. Tony escorted me to a late lunch with the rest of the team and then drove for hours while I took in every detail I could.

Eventually the afternoon passed into night. The lights and highways gave way to the bleakness of unlit farms. The fields themselves looked dry, brown, and barren—there was no snow on the ground, but Korea in January was still frozen. No one was out.

Tony drove until we approached the edge of a large farm that left the lights of the main village in its dust. It was deserted. The perfect place for a murder.

"Stop here," I said.

"Mrs. de Vries, shouldn't we just go—"

"I said stop, Tony!"

Tony reluctantly pulled over, followed by the other sedan carrying the rest of our security team. Everyone got out, and while I walked to the edge of a field, the others quickly formed a queue of four linebacker-shaped men, trailing me like an absurd version of *Make Way for Ducklings*.

I shut them out as I observed the desolation. This was where my family was from? Was this their farm at one time? Did it belong to a distant cousin now? Maybe an aunt or uncle?

I honestly didn't think I would stay to find out. I didn't feel any particular kinship with this place. My mother had made her home in Chicago with Carol, my true father, the man who raised me. What was I expecting? Some kind of enlightenment? A flash of belonging?

There was nothing for me to discover here. Except, of course, her.

A shiver passed down my spine, and I hugged my thick parka around me. God, where *was* she? Was she all right? Was she...dead?

"*Eomma*," I murmured, holding out my hand so the wind could pass through my fingers. "*Eomma*, where are you?"

My cell phone blared in the night. I pulled it out, recognizing with dread the number that had appeared there more than once over the past few weeks. A payphone in the middle of a concrete complex surrounded by barbed wires.

I considered not answering. I really did.

But I couldn't. I never really could with him.

"Jane?"

I melted into the wind, and before I knew it, tears welled. That voice. Its deep, melodic timbre called to me from oceans away.

"Eric?" I whispered. "Eric, how—"

"They gave me a phone call today. Jane, what in the hell? You're in Korea?"

His voice was stilted and scratchy through the poor line from Rikers. It was morning in New York. Eric's trial started in a few days —he should be talking with Brandon or someone local. Instead, he was using his phone privileges to call me.

"I'm sorry," I whispered.

"What?"

"I said I'm sorry," I repeated louder. "Eric, I had to. The investigator is dead. Carson killed him, I know he did. Now he has my mother, Eric. He *took* her, and he's going to d-do something to her—" I cut myself off as the gravity of the day washed over me with the force of a tidal wave. More tears fell. Oh *God*, where was my mother?

"Jane, you need to come home," Eric said, his voice pained.

"I can't," I replied. "Eric, I have to find her. If I don't, no one else will."

"You can't—Jane, you can't stay there. That's exactly what he wants!"

I swallowed thickly. I was aware of the likely motives. John Carson had paraded around Chicago with my mother as if he were baiting a fish. And like the dumbest tuna in the sea, I'd bitten.

But I wasn't diving into this without help. I had four gorilla-sized security guards, and now a detective cousin on my side. I wasn't alone.

"Eric, I have to," I said. "It's my mother."

"What about my wife, Jane? What about our baby? Did you think of her?"

The fact that he had already given it a gender choked me up even more. In his mind, Eric was already imagining that future. To him, we had a daughter, and now I saw her too. I wondered if he could see her face. See himself holding her. Loving her.

I pushed the image away, mostly because I couldn't bear it. I couldn't see past the fact that the two people in the world I loved more than anything were being kept from me, locked away in one form or another. But one had a whole team of people helping to save him. The other had no one but me.

"I have an appointment the day after tomorrow," I said. "For another ultrasound check. Suejean helped me find someone in Suwon to do the basic eight-week scan, so I'll be on track when I come back." *Whenever that is.* I didn't mention that I was no closer to finding my mother than I was when I arrived. Another scan was overkill, maybe, but it was at least something I could do to assuage Eric's fears.

"Jane, be reasonable," Eric said. "Look, if everything goes the way it's supposed to, I'll be out of here today. God, I hope it's today. Just... just come home, all right? We'll go back to Korea if we need to, but we should figure this out *together*."

"Eric..." My voice was so pitiful, but I wasn't moving. There was nothing else I could do but remain where I was. I had to try. I'd never forgive myself if I didn't.

Eric seemed to sense it. "Fine, then stay there. But don't meet with anyone, don't *do* anything, okay? Not until I can get there too."

"Yes, but who knows when that will be!" I burst out. "We hope the judge does the right thing and throws out the case, but what if she doesn't? What if it's just one more person in Carson's pocket that we didn't anticipate? Eric, I have to do this *now*, don't you see? He's close. She was spotted not ten miles from here just yesterday!"

There was a long silence on the phone, and for a second, I

wondered if the unstable line had cut out. But then, Eric finally spoke.

"Jane," he said in a voice that creaked. "I'm begging you. Please come home. *Please.*"

"I'm sorry," I whispered. "I have to go."

"Jane!"

"I'll be home soon," I said. "You're safer where you are. Listen to your lawyers, and for God's sake, don't do anything stupid when they get you out of there."

"Fucking hell, Jane, I—"

"I love you," I cut him off, pushing the tears away. And then I ended the call, turned to the car, and sobbed all the way back.

SIX

2009

It was only four in the afternoon when I walked into Cleo's that Friday. Skylar was gone to New York for the weekend, leaving me to celebrate our first round of midterms on my own. The bar was still quiet. A few students hovered around the shuffleboard table, maybe two others munched on a basket of fries by the jukebox. Another by the windows was bent over a very old book.

I approached the bar and set my messenger bag on a stool. "PBR, please."

"Long week, huh?" the bartender replied.

I shoved my red cat-eyed glasses up my nose. "Midterms are over. It's time to drink."

"I can help with that," said the bartender as he left to get my beer.

"It's purple now, huh?"

I turned to find Eric Stallsmith (or de Vries, whichever it was) standing next to me. A quick glance at the now-empty table by the windows told me he was the bookworm. Huh. That was...unexpected. I would have expected someone like him to use his extra time to, I don't know, pretend to be on a crew team or something.

The bartender brought my beer, but before I could fish a crumpled five dollar bill out of my bag, Eric had already flipped the guy a crisp twenty.

"I'll get this round," he said. "Double Belvedere on the rocks, please."

I whistled as the bartender pulled a bottle off the actual top shelf.

"That's an awfully nice vodka for a poor law student," I said, though if Eric was poor, I was the Queen of Sheba.

"I don't drink crap," he replied. "Belvedere's not my favorite, but it's the best they have at Cleo's." He accepted the drink and pushed the change back at the bartender, along with a credit card. "Keep it open, Scott."

The bartender nodded and shuffled away.

"On a first-name basis? Smart," I said.

"I'm surprised you're not. You come here a lot, don't you?"

"Only when I'm too lazy to get the hell out of Cambridge. It's a little, well, square for my tastes."

Eric quirked another smile, and I was pleased when he looked up and down my outfit, which currently consisted of a pair of black skinny jeans, combat boots I'd picked up at an army surplus store just a few weeks ago, a gray and red bowling shirt tied at my midriff, and my favorite vintage biker jacket. I tipped my glasses—new frames I'd found at a local flea market—and tossed my jacket over my bag.

"You're just unique, Stan," he said, gesturing to the name stitched over my heart. "That's a good thing. Certainly not worth sacrificing for the assholes at Harvard."

"Oh," I said, surprised more by how flattered I was than because I disagreed with him. "Well, thank you. And thank you for the beer. It's delicious."

"PBR is delicious?"

I smacked my lips. "It hits the damn spot. Especially after we've been doing nothing but studying our asses off for the last eight weeks. We deserve a break and a lot of alcohol."

"Is that why I haven't seen you much? Too cool for Cleo's, too busy studying?"

I shrugged. It wasn't exactly true. Eric and I were in the same Torts and Constitutional Law classes. We just sat at opposite sides of the classroom, and I tried not to watch with too much admiration whenever he answered questions. The kid was smarter than your average trust fund baby. Really smart, in fact. And articulate. And thoughtful. Not that I had any regrets about turning him down, of course.

"Are you going home this weekend too?" I asked instead. "Seems like everyone somewhat local is taking a few days to see family with the extra day off. Yours must be missing you."

Eric just shuddered, like I'd suggested he jump into a vat of flaming acid instead of visiting the people who raised him. "No," he said a little too vehemently. Then, a bit lighter: "We don't exactly get along."

I considered the stout ball of Asian guilt that awaited every one of my calls home with the sixth sense of a fortune teller. I did wonder sometimes if she had some kind of radar for when exactly I felt just guilty enough to want to call the house line instead of my dad's cell.

"Understood," I replied. "Home isn't for everyone."

"Home is where you make it, right?"

I shrugged. "It's not the places you go, but the people you meet?"

"Something like that."

I quirked an eyebrow at him. "Is that why you gave me a fake name? Because you don't get along with your family?"

Eric had the grace to look a little bit ashamed. "Shit. You caught that?"

I turned toward him. "Skylar did, actually. She overheard the name 'de Vries' at orientation. Which, by the way, you use in class. What's going on with that?"

Eric shifted uneasily. "I...well, Stallsmith isn't a fake name. It's just not one I use a lot. It's my mother's name. Sometimes it makes certain things easier."

"Like what things?"

He swallowed and peered at me, levelling me again with that curious intensity I hadn't forgotten. Good lord, I hoped the boy was planning to be a litigator. He'd get any confession he wanted with that stare.

"Things I generally keep to myself," he said finally. "Things I'd probably need a lot more vodka to discuss."

"Well, that could be arranged," I said. "If I thought you would actually tell me the truth anyway. Maybe you'll just give me another alias."

"Is that why you left the coaster on the bar?" He grinned with the change of subject, and that curiously transformative smile lit up the bar. I grabbed the wood to steady myself. "Don't worry, Lefferts. I rescued it."

Then where is it? I wanted to ask. But I didn't. Because that, of course, would sound like I actually wanted it.

"What were you doing over there?" I asked, nodding at the window. "That book looked too old even for the used books."

"Come see."

As if it was the most natural thing in the world, Eric picked up my bag, then guided me off my stool and to his table with a gentle, yet firm touch at the small of my back. I ignored the clear admiration on his face when he noticed my bared midriff. Lord, men were all alike, weren't they? The only difference was that for some reason, this one's gaze burned a bit hotter than others.

We sat down, and I examined the book on the table. It wasn't actually as ancient as the nearly ripped cover made it seem—just a used copy of *Leaflets,* a collection of Adrienne Rich poetry.

"Well, what do you know," I murmured as I flipped through the book. "I wouldn't have taken you for the queer feminist poetry type."

"Are you a poetry reader?" He almost sounded eager.

I shrugged. "I wouldn't say that. But she came to speak at Northwestern once, and she's kind of a badass. I liked what I heard. I take it you're a fan."

"I like her stuff pretty well. I think she's ripping off the modernists a little with her formal structure, but her words are... moving. They pretty much embody perfect catharsis, in my opinion."

I raised an eyebrow. "You know your stuff, huh?"

This time he shrugged. "I majored in English at Dartmouth. Wrote my honors thesis on Yeats. But I'm no professor."

"Do you write it too?" I prodded, unable to help myself. Lord, if this boy was a poet, no wonder he had half our classes, female and male, tongue-tied during lectures. From what I could tell, he left nearly every class with a different girl trailing after him.

Eric took a measured sip. "I do."

"Can I read it?" The request toppled out before I could stop it. This was a game, of course. He was giving me his best dating pedigree right now, the poetry-loving garbage that probably lured every woman under thirty in the Boston metropolitan area into bed with him with a single verse.

I still wanted to know, though. I couldn't help it.

Eric just fixed me with a gaze that was maybe a little harder than before. "Maybe."

"Come on," I pushed.

"Tell you what," he said, tucking the copy of *Leaflets* away. "Let's write one together. Right now."

"Ah...I'm not really the poetry type," I said. "Give me a sewing machine, and I'm all over it. But me and words? I can write papers, but that's about it."

A sly, yet sweet smile emerged. "I bet you could handle it, Lefferts. Come on, we'll just do a quick limerick. Five lines. First, second, and fifth rhyme with each other. Third and fourth together. Easy."

I looked at him with obvious disbelief, and he started to laugh. The sound made my whole body feel about twenty pounds lighter. Damn. How could I say no to that?

"All right," I said. "You start."

Eric grabbed a napkin from the center of the table and pulled a pen from his coat pocket. A small black book stuck out of that same pocket. I wondered if that's where he kept those poems I was suddenly desperate to read.

"Eric and Jane's poem," he said before writing the date next to it on the napkin. He gave me another sly smile that made my knees feel like water. "We're making history right here, you know."

I rolled my eyes. "Just get on with it."

"All right, all right. How about..." He tapped his mouth—which was distractingly full—with his pencil. "Okay, I got it:

Jane wished to take on the world.

I smirked. "Okay, okay. Um...put down: 'With looks that were purely absurd.'"

"Looks?" Eric questioned. "No, I don't think so. First of all, it's patently false, and I don't believe in writing bullshit. Poetry is the truest form of art. And secondly, what do your looks have to do with your goals?"

I rolled my eyes. "Fine. Taking over the world is absurd too. So we'll write that."

He chuckled. "How about this?"

Jane wished to take on the world
though her high hopes were maybe absurd.

I shrugged after another long drink of my beer. "Works for me."

"Now, a transition." Eric scratched the next line:

Eric saw her one night,

"And she put up a fight," I continued, enjoying myself now. "But he only thought, what an intriguing girl."

I stilled as he wrote down the remainder of the poem, polished the language a little, scratched out a few words, then turned the napkin to me to review the final product:

> *Jane sought to take on the world.*
> *Still, she thought her high hopes absurd.*
> *Eric saw her one night.*
> *Though she put up a fight,*
> *He only thought, what a pretty girl.*

Pretty girl? I had been called a lot of things in my short twenty-one, almost twenty-two years on this planet. Some names not so nice by people who didn't care to see an ambiguously raced female with a penchant for speaking her opinions aloud (such as my mother). Some other names from people—mostly men—who wanted to see what was under the glasses and leather. Some of them were even nice.

"Fairly cute."

"Interesting."

"Unique."

But even my father, with his penchant for rhyming nicknames, called me "Plain Jane." I could gussy up my face with eyeliner and red lips all I liked, but beauty was something I never aspired to.

"You thought I was pretty, huh?" I tried to make it a joke, but my voice broke a little. Ugh, what was wrong with me? Where was my bravado when I needed it?

Eric leaned across the table to study me with interest that, well, if it wasn't genuine, would have been damn hard to fake. "I'm thinking it now."

Oh, he was good.

Too good.

This guy had heartbreak written all over him. He'd probably already cut a path of it clear across Harvard Square.

Unfortunately, I wasn't sure I cared anymore.

Slowly, he reached out and touched a loose piece of purple hair that had drifted down around my face. "Pretty," he murmured as he tucked the strand behind my ear. "Girl."

Before I could stop myself, I batted his hand away. "You know what? You don't need to throw lines at me."

Eric frowned. "What? Who said it was a line?" That dreamy look that had been in his eyes two seconds ago was gone. The one that replaced it was much more familiar—annoyed. Turned on, still, but mostly annoyed.

Because, of course, I'd said what I was thinking. Just like the rest of them, he couldn't fucking handle it.

That was fine, I decided. Much easier to negotiate than this poetry crap.

"Do me a favor, will you? I think we both know what you're doing. Because you're not Prince Charming any more than I'm a Disney princess. You don't need to charm me, so let's stop the games."

"Would you rather I get you sloppy drunk and tow you across the yard to my room?" he said, unable to keep the disdain out of his voice completely, though his eyes clearly sparked at the idea. "I could put a sock on the door, if you want. Let my roommate know to clear the fuck out for the evening."

I tossed back about half my drink. *Don't let him see you crack.* "Well, at least then you'd be honest, my preppy little crew captain. I don't know what you're playing at with this poetry crap, but without it, we can just get down to business. Fucking, I mean. After all, that is what you want, right?"

"Fucking hell," he muttered. "You're very direct, aren't you?"

Ah, here it was. The moment of truth. Some men could handle it, others couldn't. Just call me the Colonel Jessup of dating.

"Do you have a problem with that?" I asked.

Eric threw back the rest of his vodka and set the glass down on the table with unnecessary force. "Not in the fucking slightest."

Sudden, unexpected relief flooded through me. I had my defenses up, sure, but I hadn't realized until right then how disappointed I would have been if this strange, unreadable boy's interest broke from just a bit of challenge. The fact that it didn't—the fact that he actually seemed more determined to be around me after I pushed his limits—was incredibly satisfying.

"Hey, preppy," I said, grabbing the edges of Eric's chambray shirt and appreciating the way the color brought out a tiny bit of blue in those gray eyes.

He looked down at my hands, then back at me with a hard, electric gaze. "What's that, gorgeous?"

I smacked my lips and batted my eyelashes with my very best Betty Boop impression. "Time's a tickin'. You want to get out of here or not?"

For a moment, he didn't say anything, just engaged in a stare-off that would have put any tomcat to shame. Then, finally, he leaned toward me, brushing his cheek against mine, and growled in my ear: "Grab your bag and get moving, pretty girl. Or else I'm carrying you out of here myself."

SEVEN

Present

After having yet another particularly vivid set of dreams about Eric and me the night before, I couldn't stop thinking of that first, furious night. The way he had called me pretty girl all night long, imprinting my mind with the term the way he penetrated the rest of me. We didn't sleep that night, and by morning, I was sweaty, sore, and completely his.

Maybe it was that fury that drove me as I reluctantly took Eric's and Cho's advice to lie low while Cho poked around the towns where the Hwaseong murders had occurred, looking for connections to John Carson. Follow the money, said every investigator I had ever worked with. So while I waited, that's exactly what I spent the next day doing, much to Tony's relief.

"Here's what I want to know," I said to Skylar as I clicked through a few more pictures on my computer. "What in the hell was he doing in South Korea to begin with? I can't find anything. How can he be such a fucking ghost?"

I was steadily building my own digital notebook of research, listing every known company in every village and neighborhood in Hwaseong connected to those crimes. Chariot might have been private, but there had to be *some* records of its holdings, right? And maybe if that history couldn't tell me exactly why John Carson was spending so much time in Korea in the late eighties, maybe it would tell me why he came back. And where he would have taken my mother.

Unfortunately, since Chariot wasn't a publicly traded company, I had absolutely no access to that information either unless we could find a private investor willing to divulge the information. Another dead end.

"Hold on," Skylar said as she stirred a pan of scrambled eggs, chatting at me through her iPad.

It was about seven in the morning back in New York, where they were awaiting Eric's hearing. She beckoned to someone off the screen.

Brandon appeared, and with a horsey grin, he carried me over to what looked like the other side of the counter in the palatial Airbnb they were renting.

"You're in luck," Brandon said.

I sat up. "Tell me everything."

"Well, as you know, private companies don't have to report shit to the public. But they still have to be held accountable to their investors, if they have any. And, as it happens, Chariot had one investor Carson couldn't quite shake after he took over. Her name was Celeste de Vries."

My jaw dropped. "*What?*"

Brandon clicked his tongue. "Eric really should have spent more time with his grandma before she died. He might have learned that he was about to inherit a quietly effective five percent of Chariot Industries. Celeste apparently invested in Carson's company on the ground floor."

"What? Why would Celeste invest in Chariot?"

Brandon shrugged. "Honestly, I doubt she was the one who did it initially. It looks like Eric's grandfather initially invested in 1983 or so. Eric said that's right about when his father and Carson were both tapped. Granted, I don't know all the ins and outs of the Janus society, but I wouldn't be surprised to hear that all the members support each other's business ventures. They are probably all constantly sticking fingers in each other's pies." He held up a handful of papers. "Nina brought these over last night when we arrived in town. Apparently they were in the files collected from Celeste's old apartment. "

"What are these?" I looked eagerly at the screen, craning my neck as if somehow that would help me see the blurry files better. Fucking technology. Maybe everyone was right. Maybe I should have stayed in New York.

"Reports for the last twenty-five years or so. These are the ones from the late eighties. Right after John Carson took over. Give me a second; I'll scan and send you the encrypted files."

A few minutes of chatting with Skylar later, my screen faced her and Brandon while they ate breakfast, and I looked through the pdfs Brandon sent.

"Here's Johnny," I sang as I clicked around, seeing signature after signature of the same pompous name I was coming to hate.

"What?" Skylar asked, clearly befuddled.

I shook my head. Was I the only one who thought it was funny that my maniacal biological father shared the same name as the legendary talk show host?

"Chariot Technics," I murmured, looking through a list of acquisitions from 1987 and '88. "Carson Electronics. Parthenon Chemical. God, look at all these loopty-loos. He was really trying to say something with his autograph, wasn't he? Damn, he really bought up the joint too. How many subsidiaries did he found?"

"Carson wanted to expand when he took over, but he probably wanted to do it quietly," Brandon said.

"He wanted something," I replied. "Chariot operated in the red for three years after these. Jesus, what kind of business model is this?"

"A smart one," Brandon said. "All those companies you just

named make different parts necessary for a bunch of things that Chariot sells. He was cutting out all the middle men. It made it possible for Chariot to reenter ammunitions and basically take it over. Especially with the Asian market."

I clicked a few more times. "These are all located in Hwaseong too. I guess we have our connection to this region." There were a few outside the limits of South Korea's most populous province, but nearly all of the companies newly acquired during that period were here. Except one. I frowned as I scrolled through the list of investments from 1989. "What's KEPCO E&C?"

Brandon stilled on the screen. "What?"

"In 1989, Chariot purchased a whole bunch of shares from a company called KEPCO. What's that?"

Skylar was watching her husband curiously as he set down his fork.

"That's the Korean Electric Power Corporation," Brandon said. "It's still majority owned by the South Korean government, but they opened it up to foreign investment in 1989."

"They're headquartered in Seoul," I said. "But it looks like right after that, Chariot also leased a bunch of land in...let me see..." I typed an address into Google Maps. "Goseong is up in the northeast, close to the North Korean border."

Brandon started. "Wait, what?"

Skylar put down her mug of tea. "What is it?"

"Hold on a second."

While Brandon got up to find his own computer, Skylar and I blinked at each other through the webcam, then waited patiently while he clicked around. When he looked up again, he wore a very peculiar expression.

I frowned. "What's with the face, Colombo?"

Brandon swallowed. "That site in Goseong is home to a nuclear reactor. Started in the late seventies, abandoned when KEPCO ran out of funds to make it work on their own, and then finished in late 1989."

"But that would be for energy, right? Do the South Koreans have nuclear weapons?"

Brandon shook his head. "They have the abilities, but they signed non-proliferation treaties. Their neighbors to the north, though, haven't been so obedient. I'd have to check with Ray, but I'm pretty sure that everything those companies made together adds up to nuclear weaponry. Well after South Korea agreed to stop producing."

I sat back. "Come again?"

Brandon abandoned his computer and edged closer to Skylar's webcam. "I'm not a UN inspector or anything, Jane. But I'd bet money that John Carson was involved in nuclear weapons production in the late eighties. And given the proximity of that reactor to the border, I'm starting to wonder if it was maybe something to do with the North Koreans, not the South."

"Brandon, that's kind of a lot of jumps, don't you think?" cautioned Skylar, though she looked just as terrified as I did.

"Red, this is just a working hypothesis. But here are the pieces: In 1985, South Korea joined 189 other countries in non-proliferation. We know that North Korea asked China and the Soviets to help them establish nuclear energy capacity. Initially, they both said no...but then Russia said yes. And we also know that quickly developed into warfare technologies. But the how is still a bit of a mystery."

Skylar and I both remained still.

"What if...what if...John Carson had a hand in it?" Brandon continued. "He inherits a small munitions company in the mid-eighties, but now Chariot runs at two of the nuclear laboratories here on the Eastern Seaboard and funds several of the other major nuclear research centers. What if he was engineering nuclear proliferation in North Korea to line his own pockets? Until everything with the Soviets went to shit at the end of the Cold War?"

"He was planning to..." I shook my head. "You don't think he was planning to sell nuclear weapons to the North Koreans. Really? That would be straight-up treason."

"It would. But John Carson doesn't strike me as someone who

cares much about the rules. And like you said, he was in the red. He was trying to grow, at whatever the cost." Brandon shrugged. "Like I said, it's just a hypothesis."

"It doesn't explain what he was doing with the women in 1987," I said.

"No," Brandon said. "But it explains what he was doing in Korea to begin with. It explains why he left. And it explains why maybe he wouldn't have wanted anyone to know he was there in the first place." He tapped a pen on the desk. "These murders...didn't you say they stopped for a couple of years?"

"After 1989," I confirmed.

"Right after the Berlin Wall fell," Skylar added.

"So, think about it. The USSR collapses in the early nineties. Carson and Eric's dad pull out of the deal as the Russians step back from their own work in Pyongyang. Skip forward a few decades...I wouldn't say those threats were ever neutralized, but now the Russians and the North Koreans have been a lot more...active together...in recent years," Brandon narrated. "Especially considering how, ah, warm the current administration here is toward their endeavors. So maybe that's why Carson's in Korea now, Jane. Maybe it has nothing to do with your mother. Maybe he's just checking on his investments after biding his time for the last thirty years, and she just happens to be with him."

EIGHT

2009

"How predictable," I remarked as Skylar and I exited Torts.

"I think his name is Keith? That guy I met at Great Scott about a month ago." I held out my phone, which currently had a picture of a medium-sized erect penis on the screen.

"Jesus!" Skylar averted her eyes. "Jane, holy crap. You could have warned me."

"Why? It's really not even that big. He trimmed his hedges so much it shifts the perspective." I examined the picture again with academic interest. "Haven't you ever gotten a dick pic before?"

"No!"

I tucked my phone away. "Patrick hasn't ever sent you a dirty picture or two? Even with the long distance? Good God, how do you guys keep the fire otherwise?"

As if she needed the reminder, Skylar checked her phone for what had to be the thousandth time that day. I sighed. My roommate had serious issues with her boyfriend, who, from what I could tell across the hall, seemed like a philandering asshole. I mean, living free is well and good when all parties consent, but my roommate was the most monogamous creature on the planet. A one-track pony, so to speak. So, you tell me what to think when your man routinely waits two days longer to call you than he says he will, but constantly butt-dials from very loud nightclubs with a bunch of ladies squealing in the background. It didn't sound like "working late" to me.

"He was supposed to text me this morning," Skylar muttered, refreshing her messages yet again. "I was planning to go down again this weekend." She shoved her phone away with a defeated sigh. "But no. No dick pics from Patrick. He's too busy with work for that kind of thing. He's too busy to call, period."

"Work, huh?"

Skylar glared through the windows at the frost that matched her own expression, and I let it go. She and I got along pretty well, much to my surprise given our obvious personality differences, but we weren't quite at the "criticize each other's life choices" stage. We'd get there eventually.

"It'll be fine," I said. "He's probably just busy."

I pulled out my phone again as we exited Austin Hall. Our study group was meeting to split this weekend's reading before we dispersed for a much-needed Friday night out.

"I thought you were seeing that Eric guy these days," Skylar said. "Why are other guys sending you pictures of their genitals?"

"Hey, hey, hey, this isn't on me. I don't know why he was suddenly pornographically inspired. And I don't know if I would call what Eric and I have been doing 'seeing' each other," I said as we made our way down the path to the law library. "Unless that's a new euphemism for banging like bunnies."

One of Skylar's red brows rose. "Is that really all it is? What happened to the poetry?"

Okay, so I'd told her about that. And also about Eric's tendency to write new ones on my skin after we'd just made our own "poetry," as he called it. Multiple times. Okay, at least ten in fourteen days.

It had become kind of a game. Post-orgasmic limericks. Who

could create with the worst puns to dispel the electricity that never quite seemed to dissipate? The guy was addictive. It was becoming a problem.

And then, of course, there was that moment after our con law class two days ago. The one when, just after he had smiled and grinned and chatted away with Catie Sparler, the former Ms. Delaware, he had grabbed my hand on the way out and walked me all the way back to my apartment. Right when half the law school was pouring out of the building for the day.

Suddenly, I was right back in high school, with every student within fifty feet wondering what the hell Decker Carlson was doing with the weird girl and her nose ring.

That wasn't exactly booty call action. And so I'd been ignoring Eric's calls and avoiding him since. And he hadn't done a damn thing to change it.

But before I could tell Skylar again that Eric and I meant nothing, we were interrupted by the Energizer Bunny himself bounding down the path after us.

"Crosby! Lefferts! Wait up!"

We stopped in the library doorway, and Eric grinned as he sidled past me much closer than necessary. The buttons of his wool pea coat scraped across my leather jacket, and he paused, trapping us both there for a moment.

"Hey, gorgeous," he murmured. "I was trying to catch you after class, but you ran off. You busy later?"

Was I busy? Well, I was trying to be. And not with this walking ad for Scandinavian virility who was undoubtedly going to break my heart if I let him get any closer.

The problem was that I couldn't seem to keep that resolve when I saw him. Which is exactly why I'd been avoiding him in the first place.

"I...don't know," I said, shooting for aloof and failing miserably. Ah, fuck it. "What time?"

There went my resolve. God, he smelled so good, and those eyes of his shone so brightly.

"Ahem."

We followed Skylar into the library, pausing our conversation until we were in the study room our group reserved on Fridays.

"Lord, there you are," our friend Cherie said as we all piled in. "We need to make this snappy. I have a date tonight."

"So do I," Eric concurred. "A really hot one."

I smarted. He had a date? Hadn't he just asked me my plans? Was that for later, after he was done with a girl he actually wanted to be seen in public with?

But before I could spiral completely, I found Eric grinning at me with open intention. Oh...he meant me. Right?

He picked up my hand and pressed a kiss to my knuckles before cradling it in his lap. The knot in my belly relaxed. A little.

"Good lord, could they be any cuter?" Cherie asked Andre, another student.

"Looks like opposites do attract," he replied.

Eric just calmly squeezed my hand, but inside, I was spurting irritation. Opposites attract? What the hell was that supposed to mean? Yeah, sure, Eric and I were as different as fire and ice, but only I was supposed to say shit like that. Not some passive-aggressive law student who didn't know us from Adam. Was I really such a freak that people had to comment on the fact that someone like Eric would ever be attracted to me?

Goddammit. I was too old for this garbage.

Nevertheless, I spent the next forty-five minutes stewing while we pored over today's lecture notes and divvied up the readings at last.

Opposites attract. Opposites attract. What in the hell?

"Picture, please!" Cherie pulled out her phone. "I promised my parents I'd send them photos of our group."

"Cherie," I said. "My love. We are studying, not drinking. And I would very much like to be doing the latter, so can we just go, please?"

"Hear, hear," Eric said with a squeeze of my knee.

"Jane, don't be a spoilsport. It'll take one second."

I grumbled the entire time, but eventually complied for a giant selfie with the rest of the group, mashed together in front of the whiteboard.

"Send me a copy too," Eric said.

"Me too," Skylar piped up.

"Take one for me, I guess."

I unlocked my phone and handed it to Cherie, who immediately fumbled it and dropped it on the table. And there, of course, was good old Keith's extremely mediocre penis, splashed across my screen for everyone to see.

For a solid five seconds, the entire table was stone-still.

"You, ah, have something you want to share with the group, Lefferts?" Eric asked, his voice betraying not one iota of irritation.

I swallowed. I had nothing to feel bad about. Right?

"Oh, Janey," Skylar muttered under her breath.

"It's...it's..." I stammered.

"Note mine," Eric finished dryly to the rest of the group. He leaned toward Cherie and another girl conspiratorially. "To start, I'm a lot bigger than a four-inch hot dog."

The two of them tittered as if on command. I scowled. How nice for Eric that I gave him a chance to brag openly about his penis to whatever female company was present.

So instead of apologizing and deleting it, I reexamined the picture. "That's a little harsh. Keith here was solidly average. I bet he measured five point one six inches on the dot." I winked at Cherie. "Besides, it's girth that matters, am I right?" And then I shrugged at Eric. "Old lover. What do you want me to say?"

Eric's expression wasn't quite as relaxed as before. "Do we want to know why you have the average American cock length memorized, Lefferts?"

"You should be grateful," I said, purposefully deleting the picture in full view of his sardonic gaze while telling myself it had nothing to do with mitigating Eric's potential jealousy. Then I turned to him with a cocky grin—pun intended. "It's how I know you are, in fact, very above average." I winked at the other girls. "Maybe you'll get lucky one day too, ladies. Eric's pretty open with his gifts. Isn't that right?"

Finally, Eric's affable, relaxed mask broke. He looked like he wasn't sure whether he wanted to kiss me or spank me.

"Prove it," he said as he stood. "Excuse us, everyone. Come on, pretty girl."

"Oh, lord," Skylar muttered. "There they go again."

It was dangerous what this man was able to do to me with just a few words. Even his text messages had a similar effect. Over the last two weeks, since that night at the bar, I'd tried to keep him at arm's length. It just hadn't worked very well. Or at all.

There had been the next night at Cleo's. Two rounds of shuffleboard, and he'd grabbed my hand and dragged me out of there to the raucous jeers from our classmates.

Then there were the times he sat next to me in class. I'd take notes, but I still couldn't remember anything the professor said. Once, we'd barely made it to the end of the hall before Eric pulled me into the custodial closet and clamped a hand over my mouth while he had his way with me.

And then two nights ago, of course, when he'd shown up at my apartment, wet and chilled through after a night run along the Charles. Skylar had opened the door, then grabbed her bag and left with a knowing smile. I, however, had been frozen on the couch as he stalked toward me.

"Bedroom, pretty girl," he'd said.

And off I went.

Opposites attract, eh? Yeah, maybe a little too much.

Like I said, heartbreak. Everywhere. It wasn't a question of if it was coming. It was when.

But instead of denying him the way I should have, I gathered my things.

"Girl, good luck," Cherie whispered as I followed Eric out. He didn't even say goodbye.

"What the fuck was that?" he demanded as soon as we were outside the library, both of us still fastening our coats. "Or, should I say, who?"

I scowled. "That is none of your business."

"None of my business? It's none of my business why the girl I'm seeing has a picture of someone else's dick on her phone?"

"Are you serious right now?" I shot back. "You want to tell me there are zero dirty pictures of your conquests on your phone right now, Don Juan? I've seen you at the bar. Hell, I've seen you after class. They're like flies. Ms. Delaware is just dying to model her sash for you."

Eric's glare basically cut through every layer of clothing I had. "Is it serious? You and the junior salami?"

I shook my head. "I can't believe this. We have been...whatever we've been doing...for two weeks! I'm your booty call, not your girl-friend. You have no right to interrogate me here, boy-o."

"Well, maybe I want the right."

"Maybe?" I shook my head. "Spoken like a true bullshit artist. Tossing hypotheticals around like confetti instead of speaking with basic clarity. Tricking women into thinking it's the real thing while maintaining plausible deniability. Well, you know what? That shit doesn't work with me. I told you. I don't play these games."

Eric's face blackened. With lightning speed, he backed me up against the brick wall.

And then he kissed me. Eric was great in the sack, of course—as talented with his tongue, even, as other parts of his body. But this was something different. He wedged me against the wall, his mouth plun-dering mine to the point of bruises, tongue diving, possessive, full of intention.

Mine, it said. *And don't you fucking forget it.*

Then, just as quickly, he released me, allowing my legs to drop to the ground just in time for me to realize they had somehow wrapped around his waist to begin with.

"How's that for clarity?" he asked in a hoarse voice. It was cold enough that I could see his breath, white in the late afternoon chill.

I couldn't even reply, but my breath still mingled with his.

He pressed his forehead to mine. "Let me be very explicit about one more thing, Lefferts. If there are any other dicks on your phone, I want them erased."

I scowled. "Why?"

He stepped back, maybe to give me some space. Maybe for himself. "You really want me to explain that? Right now? Out here?" He gestured at the students walking by who were already peeking at us curiously.

I opened my mouth to dare him to say it. Do more than just hold my hand, like he'd held so many others. Say the one thing boys like him weren't supposed to say to girls like me, and definitely not in public. I like you. I like you more than just sex. I want to be with you more than just at night.

I want you.

"What are you afraid of?" he asked, so low it was almost a whisper. I almost didn't hear it.

I took a step toward him. Then another. And then...turned and started walking down the path, ignoring the throbbing in my chest, my gut, and yes, between my legs. This was so confusing. Everything with this guy was so confusing.

But when he didn't immediately follow, I still turned around. "Are you coming or what, Petri dish?"

Eric tipped his head to one side. "Petri dish?"

I shrugged. "You know. For all the specimens you've collected."

He opened his mouth in shock, but though his expression darkened again, there was a new glint in his eye I hadn't seen before.

"You're going to pay for that," he said as he caught up.

I looked up and batted my eyelashes, completely back in the game now. "Promise?"

Eric's scowl deepened for a moment, then gradually shifted into a sly smile that lit up his entire face. "Oh, yeah," he said. "Abso-fuck-ing-lutely."

NINE

Present

I sat in the waiting room, drinking cucumber water delivered from the tired-looking receptionist and rechecking my messages for any news about court. The hearing had been delayed by multiple motions, or so said the flurry of texts Skylar had sent while I slept. But I hadn't heard anything new in over an hour.

Eric, notably, had not called again, though he was undoubtedly allowed at least another phone call or two since we spoke on the edge of the field. He was still angry, then. I couldn't blame him.

It was a quarter to six in New York right now. Nearly two hours after the court was set to reconvene *again*. Fifteen minutes after they would have likely dismissed for the day. Either the trial was happening or it wasn't.

ME: YO! What is happening? You are done now, right?

My phone buzzed almost immediately.

SKYLAR: Srry, yes. Judge ordered recess. Reconvening tomorrow at eight. Ill call after talk 2 Eric + attny.

I frowned. Skylar wasn't usually one for truncated texting. She was in a hurry. The question was why? There were only a few reasons why the judge would want to reconvene later. Number one: the trial itself was under investigation.

It wasn't exactly what we had hoped for, but it was something. Another text from her interrupted my pondering.

SKYLAR: want me 2 tell him anything?

I stared at the text for several minutes, unsure of what to say. So, she knew he was upset, then. She knew he didn't want to talk to me.

Tears sprang—worsened, I was sure, by the torrents of hormones flowing through my body. I set a palm over my belly, which at this point, maybe looked like I had eaten too much pizza. But it was different. *I* was different. Eric was missing it, and it was my fault.

Just when I had sucked in enough deep breaths to stem the tears and started to type a few updates on John Carson—we had sent the list of companies and our thoughts to Detective Cho last night and he was investigating the sites today—my name was called.

"Mrs. de Vries?"

"Hi. Yes, I'm here. *Yeoboseyo!*" I ignored the nurse's cringe at my terrible Korean as I stood.

"Hello," she said in excellent English. "Follow me, please."

I followed her to an ultrasound room in the back of the office. Like the front room, it was plush. Very plush. Likely a lot plusher than most eight-weeks-pregnant ladies would be getting anywhere else. I hadn't been through this process myself, but between Suejean and talking with my best friend through her own pregnancies, I knew that most OB/GYNs left this work to an ultrasound tech.

Bridget, I realized. Give the executive assistant to the DVS chairman a task, and she definitely gets it done tenfold. Suejean had passed the name to her, and the plucky woman had ensured that her boss's wife would receive five-star service to soothe my harried mind —and probably the irate chairman behind bars. I definitely owed her a giant flower arrangement when I got back to New York. And probably a raise on Eric's behalf.

"Dr. Han will be with you soon," said the nurse. "Please change into this." She handed me a hospital gown and instructed that I should wait up on the table after I was finished.

I changed quickly, shivering like a frozen fish on the exam table while I waited. In my purse, my phone buzzed with a call, and I scramble to get it. *Eric*, I prayed, suddenly desperate to hear his voice, even if he was angry with me.

But it wasn't him.

"Detective Cho?" I answered. He was a distant cousin, but he hadn't instructed me to use anything other than his title at this point.

"Hello, Mrs. de Vries."

Apparently the formalities extended both ways.

"It's pretty early for a check-in, Detective," I said. "Have you been to all the sites already?"

There was an awkward clearing of his throat. "I have updates on some progress. Your security—they are with you?"

I frowned. That was a weird question. "Ah, well, I'm at a doctor's appointment right now, but Tony and the guys are in the waiting room."

"Good, good." Cho spoke hurriedly, almost distracted. "Mrs. de Vries, we found John Carson's rental car. It was at the second address you provided. I think you are correct about Mr. Carson's business interests here in Hwaseong."

"So...did you find him?" My heart leaped. Could it really be this easy? Was it possible that my mother and I could be on a plane back to New York today?

"We watched the building until he came out," Cho replied. "And then we followed his car. But he...unfortunately, he lost us. There is a call to other police to look for him right now. I will keep you updated. But you should remain with your security and stay at the hotel after your appointment."

"And my—" I was almost afraid to ask as my heart sank. "My mother? Was she there?"

"I'm so sorry," Cho said. "But your mother was not with him."

My heart sank. The resignation in his voice was clear. I had a feeling that Cho was going to be searching rice paddies for her body before he looked for a live woman.

No, I insisted to myself. *Not yet.*

"Okay," I said. "Well, thank you for updating me. I really appreciate it. And...Detective..."

"Yes?"

"Um...be careful." It felt so strange, almost like I was mothering a man who, despite a distant family connection, was little more than an acquaintance. *Ha*, I thought. These instincts were in me somewhere.

But he was taking on a lot on my behalf. I was grateful.

"I will call later, Mrs. de Vries," he said, then promptly hung up.

"Mrs. de Vries?"

I set the phone in my bag and hopped back on the table as the doctor poked her head through the curtains. She offered a kind smile.

"Hi, Dr. Han," I said, pulling the paper sheet over my legs. "Thank—thank you for taking me on with such short notice."

The doctor nodded. Like the rest of her staff, she looked tired— she was seeing me well outside of normal operating hours, likely because of a large bribe from Bridget's office.

"I told my OB/GYN that I would keep up with my schedule," I said, a bit lamely, not mentioning that at this point, my OB/GYN was my cousin. "She said an ultrasound at week eight of my pregnancy was standard. I just want to assure my husband I'm staying with the plan even while traveling." I didn't mention that the irate father would probably interrogate me like crazy about it when I got home.

Dr. Han gave me a calm, indecipherable look. "Yes, that is standard. I will print a copy of the pictures and provide a digital copy for you to bring back to the United States when we are finished." She pulled out a bottle of gel and raised the wand. "Can you bare your stomach, please?"

I managed not to flinch when she squeezed the cold gel just under my navel. She spread it around with the wand, and almost immediately, a hushed, rhythmic sound filled the tiny room. On the monitor next to us, a screen full of static appeared, in which I could make out a large black space, intermittently spread with static-filled shapes.

"You see this?" Dr. Han said, pointing at the black space. "This is your uterus." She moved the wand some more. "And there...is your baby. You see the movement?"

I did see a tiny flicker. Something shifting in time with the thrumming sound.

"That is the heartbeat," Dr. Han said. "You can hear it? That is your baby."

I said nothing, just stared at the screen in awe. It was hard to make out the shape—it was really no bigger than a nut—but the movement was clear, as was its rhythm. There he—she? It?—was. This tiny little thing. The product of Eric and me. Together.

"Holy shit," I whispered, unable to keep another round of tears from welling up. I swiped at them hurriedly, but Dr. Han didn't seem bothered. "It's...wow."

The doctor took a few more pictures, checking for initial abnormalities and things like that (so she said). But the baby was small, and she said there wasn't much to do until my twenty-week scan.

"Everything looks good," she said. "Very healthy. You will need to have a blood test, usually between ten and thirteen weeks. Will you need an appointment here, or will you—"

"I'll be home," I said with more assurance than I felt. "I...I'll be home." I had to be.

The doctor nodded again, then pressed a few buttons and printed out a strip of shiny photos from the ultrasound. She handed them to me. "For you and your husband." She handed me a cloth as well to clean up my stomach, then hopped off her stool. "I will go retrieve the digital copy and return."

I nodded, too entranced with the photos to speak.

"Hey," I whispered, staring at the blurry black-and-white photos. "Hey there, tiny cellular cluster. One day you will be an actual person. And I am going to be ridiculously happy to meet you."

I got dressed, staring at the pictures on the table the whole time. Just when I finished and had picked them up again, my phone buzzed in my bag. I jumped, almost dropping the ultrasound pictures before I managed to check the new text message.

SKYLAR: Major news!! The judge turned the case over to the Brooklyn DA's office because of the conflicts with the Manhattan DA. Brooklyn is declining to prosecute.

I read the words four more times before I fully comprehended what was happening.

The initial corrupt judge. Apparently there had been more questions with the DA handling the case, hence the multiple motions today. And now a switch, which meant...

My phone rang. I answered it immediately.

"Sky?"

"It's done, Jane," my friend said. "Over before it even began."

The pictures in my hand seemed to glow.

"Where is he?" I sobbed. "Sky, I have to talk to him."

"Oh, Janey," she said. "I—I honestly don't know. They literally just dismissed, and just left the gallery. They might be processing his release right now."

My heart squeezed. Did he know? Would he be able to check his messages soon? I desperately wanted to be there, to be on the other side of those doors when he was released.

"Sky," I said. "Call me back when he's with you, okay? I need to do something right now."

We hung up, and then I turned to the ultrasound screen and snapped a photo of the shot the doctor had taken. I sent the picture to Eric with the caption. *We miss you.*

Then I called his phone, which, of course, went straight to voice-mail after two weeks in a box.

"Eric," I hiccupped. "I know you won't get this for a while, but... oh, Eric, I'm at the doctor's office. And I saw her. It. Whatever she is, but *her*, I heard her heartbeat! She's just...oh my God, Eric, she's only a little peanut, but she was real, you know? And I...God, I'm so sorry you're not here, but I swear, as soon as I find my mom, I'm coming home. *We* are coming home to you. I'm staying safe, I promise, and I'm *so* glad that you're safe now too. Get some new security since I stole yours, okay? Promise me that you'll keep yourself safe until we're together."

I paused, took a deep breath, and then continued with the words we often found so hard to say to each other. Words I had always struggled to accept clearly when he had said them, but which I desperately wanted to hear. As I stared at the picture of my daughter or son, I knew I didn't want to continue in that tradition. I wanted to be the kind of person who was open with my heart. For her. For him. For my family.

"Eric," I whispered. "I-I love you. I love you so damn much, and I promise you that once I come back, I am *never* leaving you again. I'll stop calling you Petri dish. I won't force you to eat kimchi on every-thing. And I won't run. I just want us to be a family, because that is what we are. I promise you. I just need to get all of that family back, okay?"

I paused again, realizing the idiocy of talking to a machine like it was going to talk back.

"I love you," I said once more, then took a breath and repeated it one last time for good luck. "I love you. Like the water I drink. Like the air I breathe. Corny, I know, but I'll come home to you soon and let you write the poetry. I promise."

Then, reluctantly, I hung up. The words weren't enough, but they were all I could offer. I'd come up with more one day. I'd try it every day for the rest of my life if it would help him know what he really meant to me.

"Touching. Very touching."

I screamed at the sound of a deep, sonorous voice. From behind the thick door stepped a tall, familiar form.

John Carson, looking like the grim reaper himself in pure black and a black trench coat with the collar turned up on both sides, separated the curtains and entered the room, followed by two stocky Asian gentlemen and another tall white man with a hooked nose.

"Daughter," he greeted me. His voice was calm as he took in the room and the pictures on the table.

I scrambled immediately into the far corner. "What—what the hell are you doing in here?" I looked beyond him. "How did you get past my security?"

"I hear you and that pathetic excuse for an investigator were looking for me." Carson turned the monitor so he could have a better look at the picture, examining it with distant interest, like he was evaluating a map or a blueprint. He turned back. "He found me, of course. But he shouldn't have."

And that, I realized, was as close to an admission of Lawrence Kim's murder as I was going to get. I looked longingly at my purse, wishing I could grab my phone.

"Get out," I said with as much bravado as I could muster. "The doctor is going to be back any second too. And my security will wonder where I am."

"Your security team was no match for a former KGB operative and the rest of my team, I'm afraid," Carson replied, leaning toward the screen. "And your doctor, well, she is quite indisposed as well. Now, I'm not a medical professional, but I confess, I don't see anything here. Do you have a cyst or something? Some kind of medical emergency?"

"I'm pregnant, you idiot," I retorted, realizing only too late that I probably should have kept that to myself.

His face blackened completely. Of course. It was only a few months ago that Eric and I had explicitly been warned about the dangers of procreating. The man was a eugenicist monster, so dead-set against the mingling of his own gene pool with his sworn enemy's that he had absolutely forbidden our marriage. I hadn't really believed that song and dance...until now.

"Daughter," he said again as he seethed at the ultrasound machine. "So you and your 'paramour' have done your very best to flout my orders."

"Your *orders* don't mean shit," I snapped. Fuck. Why hadn't I allowed Tony to come back here with me? What in the hell had these goons done to him?

His dark, deceptively hazel eyes—so unnervingly like mine—narrowed. "Is that right? And how is the de Vries spawn taking it while he rots in jail?"

"You didn't really think that was going to last, did you?" I cut back. "Those were trumped-up charges, and you know it. It's over. He's getting out now that they moved the trial away from your bribed prosecutor and corrupt judge."

Carson smiled then, and the sight of it turned me to ice. He was the human incarnation of the Grinch about to steal Christmas. The clear, perverse pleasure he took in orchestrating Eric's stay at Rikers Island was bone-chilling.

"Perhaps," he admitted. "But it accomplished its purpose, did it not?"

I frowned. "How do you figure?"

"Well," he said. "You are here. Your worthless renegade of a *husband*"—he practically spat the word—"is not."

Realization sank in my heart like an anchor. Of course. This had been his plan all along. Separate us. Just like Eric said.

But in order to do what?

Before I could ask, Carson held up a hand, and with the flick of his fingers, gestured his henchmen inside the crowded space.

"Your mother is alive," he informed me, like he was telling me the state of the weather. "But if you care about her life at all, you'll come with me. Quietly and obediently, if that's even possible for you. Now."

INTERLUDE I

"Come now, hen. Jake is gone. It's time to move on, and I have been very patient."

"Don't call me that, John."

The voices filtered up the stairs to Eric's suite on the second floor of the townhouse. He put down the book he was reading and got up to listen. He had found a cache of J.D. Salinger novels a few weeks ago and had been tearing through them, just like he did with all the books in his father's abandoned study. But right now, Holden Caulfield could wait.

A year ago, unannounced visitors were a common thing. His parents had been the center of a thriving social scene on the Upper East Side. If they weren't attending formal functions at his grandmother's penthouse or others within their social station, Jacob and Heather had hosted dinner parties themselves. Eric preferred the latter—it allowed him to sneak away with friends or even with a good book when he was finished with his meals, maybe eavesdrop on the adults from his favorite spot on the landing. He would sneak glimpses of his parents laughing in the reverie, occasionally catch a glimpse of the way Jacob would flirt with his wife when he thought others weren't looking. They were the couple everyone wanted to be. And how proud Eric had been of the fact.

But that was before. Since Jacob's untimely death, the townhouse had been a tomb, haunted by the ghost of Jacob's laugh, buried by his wife and son's sorrow.

Eric wasn't an idiot. He knew his mother was the object of interest to the men in her social circle. A few months after the funeral, the maid had opened the door to more than one man looking for Heather. Most of them, to Eric's relief, were turned away.

This one, however, was more stubborn. This time, Heather had come to the door before he would leave.

Eric crept out of his rooms and crouched at the top of the stairs, hidden in the shadows of the railing, but fully able to hear the conversation and watch the feet pacing the stone tiles.

There was a long chuckle. "Didn't Jake call you that? Seems like someone should keep it going."

Eric smarted. Dad called Mom a lot of nicknames—hen was just one of them.

"John..."

"I'm not afraid of ghosts, Heather. And I'm certainly not afraid of his."

There was some more pacing. Eric caught the gleam of a black men's dress shoe.

"I've waited long enough, Heather. It's time."

"John, please. You can't still be angry about something that happened more than fifteen years ago. I don't owe you anything."

"Angry? I'm not angry. Like I told you, I've been very patient. Waiting for what was rightfully mine to come back to me."

The shadows at the bottom of the steps moved.

"Let me go." His mother's voice was as weak as ever, but it bore a chill that Eric had never heard before.

"Not until I get the answer I want."

"John, please. I said let me go!"

Eric didn't wait another second. He scuttled down the stairs two steps at a time until he landed in the foyer with a crash against the big oak table in the center. The vase of roses wobbled, but didn't fall.

The man turned. He looked vaguely familiar. Tall, with a slightly hooked nose, curly hair that was mostly a dark brown, and greenish eyes that seemed to shift in the light. Like quicksilver.

The man dropped Heather's wrist, and she stepped back immediately.

"Ah," said the man. "Eric. The young sea sprite. It's nice to see you again, boy. Been a while, hasn't it?"

Eric stepped between them, allowing his mother to wrap her fragile hand around his arm. He would have liked her to pull him back and cage his shoulders with her arms, the way she used to do when he was small. But he was too big for that now. Last summer he had had a growth spurt, and now, at nearly twelve, he was nearly five-seven, at least an inch or two above his mother. Now he had to guard her.

He was not, unfortunately, taller than this man, who seemed to loom over them both like one of the gargoyles hanging off St. John the Divine.

The man smiled. It wasn't a nice smile. It felt like a knife was slicing down his chest. Eric pressed a hand to his sternum, but he couldn't look away.

"Your mother and I were speaking," said the man. "I admire a man who stands up for himself, but let's be clear. You won't win this fight, Triton."

"Who's Triton?" Eric managed. "My name is Eric. Who are you?"

But the man didn't answer. Instead he just pushed up the sleeve of his jacket and checked his watch. It was identical to the one his father used to wear. Above that, Eric caught sight of a thin chain bracelet with a gold coin.

"This is a conversation between adults. I'll give you one second to move," said the man. "And then I'll do it for you."

Eric gulped. But his mother didn't try to move him. She needed him. His dad, wherever he was, needed him too.

So he went against every impulse he had and met that terrible green gaze straight-on. "No."

The man's smirk disappeared. "Very well."

Eric braced himself—for what, he wasn't sure. A blow to the cheek? A twist of an arm? Something worse? But before he could find out, there was a harsh rap at the front door. Everyone froze.

"Oh, for heaven's sake," came a voice through the door. "Has all propriety evaporated? Garrett, will you please open the door since my daughter-in-law's maid can't be bothered to do her job?"

For once in his life, Eric was glad to hear the familiar, irritable voice sounding from the other side of the thick oak. Keys jingled, and a few seconds later, the door opened as Garrett, the old butler, held the door open for Eric's grandmother: Celeste Annika van Dusen de Vries.

"My goodness, Heather," she said as she walked in, brushing rain off her Burberry coat. "Is it the fashion now to force your guests to stand outside like common solicitors?"

The older woman stopped when she realized the foyer was actually full of people. Her sharp gaze sliced through the tension, landing on the visitor, John, after touching on her grandson and his mother.

"What in the world..." she muttered. "John. I don't know what you are doing here, but you are not welcome. I thought I made that clear at the funeral."

The man's nasty smirk reappeared. "So you did. But this is not your home, Celeste."

"It's de Vries property, just like the penthouse. That didn't change with Jacob's passing."

The man quirked his head, like he was measuring whether or not to continue this argument. "You can't protect her forever, Celeste. You're not Heather's keeper."

"Perhaps not," she said evenly. "But I do have a vested interest. Much like I do in Chariot, don't I?"

For a long time, the man didn't speak. Grandmother glared. And much to Eric's satisfaction, the man looked away first.

He turned to Heather. "Until we meet again, hen. Triton." And then, with an awful, terrible wink at Eric, he left.

It took ten full breaths before Eric could even hear his mother's voice again, waging yet another weak argument against his grandmother. Eric rolled his eyes. There was no point to arguing with Grandmother. She always won. She was a force of nature herself.

"You know why I'm here," Celeste was saying. "You haven't been answering my calls. Things are falling apart. And now I see that parasite in your home with Eric guarding you like a puppy? It's a good thing I showed up when I did."

Eric turned to find his mother falling back into one of the antique chairs in the foyer.

"Celeste." Heather's voice was barely above the echoes of shuffling footsteps. "Please. I just need more time. We need more time."

"You've had nearly a full year." Celeste looked at Eric. "The boy needs more guidance than he is getting. He is my sole heir. It's time to accept the proposal and for Eric to come where he belongs."

"Celeste, please—"

"John Carson is not going to leave the matter alone," Celeste continued. "You know that just as well as I. Since Jacob's death, he has become a man obsessed, and I'm sorry to say, no amount of money will put him off. You have only a few choices here. Eric will be safer with me. You will be safer married to Horace."

Eric watched their interaction like he was witnessing a tennis match. What was happening? Safer with Grandmother? Married?

His mother's arguments fell again and again, and with dread building in his chest, he watched her capitulate quickly, shrinking into the chair with every flattened reply.

"Come, Eric," Celeste beckoned. "I am on my way to Westchester for the weekend." She said the word like it was something different from what everyone else meant, with extra emphasis on the final syllable. Week-end. "Garrett will escort you to your polo practice this afternoon, and then we will return for your things."

Eric shook his head, finding his voice at last. "No, Grandmother. I'm staying here."

Celeste simply pressed her pink lips together and shook her head. "I'm afraid that's out of the question, Eric. De Vrieses do not renege on their promises. Your mother made me one, and that was on your behalf."

"It's just a missed practice," Eric argued. "Mom's upset. She needs me—"

"She needs you to let her be," Celeste cut in irritably.

"No," Eric said, this time forcefully enough that his voice cracked. That had been happening more and more lately. "I—I know what you're doing. This isn't just polo, Grandmother. You're—you're taking me away. It's because of that man, isn't it? He wants something from Mom, doesn't he?"

"Oh, Eric," Heather murmured, shaking her head.

The older woman's eyes narrowed. "You heard, did you? Eavesdropping is quite unbecoming of a young man like yourself, Eric. I see we have more work to do than I anticipated." She glared at Heather, as if Eric's shortcomings were yet another indication of her character deficiencies.

Talk back, Eric wanted to say to her. But instead, Heather gazed at him. She reached out like she wanted to stroke his cheek, but dropped her hand almost immediately.

"I'm afraid not," she murmured. And then, to Celeste: "He'll go. I'll have his things sent tomorrow."

Celeste nodded and turned to the door. "Very well, Eric, let's—"

"On one condition," Heather continued.

Celeste turned and raised a wry silver brow. "What is that?"

Heather's gray gaze flickered nervously between her mother-in-law and her son. "He stays here. In New York."

Celeste opened her mouth to argue back. It just wasn't done, she would say. Every de Vries heir for generations had attended the same boarding school in Europe. What right did Heather have to break such a longstanding tradition?

But Heather rattled on with more energy than Eric had seen since the funeral, where she had collapsed across his father's coffin just before it was lowered into the ground.

"It's what Jacob and I planned for him," she insisted. "He's an American, Celeste. He belongs here. And if I'm going to give him up, I refuse to do so completely. He needs to be close to his mother. To his family. Not far away from everything he knows. I won't let him lose that."

Too. The word was unspoken, but there, nonetheless. On top of his father, she meant. On top of her.

Eric swallowed thickly. Part of him wanted to run to the back of the house, sneak out the fire escape he wasn't supposed to climb on, and disappear into the city. He could leave New York, jump on one of the boxcars that his family owned. Ride away on a boat or a train or a truck and never return to this place, this city full of death and anger and sorrow.

But he knew he wouldn't. This conversation, this family—they were like chains on his legs.

Like she was a balloon that had just expelled the last of its helium, Heather sank to the chair once again and looked on wearily as Eric fetched his coat and put on his shoes. Was this really happening?

"It's better this way," she said. "You'll see. Grandmother is so much stronger than me. She has things to teach you."

She had been so sad for the last year. She hadn't even bothered to hide the empty bottles of vodka in the bedroom, leaving them for the maids to clean up each morning. Outwardly, Eric's mother was as beautiful as ever. But a light had shined in her eyes once. Eric realized now it wouldn't reappear.

"I'll see you when you return," she said softly. "We'll make a proper goodbye of it then."

She watched apathetically as Garrett hustled Eric into his coat and out the door. The air was full of "see you soons" and "in a few days." But when Eric turned, just before the door closed behind him, he caught a glimpse of Heather falling forward in the chair, face crumpling into her delicate hands. He wasn't sure if the wail that sounded after the locks clicked was a distant siren or his mother.

Inside Grandmother's Rolls, he turned to the old woman angrily. But before he could speak, Celeste spied the coin hanging around his neck.

"Take that off at once," she ordered, holding out her hand.

Eric's face screwed up in confusion. "What? No! It's mine, Grandmother."

"No, it belongs to me," she said. "If you recall, Garrett offered it to me at the funeral, not you. In fact, it belonged to my husband, who gave it to your father." Her hand beckoned insistently. "I offered it to a child mourning his father. But you are not a child any longer, Eric. Give it back."

Eric's eyes shone fiercely, glittering with rebellion. His entire life, everyone had been telling him what to do. At least his father used to jump in, shield him from the worst of it. He had taught him how to break the rules as much as how to obey them. Taken him to play catch in the park when he was supposed to be learning how to fence. Gotten pizza or Gray's Papaya for dinner instead of eating *coq au vin* at the penthouse.

Dad would have let him keep the necklace. Eric was sure of it.

But Dad was gone. And his mother had let Eric go too.

There was no one else in his life but Grandmother, whose sharp, unwavering expression told him she, out of all of them, wasn't giving up.

So, with a deep sigh, Eric unclasped the coin from around his neck and dropped it into her waiting palm. Maybe one day he'd find the courage to fight her. But today was not that day.

Present

Eric paged through the now-worn journal for what had to be the hundredth time. It was amazing how beat up the small black book had become in just a few days since his mother had given it to him. But when there was nothing to do but pore over the thing, he had practically memorized its strange, fragmented contents.

It was the journal his father was probably never supposed to keep. He had read the others, the ones intended for public record, the way all the de Vrieses kept papers to be stored eventually at endowed libraries or in state historical records. They were a "family of record," as his grandmother used to say. Everyone was taught to act like it.

It was a habit that, even in his years apart from the clan, Eric had never been interested in breaking.

But unlike those records, which represented history written by its victors, this journal was something different, almost reading like a supplement to those more official histories. Its entries were chronological, but there were often months, even years between them. It was full of clues that historians usually sought between the lines of standard sources. Coded phrases that others would have read as non sequitur comments or the idiosyncrasies of a rich, frivolous man. But Eric suspected they masked secrets that his family would have wanted to hide. As such, they were infuriatingly opaque.

April 22, 1982

Johnny's been tapped to make croutons. Three days of fighting, and I still don't know if it was worth it. Did he know I wouldn't have walked away otherwise? It's better to keep him close. He doesn't like being pushed out.

Tapping for croutons—that was obviously in reference to Janus, which tended to be shrouded in Caesar salad references, or something like it. The timing was right. In 1982, Jake de Vries would have been approximately twenty-two—a senior in college. But Johnny... was that who Eric thought it was? John was such a common name, that he couldn't know for sure. But why else would his mother have given him the journal? The investigator had determined that Carson had also attended Princeton, just like Eric's father. Had he been tapped there too?

August 28, 1983

Picked up Heather by the lakes. She was crying—I don't want to even ask what J did this time. I should let her go, but I can't. She deserves more than what he can give her. She deserves more than me too, but I'm determined to be better for her, no matter what Mother says.

Eric kept coming back to that one again and again. As far as he knew, his parents had met sometime in college, when his father was a senior and his mother just a freshman. She teased him about it incessantly—that he spent his weekends traveling to Princeton during those years instead of partying in New York as a young man. The stories had charmed a young Eric.

But if all that was true, who was this J? The one who hurt her?

September 8, 1983

Dad died today. He knew it was coming, apparently, even if the rest of us didn't.
No one brought salad to the wake, but they asked me to toss some almost immediately. Johnny wouldn't eat. I won't pretend it didn't hurt, but it wasn't a surprise either. Poor guy can't catch a break, or so he thinks.

Again with the salad references. Eric thought he understood that some. None of the Janus members had come to the funeral, but maybe his father had been summoned to a meeting? Something like that. But he didn't understand why Johnny, whom he suspected was Carson, was so upset. What hadn't he received?

There weren't any entries after that for a while. Jonathan de Vries's death from an aggressive lung cancer wasn't something Eric knew much about, but he knew it was sudden. Perhaps it shouldn't have been such a surprise, given the man was a lifelong smoker and cigar connoisseur. But anytime the subject came up when Eric was a child, someone changed it—even faster if his grandmother happened to be in hearing distance. The gap left in the family was still evident, even more than thirty-five years later.

May 11, 1985

Heather is pregnant. Bad timing, of course, with her gradua-tion coming, but I'm over the damn moon. Maybe it's just the thing to put all this ugliness behind us. Maybe Johnny can finally forgive the past and move on.

Again with the Johnny. What past? What had happened?

But that wasn't the only interesting thing about the entry, which basically marked Eric's own conception. His parents had also gotten married in 1985. A perfect June wedding. His mother had always played off the simple wedding at St. Mark's as their own choice— neither of them wanted the fancy affair that no doubt Celeste would have desired. But she was also pregnant, a fact that had been skated over his entire life. He had once wondered how much of their marriage occurred to right that social wrong. But there was something gratifying in seeing just how, well, dedicated his father really was to the two of them.

January 8, 1986

Heather did famously. Strong girl.
Eric is a solid little brick. The doctors say he can't see anything
yet, but he knew who I was when he looked at me. Gray eyes,
just like his mother's. I swear he has my hands. How could
someone this small own so much of us already?
J offered me his wishes, but I wonder if it's to make sure I'm
going with him to Suwon. He's nervous about the Russian
deal. I just wish it wasn't happening now. I hate to leave
Heather and the boy so soon.

Eric brushed a finger over the entry—one of the few written testi-
monies of his father's devotion on the day of his birth. He'd spent this
last one with Jane during visiting hours, wishing to God he had some
means of bribing the Rikers guards for some conjugal time with his
wife.

His eyes lingered on the words before dropping to the final
sentence. What deal with the Russians? What was his father and the
mysterious J doing in Seoul at the end of the Cold War?

Unfortunately, he wasn't going to find out. There were only two
entries left intact, as several pages had been ripped out of the book
near the end, and they were nearly two years apart.

January 30, 1987

All the transport between Hwaseong and Goseong is in place.
Honestly, if it wasn't Johnny asking, I wouldn't be anywhere
near this. But I don't know what else to do. He just can't seem
to let her go, even with this new racket with the airline. Those
girls seem like trouble too.
But Heather is worth it. I'd blow up the planet for her and
Eric, much less a few Ruskies.

Was the airline the same one Jane's mother and her friends

worked for? The dates lined up, just a month or so from when Jane was likely conceived.

But there was nothing more than a final entry, written in a much more jagged print, almost like Jacob didn't want to be writing it at all.

December 27, 1989

Home, home. Heather won't talk to me for missing Christmas, but it couldn't be helped. We had to clean things up. Everything's gone to hell now that the Soviets are done for. J thinks Gorbachev can still pull the country back together—he won't forgive me for thinking otherwise.
The ships, the trucks, everything is back where they should be.
J and I are done for good.

After reading the last cryptic lines again and again, Eric finally set the book on the visitors' table with a smack. The words meant no more to him now than they had two days ago. What had ended the strange friendship, fraught as it was with animosity? What in the *hell* did it have to do with DVS and the fall of the Soviets?

Eric turned to the door of the visitors' room. He needed to talk this through with someone. What in the *fuck* was taking them so long? He'd been in the courthouse jail all fucking day while the lawyers played courtroom tennis. Was he going back to Rikers tonight or not?

His suit—the one Jane had brought him during her last visit—fit poorly. Too baggy around the waist. He had undoubtedly lost weight over the last two weeks. The food at Rikers was fucking disgusting. The coffee was the worst of all.

The door opened, and Eric lurched in his chair. Fucking hell, he was a jumpy mess.

"What's going on?" he barked before everyone had even filed inside. Levi Gellert, the primary counsel on his defense team, followed by Skylar and Brandon, posing as counsel but really there for moral support, and the bailiff.

And one person...one person *still* missing.

What if it had gone terribly? What if, by some fucked-up chance, he had been sentenced to years and years away, without even saying goodbye to his wife?

"She's still not back?" Eric demanded. "Jesus Christ, Skylar, does she even know the trial is happening?"

Something deep in him deflated. He knew it was unfair, but a part of him hoped that Jane would choose him over her lying, emotionally abusive mother. Because really, that's what Yu-na was, in his opinion.

Skylar sighed. "She knows, Eric. We've been in contact for the last few days. But she still hasn't found Yu-na. I just spoke to her, and she was at a doctor's office. Getting—getting the ultrasound done."

Eric stiffened. "She's at the doctor without me too?"

Again, unfair. But good God, couldn't the woman wait for him for *anything*?

Skylar took a seat in front of him next to the other lawyer. "Eric, you know she wants to be here. She's just trying to do the right thing."

Eric sucked in a deep breath, trying to calm himself. It didn't work. So he did it again. And again. "Crosby," he said finally. "We've been friends a long time. I like you. You know I do. But I swear to God, if you don't stop defending her decision to run off like an idiot without *anyone* there to help her, I'm going to—"

"You're going to stop it right there, chief." Brandon cut in front of Skylar, with a dangerous tone Eric recognized. He recognized it because the same possessive emotions that powered it were pumping through his veins right now. It was primal, this feeling. Fucking terrifying the way it wouldn't abate.

Which was why, of course, Eric didn't hold back. His chair legs screeched on the linoleum as he stood up in a rush. "Stop *what*, asshole? Stop asking completely reasonable fucking questions? Stop wanting the right to know where the fuck my wife and unborn child are? Jesus fucking Christ, Brandon! You're telling me you wouldn't be losing it if Skylar ran off with Jenny and you were locked up?"

"Eric," Brandon said through gritted teeth, trying and failing to maintain calm. "Man. Breathe. Just breathe, and tell us what you want, all right?"

"What I *want*? What *I* want?" Before he could help himself, Eric lunged over the table at Brandon, and just managed to snag his tie before the big man could jump out of reach. "I want to get the fuck out of this rat trap and *find my fucking wife*! THAT'S WHAT I WANT!"

The two men seethed at each other—Eric for want of control, Brandon trying desperately not to react the way he was trained. Eric knew he was playing with fire. Brandon had been raised on the streets. He was seriously tempting fate here—when it came to fight or flight, Brandon would always choose the former.

"Careful, brother," Brandon said, his tone walking the line between compassion and threat as he unwound Eric's fingers from his tie. "It's not me you're mad at. Remember that."

Eric sucked in a breath, and as the new oxygen flowed into his overheated brain, he found he was able to let go of the silk. Like he was releasing a lifeline, he slumped back into his chair and fell forward to cradle his throbbing head in his hands. He was going crazy in here. He really fucking was.

"Please," he begged. "Give me some good news. Tell me I can get the fuck out of here."

"You can get out of here."

At the sound of Levi Gellert's voice, the three of them all turned to face the oddly calm attorney.

Eric sat up, unsure if he was imagining it. "I—I can?"

Levi nodded. "Everything is finished."

Eric turned to the bailiff. "I'm free to go?"

The large man simply nodded.

Eric was done with words. He was done with waiting.

He jumped up, and without another word, strode out of the room, the bailiff jogging behind to escort him out properly.

"Eric! Eric, where are you going?"

He didn't know who called the words. Whether they were male or female. His lawyer, the police, or his friends. Nor did he answer. Because all he knew was that he needed to get out. He needed to find transportation.

He needed to find his wife.

PART TWO

COUPLET

I floated on the jetstream
A pillow
A mist
And flew within your thoughts
'Til I wondered if you existed
At all.
But the dawn, it called,
An echo
A gleam
And I heard your voice cry out for me
And followed it, a flame
Snuffed.
Out.

"Jetstream"
—a poem from the journal of Eric de Vries

TEN

2009

"We can't stop fighting."

I pushed my black and white polka-dotted glasses up my nose. Skylar was staring gloomily out the window of our apartment. Outside, the first real snow of the year was falling on the fire escape, and with her knees pulled up to her chest, perched on the sill in her preferred oversized lounge clothes, she looked more like a Dickensian child than a Harvard law student.

"You and Patrick?" I set my textbook down on the coffee table. These conversations were becoming as predictable as the moon's cycles.

She turned with sad green eyes. "Yeah. He's...he says it's me. He says I invent reasons to be upset with him."

I scowled. "Well, that's textbook gaslighting if I ever heard it."

"What's gaslighting?"

"It's..."

I tapped my lip with my pencil, trying to remember how my dad described it. It helped sometimes, having a father who was a shrink.

He gave me a vocabulary for these things pretty early, although one of the most awkward conversations of my life was his version of the sex talk a month before I left for college. Well, that one was less about sex, which I already understood, and more about men. And some of the things that they could do to make women stay in terrible relationships. His greatest fear for me, he always said, was that I would settle for someone who would convince me I was worth anything less than the best. That I would stay when I didn't have to.

As cringe-worthy as I'd found that conversation, that's how I learned about gaslighting. Dad really was before his time in so many ways.

"It's when someone tries to make you feel crazy," I said. "Unstable, hysterical, etcetera. Like everything you think is all in your head."

"Why's it called gaslighting?" Skylar wondered.

"Hell if I know."

But she had already pulled her phone out to check Wikipedia. "It says here it started with a play written in the forties called *Gaslight*. A husband convinces his wife she's crazy by manipulating things in their house. Like turning down the gaslights." She set her phone down. "I don't think Patrick is doing that. He just gets frustrated with me. I guess I'm taking this long-distance thing harder than I have to."

"Or he is and he's projecting his fears and missteps onto you. Why else would he constantly be accusing you of cheating when you practically live like a nun?"

Skylar's sharp look told me I had overstepped. We were growing closer, for sure, but I needed to back off.

"We just fight," she said, rising from the windowsill and padding into the kitchen to make herself some tea. "Like strong-willed people sometimes do."

"Sounds familiar." I followed her in and took a seat on the other side of the L-shaped counter.

"You want?" She held up a box of green tea.

I nodded.

"So, you and Eric..."

"Like jackals."

"Yeah, I noticed. You're not exactly nice to him during study group."

"I think it's the perfectly cut hair," I replied. "Or maybe the ironed shirts. I just want to, I don't know, put a wrinkle in there somewhere. The guy is immovable."

"Don't you think maybe you're just looking for a problem that's not really there?" Skylar filled the kettle and set it on the stove.

"Now who's gaslighting?"

Skylar chuckled. "I just mean, he seems to really like you."

"Sky, we've been over this. Guys like Eric don't 'really like' girls like me. They are fascinated by us. Until they aren't. I'm an amusement, that's all."

But Skylar just rolled her eyes. "What's the word for gaslighting yourself? Delusion?"

"Hey! I resent that."

"Janey, this isn't high school, and Eric isn't like the suburban kids you went to school with. He's from New York, like me. I promise you, he's seen all types, even if he did grow up on the Upper East Side or wherever."

I considered arguing that people were people, and bigotry existed as much in the city as out in the middle of nowhere. Growing up in New York didn't tell me a thing about how prejudiced Eric was or wasn't.

Skylar poured us both mugs of tea, but before I could say anything more, there was a knock on our door.

I frowned. "Are you expecting anyone?"

Skylar shook her head. "Maybe Rob down the hall wants to 'borrow another cup of sugar.'"

I snickered. Our neighbor seemed to bake more than anyone I had ever met, if his constant excuses to stop by were any indication. "He can make all the midnight snacks he wants. He's not getting your cookie or mine."

The knock sounded again.

"All right, all right. Keep your pants on." I slid off the stool and opened the door. "Rob, I'm telling you, all that sugar is bad for your—oh!"

Eric stood on our ladybug-covered welcome mat, looking magazine-perfect in a pair of jeans, Sorel boots, a thick wool coat, and just a touch of snow quickly melting into his tousled blond hair. He looked way more delicious than someone walking out of an L.L. Bean catalog had any right to look.

"Who's Rob?" he asked with a frown. "And why would his pants be off?"

I narrowed my eyes. It had been almost two weeks since his little possessive spat with the dick pics, and I'd made it very clear that this couldn't be anything more than a leisure activity for either of us. When he didn't like that, I ended up ghosting him again. Or trying. I still couldn't quite let him go. Especially at one in the morning. On a Saturday night. And, the following Wednesday. And, yeah, okay, Friday, Saturday, and Sunday night too.

Did I say ghosting? Maybe more like haunting.

"Did—did I forget something? Were we hanging out?" I purposefully avoided the word "date," like I usually did, since Eric and I rarely made it out of either of our apartments whenever we met up.

He cocked his head. "Hello to you too, pretty girl."

As if on command, I flushed. The boy tended to do seriously dirty things to me whenever he used that particular phrase. Just two days ago he tied me to his double bed just to prove a point before he wore me out over the back of his couch. Talk about thinning the line between love and hate.

That curiously magnetic smile appeared, and just as quickly, my toes tingled. Dammit, how did he do that? His whole face completely transformed whenever he grinned.

"What the hell are you doing here?" I didn't mean to sound that curt.

One blond brow rose. "Why? Did you have other plans? With Rob, maybe?"

"I might have." Right. You were "planning" to watch reruns of *That Seventies Show* and gossip with Skylar about the hot barista at Peet's.

"Like what? Being rude and not inviting someone in? Hiding someone?" He poked his head over my shoulder and waved. "Hey, Skylar."

I backed up as he pushed past me into the apartment.

Skylar just waved back awkwardly. "Hey, Eric. I'm, ah, just going to head back to my room to study some more."

We waited until her door closed, and then I turned back to Eric, who was now watching me with irritatingly pleasant curiosity.

"Do you always just barge into people's apartments like you own them?" I demanded.

His gaze seared over my otherwise unremarkable outfit of black leggings and a Joan Jett shirt. "When they don't answer my texts, I do. Where have you been? After class yesterday you bolted."

I scowled. "I don't know. Living the normal life of a first-year law student? Class. The library. Trying not to kill myself with paper writing."

Did his face whiten a little when I said the words "kill myself"? I blinked, and it was gone.

"Look, if you don't want to hang out anymore, I get it," he said, pacing around the couch. "But you came to my apartment Wednesday night, Jane. You came to me after you said you wanted to call it off. Again. And then you took off. Again. Did you really think I was just going to let you jerk me around?"

He unbuttoned his jacket, revealing a heather-gray sweater that hugged his trim body in all the right places. And lord, his legs looked impossibly long and scalable in those jeans. The fact of it should have been infuriating—how dare he make me enjoy his yuppie J. Crew aesthetic this much?—but instead I couldn't stop ogling.

"You seemed to like me jerking you around on Thursday," I said coyly, trying another tactic. Eric could be distracted with the right words, or so I was finding out. I could make this easier on us. Get it out of our systems and make an excuse about why we both needed to leave. Two birds, if you will.

His eyes closed, and I could tell he was fighting the urge to push me down to my knees like he had less than forty-eight hours ago. Ha! Victory me.

But then his eyes opened with a renewed, steely edge. "No. I..."

I sidled up to him and slyly slipped my hands around his ribs, toying with the bottom of his sweater. His skin was soft, and my fingers brushed the golden trail of hair that disappeared under his belt buckle.

"Come on, Petri," I purred. "Be honest. You didn't come here to talk. So let's just get this over with, and give in to what we both want. Stop beating around the bush and pretend to be people we're not."

He stared up at the ceiling as I floated my lips over his tightened jaw. When I arrived at his mouth, I opened mine so he could suck on my tongue when I dipped it inside. I moaned. He groaned much louder before gently pushing me away.

I clicked my tongue, catching my breath. "You're just making this harder on yourself. I'm right here. Easy pickings, dude."

"Why?" he asked. "Why do you do that to yourself?"

"Do what?"

"Treat yourself like you're nothing and ask me to do it too."

Well, that definitely killed the mood. I stepped back and crossed my arms. "Just because I'm open about what I want sexually means I think I'm nothing? I definitely don't think that. But apparently you do."

Eric groaned again, but not in a good way. "That is not what I said, Jane."

"You just did. You made the assumption and put that shit on me."

"I made assumptions? What do you call what you were just doing, huh?"

"I don't know, Petri, how about seduction?"

He rolled his eyes all over again. "Lefferts, if that was seduction, then I'm the fucking mayor of Boston."

"If you're looking for some sex kitten to wind her tail around your leg, you're sniffing up the wrong pussy, my friend."

"Jesus Christ," Eric muttered.

"Hey, man, I've never pretended to be anything I'm not, so if you're looking for a coquette, why don't you hop on down to Cleo's, or better yet, just wander around the T-stop and flirt with the undergrads. I'm sure you could find some jailbait seeking Prince Charming."

My tone had gone from bitter to playful in less than a second. Suddenly, I found the idea of him doing that absolutely reprehensible.

Eric rubbed a hand irritably at the back of his neck. "Why do I do this?" he mumbled to himself.

I swallowed back the lump in my throat. The one that told me to apologize.

Eric opened his mouth a few times, like he wanted to say something else. Finally, he just shook his head. "For the record, I didn't come over here for sex. You put that on me, if we're talking about assumptions. I came over here because I wanted to see you. No innuendo. Just for the pleasure of your goddamn company, all right?"

Both of our mouths quirked. Neither of us missed the irony of that particular statement.

"Now," Eric continued. "Tomorrow is your birthday, right?"

I blinked. That was definitely not what I was expecting. "Ah... yeah. Yeah, it is."

Eric pulled a package from his coat pocket and tossed it onto the table. "You're a pain in the ass, Lefferts. But this is for you."

I stared at the package, unsure of what to say. No one aside from my parents had given me a birthday present in years—not since my tenth birthday party, after which my mother had told me I was officially too old for such celebrations. Honestly, I think it was more because she didn't want to worry about little girls ruining her precious Ethan Allen couch anymore.

"I...thank you," I said weakly. What new game was he playing here?

"One day, maybe you'll tell me why you think everyone is out to get you," Eric replied, shoving his arms back into his coat with unnecessary force. "But until then...happy fucking birthday, Jane."

Then, abruptly, he turned and left. I listened to his footsteps echoing down the hall.

"Are you going to open it?"

I didn't realize I had been staring at the door for probably a minute or more until Skylar's voice stirred me. "Huh? Open what?"

My roommate pointed to the package Eric had left. I walked over and picked it up. Wrapped in nondescript brown paper, it was clearly a book. Attached was a note that simply read in Eric's curt script:

Happy birthday, pretty girl. Meet me here tomorrow night to celebrate.

— Eric

I unwrapped the package, wondering what it was. Inside was a book, and the sight of it made me chuckle.

"What is it?" Skylar asked, coming to stand next to me curiously.

"*Twenty-One Love Poems*," I said, looking at the plain white cover. "By Adrienne Rich."

Skylar frowned. "I don't get it."

"She's a..." I started to explain about the poet. About the irony that Eric even knew her at all. About the fact that he had been reading *Leaflets* when we first started...whatever this was, just a month or so ago. "Inside joke."

I flipped the book open, and two pieces of paper fluttered to the table.

"Bookmarks?" I asked as Skylar picked them up.

"I don't think so." She handed them to me.

They were tickets for a concert. Some band I'd never heard of at Great Scott, my favorite venue in Boston. For tomorrow night.

"This...this seems like more than just a fling, Janey," Skylar said. "Someone who just wants one thing doesn't give you a book of love poems and concert tickets for your birthday."

I looked back and forth between the two gifts, still unsure what to make of them—their presence or the obvious thought behind them.

"Will you go?" Skylar asked.

"Yeah," I said. "I think I will."

ELEVEN

Present

"You're not going anywhere."

The voice was a mere echo, the ghost of a warning. Its owner had vanished by the time I finally managed to open my eyes again, conflated with the visions of Eric's hurt expression.

Was this why I had always been convinced someone was out to get me? Did some part of me, buried within half my DNA, know that out in the world lay a monster, waiting to capture me at just the right moment?

What an idiot I had been my entire life, running from demons like high school bullies and one-night stands. What a privileged fool. What a joke.

Shadows dragged through the blinds at the window, casting a yellow-orange light through the slats that told me it was nearing sunset here in...well, wherever this was. I had been drugged in the car for who knew how long, but I was still willing to bet I was somewhere in Hwaseong. Unless...*oh, God.* Visions of the map of South Korea, that tiny speck that marked the Goseong plant, throbbed in my mind.

What if that's where I was? Or even farther? Across the border, maybe?

All day. I had been here all day, lying on this cot. Freezing in this dusty room. The reality was I could be anywhere. And no one would be able to find me.

I turned, arrested with sudden panic, though my body responded with sluggish reticence.

Drugged, a tiny voice said in my head that sounded vaguely like Carol Lefferts. *That's because you've been drugged, Plain Jane. You've been drugged and taken hostage by your own fucking biological father.*

And there could only be one reason for that. John Carson wanted something from Eric.

Eric.

Just as dazedly, another thought occurred to me. If I was a hostage, maybe I was with someone else.

"*Eomma?*" I croaked as I turned over on my cot. "*Eomma*, are you here?"

There was a groan from the other side of the room. With Herculean effort, I managed to drag myself up, though the blood rushing suddenly from my head almost knocked me back down. Everything ached. And everything was blurry. My glasses had been taken, so I was left to my own poor vision. But it wasn't, thankfully, bad enough that I couldn't see movement on the other cot.

I looked out into the thin afternoon light and tried to take in my surroundings.

It was a small, bare white room with some kind of tiled floor. Our two cots were shoved against opposite walls, each with dark rumpled blankets that barely kept out the January chill. I could make out small heating vents on the floors, plus three barred windows with the blinds drawn. There was a plastic table with a chair in the other corner.

"*Eomma!*"

My limbs wouldn't work. I couldn't walk properly, but I did manage to crawl across the room, a few scant feet that felt like miles.

When I reached the other cot, I collapsed at the edge breathing heavily and touched the blanket-covered lump.

She turned. And it wasn't until I saw her face, with a mosaic of bruises up and down her left cheek and a nasty, half-healed cut above her lip, that I finally exhaled fully.

"*Eomma*," I whispered as I fell over her small, solid form. "Oh my God, *Eomma*, it's okay. I found you. It's okay."

"Jane?"

Her voice was hoarse, almost unrecognizable. Her eyes widened, pupils severely dilated as she took me in. This close, I could see that her hair was brittle, her skin blotchy and shiny at the same time. It was clear by the way she half looked through me that she wasn't entirely certain I was real.

"It's okay, *Eomma*," I said, grabbing her hand and pressing it to my cheek. "I'm real. I'm here. I'm...we're going to get out of here, okay? I'll figure something out."

But her eyes only widened in pure panic. "Jane, you must—oh, you must..." But she couldn't even finish her sentence before a stream of Korean poured out, like her hard-won, nearly perfect English was simply too much to bear under the strain of everything else.

"Shhh, shhh," I whispered, rocking her to me with the awkward, stunted movements my body would allow. "It's okay. It's going to be okay."

She calmed slightly, and I felt her body wilt against me. We remained like that for a long time.

Eric, I pleaded mentally. *Eric, please help us.*

But, of course, no one answered. Eric was furious with me and maybe even still behind bars, depending on how quickly he was processed. Who knew if he would even come at all once he was out. All I had to help me here was a third or fourth cousin with a minor interest in an old serial murder case. That was it.

Before despair could overtake me completely, the door to the room opened, and a familiar figure entered—not John Carson. The goateed, eminently punchable face of Jude Le-fucking-tour.

"Well, well, well, our little butterfly emerged from her cocoon."

He strode in, followed by a much larger man carrying a tray bearing two bowls. The smell of noodles and broth filled the room, and my stomach growled in response. How long had it been since I'd eaten anything? Hours or days?

My head swam. I just curled more into my mother's cot.

"Jude," I said through thick lips. "Or should I call you Hermes?"

I looked over his blurry form as critically as I could. He no longer wore the splint over his nose, but was that a bit of bruising still evident around his eyes? Eric had really gotten him in Lucerne.

Good lord, was that only three weeks ago?

"You'll cooperate if you know what's good for you," Jude said with a leer. "None of that smart talk. Not without anyone here to protect you."

I glared. "How's your nose, Jude? Are you ready to have some other things broken?"

He touched his face self-consciously and grimaced. "Why? Are you going to do it, Tinkerbell?"

I cocked my head. "No, but I wouldn't want to be here when Eric shows up. My guess is he'll want to break something else too."

It was bravado, of course. My failsafe. My default mode. Even if Eric were coming, he wasn't a fighter. In spite of his admirable take-down of Jude in Lucerne, I had a feeling that side of him only came out when pushed to the extreme. And I also knew he didn't particularly like it.

"*Triton* is every bit as much a coward now as when we were young," Jude said, as if he were reading my thoughts. "Still scared of his own shadow. Still falls for the nearest bit of street trash. His own Madame Butterfly." He looked me over. "Such a cliché. You're even pregnant with the lieutenant's child, aren't you?"

He bent down and tapped my nose. I batted his hand away with slow, stupid movements that made Jude laugh. I tried to spit at him and failed miserably. Jude stepped back, chuckling as he leaned over to check on my mother, who had gone back to feigning unconsciousness beside me. I hoped.

"How unfortunate for Triton," Jude remarked languidly as he turned his attention back to me, "that this piece of trash already belonged to someone else."

"Then why am I here?" I asked. "Why not just kill him and be done with it, since that's obviously what Carson wants?" It was a classic technique. Ask the questions you already knew the answer to. "Because you need him, don't you? You and your stupid society. Eric has something he wants. The question is, what?"

"Triton owes a debt," Jude replied gleefully. "A very big one, not that it's any of your business."

"I'm here, aren't I? I'd say that makes it my business."

My words came faster, less slurred. Adrenaline was taking the place of the wearing-off drugs. Vaguely, I wondered what I'd been dosed with. In the car, it had been a clap of something over my mouth —a handkerchief soaked with chloroform and probably something else to maintain the effect. Here, it was something milder. Perhaps a fucked-up cocktail of benzos to keep me calm and sluggish, maybe ketamine.

"You could let me contact him," I tried again. "I promise he'll be more amenable if you let me speak. Tell him I'm all right."

It was never going to work. But I had to try. My mother's body moved slightly behind my head, and I set a hand on her covers, looking for her solid warmth. I could barely feel her bones through the thin blanket. God, how much weight had she lost here?

Jude just shook his head, as if the suggestion were little more than a small child requesting ice cream for breakfast. "It's almost cute, Cio-Cio San. But you're not *that* stupid. You're bait, pure and simple. So be a good little worm, and eat up. Can't have our prime night-crawler shriveling up too much."

He gestured behind him, and his gorilla helper brought over the tray of soup. Jude set one on the table for my mother, and held up the other, bending over me to hold it to my lips.

"I'll even help you, since your motor function seems a bit... deprived...at the moment," he said. "Carson wants you well-nourished. Generous of him, isn't it?"

I kicked out, causing Jude to spill the broth all over himself. He seethed, looking down at the mess of noodles all over his perfectly cut wool pants.

"That," he said, "was unnecessary. Not to mention wasteful. Your lovely mother won't be getting dinner now." His hand snaked out and grabbed my jaw, forcing me to look at him. "Anton. Hold her."

The large man smiled, and then I was lugged off the floor, shoved onto a chair at the table, and held there by a pair of arms that each seemed bigger than my entire torso while Jude secured my wrists and taped my ankles to the chair legs. When I was well and properly bound into place, Jude bent down again so he was only a few inches from my face.

"When you learn to behave, maybe we'll let you go," he informed me.

"You look like you pissed your pants," I said.

Immediately, I received a harsh slap across the face. From her cot, my mother squeaked.

"Would you like to go on?" Jude asked through gritted teeth. "I happen to know Anton would love to have his turn. And I hate to tell you, but he's not nearly as nice as I am. It's why he's Carson's favorite."

I said nothing, but only because the lump on the cot began to shake.

"That's what I thought," Jude said with satisfaction. "Now it's time for dinner." He accepted the second bowl from Anton and held it up to my lips. "Drink."

I eyed the soup. It smelled so good—the ubiquitous instant noodles similar to the kinds my mother had always kept in stock in our house for easy meals and after-school snacks. But addled as I was, I wasn't stupid.

I shook my head. "No, thank you. I'm fine."

I wasn't fine. I was starving. I was hungry literally *all* the time now that I was pregnant, and I probably hadn't eaten in, what, twelve hours? The growl of my stomach filled the room.

Jude's eyes narrowed. "That's not an option, I'm afraid."

If I hadn't been sure he was drugging me with the soup before, now I was. "No."

His eyes closed for a moment, as if he was gathering his patience again. It was a small victory, but I would take it. Even if I'd regret it seconds later.

"Hold her nose," Jude said finally, standing back up.

My eyes widened as Anton circled around the chair and proceeded to close his broad hands over my nose, cutting off my air supply unless I opened my mouth. Jude stood poised with the bowl over my lips, and as soon as I opened them for a single breath, he wrenched my jaw the rest of the way open and proceeded to pour the broth down my throat.

I coughed, hacked, my body shaking against the onslaught. But some of it made it down, much to my dismay.

Jude stood back, observing with humor. "Had enough? Or are we going to cooperate now?" He looked back at the bowl. "There's quite a bit more where this came from. Waterboarding by chicken stock. Very elegant."

My choice was clear. Drown in lukewarm broth or allow at least some of it down.

Survival won.

Less than fifteen minutes later, I was asleep again, wrapped in a shroud of perilous dreams filled with probing hands and my cries in the dark. I didn't know which parts of it were real. And at some point, I no longer cared.

TWELVE

Plaster dust accumulated in the corners, drifting across the tiled floors like snow. Through two small windows, both barred, I caught glimpses of barren fields in one direction, and some sort of large facility in the other. But whatever they gave me worked fast. One moment I'd be awake, asking for my mother, for Eric, for my dead father. The next I'd be surrounded by arms like tree roots, a waterfall of broth drowning my words. Then a sudden sweep of black, a bleary curtain that faded the winking winter sun.

Sometimes I fought them.

But they fought back.

The man with the goatee.

The other with the Russian accent.

"*Eomma?*" I croaked, barely able to form the word through numbed lips and a paralyzed jaw.

A lump across the room turned, and the tired, aching moon of my mother's face appeared, her eyes deeply set into her wan skin, like two craters seen from space.

"*Eomma.*" My voice was a whisper slashed through.

She moaned, but her eyes didn't open. My eyes closed too, and I dreamed I could feel her touch on my cheek, like I was a small child, while a deeper gnaw of hunger filled my belly and my bones ached with fatigue. We shared a collection of fevered dreams, unsure of how long they lasted, how much time had passed. Yu-na and I twisted on our cots, tortured mirrors of deliria.

The hours grew long. I wondered when the days would turn to weeks. Or if they already had.

The past blurred with the present.

"Eric," I whispered as my eyes fell heavy again.

It was only in my dreams that he appeared. But it was also in my dreams that I started to scream.

2009

The T screamed away after I got off at the Harvard Avenue stop. Across the tracks, a line spilled from under the awning of Great Scott. I looked around, feeling shy, though I had been to this bar uncountable times by myself.

"Hey, pretty girl."

I turned, and there he stood, a beacon of white and blond in a sea of black and spikes.

Eric smiled.

I melted.

"Glad you showed," he said. "Happy birthday, gorgeous."

Gorgeous? I wanted to ask. He had used the term before, but, like "pretty girl," no one in their right mind had ever called me such a thing.

"Well, no use wasting perfectly good tickets." I held up the two pieces of paper.

"Good," Eric said. "You brought mine too. They're sold out, you know."

I smirked. "Who says I kept it for you?"

But he didn't even react. "Come on, Lefferts."

Eric held out a hand. And eventually, I took it.

From inside the bar, flashing lights. A bass line like a wood-pecker. The singer whistled a warning.

I handed our tickets to the doorman, who ripped them and handed Eric back the stubs, then stamped our wrists with octopi.

We fell into an oblivion of bodies and bass lines. I pushed away their sweating skins, clutching instead the dry palm that guided me through the masses. Wherever he went, Eric shone. A bright light. How could I tell him that sometimes it was too bright? That sometimes it blinded me.

Present

Blinded. That's what I was. The sun, shining through the shades, speared my weary eyes. I didn't want to sleep anymore, but I couldn't take the yellow-white shards, the way they seemed to stick my brain like skewers.

"Is it done yet?"

Who said that? The voice was familiar. On some level, my whole body seemed to recognize it.

I rolled over on my cot, cold and clammy, but also hot and sticky. The room was freezing, so my toes and forehead—the two parts of my body exposed in the winter air—were frozen while the rest of me sweat out the effects of my ongoing anesthesia.

Nausea roiled through my system. The broth was wearing off again.

The door to the room was open. *Arrogant*, I thought blearily. It was right there. I could just walk right out. They thought we were incapacitated to the point where they didn't even bother to lock us up properly.

Well, they were right.

"I thought I would wait on that, Titan," a voice I recognized as Jude Letour's said. "It seemed a hasty decision. After all, you might want to dote on it in the end."

"Do it." Carson's voice was steel compared to his underling's. That's who I heard before.

My eyes were shut, but I could still envision those icy hazels clapping on me inside the ultrasound room. I placed a hand over my mostly flat belly. In response, it grumbled. How long had it been since I had eaten solid food?

"What about Triton? Has he responded?"

"He's out, but unreachable. I'm not worried. He'll be here."

"He'd better. We need those boats. Everything is ready to transport, but I've got NIS sniffing around the plant. We need everything out of the country yesterday. Do you know he called the CIA on you?"

There was a grumble, something I couldn't quite understand.

"Forgive me for saying this *again*, but don't you think there is perhaps an easier way? Triton is so unpredictable, and the girl is difficult at best—"

"Triton lost his rights to her a long time ago. But she's his fatal flaw. The child—well, that's just for good measure."

There was a shuffle that covered their voices as I strained to hear what they were saying.

"I've got a meeting in thirty minutes to smooth the passage," Carson said. "Get it done, Jude. I don't want to come back without it finished. Otherwise he might not cooperate."

Footsteps left the outer room and a door slammed behind him. A few minutes later, a shadow appeared in the door—Jude with the Russian attendant behind him. He carried another tray bearing soup, which Anton carried over to my mother, and a vial and syringe, which Jude brought to me.

"This," he grumbled, "is a bit out of my realm if you ask me, princess."

"Then why do it?" My lips could barely form the words.

Jude's eyes narrowed. "Shut up."

I watched as the attendant pulled my mother up roughly and instructed her to eat her soup.

"*Eomma*," I croaked. "Don't do it."

But her eyes barely registered me, dilated like saucers, and she sipped lamely at the bowl like a sick puppy.

"Since you're awake, that will make this easier," Jude said. "If you'll just cooperate." He affixed the vial to the syringe, then pushed the stopper enough for a drop or two of the clear liquid to pop out the top of the needle.

"What is that?" I asked.

"Nothing so bad, I promise you. Just a little something to help you relax."

"I—no." *Protect the baby.* These kinds of drugs couldn't be good for it. I didn't want more. I didn't want any. "No, please. I'll stay here. I won't fight, I promise. Just...please don't give me anything else."

Something like regret crossed Jude's face. But only for a second. "I apologize," he said almost formally. "But it's out of the question."

He pulled down the blankets to bare my arm.

"No," I said, finding more strength than I thought I had to yank my arm out of reach. "*No!*"

"Anton," Jude called irritably over his shoulder.

I watched over Jude's shoulder as my mother slumped back onto the bed.

"What did you give her?" I squawked, scooting back into the corner of my cot. "What the hell are you doing to us?"

"Hold her down," Jude instructed Anton in a bored tone.

Anton did as he was told with brusque, efficient movements, though his face twisted into a cruel parody of a smile.

"What do you want?" I cried. "Eric is going to come, you know. He *will*."

Jude just bared his two rows of capped white teeth in triumph.

"Oh, my little concubine," he said as he tapped the side of the syringe. "We're counting on it."

"You're going to regret this," I warned him.

At that, Jude just shook his head. "You really are clueless, aren't you? To a man like Titan? Like me? There is no such thing as 'no.'"

There was a sharp jab in my arm. I jerked away, but only so much as my weakened limbs could manage, which wasn't much under Anton's strong hold.

"Triton has to learn that his actions have consequences," Jude said. "He has to pay for abandoning his post like this. For going against the orders of his Caesar. He'll pay for everything that he's done and everything his father did too."

"*You'll pay,*" I slurred.

Jude just smiled as darkness swallowed me again.

2009

I took a long swallow of my beer. PBR, of course. Eric knew what I liked.

"I don't understand. You said that's what you wanted too. Just sex. No strings. Easy." I traced a finger over the condensation on the beer can. "This doesn't seem easy to me. Birthday presents. A concert. This is much more."

"Maybe I want more." Eric took a long sip of his vodka and watched my reaction. "Maybe I want everything."

The music behind us seemed to drop a few decibels. Eric's gaze didn't waver.

"When was your last girlfriend?" I wondered. "Is this some kind of test? Reaching your quarter-life crisis and deciding you want to try to gut it out for once?"

Eric frowned. "What the hell does my last girlfriend have to do with it?"

Ah, so I'd hit a sore spot there.

I drained my beer and set it on the bar with a loud bang. "Why won't you tell me? Have you even had a girlfriend before, Petri dish?"

He swallowed another large sip of vodka. "Have you had a boyfriend?"

"I have. A few, actually."

I leaned against the bar, watching the crowd instead of my date. It was the usual you would see here. Indie rock enthusiasts mixed with a solid contingent of punk fans Where every non-Red Sox lover in Boston conglomerated on the weekends. A meeting of like misfits.

They were my people. But they definitely weren't Eric's.

"Bad breakups?"

I drummed my fingers against the bar top. "You could say that."

"Am I anything like them?"

I turned to look at him. "No one I ever took seriously."

Maybe on the outside he was like those boys. The ones who came from the upper-middle class families in the Midwest. Who wore IZOD and played golf. Who hated anything spicy and thought Dave Matthews was the epitome of alt-rock.

But if I was being totally honest, I knew Eric was still different. Those boys dripped mediocrity, but Eric loved the best. Everything about him shone in a way those boys never had. And while they had talked me into the backs of their cars, toyed with me year in and year out, Eric never did anything but look me in the eye.

But the best liars could do that. They could fool anyone into thinking they were the genuine article, then burn it all up for the fun of it.

"We've been over this a million times. I know how this goes," I said bitterly. "High school. College. It doesn't change. The reality is that guys like you do not stay with girls like me. Why are you trying to force this into something it's not? Don't you remember Pretty in Pink?"

"As I remember, the preppy kid got the girl in the end." Eric smirked. "Actually, I always thought the record store owner was the hottest one. Spiked hair and all."

But I wasn't about to be dissuaded. "Everyone knows that Andie should have ended up with Duckie, not Blane. He's the one who showed up for her. Supported her. Loved her. That's not up for debate. That's canon."

Eric's disgust was visible, and for a long time, he didn't speak, just turned his drink back and forth between his fingers. Finally, he looked up. "Do I look like I'm in high school, Jane?"

Some men in their twenties did, in fact, look like they were still prepubescent. I remember being genuinely shocked when I started college in a dorm full of gangly, baby-faced man-children. And they acted like it too. Especially when they whispered behind my back as I walked through the halls.

But I knew the way Eric's body, taut and lean, had filled out in all the right places. How many times in the last month had I given myself permission to admire the smattering of gold hair over his chest muscles, run my fingers over the flat plane of his stomach, enjoyed the sandpaper hum of his unshaved cheek against mine?

Eric's gaze didn't waver. Instead, it captured mine right back. Boys, they couldn't look a girl like me in the eye. But Eric wasn't a boy. He was a man.

And now I couldn't look away if I tried.

"No," I said. "You don't."

Present

"Don't," I moaned, though don't *what*, I had no clue.

My stomach hurt. Everything contracted, like menstrual cramps times ten.

Other things hurt too. My thighs ached, like they were bruised or overworked. My lower back felt like it was on fire. What was happening to me?

"She looks terrible." Carson again, his voice dripping with something else. Disgust, maybe. "Is it done?"

There was that question again. Was *what* done?

"It is," Jude replied. "Well, it should be in progress. Anton inserted the pills after I gave her the sedative. Took a little too much pleasure in it, if you ask me. She fought uncommonly hard for someone under that much dope."

There was a grunt. "Give her the Valium mixture once it's finished. *She* won't cooperate if she's too upset."

There was another uncomfortable shuffle. "You know, Titan, I don't think I would be quite human if I didn't voice at least some concerns about your...tactics."

"That is *not* your concern, Hermes."

"God knows I can't claim much of a moral compass for myself, but really, is this necessary? Disciplining obedience, I understand, but I hardly see what the child—or her, for that matter—has to do with Goseong."

A long pause. A few cracking knuckles.

"Triton needs...convincing. Of my authority, which he has repeatedly refused to acknowledge. And he was also warned *explicitly* about the costs of procreating. That's personal, yes. Deeply so. Eric, however, is even more incalcitrant than his father."

"Funny. I'd heard that Jacob was a good man, all things considered."

There was a scuffle. A bang as some kind of furniture fell to the floor, the thud of a body slamming against the wall.

"All right, all right!" Jude squeaked in a strangled voice. "All *right*. Message received. Jacob de Vries was scum of the earth, that's the party line. I get it!"

"Jacob *de Vries* never met a single possession of another man's he didn't covet or outright steal." Carson's voice was strained as well, almost as if the name itself was too much for him to say. "He was a thief. A liar. A scoundrel. He took absolutely *anything* he wanted."

"You mean anything *you* wanted?"

Another scuffle. The sound of broken glass.

"A joke, a joke!" It seemed Jude couldn't help poking any bear himself, even if it was one of the most dangerous men on the planet. "Terrible family, terrible man. Rid the earth of all of them, of course, of course."

"Just finish it. You have Anton at your disposal. I have a rendezvous at the border. When I get back, I want everything cleaned up. Torch the buildings. Nothing left. The boy is en route, and I don't want him distracted by any of the evidence. Is that clear?"

Jude must have nodded, because the next sounds were of a door opening and closing as Carson departed.

My stomach cramped again, this time making me moan. A blood-stain blooming across the white sheets.

"Help," I whispered as I watched my body fall apart. The blood flowered, a garden of red. "Help!"

A shadow appeared in the doorway.

"Anton," Jude called. "Come in here. It's started." He turned to me with equal parts disgust and pity. "I wonder," he said, "what will Triton do when he finds you like this? Will he still want you, ruined? Will you be his 'pretty girl'? Will you still be his 'Jane'?"

2009

"Jane. Jane!"

I broke out of my daydream, lost as I had been in the hum of the crowd.

"Were you even listening to me?" Eric demanded, now visibly frustrated. "It's one thing if you're going to push me away, but if you're just not interested at all, I'd like to know right fucking now."

I blinked with sudden panic. "No. No! That's not...sorry, I was just lost in thought."

Eric frowned. "I don't deserve this."

But instead of leaving like I expected, he snaked a hand around my waist and jerked me off my stool. Then he covered my mouth with a searing kiss. Every cogent thought I had flew from my head, and all I could sense was him. His lush, hungry mouth, his grasping, seeking hands, his hard, strong body pressed completely against mine.

When we broke apart, we were both out of breath, heaving like we had just sprinted a mile.

"I'm trying here," Eric said as he pressed his forehead to mine. "I'm trying to make something real with you. I haven't done that in a very long fucking time, but with you, I want it again. So fucking bad. With you, Jane. Is that clear enough?"

I swallowed. I wanted to say yes. Oh, God, I wanted to say yes to him, to everything he claimed. I wanted to believe.

But the room came back into focus, and we were suddenly the center of attention. People were staring. Many with confusion. The same question written clearly across their curious faces that was constantly running through mine: What is he doing with *her*?

"Don't look at them. Look at me."

Eric's voice was strong, solid. The vibration of it rumbled through his chest and into mine.

"Pretty girl. Look. At. Me."

So I did.

His steely gray eyes held mine as his hands roved my body, hiding nothing from any onlookers. His kiss swallowed me whole, daring me to think or feel anything else but him.

My cracks gaped.

My heart expanded.

Maybe the world was wider than I thought. I was so young, after all. Maybe this was what it meant to grow up.

THIRTEEN

2009

We toppled into my apartment, a writhing mass of arms and legs and mouths, our voices punctuating the dark through hot breaths and torrid kisses.

"Is Skylar here?" Eric heaved.

I barely managed to lock the door before I was shoved against it. "She's in New York."

Eric's teeth found my neck with a sharp bite. I jumped, but he just held me tighter, his front pressed against my back, cock pressed against the curve of my ass.

"You're such a vampire," I teased when he nipped me again. "Ah!"

"Fair enough. I'd probably eat you alive if I could." His teeth scraped over my pulse. "You are pretty fucking addictive, gorgeous."

Before I could respond, I was flipped around, back to the door. With a movement that belied arms stronger than they looked, Eric picked me up and wrapped my legs around his hips.

"Not wasting any time, are you?" I asked playfully as he carried me into my bedroom. "Ahh!" I shrieked as he tossed me onto the bed.

"Get undressed," he ordered. "You've made me wait long enough tonight. Do you know how hard I was, watching you dance?"

I raised an eyebrow as I rolled off the other side of the bed and stood up. "Come off it. I'm a terrible dancer."

"You're very...vigorous. And you sweat enough that your shirt was practically transparent by the end of the stupid concert."

I looked down. Shit. He wasn't wrong.

"Jane," Eric said. "Take off your fucking clothes."

For once in my life, I did as I was told, yanking off my boots, jeans, ripped t-shirt, tripping over things when I caught a look at him also hurrying out of his own garments. God, he was beautiful. Long, lean, fully formed. Not gangly like so many men my age, nor stacked with unnecessary muscle or bulk. He was...perfect. With one particularly perfect appendage that I couldn't help but crave as he removed the last of his clothing.

Eric noticed me ogling, and with a smirk, pushed his hair back from his face. "You have a condom?"

I sucked on my lower lip as I knelt on the bed. "How about a box? You know I'm always prepared, Petri dish."

He rolled his eyes, then crawled across the mattress toward me. "Don't remind me."

"Do you need to double up?" I teased even as my hands naturally found his waist. His erection slid between my legs, hard and as ready as I was. Lord, it would be so easy for him just to slip in with nothing at all.

For my impertinence, I received a sharp pinch at the waist.

"Enough of that," Eric ordered as he delivered a light swat on my ass. "Right now it's time for some retribution."

"Retribution? For what, pray tell?"

Another nip at my shoulder. Another sharp suck on my neck.

"For making me wait. Where's the condom?"

I reached over to my nightstand and procured said condom, which Eric promptly rolled over his cock. Roughly, he shoved me to the bed, then arranged my legs around his waist so that the tip of him just teased my entrance. I arched my hips toward him, not willing to wait any more than he wanted to.

But his hands kept my thighs in place with an iron grip. Once I gave up the fight, one slid up my stomach between my breasts. His fingers spread wide across my chest, sliding up my skin gradually until they encircled the base of my throat. Eric looked me over, like a hunter appraising his kill. His cock twitched, just barely teasing me. I moaned.

He slid inside, maybe an inch, maybe less. The hand around my throat tightened.

"Have you ever used a safe word, Jane?" Eric asked. All humor had disappeared from his face, his tone. His eyes were sharp with desire...and something else. Something slightly dangerous. Something that called to my bones.

I stilled. I was young, but not completely ignorant. After playing it pretty damn safe through high school, I had gone a little nuts, exploring the sides of my identity that would have horrified my mother and gravely disappointed my genial-to-a-fault father. Chicago was a big pool to swim in. There were so many fish. Band members, TAs, frat boys, football players. They all had a little something different to offer. And they were usually more than willing to let me take what I needed and move on.

Safe words, though? They hadn't really been a part of those... fishing expeditions.

"Have—have you?" I asked.

I had heard about situations like this. Dominants. Submissives. Secret underground lairs where men and women explored their kinks and penchants for leather and chaps safely. But hearing and seeing weren't the same thing. And seeing and experiencing were miles apart.

Eric was suddenly guarded. "No. I haven't been with anyone who's...inspired them."

What did that mean? Not for the first time, I wondered just how experienced Eric really was. He had moves that no man under the age of forty really should know.

I cleared my throat. His hand fell away. He sat back up suddenly, palms up on his knees in a strangely meditative posture.

"What if I told you that when I'm with you, I think about shit that has never crossed my mind before. Not with anyone." He exhaled sharply. "It makes me...distracted."

I swallowed and eyed him back, wondering if I should just come clean. What would Eric, this clean-cut image of perfection, say if I told him I imagined him tying me up on the floor and leaving me there, just to show me he could? That more than once I'd pleasured myself in the shower or late at night with thoughts of his hand pinking my thighs, fingernails scraping lines down my shoulder, or palm delivering a harsh slap across my face? That I'd spent more time recently perusing whips and floggers on a sex toy website than studying for our upcoming final exams?

Distracted. Yeah. He wasn't the only one having unfamiliar fantasies.

Eric leaned in so that his nose touched mine. His hand returned to my throat. He was caging me completely—assuming complete and utter control.

"I'm becoming a man obsessed." His voice rumbled against my skin, low, and sounding much older than his twenty-three-ish years.

"Is that healthy?" I wondered, though my voice was growing weak all over again.

"Is it healthy to deny yourself a basic need?" he asked. "That's what it's starting to feel like. What you are starting to feel like."

I swallowed again, this time with more difficulty. My hands were in his hair now, gripping tightly. Whether I was keeping his mouth close or holding him away, I wasn't completely sure. But I wanted... oh, God, I wanted more.

"I think..." he said as his fingers returned to my neck, pads pressing into my skin as if testing their imprints, one at a time. "If you're willing...we should try it."

"A safe word?" I asked. "What are you planning to do that would require me to have one?"

He inhaled, like a predator finding his prey after days on the hunt, but still holding off the impulse to simply dive into the feed. "I'm not sure yet. But you can trust me. Just...look, you let me do... whatever I'm going to do...and if you don't like it, you say the word. And I stop. No questions asked." He pulled back once more, the quick movement making his blond hair flop boyishly across his forehead. His eyes were suddenly earnest. "Call it a new beginning. Isn't that what tonight is?"

I considered the tickets. The book. The fact that he had been waiting there for me, waiting to adore me in front of everyone we knew and everyone we didn't.

Maybe he was for real.

Maybe people like me could find happy endings.

Or one. With him.

I tipped my face up and licked his lips. Eric growled again, and his other hand tightened on my thigh.

"What's the word, pretty girl?"

I smirked. "Erie."

He frowned, and I almost started laughing.

"As in scary?"

I shook my head, chuckling. "As in the lake. My folks like to visit there. I have very not sexy memories associated with family vacations."

He considered it for a moment, then nodded with a chuckle. "Erie. Okay?"

Somewhat nervously, I nodded. "Okay."

And then, before I could say anything more, he covered my mouth with a kiss that recalled all of the ferocity with which we entered the apartment. Eric stole my breath, and it had nothing to do with the iron palm at my throat.

I was completely at his mercy, and I had never been more turned on.

"Is it fucked up how I want every bit of your pleasure?" he asked as he sat back up, though the hand at my neck held me down.

His cock found my entrance and slipped in again, just slightly. He stared at it, his fingers tightening under my jaw, his thumb finding my clit. I gasped, feeling the excitement of ecstasy and alarm flooding my system. Who knew sex could be like this? So exciting. So all-consuming?

I shook my head. He wanted my pleasure? Well, I wanted him to have it. For the first time in my life, I was actually able to give some control to someone else. Without thinking too hard about exactly why I would want that—the effects of living in a society that always wanted to control me undoubtedly had something to do with it—I could freely and safely embrace the fact that I did.

The idea was intoxicating.

Eric pushed in deeper, finding his seat within my heat. Slowly. Methodically. The hand around my throat tightened a bit more while the other one intensified its movements over my clit. He started to move, started to drive me with each thrust, each pull. Mine, they all seemed to say as his eyes traveled over me, taking in each subtle response I gave to his ministrations. All mine.

It was too much. It was almost too much to bear. I squeezed my eyes shut. And for that, I was rewarded with a sharp slap across my cheek, followed by a tingling that seemed to be linked directly to the heat emanating from where our bodies met. I jerked, my entire body arching up under his as my eyes shot open again.

"Jane." Eric's voice was an omen. A promise.

I struggled slightly, fighting his touch. But he held me in place, constricted me deliciously against the mattress. His hands, his body, his cock all pinned me in place. There was no escape from this. My fight was only for me.

"Don't you look away, gorgeous. Don't you dare look away from me when I'm fucking you."

Eric pushed forward harder, spearing me completely. The hand around my throat tightened that much more.

"Why?" I demanded, nearly having to croak. "Why does it matter so much that I watch?"

He stilled, hand braced around my neck, cock throbbing between my legs.

Then he bent down and kissed me, slipping his tongue in to taste all parts of me. He pinched my clit and drove deeper than he ever had before.

"Because," he whispered. "I'm going to fall apart here, pretty girl. And I need to know you've got me when I do."

"Oh!" I cried as I came suddenly, without warning, like a clap of thunder in a rainstorm. "Oh, God!"

Present

"Oh, *God!*"

The words escaped with a tortured breath as the world swam around me, luminous shapeless figures in a sea of dusty white cold.

It hurt. Everything hurt. I was a mess of pain.

"Help her! She needs help!"

My mother's voice was throttled, a shredded version of its normal ferocity. I opened my eyes, and a blurry figure waved from a dark lump across the room. The room was a static rendition of itself, like an analog TV set with poor reception.

I moaned again and turned over, clutching my slick belly as another round of throbbing pain seized my midsection. "Ummmmmmmm."

Footsteps slapped the tile and pounded through my head. Harsh hands turned me onto my back and yanked the blankets from me. The cold wrapped me in its frigid grip, contacting the wet mess and wracking my body with shivers.

"Noooo," I wailed. "Stop!"

My stomach seized. Everything shook. But the world swirled

together, and nausea overtook me, so I squeezed my eyes shut, willing the spiraling to stop while I focused on bearing the pain. It came and went, contracting heavily like waves. But it hurt. Oh, God, it hurt more than anything I had ever experienced.

Voices rode through my mind like on the tail end of a bad trip, diving in and out of dreams and reality.

"She's finally losing it." The deep voice spoke with a curious blend of regret and relief. "I'll tell Carson. Anton, clean her up."

There was a rattle of obstinate Korean, a woman and a man's voice.

"Just do it!" shouted the woman finally, in English. "She will die if you do not!"

Yu-na? *Eomma?* Was that her name?

More hands. A cold, wet fabric. Gauze or cloth or sheets shoved between my legs.

"Ummmmmmm," I moaned again, writhing into myself.

"Can't you fucking give her something?" A man's voice, the first one, hovering closer, speaking with something close to panic. "She can't die, Anton. Carson will fucking flip out."

"She won't die." The voice was heavily accented, sharp and clipped with fear. He had gotten more than he asked for. He was scared, even if he liked pain the other times.

"She better not," said the other man, a man I knew. *Hermes.* A name, hanging by the wings of a Greek god, floated through my erratic brain. "Give her something," he said again. "Calm her down, Anton. All that thrashing around can't be good for her."

"Go," said the Russian, angry now. "Let me do my job."

"Fuck. *Fuck.* She better be alive when I get back with the medic, Anton. Otherwise *you'll* be responsible, not me."

"Shhhhh." I didn't know who said it, but a prick in my elbow made the world fade away again, though the pain still remained, like a shadow I couldn't escape.

2009

"Shhhh."

Eric stroked the top of my head while outside, another new snowfall filtered through the streetlights. Boston was quiet, insulated by a mantle of white.

My glasses sat on the table, having been removed at some point—by me? By Eric—during one of our bouts of passion. Outside our cocoon of sex and warmth, the world was blurry. But here, in this bed, it was crystal clear. Eric and I gazed at each other with openness. Hope.

And for the first time, I examined him without looking away.

"That was..." He shook his head. "You know what? I don't want to describe it. It will just sound trite."

"God forbid we sound trite," I joked, though I understood what he meant. Some things, you can't comment on. Some things just need to stand on their own.

Though in all honesty, this was the first of those things I had ever encountered in my twenty-two years. It was a little overwhelming.

"Tell me about your life," I said instead. "Your family. You're from the Upper East Side, right?"

Eric didn't answer. Instead he toyed with a strand of my hair, winding it around his finger, dropping it in a tight curl before it relaxed into its natural wave. I didn't even want to think about what I looked like at the moment, after rolling around the sheets for the last who knew how many hours. It was probably close to three or four a.m., and the effects of drinking, snow, and sex had likely not been kind. My thigh was probably bright pink, and the spot where his palm had met skin again and again still smarted in the best possible way.

"Your hair is so...alive," he said as he examined the bright purple, twirling it again around his fingers again.

"That's one word for it," I said. "I probably look like a hungover hair band groupie right now."

Eric just rolled his eyes. "I wasn't talking about the color. More the texture. It has its own personality." He stopped his movements. "Would you give me a lock?"

I leaned back. "Who are you, the Duke of Cumberland? You want a lock of hair to ride into battle?"

But Eric didn't bat an eye. "Come on, I want one. Like a talisman." He combed through another piece. "I wouldn't mind carrying a reminder of your bravery with me wherever I go."

I was quiet for a moment. I had been doing things to my hair since I was old enough to sneak boxes of drugstore dye past my mother. She had been freaking about my hair my entire life, even when I was a small child and she would spend hours combing through the wavy tangles. It was so unlike her own beautifully straight black hair. *Just like your father's*, she would say irritably, over and over again.

Even then, I was difficult.

The comment never made sense, though. Dad's hair was a thin, scraggly auburn. Nothing like my thick, naturally brown-black waves.

Brave, though. Did dyeing my hair make me brave?

Crazy.

Try-hard.

Attention-seeker.

Teachers, friends, students, etc. Everyone had something to say about my penchant for out-of-the-box fashion and style.

Brave. That was a first.

"Tell me," I changed the subject. "Your family. Do you...do you get along with your folks? Your dad, maybe?"

"Well, that would be hard, since he's dead." Eric focused hard on the hair between his fingers, even pulling it a little so it pinched.

"Jesus," I said. "I'm sorry for that. What...what happened?"

He stilled. "It was a long time ago. I was around ten, eleven. But I think...that's best saved for a night where we consume at least a bottle of wine each. And maybe not a story to start at almost four in the morning."

I shrugged, as if his brush-off didn't sting a bit. "Fair enough. I don't need to know your secrets to bone you."

"I think I'm the one who does the boning, pretty girl."

But despite the playful words, his face remained solemn. I couldn't help but wonder if there was something more behind Eric's melancholia besides the death of his father. Granted, that was no small loss, but I had known other people who lost a parent or close person as kids. Children were resilient. They never really recovered, but they bounced back better than people gave them credit for. Eric's stolid face masked something deeper, a mark of tragedy that, for whatever reason, felt more recent.

But what did I know? I couldn't force him to bare his soul. Not when I was nowhere close to giving him mine.

The thought was terrifying. But suddenly, I wanted to do anything I could to wipe that sadness off his face.

"Here," I said, tossing back the covers.

"I get a show, huh?" Eric watched with open admiration as I padded naked to my desk, which was covered with scattered sewing supplies.

I rolled my eyes. "Don't get too excited, Petri dish."

"I really fucking hate that name, you know."

"Which is exactly why I'll continue to use it."

I grabbed a pair of scissors and walked back to sit down in front of him. From under my mane, I pulled out a lock of purple hair and measured out a solid few inches, enough to curl on its own.

"Here," I said offering the scissors to him. "When you need a bit of bravery. Or maybe bravado is a better word."

"Sometimes they're the same thing."

Eric took the scissors and snipped the lock just below my fingers. He cradled his gift in his palm, rocking it slightly back and forth before he accepted the tiny rubber band I procured from my nightstand.

"Thanks, gorgeous," he said as I wrapped the elastic around one end of the lock. He took it, then reached down to the floor to grab his wallet from his jeans. He tucked the lock between a few bills. "For safe-keeping. Now I can take your bravado with me everywhere."

A part of me shouted that this couldn't be real. That this was a bubble, and at some point, it was obviously going to pop. A lock of hair in his wallet? I shouldn't fall for this, right?

But instead, I toppled right back into his arms when he returned to the nest we had made.

"You'd better treasure that," I said as he wound the rest of my hair around his fist and trapped me under his solid, wiry form. "I just maimed my perfect coif for you. I hope you appreciate thesacrifice."

"Ah, Jane," Eric said before his lips closed over mine. "Haven't you learned yet? I appreciate everything about you, pretty girl. Every single fucking thing."

Present

"Pretty girl. Come on. Come on, gorgeous. Fucking hell, Jane, you have to wake up!"

A new voice sounded. A different voice, one that wasn't angry or condescending or disgusted.

It pleaded with me. But this was a voice that never, ever begged. Not with me.

I was dead.

She was dead.

Maybe this voice was dead too.

I hoped he was alive, but I wasn't sure that what I wanted mattered anymore.

"Jane! Oh, Jesus. Jesus *Christ*."

I had failed us both. They were calling for me, voices through the dreams, through the memories, through days and years I couldn't tell apart anymore.

"What the *fuck* did you do to her?"

"I did not do anything. I saved her *life!*"

"Eric, man, he's just a medic. Ten to one, he's a captive just like they are."

"Yeah, but why in the fuck would they need a medic?"

The bed sank, a weight beside my body. *They were back*, a voice realized deep within me. Back with broth. Back with noodles. Back with fuzzying substances and impersonal, bruising hands that forced my legs apart and penetrated those deep spaces.

But the hands that framed my face were gentle, not prodding. The breath against my cheek was warm and smelled of mint, not cigarettes. A whiff of cologne. Light. Linen.

Eric's face was a golden light, a floating, concerned mask as bright as the sun.

"Jane," he whispered, his voice shaking with pain and emotion. His hair flopped forward. "What happened? Oh, God, can you even hear me?"

"She is going to be okay," said the accented man.

I made a face. I knew that voice. It was the one that belonged to some of the impersonal, prodding hands. The one who whispered hushed Korean prayers as it did *something* down there while the others fled. Had he done this? Had the others, the ones who put something *else* there too?

Eric's face, though, still consumed my vision, growing clearer with every second.

Too clear.

Too much.

"You're not real," I murmured, amazed at how very soft the hair under my fingers felt.

Gentle hands stroked my face.

"Shhhh, gorgeous, I'm here," said the vision. "Don't say anything. I'm here. And it's going to be all right."

"I don't care if you're not real," I mumbled as I lifted my face toward his light. "I'm just glad you're here at all."

FOURTEEN

2009

"Do you have anything to eat?" Eric asked as he opened the fridge. "I'm starving. You kind of sapped my energy, you know."

I lolled over the countertop, purposefully pushing together what little cleavage I had. Okay, it wasn't much. I was a B-cup on a good day. But Eric ogled cooperatively.

This wasn't hard, the ooey gooey stuff. The "pleasing my man" thing. Twenty-four hours after I had watched this boy literally take a lock of my hair like a knight accepting his lady's favor, I was all in. Head over heels. Stick fifteen forks in me. So done I was practically charred through.

After spending the last twenty-four hours doing nothing but alternately fucking like monsters and cooing like doves, we were both, apparently, finished with the pretense of push and pull. By some strange magic, the boy was more beautiful now, and that was really saying something. And he, apparently, thought the same of me, since whenever I caught him looking at me, he positively glowed.

I still couldn't believe I'd actually given him that lock of hair. Who was I, Lady Guinevere?

"I need actual sustenance," Eric said as he leaned over and nipped the curve of one breast. "I'd live on this if I could, but it's just not possible, gorgeous."

I grinned. I couldn't help it. Eric preened at my open adoration of him as he turned back to the fridge. Good God, how had I gotten this lucky? The way the man filled out a pair of boxer shorts should be illegal. Meanwhile, I was also fucking alight, like one of the lanterns that kept Harvard Square twinkling even in the dead of winter.

Outside the window, the snow cloaking Cambridge shimmered with said lights.

Was this what it felt like to be in love? Okay, maybe it was a little early for that word, but I honestly wasn't sure I could call it anything else. I'd never said it to anyone, never felt anything like it. I felt free even though another part of me was completely at this boy's mercy. Eric could snap his fingers, and I'd bend right over this counter if he asked me. And at the same time, I felt like I could jump right off that fire escape and soar.

On your knees, he'd said more than once last night.

I hadn't knelt. I'd practically jumped to the floor.

Come here, he'd ordered from the head of the bed.

I'd fucking flown.

A lock of hair. I had given him a lock of fucking hair.

I helped Eric mouse through what little Skylar and I had, shoving him aside and sticking out my ass, earning a swift swat across the cheek. I looked over my shoulder to find him grinning.

"If you wanted more, you could just ask," he said, rubbing his palms together.

I wriggled my hips at him. "Aren't you a little presumptuous? Maybe I want you to leave now that I've had my fill of you."

Another sharp smack. This time I jumped. Eric laughed and pulled me back against his chest.

"If that's true," he said as he cupped my breast through my thin shirt, "then I've got a lot more work to do."

I sank into his warm touch, allowing him to encircle me with his solid form.

"I do, however, need something to eat. Besides you. Do you actually have anything other than ketchup and fermented cabbage?" He toyed briefly with my nipple, then kissed my earlobe before releasing me. "Or do I need to venture out to get us some appropriate sustenance?"

I opened the fridge again and pulled out the only box that wasn't a condiment. "All we have is some...I don't know...I think there is something in here. Skylar's, but she forfeits rights to her takeout."

I handed Eric the container, which he opened. His stomach growled, and mine answered. Sex burned a lot of calories—especially the kind that he and I had.

"I think it's Greek," I said as I bent back to the fridge to pull out some of the kimchi he mentioned and a carton of eggs. "I can make us some noodles too. I have a lifetime supply in the cupboard."

When I stood back up, however, Eric was still staring into the box like it contained the mysteries of life.

"Oh, sorry," I said. "Is it moldy?"

I peeked in. It was not. I frowned. Eric still hadn't moved.

"It's spanakopita, Petri dish, not a pensieve. What's wrong with you?"

When the nickname still didn't provoke an answer, I was officially worried.

"Everything okay?" I asked.

Eric blinked and swallowed. His eyes refocused on me. "What?"

"Got something against Greek food? It's okay, it wasn't that good anyway. You should come to Chicago during spring break, after the winter storms are over. I'll take you to Greektown, and we'll get some spanakopita that's not a mushy mess. I know this one place, it will knock your socks off..."

I was babbling nervously. Something had happened, and I really wanted to know what. Was he regretting the last twenty-four hours? The tickets, the lock of hair, the mind-bending sex? It was overwhelming, but surely he didn't regret anything?

Did he?

He looked up. "We'll get what?"

I swallowed. "Um, Greek food. You know, since you're not happy with Skylar's takeout, plus you've got that classics fetish?" I was trying to sound laid-back, but to be honest, his lack of response was starting to freak me out.

Eric frowned. "How did you know that?"

I rolled my eyes. "Eric, you have like twenty books of Greek and Roman poetry on your bookshelf. You didn't think I missed that, did you? I am reasonably observant."

Again, he didn't respond, but that empty mask was hiding some serious gear-turning.

"Eric?" I ventured once more. I reached out to touch his hand. "What the hell is wrong?"

Suddenly, he was all movement, looking from side to side, tossing the box on the counter like it was a hot pan and darting around me toward the bedrooms.

"I...I need to go," he said in a hurry. "I need to get out of here."

I followed him back to the bedroom, where he was digging through the clothes on the floor.

"I'm going to get some real breakfast," he said curtly as he yanked on his shirt. "We'll—um, we'll talk later, okay?"

"What? What happened to eating me for breakfast?" I was trying to be playful, but failed miserably. When your voice cracks like the San Andreas Fault, it's sort of a giveaway.

But the time for flirtation was over anyway. Eric was too busy pulling on his pants, then shoving his feet into his shoes without even bothering to look for socks. Almost out of solidarity, I pulled on my neon-green bathrobe, wanting to cover myself up too. The room felt unaccountably cold.

"Eric?" I tried once more. "Eric, what's wrong?"

He pulled on his jacket and tossed a scarf around his arm before stopping, finding me staring at him.

"Eric, I'm kind of freaking out here," I said, pulling on a bunch of loose purple hair. Shit. In this bathrobe I probably looked like a Fraggle. Honestly, it was the first time I'd ever worried about how I looked the morning after. "I—what happened?" I tried yet again. "What did I do?"

He looked me over with an expression I couldn't read. It was almost like he had just realized I was there. Was that regret? Sorrow? Fear? I didn't know him well enough to interpret.

"Jane. I'm—fuck, I'm so sorry. But I—I can't do this. I have to go."

He pushed past me and dashed out of the apartment. The slam of the door catch woke me out of my stupor. What in the fuck had just happened?

No, I decided. He didn't get off that easy.

Before I could stop myself, I was running out of the apartment, chasing him down the hall in my purple and green glory. When I heard the elevator doors close, I beelined for the stairs, doing my very best to beat him to the ground floor despite not exactly being an athlete.

I reached the ground floor just as the elevator doors opened, and Eric stepped out looking like a scared deer when he saw me shuffling toward him in my Jesus sandals, scruffy robe, and purple hair a mile high.

"Hey!" I called out while I sucked in breaths. "Eric!"

"Jane, go back upstairs. I told you, I'll call you later."

I knew he wouldn't call. He couldn't even meet my eye as he walked out of the building. I was something of an expert in brushoffs —giving and receiving them—and this had supreme ghosting written all over it.

The biggest difference was that this one was really, really going to hurt.

So I followed him out into the snow, caring absolutely nothing for the other students entering and leaving the building on the otherwise calm Cambridge street. Jesus fuck, it was cold out here. My toes were already turning white. Why hadn't anyone warned me about the sudden onslaught of the New England winter?

"Eric!" I shouted.

He stopped at last, barely covered himself with his coat. I held out his gloves, which he took blindly. But I didn't let go right away, instituting a kind of tug-of-war that forced him to talk to me.

"What in the hell is going on?" I asked. "Where are you going?"

Eric tugged on the gloves, then scowled when I wouldn't release them. "Jane, can I have my gloves, please?"

He was so painfully formal.

"No," I snapped. "Not until you tell me what the hell is happening here?"

"Jane." Eric glanced around. Ah, there was the look. The worry that someone would spot him. Well, fuck that. We were way past that now.

"Eric," I responded. "Where are you going?"

He tugged on the gloves again. Again, I didn't release them.

"Home," he said through his teeth.

"Home? Home?" I yanked on the gloves, but this time he wouldn't let go. "Listen, I know last night was a lot. But I thought—those tickets, Eric. The lock of hair. They all meant something to me. Didn't they—didn't they mean something to you too?"

I hated the way I sounded. Pathetic. Pleading. Like my entire life's happiness hinged on a man, of all things. It didn't, but I didn't like feeling as if he had my heart cupped in those cold hands, and with one squeeze, he could break it.

He looked at me for a long time, long enough for the silence to settle around us like the snow, for the sound of voices in Harvard Square to filter back to us. His grip on the gloves tightened, but he didn't release them. Neither did I.

"It did mean something," he admitted finally. "But I'm sorry. Jane, I can't do this with you right now. I thought I could, but I just can't."

"You can't do this? I'm pretty sure it's already done," I said bitterly. "Unless that's the point. You worked as hard as you fucking could over the past few weeks to screw the crazy-haired girl with the weird clothes. You broke down every barrier I had until, what? You got what you wanted? Break the purple-haired freak for some fun before finding some pearl-clutching heiress to pair up with?"

Eric shook his head helplessly, gray eyes widening. "No, Jane, wait...it's not you, I swear. It's me, it's—I—"

"'It's not you, it's me'?" I parroted cruelly. "I might only be twenty-two, but come on, Eric. Even I'm tired of that stupid line."

"Jane, I—look, if you want to know the truth, I just got out of a relationship before coming to Boston, okay? I thought I was ready to move on, but maybe I'm not."

"You just got out?" I asked. "How long ago?"

"A year and a half," he admitted.

"You just got out of a relationship a year and a half ago?"

He opened and closed his mouth a few times, but then, slowly, nodded. "I—it was a hard breakup. I swear, Jane, I just need some space, a few days, maybe a couple of weeks. I'll come back around, I promise."

"A few days? A few weeks?" I was repeating everything he said like a goddamn myna bird, but I couldn't help it. I was too shocked. Who was this person?

"Jane, I swear to God, I'm not trying to hurt you."

"Wow," I replied. "I must have been quite the thrilling fucking chase for you to go after it for a month, you fucking lab experiment."

"Jane, come on..."

But I was done listening. I dropped the gloves, not even caring when the sudden release caused Eric to stumble back a few steps.

One tired line after another. Why couldn't he just be honest? Say what was so plain to me: babe, I'm just not that into you. We had some fun, and now it's over.

As excuse after excuse poured from his sorry, stupid mouth, I swiped a layer of snow off the bannister of my building, packing it in my hands meditatively. And then without thinking, I turned and hurled the snowball directly into his face.

"Hey!" Eric shouted. "What the hell!"

"You're all the same," I snapped. "Just want to fuck and run. But you know what? At least the others were honest. They didn't even feign like they wanted something more than sex. No sweet-talking, no playing house. They just wanted sex. You want to break hearts too. Well, you know what, you fucking sorry excuse for a lab experiment? You can't have mine. Not now. Not ever."

I threw another handful of snow at him, then another, and another, until my hands were freezing, and he was too busy dodging snowballs to offer any more excuses or cries of innocence.

Except maybe one.

"Jane!" he cried, though the layer of white muted his shout. "I'm sorry!"

I let the door slam behind me. I no longer cared.

FIFTEEN

"I'm sorry, baby. Oh, *fuck*, I'm so goddamn sorry. Detective, what the hell is wrong with her? Why is there so much blood?"

I moaned as I tried to sit up on the cot. My entire body felt like it was on fire, and my vision was even worse than before. My head throbbed like I'd been clocked in the temple.

"Eric?" I asked. Was it really his face I'd seen earlier? His voice that had comforted me?

A tall shape squatted beside me. This close, things were a little clearer. Behind him, blurry shapes moved all around the room, looking more like dark, shapeless snowmen than actual people. How many were there? Five? Ten? My head hurt too much to count.

Eric. Eric's face. Eric's golden face. He bent down until he was almost in full focus and I could almost ignore the pain.

He looked like he'd aged ten years, with tiny crow's feet more apparent than usual around his eyes, the lines across his forehead in high relief, and haggard circles under his normally bright eyes.

"Hey, gorgeous," he said in a voice that was a *lot* calmer than he looked. "You're awake." He exhaled and cupped my cheeks gently. "I'm here now. Can you—shit, can you tell me what's wrong? There's an ambulance on the way."

"I don't feel very good," I mumbled. Who was I kidding? I hadn't felt good in days. Everything about me was completely wrong.

"Jane, they—they gave you something. A few things, looks like. They split just as we arrived—I think one of them saw us coming down the road. Do you know what they gave you?"

"They gave us a lot of things." I shook my head. "I dunno what. Where's *Eomma*? Where are we?"

"She's—Cho is helping her out to the car, see? You're at an abandoned farm outside of Jinan. Carson's owned it since the eighties. Cho thinks he used it to run a local prostitution ring when he was in town."

I squinted, and barely made out the figures on the other side of the room. One of them—I guessed Cho—looked up from where it was helping another figure from the other cot.

"I can't see," I said. "They took my glasses."

"Shit," Eric muttered. "You can't see anything?"

I shook my head, though the movement made it hurt even more. "You're all blurry."

"She's in a bad way," he called to someone else across the room. "What's the ETA on the ambulance?"

I couldn't make out the response.

"*Jane*," my mother called vehemently. "Who is—get away from —" She broke into a string of Korean while standing up, pointing at me, then Eric, as blurry Cho towed her out of the room.

I looked away as her voice faded. No, I couldn't listen to that now. Everything was no with her. My whole life, just no. No to my hair. No to my clothes. No to my husband. No, no, no.

I just wanted to stay here, in the quiet. Two hands clasped my cheeks, and when I blinked—verrrrry slowly—Eric's face filled my vision once more.

I relaxed. And then stopped, because everything hurt.

"Yu-na is pretty out of it too," Eric said. "Jane, what did they give you guys?" He looked down at me, and through my haze, I registered the barely concealed fear playing across his features.

"You're so pretty," I murmured as I reached a weak hand to play over his lips, which cooperated with a slight smile. The lines across his brow seemed to deepen. "Don't worry so much."

"Maybe I won't if you tell me what they gave you, gorgeous."

He looked away again. *No, don't look away*, I thought.

"Tony, did you find anything?" he called.

Another familiar voice responded, but I couldn't understand it. The tone, however, didn't sound good.

"They gave us a lot of things. In all different places." I could hear how thick-lipped I sounded, like I was speaking through water. But no matter what, I couldn't manage to articulate properly. "A lot. Check—check the soup."

"The soup? Tony, did you find soup?"

"I'll check the kitchen."

I tried to look around to help them, but even the movement of my eyes made me dizzy. I closed them.

"Jane." Eric's deep voice was more strained. "Baby, you have to stay with me. Don't go to sleep yet."

"You never call me baby." My eyelids felt weighted by anvils, but I managed to open them again. "You must be really worried. Where's the guy?"

Eric's face screwed up in confusion. "What guy? Do you mean Jude? Carson?"

I shook my head and immediately cringed. Oh, that hurt. "No, they left. The Russian. They called him Anton. He—he was the one who—gave us the—" I slumped against the wall, just barely missing smacking my temple on the concrete when Eric's strong arm propped me up again. Oh, his chest. Yes, that felt good. That was the place to be.

"The soup," I mumbled again. "Check the soup."

My eyes closed again, and the room went black. The hands around my shoulder stiffened.

"Jane," Eric's voice hummed pleasantly enough next to my ear, though I could still sense its strain. "Jane, stay with me, okay. Cho, do we have an ambulance on the way?"

"Yes, it is coming."

I sniffed. Something smelled wrong. There was him, of course, full of light and linen and the cologne I loved so much. Tom Ford.

"You smell like money," I bleared, and Eric's chuckle vibrated under my cheek. But when I sniffed again, that other scent was back. Something metallic. Something...wrong.

The man. Jude. Carson. He had said their names. Where—where had they gone? What had they done to me?

Get it done, he said.

Bait, he said.

With more energy than I thought I had, I pushed off Eric and sat up, the sudden motion causing another sharp stab in my belly. "Oh! No, Eric, that's—ah!—that's what he wants. He's—Eric, you have to get out of here."

"What? No, Jane, I'm not going anywhere. I'm here for you, all right? *I'm not going anywhere.*"

"Bait," I wheezed. "I'm...bait. He said that I'm—he's here for *you*. Owwwwwww!"

I moaned as I collapsed back against the wall. The pain made me wake up again, more attuned to my surroundings. I looked down, finally finding the source of that terrible smell.

Blood. That's what it was. Lots and lots of blood, enough that my blankets and the sheets tangled with my legs were soaked.

"Why—oh, God, is that...is that mine?"

Eric's face told me everything I needed to know. "Tony!" he shouted, though he didn't look away. "What's the ETA on the fucking ambulance?"

"Two minutes, sir!"

"I—I don't know—what's happen—what did they do..." I

mumbled, unable to say much more than that. God, I was tired. *So* tired, and yet, I didn't want to go back to sleep, back to those terrible dreams that reminded me just how much I had to lose. I couldn't go through that loss again. I couldn't.

"Jane? Look, gorgeous, I need you to stay awake, all right? Help is on the way, but you have to stay awake."

"You have to...you have to get out of here," I mumbled. "He'll be back." Another massive round of pain clenched my belly, and I curled into myself like a shrimp and cried like I hadn't since I was a child.

"Tony!"

"One minute!"

I sank back into the bed, no longer caring about the metallic scent of blood in the air or the fact that even Eric's face seemed to be fading away.

"I'm so tired," I said into my sweat-soaked pillow. "So...so tired."

"Jane, just hold on! Fucking hell, Tony, her pulse is dropping!"

"They're here!"

There was a rush of activity as another several blurry figures burst into the room. My eyes opened one last time as I was lifted from the bed and transferred to another. They rolled me out into the cold, Eric jogging beside me. I began shivering violently the second the January air hit my soaked, shriveled body. His face. I could only focus on his face.

"Is she going to be all right?" Eric kept asking as he followed me into the back of the ambulance.

An EMT looked up and rattled off machine-gun speeds of Korean while he took my vitals and tried to push Eric away. He was one of the few I'd met so far who did not speak fluent English.

"Just try it," Eric snarled at him. "I'm not going fucking anywhere."

Cho, thankfully, appeared in the doorway next to Eric, listening intently, and then translating.

Eric just watched with obvious dread. "What?" he asked. "What is it?"

"The EMT wants to know," Cho said. "Was she pregnant?"

"Was?" Eric asked, dumbfounded, though the arms around my shoulders squeezed a little tighter.

"No," I moaned, holding my waist. "It's—she—no, *please!*"

Cho looked regretfully at Eric. "Was," he said quietly.

Behind me, Eric sucked in a tight breath. Energy seeped from my body, and the edges of my vision darkened once more. I fell back into the pillow, blinking as the monitors in the ambulance flashed on and started going off loudly all around.

The EMT shouted again in a frenzy, trying to push Eric out of the way.

"Get the fuck off!" Eric roared back.

"Mr. de Vries, she is failing," Cho translated. "You have to leave now so they can help her!"

"Over my dead body, Cho."

Vaguely I registered doors closing, the rumble of an engine. Movement. Movement of bodies around me, of the floor beneath me. Everything started to numb.

"Jane! Goddammit, Jane, stay with me, do you hear me?"

"I can't," I whispered. "I'm sorry." God, I just wanted it to go away. I wanted to sink into the nothingness that beckoned and never return. Anything would be better than this, than the stabbing pain in my belly, the nausea, the lightness, the fatigue.

The complete and utter desolation that awaited me on the other side.

Do you really want to give in, pumpkin? Is that your style? My dad's voice questioned me, even from the grave.

Oh, Daddy, I thought with an inward smile. *That was always your problem. You loved me, but you never knew me at all.*

"Jane!" Eric shook me slightly, ignoring the shouts of Korean around him. "Jane, listen to me!"

My eyes opened once more, my vision clouded not by pain, but by the fathomless gray eyes full of love and fear.

And really, didn't those things always go together? At least with us?

"You listen to me," Eric ordered. "You *listen*. I refuse to let him kill one more person I love. And you? I love *you*, you stupid, stubborn, headstrong girl, more than anyone or anything I have ever loved in my entire sorry life. *I love you*, Jane Lee Lefferts de Vries. With everything that I am and everything that I will ever be! So you are not allowed to leave me in this world, because if you do, I'm not staying behind this time. You go, I follow. And I'm not ready to die yet, Jane, so you have to stay!"

My eyelids fluttered, and Eric pressed me to his breast, giving me one last inhale of his clean, masculine scent before he was pulled away. It was the perfect way to go.

"Do you hear me?" he kept saying. "Do you hear me, woman? I love you, and I can't live this shitty fucking life without you. So you have to stay with me, Jane. I'm begging you, pretty girl. Stay with me!"

I fell back. The world was a scream.

"Oh, Eric," I murmured. "I love you too."

The words were my goodbye.

SIXTEEN

2009

"Jane? Are you all right? It's not like you to miss class, and you weren't in class this morn—oh!"

Skylar stopped short in the doorway of the bathroom when she found me standing in front of the mirror with a pair of scissors like a serial killer.

It had been not quite two full days since the snowball fight with Eric. I had spent most of Sunday drowning my anger and sorrow in cheap tequila—the last of which I'd chased with some orange juice this morning instead of going to classes. Hey, hey, hey. It's kind of a breakfast, all right? And this was my first honest-to-God broken heart. It wasn't the easiest thing to bear without a little help from Señor Cuervo.

Skylar's big eyes flew all around the bathroom, taking in the abandoned green bathrobe on the toilet, Eric's shredded t-shirt in the waste bin, the empty bottle of tequila perched on the sink. Okay, so maybe I had a lot of help from my Mexican friend.

That might have been alarming enough, but I was pretty sure it was the bright purple hair clippings scattered all over the bathroom like feathers that really evoked concern. In my drunken grief, I had gone full GI Jane.

Skylar dropped her bag like she was preparing for battle. "Had a weekend, did we? Is your, ah, makeover why you missed classes?"

"No," I said as I snipped. "The makeover is just for fun. I missed class today because I decided I'm dropping out." I cut just a few more strands, then dropped the scissors in the sink with a clatter. That was the best I could do without a mirror behind me. Or, you know, a professional hairstylist.

I eyed my reflection carefully. I really wouldn't be able to put any black in there for another few weeks—not unless I wanted my heavily bleached hair to fall out from stress. But I wasn't really feeling the pixie look. I looked too much like an anime figure. Like a little girl.

Maybe I just needed to buzz it all off.

Skylar, to her credit, didn't leave. She just raised one wry red brow. "Oh, really?"

"I don't belong here," I said as I turned to the box of hair supplies on the toilet. "Look at our class. Everyone there is named Lindsay or Someone the Third. Or..."

"Crosby?"

I stood back up with the clippers. "You know what I mean."

Skylar rolled her eyes. "I think you are overstating things a little bit. Obviously Harvard has a legacy problem, but our class is the most diverse in HLS history. It's not perfect. But you aren't exactly Ruth Bader Ginsburg in a hall filled with men. What really happened?"

I swallowed as I turned toward the mirror. "Does anyone else in our class look like me?" I wasn't talking about my ethnicity. I was talking about the whole package.

Skylar didn't answer for a long time, so I plugged in the clippers and brought them to my temple, ready to push them through the hair on the right side of my head. The buzz filled the bathroom, but just as I was about to start, Skylar reached over and turned them off again.

"Hey!" I protested.

She took the shredded t-shirt out of the trash. "Is this about Eric?"

I scowled. "You mean that human golden retriever picked out of a VD awareness pamphlet?"

"Oh good, we're back to that again." She dropped the shirt back in the trash.

"Why? Did he say something?"

"Well, he didn't look so great in class. Very...tired. I'm guessing something happened between you two."

"Oh, something happened all right. Our fake-haloed lab experiment decided he needed to expand his sample size on Friday. He was probably tired because he was out collecting specimens too late last night."

Skylar's mouth dropped. "Did he really say he wanted to see other people?"

I was about to say yes, but realized I couldn't. Because even though I was angry, I didn't want to lie. Unlike him. So instead of answering, I turned on the buzzers again.

Skylar promptly turned them off.

"Sky!"

"Jane!" She stood like a tiny Peter Pan, her hands on her hips. "You're not doing this. I'm not letting you throw your life away because of whatever Eric did or didn't do. He looked really upset, I'm telling you. I don't know what happened, but maybe you two just need to—"

"Skylar, stop," I interrupted. "This is on him. He came over this weekend, laid on his charm sooooo thick for my birthday, and then dropped me just as soon as I let my guard down. He couldn't have been plain enough about it. His exact words were: 'I can't do this.'" I crossed my arms. "And then he fucking left. That was it."

Skylar's jaw dropped along with her hands off her hips. "Wow," she said. "I'm—wow, I really wasn't expecting that. And that's...well, when I approached him, that's not exactly what he said."

"Oh, really? And what was that?"

She blinked sadly. "Just that it had been a rough weekend. And that he knew you deserved better." She toed her shoe on the tile floor. "He sounded very sorry. Maybe it was just a moment of weakness, you know? Some guys get kind of awful when they're overwhelmed with emotion."

"Is that how you know Patrick loves you?" I snapped.

Skylar didn't say anything.

I sighed. "I'm sorry. That was low."

"It was," she agreed. "But you get a pass because you're drunk and in pain. To make it up to me, you can talk to Eric. I think he's hurting. I think he misses you."

"Well, then we're both idiots," I said, a little too harshly as I turned back to the mirror. "The only difference is that I'm learning from my mistakes. I'm not spending the next three years being laughed at. Absolutely not."

Skylar watched me carefully as I turned on the clippers, and this time I managed to push them through one solid patch of purple just above my ear. It fell to the floor with the rest, leaving a plowed stripe of black-brown fuzz in its stead. I snorted. It might seem ridiculous now, but this was going to look badass when I was finished.

"Jane," Skylar said a little louder. "You realize they will laugh if you leave too."

I paused, mid-stripe, then kept going. "Who cares? I won't have to see them." Him, I should have said. I won't have to see him.

The look on Skylar's face told me she was thinking the same thing.

"I'll make you a deal," she said once I was finished buzzing the rest of that side of my head, leaving myself with an asymmetrical bob that was half dark growth close to my scalp, the wild remnants of my bright purple waves cut to my chin.

I turned the clippers off and put them on the sink's edge. "What's that?"

"I help you clean up this disaster, and you come with me to class this afternoon. And then, if you really want to quit, I'll help you write the petition for tuition reimbursement myself."

I put my glasses back on, dizzied for a moment by the way the entire room suddenly came into sharp focus. Fuck, she was right. I was still kind of drunk. Well, whatever. Might as well take the new do out for a spin.

"Fine," I said as I started to clean up the clippings. "But I'm holding you to that."

I squatted down to start sweeping the fallen remnants of my hair into a pile. Skylar watched for a moment before she helped too.

"I'm sorry," she said quietly, rubbing my shoulder. "But I'm here for you. We'll get through it together, Janey. It's going to be all right."

Present

"Is she going to be all right?"

"Mr. de Vries, she is stable. That is all we can promise for now."

"Stable? *Stable?* She's in a coma, for Christ's sake!"

"She lost a lot of blood, Mr. de Vries. We are sorry, but your wife has a very rare blood type, B-negative. Less than one percent of Koreans have this blood type. O-negative, universal, is also rare here. We have put a request in with some other hospitals, but these things take time."

"You need blood? I'm O-neg. Where's the fucking needle?"

"Mr. de Vries, we cannot just accept blood from a stranger—"

"I'm not a stranger. She's my *wife*. I'm not going to lose her. Do whatever tests on me you like, but do them fast. She's—fuck, I can't lose her—"

"Mr. de Vries..."

2009

"Mr. de Vries? Mr. de Vries!"

The entire class was staring at Eric while the professor tapped irritably on her podium.

Skylar and I had taken seats near the back today, and so it was with some delight that I enjoyed watching Eric in the front, casting his eyes from side to side, looking for something. Was it me? Probably just seeking out his next prey, but a part of me liked the idea that maybe I was the reason the Rising Star of Torts wasn't paying attention for shit.

Still, he'd managed to answer the occasional Socratic question until now. When he had spotted me. Idiot. How hard was it to see the bright purple beacon in a sea of black and beige?

"Ground control to Major Tom," remarked the professor one last time, to the general uproar of the class. "Will you come back to us?"

Eric shook his head, then broke our gaze and turned to the front. "Sorry, Professor," he said, then cleared his throat.

Before he could answer the question, however, the class ended.

"Come on," I said to Skylar. "I just want to go back home."

"What about study group?" she asked as we put on our winter wear.

"Please." I shook my head. "Do I seem like I'll be in any condition to sit across from that jackass for an extra hour? I just want to be alone. I'll study by myself better anyway."

Skylar sighed, then wrapped her scarf around her neck. "All right. I'll get your share of the readings for you."

I nodded, then dashed out, still buttoning my jacket and looking for my yellow beanie in my bag. Now I was the idiot. Because, of course, in my hurry to leave, I didn't look up. And instead plowed right into the one person I was trying to avoid.

"Whoa there."

I jumped back. "Do I look like a horse to you?"

But Eric, apparently, had no comebacks. "I waited for you outside your Contracts class," he said. "Where were you?"

"I was at the law offices of it's none of your fucking business," I snapped. "What's with the third degree? Can't quite get your hooks out now that you've decided to catch and release?"

Eric just looked me over, like he was checking for bruises. "You cut your hair."

I swallowed, putting a hand up to my shorn mane. "Observant, aren't you?"

Lord, my mother was going to freak when I came home for the holidays. Dad, of course, would just take it in stride. I could hear him already. *Nice do, kiddo. Starting a punk band?* But Yu-na would probably just complain about how I needed to wear a hat now wherever I went. She'd probably resent the fact that the winter would require it anyway.

"Why?"

My eyes flashed. "Because I felt like it. When I decide to do something, I actually fucking do it."

Eric's expression, however, didn't waver. I hated it. I hated the pity I saw there. The concern. What right did he have to look at me that way when he had caused the whole fucking problem?

"Did it...did it have anything to do with me?" he asked.

"Are you serious right now?"

Eric toed the ground nervously, but he didn't look away, even as our classmates exited the building, eyeing us curiously. "Look, Jane, about the other night. Let's go somewhere and talk. There are things about me that—"

"You know what?" I broke in. "No. Whatever bullshit you're going to use to pathologize your behavior, I don't want to hear it. You made your choice when you walked out."

"Jane—"

"What are you expecting here?" I continued forcefully. "Do you think your cock is a magic wand? All you have to do is wave it over my head, and I'll come like a rocket and forget your emotional abuse?

That only works in male fantasies, Petri dish. Bad romance novels and Judd Apatow movies. In real life, it's different. Like it or not, you are completely replaceable."

He searched my face for a long time, clearly disbelieving. But for the first time in my life, I was able to keep my bravado firmly in place.

When I had arrived at Harvard, I knew I was different. That in this world of legacy and entitlement, I'd likely get stomped if I didn't protect myself. But over the last month, this man had convinced me it didn't have to be like that. Somehow he had found the cracks in my armor and broken them down, one piece at a time. He made me admit that some people were worth letting in. Maybe one person. Maybe him.

Right before he'd run over all of it like one of the snowplows moving up and down Comm. Ave.

Still, silver linings. In the last forty-eight hours, I'd done something I'd tried to do my entire life and failed. I'd built a wall without cracks. A wall no one, not even this asshole, could breach.

"For what it's worth, I like it," Eric said. "I liked it before too, but they both look good."

"Do you really think I give a good goddamn what you think of my hair, Petri dish?"

All at once, the mask I'd seen from the first day I met him slid back into place. He was still friendly. Still easygoing. Affable. Easy.

But now that easiness seemed ice cold. The Eric I knew was gone.

"No," he said quietly. "I don't imagine you do."

I met his gaze head-on, and not one bit of me wavered.

And this time Eric was the one to back down. I was the one to stay strong.

Present

"Stay strong."

A squeeze of my hand. The hum of a machine. The mutter of a distant voice.

"Don't give up, gorgeous. Please, Jane. Come back to me."

Beep. Beep. Beep.

The first thing I saw when I opened my eyes was the heart rate monitor, with its recognizable flicker jumping rhythmically across the screen. Still blurry. Everything was blurry.

The second thing I saw was Eric.

"You're back," he whispered.

"Am I?" I asked. I still wasn't sure.

"Hold on."

A pair of glasses slid onto my face. And then, finally, the world came into focus.

Eric lay next to me on the bed, offering warmth where I couldn't get it, body vibrating against my cheek. It wasn't until I managed to look up again that I realized he was crying—terrible, silent tears that dripped down his haggard face. They weren't the first; his eyes were red-rimmed with stress and exhaustion.

"Yeah," he whispered. "Oh, thank fucking God. You're back." He pressed kisses across my brow again and again. I leaned into them. Each one seemed to blast through the fuzzy halo I was wearing.

"You're here." I blinked, my eyes opening wider. "How—*how* are you here?"

Eric swallowed—was that a chuckle through those watery gray eyes? "I—the trial was thrown out. My attorneys did their jobs and figured out that the prosecutor was being bribed by Carson. So the judge reassigned the case to the Brooklyn DA, who promptly declined to prosecute."

"Oh." Right. *Thank you, Matthew Zola.* I didn't have to say it, though. We owed the young prosecutor for more than either of us could count.

"I came to find you," Eric murmured. "Jane, why the fuck did you leave? Why didn't you just wait for me?"

My throat felt tight, like someone was squeezing it. I didn't have a new answer for him. He knew every one I had to offer.

"The—the—the baby," I managed to get out. My throat was on fire. "How—"

"I—we—oh, fuck." Eric could barely get his words out either as he clasped my head between his broad palms and touched his forehead to mine.

"We lost her, didn't we?" My heart picked up. Pieces of the last few days were coming back to me. All a haze, but I remembered the blood. I remembered the pain.

Eric's tears streamed. "Ah, *fuck*." His voice was pained as he swiped them away. "They...yeah, Jane. We...we lost her."

"M-miscarriage?"

But against my forehead, Eric slowly shook his head. "They took her. Jane—shit, I'm so sorry, but he—Carson—he had the Russian, the one called Anton." He shook his head, like the name meant something very specific to him. "They forced an abortion. They sedated you and did it, and then you got an infection. They gave you too much of one of the drugs, and then they were forced to call a medic, who was there when we arrived. But f-fuck, Jane, you almost died."

By the end of the statement, his words were bouncing over themselves like they were tripping over cobblestones.

So strange, I thought. Normally I was the one with all of the emotion. The one who spouted off, who wore every thought and feeling I had right on my sleeve. Eric had always carried us both, and yet here he was, breaking down like a child.

How long had I been out?

How long had I been in danger?

What had he gone through during that period?

"Sh-shhhh," I said, managing to pull a fragile arm from under the hospital blankets and wrap it around his waist. "It's going to be all right."

The words felt hollow. Somewhere in the back of my still-addled mind, a voice of reason cautioned: *Don't worry, pumpkin, it will hit you. You'd better be ready when it does. If you push against a tidal wave, it will only knock you over.*

Dad? Was that the voice of my dad, chiming from the grave again?

As if on cue, I heard his familiar, belly-jiggling chuckle. *Don't tell your mother, peanut. She doesn't like it when I tell her what to think.*

My mother.

"*Eomma*," I said suddenly, pushing Eric's arms away.

He sat up, swiping at the remaining tears.

"Where is she?" I demanded. "Is she all right?"

The realization that I had been in the same room as my mother for several days and hadn't done a thing to help her lanced through me like a sword. After all, what in the hell had I been here for in the first place?

"Relax," Eric said, stroking my hair. "She's going to be all right. She was severely dehydrated and malnourished after two weeks at that house, but she's on the mend in another room. They had to detox her from the sedative, but she's almost through it. She was on it for much longer than you." He squeezed my hand. "I'm sure she'll come to see you as soon as she can."

"What about Carson?" I asked, my eyes widening. "Jude? He was there too. The Anton guy? What happened to the medic?"

I hoped beyond hope that it hadn't all been for nothing. That Eric wouldn't have flown here just to rescue me. I wanted, more than anything else, for this nightmare to be over.

But instead, Eric just shook his head with clear regret. "The police took the medic into custody, and they've been questioning him, or so Cho says. But Jude and Anton left just before we arrived—they likely saw us on security footage, but your condition made it impossible to use you like the bait they intended. There has been no sign of Carson or anyone else since."

I wilted with defeat. "Then it was all for nothing. I ruined it all, didn't I?"

Eric said nothing. Even under the layer of haze, my heart ached.

"I—I—" I couldn't speak. Couldn't even think straight. *Sorry,* I wanted to say, but the word wasn't even close to adequate. What *was?*

"What is it?" Eric asked, scooting closer. He cupped my face, and his thumb stroked my cheek. "What do you need, gorgeous? Anything."

I closed my eyes and leaned into his hand. I needed a lot of things. The enormity of what I'd been through was beginning to dawn on me, but I was pretty sure it would get worse once the sedatives wore off completely. Food. Water. Shelter. Eric. I needed them all. But right now, I wanted more sleep. And I wanted one other thing.

"Home," I whispered. "I just want to go home."

INTERLUDE II

Present

Eric paced in front of the steps leading up to the DVS jet. Tony stood stolidly by their entrance, watching his boss's every move. The other security members—the two new ones Eric had brought from New York as well as the other three who had come with Jane on this journey, were already seated, nervously drinking sparkling water. Jane's detail likely thought they'd all be without a job once they reached New York. Eric still wasn't sure what to do. After all, she *had* been taken on their watch.

But for now, much like his wife, he just wanted to go home.

If they even could.

After a week in the hospital, Jane was stable—not the bullshit half-in-a-coma stable where the doctors had tried to convince him she was perfectly fine, but really and truly stable. No more fever, the infection was waning, and her face didn't look like death anymore.

They could fight this battle from New York—if they could get there at all.

They had been sitting at the military air base in Suwon for hours, waiting to get the final go-ahead to leave. But just as the pilot had started taxiing toward the runway, they had been called back. A problem, said air control, with customs.

With Carson, Eric knew. The man wanted them here, and after hearing Jane's gradual retelling of the things she had overheard between fever dreams on top of what she and Cho had uncovered, he now knew why: Carson needed DVS transport. For something. Something big.

Not that Eric gave two shits about that. Carson was still MIA, but unfortunately it had become a matter of who had the most pull with the government—South Korea's *or* the U.S. And since Carson had been actively involved with both for so long, as opposed to Eric with less than a year at the helm of DVS, Eric was losing the game. Badly.

Still, Eric had personally met with the Minister of Trade, who had assured he would do everything he could to protect their departure, even getting them special dispensation to leave from the Suwon base under the supervision of the U.S. Army's air defense battalion instead of having to go through Incheon International Airport. Eric had accepted the favor, but he honestly wasn't sure it was even for the best, considering how deep Chariot was in the military's pockets.

Because despite the fact that Detective Cho had called the NIS directly to alert them of the kidnapping, nothing had happened. No arrests had been made. It was like Jane and Yu-na's entire abduction —the abduction of *two* American citizens—hadn't happened at all.

Eric shivered in the cold, but stopped pacing when he spotted a vehicle speeding across the tarmac.

"That looks like U.S. military this time," Tony said, pointing at the truck.

Eric squinted. The closer it came, the more he could make out the even mix of air force fatigues and officers' uniforms.

"Shit. They've corralled the lieutenant colonel into this." He swore again. Lieutenant Colonel Clifford, the commanding officer of the U.S. battalion, *really* didn't like the fact that his base was being used to give in to the demands of a spoiled aristocrat and had made his impressions of Eric clear immediately after they arrived.

"Who's the suit with him?" Tony wondered.

Eric shook his head. "I don't know. More bureaucratic red tape, I'd guess."

The car pulled to a stop, and the lieutenant colonel exited, followed by a man and a woman, both in civilian suits.

"What's this about, Colonel?" Eric asked. "My wife and mother-in-law have been through a harrowing ordeal. I thought we had gotten through all the paperwork needed to get us home."

The colonel, a barrel-chested man with a beefy neck, shrugged as he gestured to the other two people who had exited the car with him. "Intelligence has a few more questions for you, Mr. de Vries," he said gruffly, clearly not pleased about the new development. "This is Agent Kym, from the CIA."

The woman reached out to shake Eric's hand. "We are working with South Korea on subjects relating to North Korean disarmament," she said in perfect English. "This is Agent Suh, from the NIS."

The other man grunted.

Eric blinked. He was beyond this kind of small talk.

"We just have a few things to ask your wife and mother-in-law before they depart," Agent Kym continued.

Eric eyed both of the agents, then shook his head. "Yeah, I don't think so. Not without our lawyer present, and he's in New York."

"Aren't you and your wife both attorneys?" snapped the colonel. "Your plane has been sitting on our runway for half the damn day. My battalion hasn't been able to run most of its drills today."

"We are," Eric said smoothly, "but my practice was primarily securities, and my wife was a prosecutor. I'm sure you'll understand that neither of us have the background to represent ourselves adequately in a unique international situation like this one." He looked back at Agent Kym. "We'll be in New York if you need us. Shouldn't that make things easier? Everyone on this plane is an American citizen. We'll be on home ground."

"Mrs. Lefferts is a Korean national," Agent Suh finally spoke up. "She never renounced her South Korean citizenship."

Eric scowled. "As I understand it, she holds dual citizenship. That means she has as much a right to return to the States as me or her daughter."

"It also means we are within *our* rights to hold our nationals subject to *our* laws, Mr. de Vries. You have no right to take her without our consent."

They glared at each other, Eric's steely gaze holding Suh's inky one in a tense challenge until Agent Kym diplomatically cleared her throat and turned to the colonel, who was becoming increasingly agitated.

"Colonel Clifford, this will only take a moment, and I know you have more pressing things to do. If you'd like to have your assistant return you to base and send him back for us, I'm sure we will be finished by then."

The colonel glanced between them, clearly battling between what he was *told* to do, likely in veiled terms, and what he felt he *should* be doing. "Hell," he muttered, tossing a hand up at all of them. "If it gets this thing off my runway, I'm all for it."

And with that, they watched as he and his underling returned to the Jeep and drove to the American side of the base.

Agent Kym turned to Eric. "Mr. de Vries, I'm sure Agent Suh would say that of course Mrs. Lefferts can and should return to her home. But for the sake and expediency of our own investigations, we would be grateful if she and your wife would answer a few questions for us before she leaves." She tipped her head to the side. "I'm sure you can understand why the CIA might prefer to conduct this kind of interview in the comfort of your jet instead of the constraints of the base."

It took a moment, but answers quickly dawned on Eric. Why Agent Kym had so brusquely shooed away the colonel. And Agent Suh was eyeing the control tower every so often.

Perhaps Eric did have some allies in South Korea after all.

"All right," he said. "Let's make this fast."

They followed him into the jet, where Eric quickly instructed the lingering security to wait outside. "Except you, Tony," he said to the big man. "You should stay."

As soon as the large men had gone and the fuselage was closed, Eric led the agents to the bedroom at the back of the plane. He knocked on the door. "Yu-na? Jane? Can I come in?"

There was a low groan, and then a raspy: "Of course you can come in, you goon. It's your airplane."

Eric opened the door with a wry smile at Agent Suh, who looked taken aback at Jane's response. Agent Kym just hid a smile.

Jane and her mother sat on the bed, bundled in a thick down comforter. Both women still looked incredibly frail and weak, but they both had color in their faces and had lost that terrible, glazed dilation.

Jane's eyes, benefiting from a spare set of glasses Eric found in her hotel room, cast sharply back and forth between the two agents. "Who are they?"

"South Korean and American intelligence. They...have a few questions." Eric made introductions, and when he pointed to Agent Suh, Yu-na shrank more against the headboard.

Jane looked about as amused by their sudden appearance as Eric had been. "What do they want? Are they aware that I am recovering from a botched forced abortion and my mother is recovering from almost *two weeks* in drugged captivity? We're kind of tired."

It was all Eric could do not to shove the two agents out of the plane right then and there.

"I think they want to help," he said quietly. "Agent Kym is from the CIA. A part, that, um, did not want the U.S. military involved here."

Jane perked up. "Zola?"

Agent Kym nodded. "A colleague of mine was in touch with Matthew Zola, if that's what you mean."

"I see. Well, we already gave our statements to the Hwaseong police," she said. "My cousin, Cho Dong-hyun, is a detective there. He is also in charge of the local investigation, right, Eric?"

Eric nodded.

"We read those files, Mrs. de Vries—"

"Lefferts," Jane put in. "My last name is Lefferts de Vries."

Eric ignored how much it hurt that she didn't take his last name the same way she did in the hospital.

Agent Kym cleared her throat again. "Lefferts, I apologize. Anyway, I'm sorry to say it, but your statements seemed...incomplete. Agent Suh and I were hoping, now that you and your mother are no longer sedated, that you might be able to recall a few other details." She leaned in. "The CIA is taking these crimes against your family very seriously, Mrs. de Vri—ma'am. We intend to follow up on everything you say. Particularly anything to do with John Carson or Chariot Industries."

At the sound of her biological father's name, Jane stiffened, and Yu-na turned white. Eric reached down to take her hand, but Jane pulled it away. She hadn't wanted to touch him since they left the hospital. He couldn't blame her, but he also couldn't say that it didn't hurt too.

"Because Detective Cho has alleged that Mr. Carson is responsible for the most famous serial murders in our country, but he also happens to supply thirty percent of our military's munitions," snapped Agent Suh. "This is a very grave matter for our government *and* our national security."

Eric opened his mouth to inform the man he didn't give a good goddamn about the national security of the South Koreans when they couldn't have been bothered to help *him* ensure the security of his wife. But before he could say so, Yu-na spoke.

"You can take it," she said quietly, handing the man her Korean passport. "I will not come back anyway. Take it and go. We have nothing else to say."

Agent Suh scowled, and once again, Agent Kym stepped in.

"Mrs. Lefferts," she said as she took a seat on the end of the bed.

"Let me assure you that no matter what, you are going home. You are a citizen of the United States, and therefore, you have its complete backing."

At that, Yu-na relaxed a little, but not much. And she tensed right up when Agent Suh began a long line of questioning—this time in Korean.

"Do you know what he's saying?" Eric whispered to Jane.

Her side-eye slipped around her frames. "Did you forget everything you know about me? I know swear words, all the best shaming phrases, and that's about it."

Agent Kym turned to them kindly, though her eyes still followed the rapid-fire conversation. "He is only asking about what happened to her. I'm sure as lawyers, you both understand the importance of going over a witness's account multiple times to be sure it is the right one."

Eric and Jane both watched Agent Suh pepper Yu-na with questions while she offered curt, if somewhat weak-voiced answers.

The exchange continued like that for several minutes until something Agent Suh said definitely got under Yu-na's skin. She broke forward, rattling off a much longer spat of Korean that ended up making the immovable agent look the slightest bit ashamed. Agent Kym just looked on with more mild amusement.

Jane's eyes widened. "*Eomma*," she whispered. "Talk about feisty."

Agent Kym blinked. "I'll say."

"What did she say?" Eric asked.

Jane shrugged. "I only caught a few words at the end, but they weren't very nice ones." She patted her mother's leg kindly. "Way to stick it to the man, *Eomma*."

Yu-na was not amused.

Agent Suh leaned forward with one more curt, cold question. And at that, Yu-na's small hand flew out from under the covers and hit the Korean agent squarely in the jaw.

"Whoa, *Eomma!*" Jane remarked, genuinely shocked. "What just happened?"

Yu-na landed Agent Suh with what must be her famous glare and Eric finally appreciated why Jane compared her mother to a basilisk. Eric would probably have gone with Medusa himself.

"He asked me," she said coldly, "if Jane and I are prostitutes."

Eric sprang up. "That's it. Get the hell *out*."

Suh rose as well, though he made no other move to leave. "You are aware that the U.S. shares an extradition treaty with South Korea," he said with a derogatory sniff toward Yu-na. "Mrs. *Lefferts* is making some very serious accusations about a very good friend to Korea. If I do not get the answers I need, my government will request her return."

"Try it," Eric growled. "I'll wrap your government in so many goddamn lawsuits, you'll be begging the North Koreans to nuke you out of existence."

"Eric—" Jane put in. "Come on, you don't know anything about international law."

"Jane, stop," he retorted. "I'm handling this."

"No, *you* stop! You're pissing off the people who are trying to help us!"

Maybe he should have been glad that she was finally feeling well enough to fight back and tell him he was acting like an idiot, but the reality was, he wanted nothing more than to get the hell out of Seoul. He wanted to get the hell out of this hemisphere.

Jane coughed again. The circles under her eyes were darkening. As soon as he spotted them, Eric sank back onto the bed beside her. Fuck. He was fucking this all up. Again.

The NIS agent's phone buzzed, and he grimaced when he pulled it out. "This is not over," he informed them, and walked out of the room.

"Eric," Jane said with a hoarse voice. "My bag. My things from the hotel. Were they recovered?"

Eric nodded. "Hold on, I'll grab them."

He retrieved her messenger bag—good God, was this the same army surplus piece of shit she had carried with her through law school?—and brought it to the back of the plane. Jane was sitting up with some pain still playing across her face, but she accepted the bag, looking visibly relieved when she opened it and pulled out a thick folder.

"Here," she said as she handed it to Agent Kym. "I think you'll find the proof you need. It's the investigator's file along with my notes and some of my cousin's."

"Good God," Agent Kym murmured as she paged through the documents. "John Carson has been—"

"Conducting illegal arms deals with Pyongyang under the South Koreans' noses?" Eric finished for her. "Yes, it looks that way. He started in the mid-eighties, but after the Soviet Union disintegrated, we think he suspended operations. He's been taking advantage of the relaxed U.S. relations with North Korea alongside the more recent destabilization of the South Korean government to continue the work. His life's accomplishment, as it were."

"This isn't just an arms deal—" Agent Kym looked up. "The nuclear facility was just the tip of the iceberg. Chariot Industries was constructing a pipeline. Mr. de Vries, I'm afraid I must take these. We will need them as a gesture of good will to get cooperation from NIS. As you might have gathered, they are feeling rather...torn...about the issue of John Carson."

"Then they might want to check the flight manifests for marked women on that list," Jane put in. "Half of those crimes were probably copycats, but the other half? They were regional flight attendants for the same airline my mother worked for in 1987. All from the same part of Hwaseong. All killed around times when John Carson was on record being in the country. And all part of the same...ring...that led to my conception."

She nodded regretfully at Yu-na, but the older woman just stuck her chin out defiantly.

"My father's journal from the period may corroborate some of these implications as well," Eric said. "I believe John Carson tried to extort him into using my family's shipping liaisons here in Korea to move weapons across the border, but it never came to fruition."

Agent Kym continued paging through the documents. "Unbelievable," she murmured. "We always wondered how the Koreans developed the bomb after the Soviets fell apart, but no one suspected it was our own defense contractors."

"It's an embarrassment," Eric said. "To the South Koreans *and* to the Americans. So you see, if NIS takes that evidence, it's never going to see the light of day." Without waiting for a response, he took the bundle of documents off Agent Kym's lap. "Detective Cho has digital copies. In the meantime, these are intended for the Secretary of Defense and the head of the CIA."

"I *am* CIA," Agent Kym reminded him.

"Then you'll understand exactly why we can't give them up without knowing exactly who is going to look at them." Eric nodded toward Jane and her mother. "My mother-in-law and my wife have been through hell over the last two weeks. Justice needs to be served. And it's become very clear that we can't trust just anyone to make sure that happens."

Agent Kym's face softened, as if she could clearly see the resolve in Eric's. She sighed, then stood. "I will notify the director at Langley," she said, softly enough that the other agent wouldn't be able to hear her. "And...no one else. You have my word. Travel home safe. All of you."

But before anyone could reply, Agent Suh burst back into the room, chattering in Korean on his phone. All at once he stopped, holding the phone away with his hand over the speakers. "No one is going anywhere. I have an order from the president herself—right here—that Mrs. Lefferts *must* be kept in the country. The plane is grounded until she comes into custody."

"What?!" Jane squawked.

"No!" Yu-na shouted.

"Carson," Eric muttered. "Absolutely *not*."

Before Agent Suh could argue with him, Eric snatched the phone out of his hand. "This is Eric de Vries, Chairman of De Vries Shipping. Am I really speaking with President Chang?"

"Mr. de Vries!" Agent Suh shouted, but Eric turned his back so he was facing Jane. Her eyes danced behind her glasses as she watched. The little minx, she was actually enjoying this.

It wasn't the president, but her assistant, who, as it happened, was able to turn the phone over to the president herself.

"President Chang? Yes, this is Eric de Vries. I understand you have suddenly decided that my mother-in-law, an *American citizen*, is not to leave the country. Is there any chance this direct infringement on American sovereignty is a request from John Carson?"

There was a pause on the other line. Then:

"That is not of your concern, Mr. de Vries. The Korean government has a right to detain any of its citizens that—"

"President Chang," Eric interrupted with an edge that had both agents in the room cringing. "I think perhaps *you* will appreciate the fact that the longer I am held up here in Suwon, the longer it will take me to sign the papers renewing the De Vries Shipping contracts in Incheon, Busan, and Donghae, among others. If I am unable to sign them, I'm afraid operations must cease until I return home. Remind me again, how much daily commerce flows through these ports cumulatively?" He looked at Jane while the president spoke, as if her tired, surprised face would reveal the answer. "About fourteen percent? Yes, that sounds about right. Or is it twenty-three, as your trade minister told me yesterday? Now, how much of the total South Korean GDP does that account for, President Chang? I wonder if our numbers will also match there."

This time the president actually didn't answer, so Eric just continued.

"Those three ports are responsible for close to eleven percent of your economy, yes. That sounds about right. Can you imagine what an extended cut on imports and exports there would do for your markets, let alone the economy?" He smacked his head. "And when you've just emerged from a recession too. Your exports are already down ten percent from years past, President Chang. Can you really afford to let go of another eleven?"

"Very well," President Chang interrupted suddenly. "I believe you are correct, Mr. de Vries. Mrs. Lefferts cannot be the same Yu-na Lee we are seeking. It must have been a grave misunderstanding."

"Must have been, President Chang. I'll let you tell your agent here the same thing. Immediately."

Eric handed the phone to Agent Suh with a stony expression. "We're leaving. Now."

While the agent grumbled a bit more, a few words from his president assured him that he indeed had to allow the American jet to take flight. The agents disembarked the jet, the security team re-boarded, and within fifteen minutes the engines were running and the plane was taxiing to the end of the runway.

It was only after the coastline of South Korea was long out of sight that Eric finally relaxed. While Tony and the other security guards chatted amiably about going home, he sank forward in his seat, rested his forehead in his hands, and exhaled at last.

AFTER THE PLANE had been airborne for about two of the fifteen hours back to New York, the door to the bedroom opened. Yu-na emerged, looking for the bathroom. Her gaze flickered sharply around the sleeping security team, landing on Eric for a split second. But a split second was all it took to convey one harsh phrase.

Your fault.

There it was, clear as day. Hadn't she warned Jane before the wedding not to get involved with Eric and his family? She knew. She had known the whole time, and no one had listened to her.

"Mrs. Lefferts—" he started, but the woman shook her head.

"No," she said, and the single word, like her expression, carried all manner of meaning. It was too late for talk now.

She disappeared into the small bathroom, then took a seat by herself. After a moment's thought, Eric got up and again entered the bedroom. Jane was asleep on the queen-sized bed, curled into a tight ball, her face shoved into a pillow while both her hands clutched the down-comforter tightly.

Eric sat down at the end of the bed, reached out to her leg, but pulled back so he could watch instead. It was something he had done several times at the hospital when he was in between phone calls with the CIA and trade minister, shaking Tony down for every scrap of information he could get, coaching Nina through her interim duties with the board, and trying to figure out how in the hell he was going to get his family home when the entire Korean government wanted to stand in their way.

Tried to touch. But never landed.

He had never felt like such a failure. Sure, they were on their way home and had managed to rescue Yu-na before she went the way of the other murdered flight attendants. But at what cost? The investigator's life? Their child's?

He would never forget Jane's face when he told her what had happened. The way it had felt as if he himself was responsible for her utter violation, not the men who had actually done it.

Your fault.

He couldn't argue with that. And he'd spend the rest of his life making up for it if he had to.

They'd get through this. They had people working with them now, not just a small-time investigator, but real people of power. The CIA. The State Department. The Secretary of Defense.

John Carson couldn't fight them all.

Right?

At that thought, Eric reached out again and set a hand on Jane's leg, hoping her solid presence would calm his anguish. But despite the fact that she was still on a combination of minor sedatives and antibiotics, Jane jerked in her sleep. Eric rubbed her leg, hoping to console her.

But she pulled away more, curling even tighter into herself, and moaned.

He pulled his hand back. She had never done *that* before.

It wouldn't last.

Would it?

Home, he thought to himself. They just needed to make it home, and everything would get better.

He only wished he could believe it.

PART THREE

TERCET

The problem with chasing the dawn,
Is its essential emptiness.
You can run after it all you want,
And the thrill will never cease,
But in the end, you'll be alone,
Never sated,
Never getting what you need.

"Vacancy"
— from the journal of Eric de Vries

SEVENTEEN

"Mrs. Lefferts, you can stay here if you like. We have rooms in the main house too, but Brandon and I thought that you and Ms. Lee would be more comfortable here."

Four nervous Korean women followed Skylar around the spacious guest house on her Brookline property. Yu-na, her cousin Ji-yeon and her daughter, Suejean, and Jane.

They resembled a queue of chickens, eyes dancing nervously around the deceptively airy space. Eric hung back in the doorway, watching the strange procession. Yu-na and the cousins spread out slowly. Jane stuck close to Skylar, hugging her friend's side, Eric noted with envy, instead of his.

His wife had barely touched him in three weeks. Not since the hospital and those first terrible moments when he'd found her in that dingy house in Hwaseong. She'd clung to him then like those moments might have been her last. And they might have been. The doctors, both in Suwon and at home, had said as much.

Eric rubbed his inner arm. He was still angry that he hadn't been allowed to donate blood. A year—a fucking year!—you had to live in the country before the Korean Red Cross would allow it, on top of a bunch of other requirements. It was only by a stroke of luck that they ended up finding a few extra pints at a blood bank in Singapore that had cost Eric a fucking mortgage payment to transport to Suwon. He would have emptied his entire account to do it. Eric had been two seconds from sticking a needle directly from his arm into hers if they hadn't found *something*.

Now that she was nearly back to normal, she'd shrunk away. He noticed it first after they left Mount Sinai and Skylar returned to Boston. She slept for most of the day, keeping to her bed while her mother listlessly roamed their apartment. Until today, neither of them had left it once in two weeks.

Eric had done his best to give her what she needed. He managed to do half his work for DVS from the confines of their apartment and had slept quietly next to her, rising when she did, waiting for her to reach out for him.

Except she never did.

It went both ways, really. They were interacting as if both of them were covered in jagged edges that could slice the other open. Or even hurt themselves. They operated with cordiality. Kindness. But always at an arm's length.

Maybe this was what she needed. A check-in with family. With Skylar. A change of scenery.

Eric wasn't sure what else he could do.

Ji-yeon and Suejean explored the two-bedroom cottage with the asserted interest that was characteristic of Jane's entire family, from what Eric could tell. They chatted about the practicalities of the space—whether the kitchen had enough counter space for a rice cooker *and* an Instant Pot or if the closets had enough room for a full-size shoe rack. Ji-yeon said she was only planning to stay in Boston for two weeks, but her two giant suitcases suggested she might be there longer. Eric was okay with that. If Yu-na had company here in

Boston, maybe it would be easier to coax Jane back to the city with him.

Because the main problem was Jane's guilt. And Yu-na was *very* good at pressing that particular button.

It had taken Yu-na exactly one week to say in no uncertain terms that she was not staying in New York. She didn't feel safe there, she said. Everything was too crowded. Too many streets for people to hide in. Too many alleys for people to jump out of. Too many people who could take her away.

Eric couldn't lie—he was ready for his mother-in-law to leave, even if it meant sending an entire battalion of security with her. But Jane, who seemed to be scared of her own shadow these days, had fought the idea of her mother returning to Chicago. For every reason Yu-na gave, Jane had an answer. Wasn't she accosted in Chicago, not New York? And just outside of her old suburban home? Weren't she and Jane sequestered in a small farmhouse next to a bunch of rice paddies, not apartment buildings?

And so, when Skylar offered the guest house just steps from her private security gate, sheltered behind the tall stone walls of the Crosby-Sterlings' Brookline compound, it seemed like the perfect solution. Ji-yeon would meet Yu-na there for a few weeks, and after that, Skylar's grandmother would probably suffocate Yu-na with blintzes. Brandon's mother wasn't exactly inhospitable either. They'd all learned about Yu-na's plight and wouldn't leave her alone for a second.

"You know there's room for you too," Skylar said quietly to Jane.

Eric had to concentrate not to glare at Skylar. He was already worried that Jane wouldn't leave her mother, and the fact that she had brought her own house-sized suitcase didn't soothe his suspicions. *Say no*, he willed Jane. *Say you need to come home. With me. Did you forget what we are? Did you forget that I'm the love of your fucking life?*

But Jane just watched her mother touch a finger to the mantle over the blazing stone fireplace, then looked out the window toward the big house and the orchard. It was pretty idyllic.

"Jane can stay?" Yu-na demanded. Good Christ, the woman had the hearing of a bat. "How many rooms?"

Eric stifled a scowl. *No, she can't fucking stay*, he wanted to snap. The truth was, he was heartily sick of his mother-in-law. He realized he could take Yu-na in small doses, but he was getting very, very tired of the way she demanded Jane's time and energy with no apparent gratitude. He understood they were both recovering from the trauma of their abduction—yes, he *definitely* understood that—but Jane was the one who had been through a legitimate medical emergency. Yu-na's detox had been difficult, but she had rebounded much faster than her daughter. She had also been no fucking help after they returned to New York. And now here was Yu-na, asking more of her daughter. For herself.

"There isn't enough room in here," Eric said. "Not with Ji-yeon here, right, Skylar?"

Everyone turned to him, and Jane's gaze was particularly sharp.

"There is in the house," Skylar offered, though she looked uneasy about it. Yeah, she knew exactly what Eric was thinking. "Anytime she likes. We have a spare room just for Jane. And you, of course, Eric."

"We have an apartment too," Eric put in. "In the North End." He knocked on the walls, like they were somehow lacking. "If we need to stay in Boston, we can go there."

But Jane's grimace made it clear what she thought of that. Hell, even he didn't like the idea. Aside from the fact that they'd be sitting ducks in that place (there was no security other than the elderly doorman), there was also the fact that it was just...pre-Jane. To him, and probably to her, the cold modern edges of his old apartment represented a life that deep inside, Jane was scared Eric wanted back. A bachelor's existence, devoid of intimacy, but still full of women.

He made a mental note to sell it as soon as possible. He wanted nothing to do with that life anymore. He only wanted Jane.

"There are two bedrooms in here," Yu-na protested. "Jane and I can share a bed, just like we did when she was a girl. She can be with her mother where she belongs while she heals."

What about with her husband? Eric was practically seething at this point. He wanted to scream, yell, shove the tiny, square-shaped woman out the door. Two weeks—*two weeks* she'd been butting in on their lives, interrupting those moments where he and Jane should have been reconnecting. Calling out in the middle of the night like a baby. Forcing Eric to spend half his nights alone, staring at the ceiling.

Her daughter was a grown fucking woman. She didn't need to be sleeping in a bed with her *mother*, of all people.

"*Eomma*, that other room is for Ji-yeon. And we are absolutely not sharing a room," Jane said, to Eric's intense relief. "You're staying out here, okay? We need a little space."

Was it wrong that Eric wanted to throw his fist in the air in victory?

But Yu-na wasn't finished.

"Space? What is this space? Space is why we ended up in Korea like we did. A daughter should be with her mother." Yu-na looked around the room, like she was expecting fucking applause. When her gaze landed back on Jane, she was practically triumphant. "You want to sleep at the big house, fine. But I want you to stay here. Family should be together."

What about my *family?* Eric wanted to snap back. God, the woman made him want to tear his hair out.

"Jane?" Yu-na's hands perched on her hips while she waited impatiently for her daughter's answer.

Jane sighed, and fatigue enshrouded her thin body like a cape. She drooped against the wall. Her face was still frail, thinner than it should be, and behind her thick black glasses, her eyes shone with fear and vulnerability. No bravado. No punch. So damn different than the woman he knew. Eric wanted to pick her up and carry her away from the tiny tyrant, away from everyone putting that look on her face.

Behind her, Ji-yeon and Suejean had peeked out of the bedroom to witness the exchange. It was plain on both of their faces what they thought she should do. Skylar rubbed Jane's arm sympathetically. Jane wilted toward her.

He had lost, Eric realized. Before anyone said anything.

"Lunch?" Jane asked weakly.

Skylar smiled kindly. "Of course, Janey. Susan came over last night and made a few extra roasted chickens with dinner. Why don't we eat, and then everyone can get settled in."

THEY WALKED BACK to the main house through the snow, where Brandon and the four kids—Annabelle, Christoph, Jenny, and Luis— were building a snowman. That basically consisted of Annabelle bossing everyone around, Christoph pointing out the deficiencies of her plans, Jenny trying and failing to roll as many giant snowballs as possible, and Luis screeching with joy every time he stuck his hands in the snow. Frequently, one of them would hurl a snowball at Brandon, who would retaliate swiftly, to their delight. And every so often, Luis toddled out to the driveaway on his chubby, two-year-old legs, causing his father to jog after him, swing him up into the air, and redeposit him in the yard with the other kids.

The children's laughter echoed around the park-like property. Everyone else smiled. Eric looked at Jane, who avoided eye contact. Behind her lenses, her eyes shone like she wanted to cry.

Fuck.

Is this what it would have been like? Eric wondered. Would their baby have been chubby like Luis? Would they have had snowball fights in Central Park next winter? Taught their kid to make snow angels the year after?

The idea pricked his eyes like needles. Eric looked away from the scene. This was the wrong place to be. Couldn't she see that? They needed time alone. Time together. Time to heal.

Jane wrapped her arms around her waist, like she too was thinking of what had been stolen from her. It was so easy, Eric knew. It happened to him all the time. A taste, a scent, a brief image. Something would bring that violation to the forefront of his mind, and like a knife, it stabbed.

Jane finally looked up to find Eric watching her, and her big, expressive eyes seemed to water even more despite the raucous laughter around them. She knew what he was thinking. She knew the loss he heard in those tinkling shouts. She knew because she heard it too.

But before Eric could approach her, use that connection to build something better, Jane turned away. Eric stopped. He didn't know what else to do.

"Are we ready to eat?" he asked, unable to take one more of this Norman Rockwell-level moment.

"I think so," Skylar said. "Shall we?"

Eric just watched Jane. At last, she nodded. His chest sagged with relief. Jane had been subsisting on little more than instant ramen for the last two weeks. Just a few days ago, her doctor had expressed concern that she wasn't gaining enough back after her ordeal, but she'd batted away his reminders like flies.

And with that, their sad, strange procession continued inside.

EIGHTEEN

"Is that all you're having?" Eric asked, eyeing the wing and spoonful of green beans Jane had taken. It wasn't exactly a king's ransom.

"I'm not that hungry," she mumbled.

"But the doctor said—"

"I said I'm not hungry," she replied, more sharply this time. "Okay?"

Eric opened his mouth, wanting to argue back, but just turned to his plate without another word. Jane wouldn't thank him for admonishing her like a child in front of everyone. She had her mother for that, after all. But he wasn't letting this go. She had to know that.

"Eric, is everything settled now on the board?" Brandon asked from the other side of the table where he was loading his plate with mashed potatoes.

Grateful for the intervention, Eric looked up. "Yeah, seems that way. Especially after the DA dropped the case. I've just been sliding back into things since we returned." He shook his head. "What a clusterfu—" He stopped short, realizing how many children were present. "I mean, what a mess the last month has been."

"Well, thank *God* for Matthew Zola," Skylar said. "I swear, he has saved us more than once. He's like our little group's guardian angel."

"If I didn't know better, Red, I'd say you have a crush," Brandon replied affably, though his tone was laced with jealousy.

"He did have a thing for her once," Jane remarked. "Remember when he kissed you, Sky?"

For that, she received a dirty, green-eyed glare from Skylar as the far end of the table went a little quieter.

"Zola *kissed* you, Mama?" Jenny piped up. "Daddy, how did you let that happen?"

The glare sharpened. "Don't pay attention to your auntie Jane," Skylar said before Brandon could reply. "She's just poking the bear."

Jane shrugged. "He's fun to poke."

Eric smiled at his chicken thigh. There she was.

"Is it fun when I point out that he had a thing for you too at one point?" Skylar said.

"I'm sorry? When was *that*?" Eric looked up sharply.

"It was for about half a second. Maybe five or six years ago," Jane said.

Now she was the one glaring. The sight of it made Eric want to kiss her. But just as soon, that beautiful fury faded.

"That's not funny, Sky," Jane murmured. "Or are you forgetting how *someone* almost got into a fistfight with the man a few months ago?"

"What?" Yu-na piped up. "Who fought with whose fists?"

"Nothing, *Eomma*," Jane now avoided the studious looks of all her family members.

"I'm going to need details about that," Suejean said conspiratorially.

Jane shook her head. "It was just a misunderstanding last Thanksgiving."

"I'll say," Eric muttered. He wasn't particularly interested in reliving *that* mortifying episode.

Skylar didn't even cower, just turned to her husband. "It was a little funny, don't you think?"

"Poor Zola," Brandon said, good-natured once again. "Always the bridesmaid, never the bride."

Jane sighed. Eric darted another glance at her. Why was she so torn up about Matthew fucking Zola? Why not her own damn marriage?

"Are you guys heading back to New York after lunch?" Suejean broke in diplomatically before anyone else could ask annoying inappropriate questions. "If I could catch a ride to the T-stop, that will take me downtown. I'm supposed to be at Mass Gen later this afternoon."

"We could just drop you at the hospital on our way back to Logan," Eric offered. "Right, Jane?"

"Well," Jane replied, "Since Skylar offered, I think I'm going to stay here for a few more days. Maybe a week or two."

A sudden quiet descended over the table.

Though his body didn't appear to move an inch, Eric's entire posture shifted slightly. "Come again?"

Jane swallowed visibly. Eric's throat hurt. He knew what she was going to say, but still, he prayed: *Don't say it.*

She, however, just pushed her glasses farther up her nose and managed to look at Eric straight-on. Her hazel eyes practically broke him.

"I just decided," she said. "I think it would be better if I were here to provide the support my mom needs. Skylar and Brandon have great security. I can help her get settled, and then you won't be bothered by us while you're fixing everything at work."

"Jane, you don't bother me—" Eric started, but Jane shook her head.

Skylar reached for Brandon's hand and looked very sorry for both of them.

"Jane." Her name hurt on his tongue. It was the longing that cut so deeply.

Jane looked up again, and for a moment, the clear pain shining through those deep hazels skewered him. "It's going to be easier this way for a bit," she said quietly. "I just...Eric, I just need some space."

"Space from me?" His voice was gutted. Just like his heart. His entire body. No, no, no, this was wrong, so fucking wrong! They had already been ripped apart for weeks, and now she wanted to do it *again*? What the hell was happening here?

But Jane wouldn't answer, just stared back down at her plate. The green beans that had only been reduced by two, maybe three. The chicken wing that was missing only a bite. She shuddered, like the idea of food made her feel sick.

Or maybe it's me, Eric thought. *Maybe she's just sick of me.*

In a sudden hurry, Jane stood up. "I'm, um, going to put my things away in the guest room upstairs. "Sky, thanks for lunch."

And before anyone could respond, she grabbed her plate, deposited it in the kitchen, and practically sprinted out of the room. Eric stared after her for a few seconds before realizing she had nothing to put away. Everything they packed was still in the car. She hadn't even brought in her purse.

"Eric," Skylar murmured.

In a sudden flurry of movement, he was up and off. "I'll, um, be right back."

He found Jane in one of the guest rooms, pacing back and forth, muttering to herself: "What are you doing? What are you *doing*?"

"That's a very good question."

Jane swung around as Eric strode in, arms crossed over his chest. He stopped by the bureau and slapped his hand on the teak.

"You want to tell me what's going on?" he asked. "What's with the sudden change of plans?"

"Come on, Eric. This shouldn't be a surprise. I did bring that giant suitcase."

"I had *really* hoped that was only a precaution."

"I—she asked me to stay—I just think I should."

Eric sighed. "I thought we agreed it would be good for the two of you to have some space."

"My mother disagrees."

"Do you?"

"I..." Jane paused. "I don't really think that matters. Look, you don't need me up there. And my mother, she needs me here."

"She does not need you—"

"She *does*," Jane insisted. "Just like she needed me in Chicago before I abandoned her there. Just like I left her rotting in that room for two weeks before I was able to find her. She needs me, and I'll stay with her until I'm completely certain that she doesn't. And if you don't like it, you can j-just—"

"Okay," Eric cut her off just as her lower lip started to tremble. "I get it, all right?"

Fucking hell, the sight of her choking up killed him even more than this ridiculous proposition. He still wasn't used to her like this, with such intense vulnerability. Had it been the gift he wanted it to be, he'd cherish every one of those tears. But he knew she was only breaking like this because she wasn't strong enough to put up her guard. Not because she actually wanted anyone to see it.

And for that, he was having a hard time forgiving himself.

Suddenly, he couldn't take it anymore. He crossed the room in three long steps, pulled her to him, wrapping his arms around her shaking shoulders. Jane stood stiffly, refusing to melt into him the way he desperately wanted. Needed. So they were both careful, static, even though they were touching. But just barely.

She needed comfort, obviously. But this wasn't doing it. Maybe it was him.

After several long minutes, Eric stepped back at last, rubbing his big hands together for a moment before shoving them into the pockets of his jacket. There was nothing more to do.

"I do have to get back," he said lamely. "The plane is on standby at Logan. There's another board meeting in the morning. What if you came with me, and then we came right back..."

He didn't even finish. The regret on her face told him exactly what she thought about that idea.

Eric sighed. "I guess…I guess I'll just go, then."

Jane nodded, took another step back, and examined her hands. "Oh-okay."

"Will you let me know when you're coming back?"

Eric willed her to meet his gaze. But she couldn't. Wouldn't? Did it even matter?

"Okay," he said. "I'll—I'll go, then. Jane, I love you."

Jane nodded. "I love you too." But the words—his, hers, all of them—were hollow. Whispers of what they should've been.

Eric's shoulders fell as he turned to the door. "I'll see you," he said, and after another few beats, walked out.

He met Suejean hurrying up the stairs.

"Hey," he said. "It's just me leaving, but if you still need a ride, I can drop you."

"I'll be right there," she said. "I just wanted to talk to her a second, okay?"

Eric nodded, and started to walk downstairs, but stopped. The voices of Jane and her cousin filtered into the hall. And something made him listen. He crept back down the hallway and waited outside the room, out of sight. Unrepentant. She wouldn't let him in. But he needed to know she was going to be okay without him.

"You're doing that procedure at Mass General tomorrow, right?" Jane was asking.

"Yeah. My mom is settled into the guesthouse, and so is *Imo*," Suejean said, using what Eric gathered was the Korean version of "Auntie" or something similar, despite the fact that Ji-yeon was Yu-na's cousin, not sister.

"Good," Jane said. "I think they'll have a good time. This place is like a bed and breakfast."

"If it's any consolation, I really do think you can go back to New York with Eric," Suejean said. "*Eomma* has been dying to visit *Imo* ever since you guys got back. And I'll be here at least a few days, so

I'll definitely check on them. Although I doubt they'll do anything but watch K-dramas and gossip."

Yes, Eric urged her. *Say yes. Tell her you'll come home.*

"Thanks," Jane said. "But I'll probably stay here for a bit longer. Just in case. Good luck on your surgery."

And just like that, hope deflated again.

"Thanks." Suejean paused. "Look, you can tell me if I'm out of line here. But I feel like I have to say something. I noticed that...well, I'll just say, I've had a lot of patients who have gone through...well, something similar. Not with the complications and the violation, of course, although I have definitely had a few. But with termination."

Eric listened curiously. He knew that Suejean was an OB/GYN, but he hadn't actually heard her broach the topic of abortion with Jane. Maybe it was to save their mothers from overhearing the conversation.

"The common refrain is to abstain from relations with your partner for at least a month," she was saying. "In your case, probably four to six weeks."

Eric nodded to himself. Okay, now this was getting interesting. That was, in fact, what the doctors at Mount Sinai had recommended.

"But I'll just say this," Suejean continued. "My patients who complain of painful intercourse post any kind of vaginal expulsion—miscarriage, birth, etc.—well, anecdotally, they are generally also the ones who avoid other kinds of intimacy with their partners."

Eric's eyes widened. This was definitely not the conversation he had expected.

"What are you saying?" Jane wondered.

Suejean sighed, now clearly the uncomfortable one. "I'm saying that there are a lot of ways to take care of yourself, and your marriage is one of them. I'm not talking about sex. I'm talking about all the types of intimacy that inform our health. Or don't listen to me at all, since I'm not your doctor."

Eric held his breath, waiting ardently for Jane's response. He could practically hear her thoughts now, wrestling with knee-jerk reactions about prioritizing men's needs over women's, and shouldn't *her* body's responses be more important than his? But Suejean wasn't talking about that, obviously, and that wasn't what Eric was thinking about either. She was simply making the point that the body and the mind influenced each other. That health was something informed by both.

And by both partners. Wasn't it?

Say you understand, he willed her. *Say you'll come home. Because, goddammit, Lefferts, you need me and I need you!*

But Jane's conscience apparently thought the answers were self-evident.

"Thanks, Suej," she said finally. Disappointingly.

"Let me know how the next follow-up goes," Suejean said, referring to Jane's next check-up with her doctor. "And be nice to Eric when you do go back to New York. He seems...well, I don't really know him, but he seems like he needs some extra care right now too."

You can say that again.

Jane sighed, full of guilt. "I'll try."

Her despondency made Eric wilt against the wall. Fuck. What was he doing? He didn't want to guilt her into being with him. Jane deserved to be anywhere she wanted. She deserved to do whatever was necessary to take care of herself. Right?

He turned to walk back down the stairs, ready to leave, but at the bottom he turned. Back and forth, back and forth, unable to decide.

Suejean was pounding down the stairs when she saw him and stopped. Understanding crossed her kind features.

"Don't give up on her yet," she said. "She needs you."

Eric swallowed. And then, full of sudden decision, he turned back up the stairs. "Tony will take you wherever you need to go," he said. "I need to take care of a few more things with Jane, okay?"

Suejean nodded supportively. "Of course."

He walked back up the stairs with dread. What would she say when he arrived again? What would she do?

He knocked on the door. For a moment, he wondered if she was asleep again, giving herself up to her inner pain and heartache.

But then the door opened, and there stood Jane, glasses off, tears tracking down her face, looking for all the world like she was falling apart from the inside out.

"I'm fine, Sky," she was saying, viciously swiping at the tears. "I'm *fine*."

"Well, I'm not," Eric said.

Like it was yanked on a string, Jane's head jerked up at the sound. Eric stood there, stuck to his place, feeling like he was about to fall apart too.

"Jane," he whispered. "Please."

"Please what?" she asked.

But he couldn't say. He didn't know.

NINETEEN

"Come home."

Home.

The word rang through Eric's head like a bell. It was synonymous with Jane, had been for months, maybe even years. It was a word he had struggled with all his life, but he remembered so clearly thinking it the first time they had spoken.

The booth. The napkin. The stupid limerick.

He had been running away from home for more than a year, since his had been stolen from him. And in a dank bar with an impetuous blue-haired siren, he had found it again.

That famous quote from Robert Frost came to mind: *Home is the place where, when you go there, they have to take you in.* But here she was, putting herself out. Running away. Closing herself off. She was afraid of their home. Maybe she was afraid of him.

"Eric, please." Her voice, normally so strong, so pointed, was barely above a whisper. She slipped a long finger under her eye to wipe away a bit more of the dewy tears building along her lower lid. Her engagement ring, with the black diamond he'd chosen for the way its sharp beauty reminded him of her, hung slightly loose on her finger. "Please don't do this."

Eric sagged against the door. The sound of her defeat? It fucking defeated him. "Don't do what? Fight for us?"

At the word "fight," her tears welled even more.

"I can't," she whispered. "I can't fight anymore. My mother. You. Please don't make me. *Please.*"

Her breaths were shallow. She looked small, several inches less than her normally statuesque five feet seven inches and a quarter. Yes, Eric knew Jane's height down to the quarter inch, thanks to his curiosity one night, just a few months ago.

"STOP SQUIRMING, you little pixie. Let me measure you."

Eric batted Jane's hands away from the tape measure he had nabbed from her work table. It was the soft one she used to measure her own waist, bust, hips, and other parts when she was making her clothes. She never knew how many times he'd stopped when he was walking past this room, struck by her sudden grace as she held the tape around her bare stomach or reached from ankle to hip. Her grace, yes, but also her focus, the way she might clench her pencil between her teeth or bite her full red lip as she read the numbers. He loved watching her work. He always had.

"I can tell you my own measurements, you know. I've done them enough times. And they are hardly pixie-sized."

"I think I need to see them to believe them."

Jane giggled with delight as Eric stretched the malleable plastic down her naked body. Down, down, down its long, lean lines, over the legs she irritably called chicken pins, but Eric called works of art. Shit, he couldn't even look at them without imagining them wrapped around his waist. Again. Fuck.

"Thirty-four and a half inches," he pronounced after he pulled the plastic from her hip bone to her ankle. "Nice stems, Lefferts."

She peered at him down her body. "What are you doing? Taking inventory?"

His teeth closed over a particularly smooth, fleshy part of her thigh. She screeched, and Eric laughed.

"Just memorizing the terrain," he replied with a grin.

She grinned back, and he honestly thought his heart might burst out of his chest.

His lips pressed back up her body, sucking here, licking there as he trailed his way back up her legs. He paused over her chest, stretching the tape between the pert nipples he loved to worship.

"Seven inches," he pronounced with a smirk, dropping a kiss on one, then the other. Jane arched into his mouth, begging for more. Eric's lips curled into a smile over the pebbled flesh. God, he loved the way she responded to him. She loved it rough. She loved it sweet. Hell, she seemed to love it any way he wanted to give it.

But he wasn't quite in the mood for domination tonight. There was a rosy tint to this evening. He wanted to swim in it.

He released her nipple with a pop, wove his tongue over her neck while drawing the tape measure over one arm from wrist to shoulder.

"Twenty-one," he observed, his breath hot at her ear.

Jane purred. "I think you might be doing this wrong. That is not what I usually get."

"I'm doing it perfectly."

"What else, Mr. de Vries?" she asked, stretching both hands upward.

Eric arched over her, relishing in the feel of skin meeting skin, the way their bones seemed to fit together like pieces of a puzzle. He looped the tape around her wrists, crossing them over her head.

"Six inches," he murmured over her mouth. That sweet, succulent, cherry-red mouth. Fucking hell, he could die right here, kissing this woman, and have lived the fullest life possible.

Jane arched beneath him, and the near seventy collective inches of legs wrapped around his waist, pulling him closer. He slipped the tape measure around her wrists a second time, then looped the plastic *through itself so he could hold her wrists securely against the mattress. He bound her. She bound him. Mutual captivity by equals.*

Her heels dug into his skin, urging him to find that dark, heated space inside her. The tip of him teased her wet entrance, but Eric held back, pushing against her wrists, the bed, luxuriating in that sweet limbo before he completely gave himself up to this woman. Before he let her consume him.

"Come," she whispered against his lips, her tongue slipping out to find his. Her kiss was a siren's call. "Come home, Mr. de Vries."

His head tipped back, and she licked his neck. And then he sank in. She was home, goddamn, all sweet, soft, slick forbidden spaces of her. Home. And all his.

ERIC TOUCHED JANE'S SHOULDER, feather-soft. "You don't need to fight, pretty girl. *I'll* do the fighting. For us both."

When she didn't move away, he drew his hand over the symmetry of her shoulder, down the flannel-covered arm. Measuring. Remembering.

Wanting.

"Sex isn't going to fix this, Eric."

His whole body jerked. "What?"

Suddenly, Jane looked angry. Well, maybe that was an improvement.

"It's the only time you suck at hiding your emotions, you know. When you're thinking about nookie."

Eric blinked and withdrew his hand. "I was not—"

"You totally were." But the fight of the words still wasn't completely there. Jane stepped away from the door, back, back, back until her legs hit the edge of the bed and she dropped onto the deep blue comforter.

"So what if I was?" he asked finally. "It doesn't mean I have to have it right that moment. I love you, Jane. I want you, sure, but it's a hell of a lot more than that. So I'm not going to apologize for daydreaming about my own damn wife. Or wanting her to come home."

But Jane just stared at her hands, defeated.

Amazing how this woman's silence was so much more deafening than any of her sharpest words.

Eric closed the door, then took a seat next to her. His weight caused her to teeter into his shoulder. He placed a hand behind her back, hoping the open movement would encourage her to sink into him like she used to.

But she just readjusted herself farther away.

"Yes, I was, thinking about sex," he admitted again, doing his best to sound remorseful for something he still didn't think he should be sorry for. "I can't help it around you. You know that."

"Because I'm so sexy right now," she said bitterly, her voice dry and hollow. "In old leggings and my dad's Cosby sweaters. I look like a Tim Burton heroine."

Eric looked her over, trying to see what she saw.

Her glasses were on the bureau, and tears streaked her pale cheeks with no sign of ruined makeup. No lines, no lipstick. Her lips were a pale, cool pink instead of the red he always knew. Her brownish-black hair hung around her shoulders in limp, uncombed waves, like she had just pulled down the perennial knot of hair that had been at the base of her neck for weeks.

And then, of course, there were her clothes. Eric didn't think he had ever seen Jane in something so banal as yoga pants, but here she was, in a nondescript pair, topped with the ugliest sweater he had ever seen. Oversized, patterned with maroon and yellow plaid, she looked like a child playing Harry Potter dress-up.

He suddenly realized that he had never seen her like this. She was nothing like the unique, stylish woman he fucking worshipped. Stripped down to nothing. Absent of armor.

And yet...he was more in love with her than ever.

"The truth, gorgeous?" he said quietly as he reached out a hand. His pinky finger touched hers. She didn't move away. "I hadn't even noticed."

Jane snorted. "Yeah, right. Mr. Poetry over here doesn't notice basic aesthetics? You love beautiful things. Maybe even more than I do."

"You're still beautiful." God, he wanted to touch her. Wanted to push her hair aside and kiss her neck. Hell, he wanted to do more than that. Like tie her to the damn bed and force her to look at him while he plunged into her, make her see the truth in his eyes. The love he could never hide. Not from her.

Another snort. "If I ever was 'beautiful,' I'm certainly not now."

"Jane, you could be covered in garbage and still look like a masterpiece to me." He gave in. Raised his hand and traced the line of her jaw with his index finger. "Pretty girl."

Jane's shoulders shook, and she looked up, hazel eyes impossibly big and shining. And so, so sad.

For a moment, Eric thought she might kiss him. Thought that maybe, just maybe, he had finally broken through that miserable shell.

"How," she whispered. "How do I really know that?"

Was she kidding? Did she really not know, after all this time, how he felt?

"Jane."

She looked away. "Please don't."

Don't what? he wanted to demand. *Don't compliment you? Worship you? Tell you all the things you're dying to hear?* He wanted to shout at her to snap the hell out of it. But instead, he just reiterated his chief objective:

"I just want to go home," Eric said again. "With you. We came up here to settle your mom, and we did. You both need some time apart, no matter what she says. And you and *I* need time together. To heal from this fucking terror of a month."

Jane immediately burst into tears all over again. "I can't," she cried. "Don't you understand that? I can't just leave her again. If I hadn't in the first place, none of this would have happened."

And that was the crux of it. Her guilt paralyzed her. Eric never thought he would see the day when this woman was stilled by the fear of her own actions. This was Jane—brazen, bold, as direct as they came.

Her tears overcame her completely, and it was then she finally rocked toward him, allowing him to wrap an arm around her and pull her into his chest. Where he had been dying for her for weeks now.

Every frustration he had disappeared. Was it sick that he was simply enjoying the feel of her again?

"No one is going to hurt her here," Eric crooned as he stroked her hair. "No one is going to hurt either of you, I promise. Ever. Again."

"It's easy to say that, isn't it?"

"It's the truth."

Jane sat up, pushing his arms away and wiping at her face. "That's what we thought before. When I had four mountain-sized security guards trailing after me. You still ended up in jail, Eric. And *Eomma* and I still ended up drugged in that fucking house!"

Well, at least she had a little spunk in her.

"That was before we had enough evidence of John Carson's treason to lock him away for life, Jane!" Eric burst out, finally unable to keep his frustrations at bay. "You told me to be the man this family made me, and guess what? I am! I'm calling in every fucking favor I can to bring that bastard to justice, I *promise* you. He's got half the U.S. government ready to arrest him."

"But he also has the other half in *his* pocket, doesn't he?" Jane cut back bitterly.

"What else do you want me to do?" Eric asked. "I'm out of ideas here. I'm doing everything I can to keep that maniac away from us so we can heal. *Together*. But I can't do that without you." He rubbed a tired hand over his face. "Jesus Christ, Jane, you're not the only one who had a shitty month. Did you forget I was literally behind bars for half of it?"

Jane opened her mouth, eyes flashing through their watery expanse like she wanted to fight back.

Do it, Eric wordlessly urged her. *Fight back, gorgeous. Fight like I know you can. Tell me I'm full of shit. Tell me my cushy stay at Rikers was nothing compared to what you went through. Tell me so you can tell yourself. So we can yell at each other and get back to fucking normal!*

But the flash of anger only turned to smoke, then died. She closed right back up and stared at her hands all over again.

"It's not just that," she said after another minute or two. Back to unnerving quiet. Back to scared.

"What do you mean?" Eric asked, taking her hand in his and not letting go. He wasn't willing to relinquish all that space yet.

"When I was there...before he...before the baby..." She looked up, and the pain in her eyes felt like a knife through his own chest. "We are killing people, Eric."

He stilled. "What in the hell would make you say that?"

Maybe she didn't need to answer. Visions of his father in the casket, Penny in the tub. Grandmother in the church. Even the investigator, Kim. Fucking hell, death did follow him everywhere, didn't it?

Was that what he was? Some kind of raven, an omen of destruction for everyone he loved?

Jane sniffed back another round of tears. "If we had just listened to him, none of this would have happened."

"If we had listened to him, there wouldn't have been a baby in the first place."

"Maybe that would have been for the best!"

Her words dropped like grenades, and Eric literally fell back on his elbows like he'd been pushed by the blast. His hand rose to his heart, flattened over his chest to calm the pounding.

"You don't really believe that," he said.

Jane didn't answer.

He considered leaving. Jog out to the car, out of Boston, away from the pain and suffering that vibrated through this room, through this marriage, through this life. For a split second, Eric wondered if she was right after all. Maybe, in the end, all they were together was pain. Maybe the best thing to do would be to cut their considerable, permanent, life-shattering losses and find a way to exist in the world without one another.

But he didn't. Because in the next split second, he also knew there was no way he could function that way. Hadn't he promised her that in the hospital? While he screamed at her to stay with him? While he had rolled up his sleeve and offered the very blood running through his veins if it would only keep her with him?

No, he wasn't leaving her now. Not now. Not ever.

"It's not that," he said. "The worst things in the world happen when we're apart, not together." He sat up again and took her hand. "Splitting us apart is exactly what that bastard wants, Jane."

When she didn't respond, he squeezed her hand between his palms. Then forced himself to look at her again, really look at her. Take in how her weakened, shrunken body folded in on itself the way people did when they believed they had no one.

But she had everyone in this house.

She had him.

Eric got off the bed, squatted in front of his wife, and set his hand on either side of her too-slim hips.

"Okay," he relented. "We'll stay a little longer. Until you know she's safe. Until you understand that *we* are safe. Together."

"You don't have to—" she started.

"Jane." He framed her face, forcing her beautiful hazel eyes to meet his. "Of course I do. You have to know I do."

The doubt shining so clearly through her face broke his heart.

"Eric," she whispered.

He popped up on the balls of his feel, and slowly, carefully, placed a tentative kiss on her lips. He stayed there for a solid five seconds, willing her to remember the love and devotion and *rightness* that he knew without a doubt.

She didn't kiss him back. But she didn't move away either.

It was something.

TWENTY

"All right, Bridget. I think that's it for today. I'll be in town for the board meeting this Friday."

As Bridget nodded through the screen, her ponytail bounced like a spring. The girl was so damn perky, it was almost painful. But she really could run the entire country from her iPhone.

"I'll let everyone know, Mr. de Vries," she said and exited the video conference.

"What about the meetings with the union reps?" Nina asked, now the sole occupant of the laptop screen. "I'd offer to take them, but to be honest, I think they would rather deal with you. Grandmother was always grumbling about how she wished Grandfather was around just to deal with the longshoremen."

Eric tapped his chin, considering. "Yeah. I hate to say it, but they are pretty old school like that."

Nina gave him a look that could only mean "no shit." She was too refined—or maybe just shy, Eric mused—to tell him flat out that the correct word was "sexist." If Jane were there, she would have jumped on that in a hot second.

He almost turned to check for his wife, though she wouldn't be here. Brandon had offered in his old attic office, which now served as storage. Eric rolled back and scowled when his chair slammed into one of Brandon's boxes of comic books. Honestly, the man was a damn pack rat.

But it wasn't just that. Eric missed *his* office. *His* apartment. He missed his own space.

It had been another two weeks since he had agreed to infringe on Skylar and Brandon's home. Not that it had done any damn good. Jane had mostly just holed up in their room, sleeping most of the day and night. Suejean assured Eric that it wasn't strictly abnormal to need extra sleep while healing, but she *should* be getting back some of her energy by now. If she didn't start perking up soon, she cautioned, it might be time to call her doctor again. Who might suggest a psychiatrist instead.

Eric's stomach growled. He checked his watch. Eight a.m. For most people, the work day was just getting started, but Eric had been up for hours dealing with issues with their European ports before the conference call with Nina and Bridget. This had become their daily ritual before Nina got her daughter off to school. They split up the work between what Eric could do remotely and anything Nina needed to be present for while he remained in Boston. His cousin was a godsend.

"Let's set up a meeting for Friday morning when I'm there," he said. "Pre-negotiations, I suppose, before the big show next week, all right? Then we can update the board in the afternoon. Who knows, maybe I can convince Jane to come with me this time."

Nina looked doubtful. "Well, it would be nice to have you back." Eric knew she was pretty overwhelmed.

But he could only shrug. "We'll see."

Nina raised a delicate blonde brow.

"These things take time," he said. "She's not exactly herself. It's good for her to be with family and friends."

"What about you? Don't you need that too? I know she's hurting, Eric, but you had your own trauma. Who's taking care of you?"

Eric frowned. This line of questioning had been bouncing around his head for too long. He was thoroughly tired of it.

"How's *your* family, Mrs. Gardner?" he asked pointedly. "Are you and Calvin getting along again?" While he had been at Rikers, his cousin had spent some time with Jane, furious over the fact that her husband delivered Eric's whereabouts to John Carson and confirmed the trumped-up charges of securities fraud to the SEC. But as far as he knew, she was back at their townhouse again.

Was it just him, or did Nina cringe? He was an asshole for asking about Calvin, but since Nina had something to say about Jane every time they spoke, it was only fair he get a word in.

"Calvin is staying with his parents right now," Nina confirmed with her version of an eye roll—the most sedate eye roll ever, but it was there.

"Really?" He had assumed that after Nina's few days staying with Jane, things had gone back to normal.

But Nina just studied her nails. "I...we are just thinking through some things."

"Like what things?"

She looked up. "It's a marriage. They're never perfect. You'll know eventually."

Eric cocked his head. "Are you thinking the big D?"

Nina exhaled daintily through pursed lips. "I... Maybe. But honestly, I don't think it will go anywhere. Every time I consider it...I think of what she would say."

Eric didn't have to ask who Nina meant. The specter of their grandmother hung around them both. Hell, her portrait was literally hanging behind Nina, watching over this very conversation with Chanel-clad superiority.

Still...

"Do you really want to make the rest of your decisions based on a dead woman's thoughts? Nina, don't forget, this was a person who thought blackmailing me down the aisle was perfectly acceptable."

"You weren't exactly fighting it, if I recall," Nina said dryly. "And really, Eric. Do you think she would have actually sold off the family's holdings? Our entire legacy?"

Eric drummed his fingers and kicked his feet up on the desk. "I think dear old Grandmother was as ruthless as they come. But you knew her better than me. I hadn't spoken to her since I was twenty-two. Not exactly the most perceptive age."

Nina peered sympathetically through the camera. "I knew her better, but she loved you best. You must know that. And I truly believe she only wanted you to be happy."

"But how could she have known that Jane was where this was going to go?"

"You can really be incredibly naive sometimes, do you know that?"

Eric scowled. "I am not."

"Eric, you went to the most prominent law school in the world. Do you honestly think Grandmother had absolutely no way of keeping track of you?" Nina tipped her head. "Believe me, I heard about Jane long before you ever brought her home. Five years, in fact."

His feet toppled from the desk. "Are you kidding? She was *spying* on me?"

"She was a wealthy old woman with control issues and an unhealthy attachment to the de Vries name. Of course she was spying on you. She watched all of us." Nina tapped a pen on her desk. "But I think originally, Grandmother was trying to be patient. She thought you would find your happiness on your own and eventually come back to the fold. When she learned of her diagnosis, well, that put a different spin on things. She wanted to do right by you before she was gone. Just...in her own way."

Eric folded forward, placing his hands on his head. "What would she think of all this now? This bullshit with John Carson? All these traps?"

Nina twisted her mouth around. "You were in college when I

debuted, so you won't remember this. But Grandmother ensured I had the best escort: Oliver Newcomb."

Eric frowned. "The pancake mix heir?"

Nina nodded. "That's right. He's a disaster now, by the way, total slave to the bottle. But back then, he was *the* escort. Except he almost didn't come with me."

"Why's that?" Eric asked, curious where this was going.

"Well, Alicia Platt thought she was half in love with him and was destroyed that he wasn't escorting her. So to dissuade him, she started a few rumors. Quite unoriginal, really. That I had slept with half the school, traded sexual favors with Ollie, even seduced his father. Can you imagine? Me at seventeen with that moldy old man?"

Eric blanched. He didn't want to imagine his cousin with anyone.

"Anyway," Nina continued, "when Grandmother found out about it, she was furious. There was only one course of action, according to her. Alicia had to be ruined to the point she wouldn't even consider showing her face in polite society again. Every rumor on the planet was put out there, every person talking. Page Six, gossip sites, not to mention every benefit on the planet. Alicia had to attend some public school on the West Coast, did you know that? Not a single admissions head on the Eastern Seaboard would take her. And on the night of Cotillion, Oliver showed up on my arm. Because Grandmother said he would."

"So, what, she ruined this young girl's future simply because she threatened one night of yours?" Eric frowned.

"No," Nina said. "She made sure I was never a target by making *me* ruin Alicia's reputation. Grandmother never lifted a finger. She just told me how to do it."

Eric honestly wasn't sure what to make of that. "I didn't know you were so vindictive."

Nina leaned forward so her face filled the screen. "I'm not, really. But I learned a bit about...survival in this world of ours while you were off reading poetry and pretending to be a layman."

Now Eric rolled his eyes. Attending Harvard and starting his own firm wasn't exactly laying brick.

"My point is: Grandmother wouldn't wonder what to do about John Carson, Eric. She'd probably just wonder why you hadn't already eviscerated him."

"Sounds a little bloodthirsty." He was joking, but only because he'd been seriously reining back the urge to kill for weeks now. It was a little odd to think it was a family trait.

Nina, however, didn't laugh. "Do you have any idea how bloodthirsty our family had to be, making a name in *shipping* of all things in the seventeenth century? In *America*? We have generations of blood on our hands, Eric."

"Why, Nina. I never knew you were such a historian."

She just snorted. "You're acting like a novice, not a legacy. Grandmother, I assure you, could be the absolute personification of vengeance when she believed anyone threatened this family. John Carson stayed away until she was gone for a reason."

Again, Penny's body flashed through his mind—but he shook it away. He didn't quite stay away, did he?

And then he saw his father, lying in that damn coffin. Lifeless and gray. And Eric wondered where his grandmother's vengeance had been then. Or if maybe she had just taken it out on Eric while raising him.

Maybe. Maybe.

"And as for Jane," Nina said before signing off, pulling Eric out of his gloom. "Somehow, you have to remind her of what *she* is to you too. That's what every woman really wants, you know. A reminder that someone cares for her. Sees her. Fights for her. Especially when the rest of the world doesn't."

ERIC SAID goodbye to his cousin, closed his laptop, then headed out of the attic down to the kitchen, where Skylar was getting Luis breakfast while Brandon chatted amiably with Jenny over cereal at the farmhouse table.

Eric accepted a cup of coffee from Skylar, took a sip of the weak, lukewarm sludge (which was being polite), and grimaced. "Crosby, where do you keep your French press? I know you have one."

"You're such a snob," Skylar said, setting a plate of eggs in front of her toddler, who proceeded to smash a handful into his mouth.

Eric shrugged. He couldn't deny it, especially when it came to his coffee. "If you're gonna do it, do it right."

"Let him, Red," Brandon said. "No offense, baby, but your coffee tastes like dishwater."

Next to him, Jenny giggled when she caught her mother's indignant expression.

"It's not *my* fault." Skylar turned to Brandon. "I'm a tea drinker, after all."

"Then just let me do it, Cros," Eric said as he poured the "coffee" down the sink. He located the bag of Starbucks on the counter and masked a cringe—he preferred fresher coffee, but he could make something out of this. "You're putting us up here. I can at least take care of the brew."

Skylar grumbled, but eventually directed Eric to the equipment he requested.

"Jenny," she said, examining her daughter's plate. "How much of those eggs has Daddy eaten?"

"None," Brandon said just as Jenny replied, "This much," roughly indicating half her dish.

Brandon held his arms out in mock innocence, but flashed a grin at his wife.

Skylar wasn't amused. "Brandon, she has to eat."

"She's a pea, Red. She doesn't need this much food."

"Well, she's going to stay pea-sized if you keep eating her food for her."

Brandon looked his daughter up and down, as if he were literally estimating her size.

"Brandon!"

"You know who you sound like right now, don't you?"

"I do *not* sound like Bubbe, you big bully!"

"Okay, okay, Red, keep your pants on. Jen, your ma's right. You need to finish the rest."

"Daddy!"

"No argument, peanut. Listen to your mother and me. Eat."

It was clear by his tone that there was no getting around it, and Jenny clearly knew it, since she immediately bent to her food. Brandon turned to Skylar with an arched brow, then flashed his trademark, "million-watt grin," as Skylar called it. It worked—his wife plainly melted in return. Then she rewarded Brandon with a tame kiss that still managed to heat up the whole kitchen.

"You're a menace," she muttered with reddened cheeks.

Brandon murmured something in her ear that Eric couldn't hear, but made Skylar's face flush even more.

"Brandon!" she said again, but this time in that way women did when they were pleased and embarrassed at the same time.

Brandon just sat back and took a large, satisfied bite of his own eggs. He looked like a king. Eric turned back to making his coffee, aching for his own kitchen on Seventy-Sixth and Amsterdam.

The family's exchange was familiar, but at the same time foreign. Eric vaguely remembered similar interactions between his parents— flirtatious admonishment between his mom and dad over breakfast or dinner. His father's teasing that almost always made his mother say "Jacob!" in the exact tone Skylar had just used. The warm feeling Eric would get in his stomach every time he caught them smiling at each other when they thought he wasn't looking.

But after his father died, it had been Grandmother and Garrett. There was no banter. No repartee. Just a cutting glare that ensured Eric ate his perfectly poached eggs and half a grapefruit.

Is this what it would have been like with Jane after the little one was born? Once, teasing had been as natural to them as breathing. Would their kid have grinned at the two of them the way Jenny was doing now? Would she have run down the stairs every morning, eager for the show of her parents' love?

The idea made Eric's guts twist. He finished pushing down the plunger on the French press, then poured himself a cup before wandering over to the solarium to sit under the snow-covered glass. The chill there fit his mood.

"Jane been down yet?" he wondered.

Skylar shook her head. "No, she's still asleep, I think."

He wasn't surprised.

Skylar joined him in the solarium with her tea. She was dressed for the office in one of her designer suits, and for a moment, Eric was envious. He missed the camaraderie of Copley Associates, but also missed knowing the ins and outs of his own shop, all his employees, and every nook and cranny of the place. DVS wasn't his. Not yet. Maybe not ever, not in the same way.

But at the same time, he was enjoying the challenges of taking over the big company. It wasn't what he imagined for himself when he originally came to Boston, but he had to admit, Jane was right. Grandmother was right. For the last five years, he had been treading water as a mere lawyer. This was what he was meant to do.

If only he could get back and do it. But he wasn't going anywhere without Jane.

"You just need to give her some time," Skylar said quietly, as if she knew what he was thinking.

Eric looked up, deflated. "It's been two weeks. Yu-na's settled with Ji-yeon. How much time does she need?"

"Pea, take your brother to the playroom," Brandon urged Jenny as she finished her breakfast. "We'll leave in a few minutes, all right?"

After the little girl did as she was asked, Brandon joined Skylar and Eric. They both turned to Eric expectantly.

Eric took a long drink of his coffee. "I don't know what to do," he admitted. "She's...look, I know she's been going through some hard stuff, but—"

"I don't think you really know," Skylar put in.

"She's *my* wife, Crosby. I found her. I sat by her wondering if she was even going to live. I think I understand a little about what happened to her."

"Do you *really*?"

"You know, I was kidnapped and tortured myself just a few months ago, if you don't fucking remember," Eric retorted. "I'm not exactly naive in all of this."

"And did you have a child ripped from inside you too?" Skylar's cheeks reddened all over again. Brandon placed a hand on her wrist.

Eric paused. "That's a little much, don't you think? It was an abortion at eight weeks. It didn't really go like that."

Skylar stood up from the love seat, walked carefully around the coffee table, and sat on it directly in front of Eric.

"No," she said. "It didn't. So let me tell you exactly how it *did* go."

"Red—" Brandon started, but Skylar batted his hand away.

"No," she said again. "I'm sick of people minimizing this, like it wasn't a legitimate trauma. Eric, you've been pretty understanding about her healing, but there are some things you don't get, even if the doctor explained it to you."

Eric scowled. "I talked to the doctors, Skylar."

"So they informed you, then, that someone Jane didn't know drugged her, inserted four pills inside her vagina, then inserted four more, thereby giving her *twice as much* as was needed to induce an abortion."

"Skylar," Brandon tried again, looking visibly uncomfortable.

Skylar, however, just continued. "So, on top of forcibly expelling an embryo as well as all of her uterine lining in an incredibly painful fashion, even through heavy sedation, these assholes also caused hemorrhaging and infection that nearly killed her. Which made a procedure that isn't exactly a walk in the park anyway completely life-threatening, on top of fucking nonconsensual. So, no, Eric. No one literally ripped a baby out of her. But to Jane, it was pretty damn close."

Eric sucked in a sharp breath, willing the pricking at his eyes to fade. It wasn't like any of this was new information. The doctors in Korea and New York had been pretty frank with him about it, multiple times. But it was different, somehow, to hear it coming from someone who wasn't just Jane's best friend, but one of his own too. Skylar had a way of cutting through the bullshit. She didn't sugarcoat things. She forced people to face them.

He didn't want to tell his friends just how many times over the past week he'd come close to breaking down himself—in the shower, in his bed—trying to forget the sight of Jane drenched in blood, or the sleepless night he'd spent wondering if she was going to come through it.

And here was Skylar, dredging it all back up again. It was all he could do not to snap.

"Do you remember?" Skylar asked. Her large green eyes hadn't wavered. "How it was for me, Eric?"

Behind her, Brandon visibly cringed at the mention of his wife's own abortion. She and Eric had been roommates just after.

Eric nodded. "I remember you were pretty down for a while, yeah."

"Then imagine something like that happening without your consent. Jane wanted this baby, Eric. She wanted a family with you. And this man, these strangers, paid by her own father—they stole that from her and nearly killed her in the process." She shook her head. "I don't think any of us can really understand what she's going through right now. I think we just have to be with her while she heals. Inside and out. On her own terms. To be honest, Brandon and I are both just humbled she felt comfortable enough in our home to do that."

She returned to the love seat and curled into Brandon while he stroked her hair thoughtfully. No doubt managing some painful memories of his own.

Eric bent forward, resting his elbows on his knees. In his mind's eye, he could still see the ultrasound photo that Jane had texted him just before she was taken.

"Fuck," he whispered. "*Fuck.*"

He had never felt so helpless in his entire life, and considering the iron fist who had raised him, that was saying something. Or maybe it was just that he also wanted to do something this time. Something different. But nothing seemed to be working.

"So what else do I do?" he wondered. "The FBI. The CIA. Fuck, even the investigator's blood, still on our hands. No one seems to be doing anything to help. Least of all me."

Skylar didn't say anything, and neither did Brandon. Then, after a few minutes, Brandon got up. Skylar stood with him, allowing him to pull her close and rest his chin on her head. For a long time, Eric had looked down on their constant need for contact. But now, with Jane, he understood it. Being apart from her just felt wrong.

Brandon's eyes closed tightly. The guy hadn't said much while Skylar talked, but Eric could see he was wrestling with the memories Skylar's testament was bringing up. They had their own losses, after all.

"You mind getting the kids to school this morning, babe?" he asked.

"Sure," Skylar said after Brandon released her. "Are you in the lab?"

Brandon shook his head. "No, Eric and I need to go do some things. We'll be back later this afternoon. I'll pick the kids up on our way, all right? Text me if you need anything at the store."

Skylar nodded. "All right. I'll tell Jane before I go."

TWENTY-ONE

The engine purred like a kitten as Brandon shifted into third gear. It was a newer acquisition, purchased sometime after Luis had arrived —a shiny blue bullet of a thing with two racing stripes down the nose.

Hello, midlife crisis. Eric smirked, hearing Jane's pointed voice in the back of his mind. She'd commented on Brandon's car collection, which had bloomed since he entered fatherhood, more than once.

"It's funny," Eric said as he admired the leather interior, "but I never really took you for a muscle car kind of guy. I think I've only ever seen you with a driver, actually."

"Well, this isn't just a car, my friend. It's a 1970 Chevelle. A classic."

Eric shrugged. The name meant nothing. He grew up in a city jammed with people, not automobiles. He didn't even get his license until he was in college and needed a way to get around rural New Hampshire. "I've never been much for cars."

"Spoken like a true New Yorker."

"Hey, a lot of people in Boston don't drive."

"Yeah, I'm from *South* Boston, de Vries." Brandon smirked and tipped his worn Red Sox hat at Eric, looking very much like someone from the rougher side of the city in a pair of worn jeans and a black fleece. "If the Sox weren't on, we were either playing pool or working on engines."

Eric knew for a fact that was an oversimplification. But despite being a lauded attorney and former investment guru, Brandon had also graduated from MIT by nineteen and now ran a lab with his foster father, an electric engineering professor. It shouldn't have surprised Eric that he liked any kind of machinery, automotive or otherwise.

"My old man liked cars," Brandon added quietly. "He taught me a few things before he got locked up. On the days he wasn't wasted, anyway."

Eric didn't press. He also knew from bits and pieces over the years that Brandon had a nonexistent relationship with his biological father, a man still in jail for assault. There was a reason why he had gone to live with Ray and Susan—the people he now called his parents—at age twelve and never left. Eric knew how that felt, the need to abandon one's previous life.

But some things from that life had stuck with Brandon, apparently.

Eric knew how that went too.

It wasn't until Brandon exited Franklin Park that Eric realized they were closer to his friend's past than he'd thought. The buildings around them fell further and further into disrepair as they drove away from the zoo and the golf course and drove right into the heart of Dorchester, the neighborhood where Brandon had grown up. Eric hadn't spent a lot of time on this side of the city in all the time he'd spent in Boston. A Sox game or two at Fenway was the farthest south he'd really ventured, with the exception of a few girls' apartments he'd visited back in his law school days.

Missing those days, Petri dish?

There she was again, teasing him. God, he wished she would call him that stupid fucking name for real. He'd slap a hand over that smart mouth of hers, tell her in no uncertain terms that it takes one to

THE LOVE TRAP   223

know one, and then teach them *both* a lesson in fidelity until the sun rose.

Would he ever get to do that again?

God, he fucking hoped so.

Dorchester was an interesting mix of cultures and money, changing the way a lot of the older neighborhoods in Boston were changing. Thirty or forty years ago, it had been dominated mostly by Boston's infamous Irish-Catholic groups, including the Westies. Now you were more likely to find Vietnamese restaurants as pool halls. As the city itself became more strapped for cash, the younger, more affluent people were gentrifying the neighborhood.

"Like a damn department store," Brandon muttered as he turned the car onto Park. "Look at that. A French bakery in Field's Corner. I never thought."

"Come on. The Vietnamese love their French pastries," Eric countered. "Fruits of colonialism, right?"

"You sound like your wife when you say that," Brandon replied dryly.

Eric's mouth quirked. He did sound like Jane, didn't he? He didn't altogether mind the idea, actually. How many times had she teased him over dinner about mixing Asian and European foods with exactly that argument?

They parked and got out. Eric looked up and down the block. There wasn't much to see—a bunch of crooked row houses in need of paint jobs, an abandoned Chinese restaurant covered with grates, and an unused parking lot across the street. Most of the signs of gentrification in Dorchester were still confined to housing costs and renovations on its main streets.

"This is it." Brandon gestured at the large, unmarked brick building behind them.

Eric looked up and down at it. "Are you planning to have me whacked, Sterling?"

Brandon snorted. "Eric, do yourself a favor and don't say things like 'whacked.' Your Upper East Side is showing."

Eric rolled his eyes. "Please. You're about as Dorchester as I am these days, my friend."

Brandon just shook his head and deliberately turned up the intensity of his South Boston accent so he sounded like a Marky Mark impersonator. "Never, never. You can take the boy out of Dorchester, but you can't take the Dorchester out of the boy."

He grinned, and Eric couldn't help but laugh with him. He felt that way himself about the city sometimes.

"So what is this place?" he asked as he followed Brandon to the entrance marked by a heavy steel door.

"It's where I come to let off some steam now and then. Get away from the estrogen running my fuckin' house. Welcome to the South Boston Firing Range."

"You're telling me that shooting a gun makes you feel more like a man?" Eric asked doubtfully. "Isn't that a bit of a cliché?"

"Maybe." Brandon shrugged. "But it helps. Listen..." He paused with a hand on the door handle. "All jokes aside. I've been where you are now."

Eric opened his mouth to ask where exactly that was, but shut it when Brandon continued.

"When that motherfucker kidnapped Skylar, I felt like there wasn't a goddamn thing I could do to save her," Brandon said. "I swear to God, Eric, I have never felt so helpless in my whole fuckin' life. Not even when I was a kid, bouncing around group homes and shit. That day, coming back to her apartment to find her missing? Seeing her blood on the floor? Not knowing where the fuck she was or how I could help her? Worst fuckin' day of my life. Bar none."

"For me, I think it was worse when I found Jane," Eric replied somewhat numbly. "If we're being honest."

Brandon released the handle. "How do you figure?"

"Because even when I found her, I still needed someone else to help her." Eric couldn't stop his voice from shaking. "She was sick and dying, and I couldn't do a fucking thing to make it better."

"You did, though," Brandon countered. "You showed up. If you hadn't, she probably would have died, right? That's something. Maybe the most important thing."

"Still. I felt so fucking worthless. I still do."

Brandon watched Eric, maybe waiting for his emotions to level again. When at least Eric was able to look at him without wanting to rip his own skin off, Brandon grabbed the door handle once more and pulled.

"That," he said, "is exactly why we're here. Come on. I'll show you."

FOUR HOURS LATER, Eric was a newly certified student of the Basic Gun Safety course at the South Boston Firing Range. By a trick of fate, they had had one available spot that morning, and so while Brandon enjoyed some time shooting by himself and grabbed some pho around the corner, Eric found himself learning to do things like dismantle and clean a weapon—things he'd never even considered until today.

"I can't believe you made me sit through all of that," Eric said later that afternoon as he and Brandon were guided to a lane at the end of the range. He had to shout above the racket of shots by other patrons. Both men carried the ear protectors and plastic eyewear but hadn't put them on yet.

Brandon shrugged. "In Massachusetts, you have to take a certified course to get a license," he called. "I don't know about New York, but you want to know the truth, I think everyone should at least know how to manage a firearm."

"I didn't realize you were such a second amendment advocate," Eric said. "You and Skylar donate a ridiculous amount of money to gun-control causes."

"Oh, I believe in gun control. There's plenty of weapons—some made by Jane's father, as it happens—that don't belong in civilian hands any more than nuclear bombs or anthrax. But I also believe in a person's right to protect their family. For their own sake as well as others'." Brandon placed his gun and Eric's rented Glock on the counter of their lane.

"What kind of gun is that?" Eric asked. "That looks like the same one the infantry were carrying at the base in Korea."

"It probably is. The M9 is the standard sidearm for the U.S. armed forces." Brandon grinned sharkishly. "It's also one of the few big enough for my hand."

Eric just rolled his eyes and put on his ear protectors. He wasn't interested in getting into a pissing contest with a guy who outweighed him by at least thirty pounds.

"I'll go first," Brandon yelled.

He removed the safety, and Eric stood back and watched his friend proceed to fire off six rounds at the target. About five landed directly in the center of the outlined "person's" chest, the other two not far from it.

"Nice," Eric remarked after Brandon replaced the safety and put down his gun.

"Yeah, yeah, thanks, Hawkeye. Let me see what you got. Barry said you were a sharp fuckin' shooter for being so green."

Eric rolled his eyes. Of course Brandon was on a first-name basis with the instructor here.

But then he picked up the Glock he'd used earlier during the live fire practice at the end of the course, and found himself comfortably holding it up. He glanced at Brandon, then looked back at the target and took a few lame shots. One hit the far side of the target. Nothing else landed.

"Come on, de Vries," Brandon chided behind him. "You can do better than that."

Eric replaced the safety and turned back to his friend. Suddenly he wasn't in the mood for this kind of joking. He didn't want to be here. He didn't want to fail anymore.

"I'm tired. Let's just go, all right. The girls are probably wondering where we are."

But the bigger man didn't move.

"What would you do if that was John Carson or Jude Letour?" Brandon asked. "If Jane was behind you, and it was either you or them? Don't think about it. Your security is downstairs. There's nothing else but you and them, Eric. What do you do?"

It was all too easy to imagine. Too easy to see Carson appearing from behind the drapes of the ultrasound room. If Eric had been there—fuck, *if he had only been there*—maybe Jane wouldn't have been taken. Maybe he could have saved her. The baby. Both.

He turned back to the counter, picked up the Glock, and proceeded to fire straight through the target. One, two, three, four, five, six. John. Car. Son. Jude. Le. Tour. One after another, Eric fired, until fourteen rounds had been discharged. All landing within maybe a six-inch radius of the head-shaped target.

When he was finished, he was breathing heavily, but his shoulders felt lighter. Slowly, Eric removed the earmuffs. The shooting range had gone silent. Brandon's mouth was open.

"Holy shit," someone muttered a few lanes down. "Did you see that?"

Eric replaced the safety and set down the gun. "Stop staring at me like that, Sterling. Did I do something wrong?"

Brandon swallowed. "Ah, no. No, you didn't."

Eric's mouth tugged to the side in a smirk. "So I did something right?"

"I'll, uh, put it this way. The only other person I've ever seen shoot like that in here was a Marine Expert Marksman." Brandon shook his head, expelling a long breath. "I think you might have missed your calling, my friend."

"Yeah, maybe I should trade Wall Street for the O.K. Corral," Eric replied dryly.

Brandon cast him a sideways look. "Hey. I didn't mean to push you. If you want to go, we can go."

Eric started to nod, then stopped. His legs felt heavy, and his finger itched. He looked back at the target. There was still one part of the head that was free of bullet holes.

"No," he said. "Let's, ah, let's shoot a few more rounds." He held up the gun again, squinting as he looked through the target with one eye, as if it would help him see it better. "I do feel like James Bond." He pressed the trigger, and the final bullet went flying through the neck of the target.

Brandon put his eyewear back on with a smile. "You feel a little better, don't you?"

Eric put on his muffs and didn't answer, pretending like he hadn't heard Brandon's question. But yeah, he had to admit to himself as he proceeded to finish off the target. He did feel better. A lot better.

TWENTY-TWO

The idea came to him in the middle of the night. Jane was asleep next to him, curled into herself like a nautilus shell, per usual. Well, her new usual.

For more than three weeks now they had been living a strange life out of Skylar and Brandon's guest room, watching everyone but them live some semblance of normal around them while Eric floated between New York and Boston. It was uncomfortable, taking advantage of someone's hospitality like this. Eric wanted home. He wanted his own bed. His own coffee. His own fucking life.

But Jane put off every suggestion that they return home.

To their credit, the Crosby-Sterlings didn't say a word. They just went about their daily routines, taking the kids to school, going to work, basically living their normally busy lives around their perennial houseguests. The perfect hosts.

Yu-na seemed to be getting right back to herself. Eric still didn't know his mother-in-law very well, but between her cousin and Skylar's grandmother's insistent nurturing, Jane's mother had definitely been stepping out more and more confidently each day, and largely without her daughter. She and Ji-yeon had hooked up with some new friends through the Korean church just a few blocks from Skylar and Brandon's house, and they had started taking daily sojourns around town with Sarah, Skylar's grandmother.

Yu-na wasn't enjoying her veritable playdates, however, she was trying to harangue Jane out of bed, and Jane wasn't fucking having it. If she and her mother had been fighting properly, that would have been one thing. But the conversations mostly consisted of Yu-na shaming her daughter's grief, and Jane just murmuring wordlessly into her pillow.

Because three weeks later, and a full five after Eric had found her in that dusty, freezing house, Jane still couldn't seem to shake the despair that had invaded her normal buoyant self. Korea had broken her. Carson had broken her. And, it seemed, she didn't believe she could ever put herself back together.

The nature of that despair, however, hadn't really reached Eric until he had overheard a conversation between her and Skylar just after he arrived home from New York that day.

"DO YOU EVER REGRET IT?" Jane was asking her. "The first one, I mean."

There was a long pause.

"I..." Skylar started. "Yes and no." Another pause. "It's not really the same thing, though."

"You lost a baby," Jane countered. "And you've told me yourself you wondered what it might have been like."

"Sure, I do. But...well, it was totally different circumstances. To start, it was my choice. When I found out that I was pregnant, I was twenty-six, broke, and I thought Brandon was married and totally lost to me. I was in no place, mentally or otherwise, to take care of a child the way it deserved, and so I thought I was doing the right thing, even if sometimes I wish I could take it back now."

There was some shuffling on the covers and a long silence.

"I should have protected her." Jane's voice was so weak, the words almost inaudible. "I should have done more somehow."

Her? Eric shook his head. She had barely been eight weeks along. No wonder she was a mess, in there imagining a child that hadn't really existed yet.

"Oh, Janey...there was nothing you could do. You have to understand that. But you have a partner to help you through it. Don't push him away like I did. That's my real regret, you know. Not treating him like the partner he always was."

JANE HADN'T RESPONDED. And so Eric had entered and Skylar had left, giving him a meaningful green look before bidding them good night. Jane had only wiped at her eyes and turned away, claiming she was too tired to talk anymore that night. Or at all. Maybe ever.

Now, Eric watched her sleep with hands pressed protectively over her stomach. Her guilt that was eating her alive.

He turned back to the book of Yeats poetry, an old favorite. It was flipped to one of Yeats's last poems, "Man and the Echo," which reckoned with the writer's regrets, written as a call and response between a man's thoughts and the echo from somewhere else.

Man

In a cleft that's christened Alt
Under broken stone I halt
At the bottom of a pit
That broad noon has never lit,
And shout a secret to the stone.
All that I have said and done,
Now that I am old and ill,

Turns into a question till
I lie awake night after night
And never get the answers right.
Did that play of mine send out
Certain men the English shot?
Did words of mine put too great strain
On that woman's reeling brain?
Could my spoken words have checked
That whereby a house lay wrecked?
And all seems evil until I
Sleepless would lie down and die.

Echo

Lie down and die.

That was the answer to guilt, the echo seemed to say. You want to lie down and die? Fine, do it. Give yourself up to the sorrow, the hopelessness. Sink into the night, if that's where you think you're going. No hope, no introspection. Just an echo chamber based on the spiral of despair that could sometimes overtake a person's soul.

Or maybe its parody, calling its bluff.

Because the poem ended with the man's voice, not the echo's. Pulled out of his thoughts by the immediacy of the world, the man abandoned his introspection for more important things:

Man.

O Rocky Voice,
Shall we in that great night rejoice?
What do we know but that we face
One another in this place?
But hush, for I have lost the theme,

Its joy or night-seem but a dream;
Up there some hawk or owl has struck,
Dropping out of sky or rock,
A stricken rabbit is crying out,
And its cry distracts my thought.

Yes, Eric thought as he read the end of the poem again, and again. Some interpreted this poem as a dismal reckoning on the meaninglessness of life. How easily one's purpose could be flung away with small distractions. But Eric saw it differently. He saw it as a description of the visceral connections between all forms of life and the pains they experience. A recollection that one wasn't truly alone.

It was this passage and ones like it that had helped pull him out of his own despair after Penny's death. His father's death. Reminders that real life existed outside the clamor and darkness of one's own thoughts.

Poetics came to mind, via an essay on Aristotle that had saved him when Penny died, so long ago. When Eric's own guilt had been eating him alive too.

Aristotle wrote that the point of reading and hearing and viewing tragedy was to help readers or listeners "purge" of emotions like fear, sadness. And, sure, guilt. People, in other words, had too many damn feelings. And if they didn't let them out in some way or another, they were eaten up by them. But most people, Aristotle said, couldn't articulate those feelings, the complicated emotions of life. That's why they needed others who could express them in words, music, art, drama. Through poetry, they faced the terrible conditions of life again and again, and in doing so, were able to let them go. Were able to purge and make way for the next round.

But despite being someone who had made her living on words as a lawyer, Jane wasn't a huge reader. She was a tactile person, kinetic. She coped with life's difficulties by living it, not passively absorbing others' impressions.

It was one of the ways in which they were so different. But that didn't mean Eric couldn't understand some of her.

Guilt. Yeah. He knew something about that.

Jane's emotions were eating her up. But her catharsis would have to come through experience, or perhaps witnessing someone else's in real time. And that, Eric thought, he could help with.

Finally.

"JANE, get up. We're going out."

It was past ten o'clock. She had been sleeping later and later every day instead of getting up earlier and earlier. Another sign of her deep depression, or so confirmed her doctor.

Jane pushed his arm away. "I'm still tired," she mumbled into her pillow, which had left a brutal red mark across one cheek. "I don't want to go anywhere."

Eric sat up on the bed and worried his lip for a moment as Jane's eyes remained shut. He could be gentle about this. He could pet her head and murmur nice things into her ear and coax her downstairs for breakfast, like he'd managed a few times before. But he'd been gentle for weeks, tiptoeing around the woman all the damn time like she was about to break. It seemed to be making things worse, not better.

Fuck it.

He yanked the pillow out from under her head, causing her head to flop down onto the mattress.

Her eyes flew open. "Hey! What the fuck?"

"I said get up," he repeated. "I have something to do today, and I need you to come with me."

She scowled, though she did grab her glasses off the nightstand and shove them on to glare at him with more clarity. "And *I* said I don't want to go anywhere. Can't you do your little errand without me?"

Eric opened his mouth and paused. Was he pushing her too much? It had only been five weeks. Maybe she needed more time.

As if in response, the grandfather clock in the hallway chimed with the hour. No, she didn't need more time to stew, pushing everyone and everything away so she could wallow deeper in her own misery. He was starting to suspect the longer she did that, the less likely it was she would ever emerge.

"No," Eric said firmly. "I can't."

With a groan, she pushed herself to sitting. Her hair was matted a bit in the back, and despite the twelve or more hours she had already slept, she still had dark, puffy circles under her eyes. She was still beautiful.

"Why are you dressed like that?" she asked through a yawn.

Eric looked down at his clothes, a comfortable pair of chinos and a tailored blue shirt. Somewhere between the suits he wore for work, and sweats he preferred at the gym and, yes, the shooting range (he'd visited a few more times since last week). A gray pea coat was tossed on the chair.

He looked up. "What's wrong with this?"

"I think you wore that exact outfit at mock trial during our third year."

He examined his clothes again, trying to remember what she was talking about. "I definitely wasn't wearing Prada at a law school mock trial. I would have at least worn a tie." He smiled. This might have been the first joke in over a week. "Are you trying to say I look like a young student again, gorgeous? Is it getting you going?"

"I'm saying you look like a just-off-work bank manager."

"I was going for respectable."

He waited for another comeback that he might volley over the proverbial net. But none came. Jane fell back into her pillow.

Eric sighed and squatted next to her side of the bed. "How's this, Lefferts? You come with me now, you can dress me however you want this afternoon."

For a moment, she brightened. Her full, somewhat paler-than-usual lips parted, and he could practically see the word "Really?" on the tip of her tongue. But then, her face fell back, assuming that same, blank stare.

"Wear what you want," she murmured. "They're just clothes, after all."

Shit. Even if this had been the first interaction he'd had with her in years, he would have known something was horribly wrong when she said that. Tentatively, Eric reached out and covered her hand with his. The one still resting over her practically concaved stomach. Fucking hell, was she eating at all?

"Jane," Eric said. "Please. I need you with me today. Your mom is already gone."

"What?" At that, she perked up again. "Where is she? Where did she go? Is she all right?"

"Relax. Sarah took her and Ji-yeon to Quincy Market, and then I think they are planning to go to a bible study at the Korean Presbyterian church this afternoon."

Jane sat up, shoving her hair back from her face. "What? Eric, how could they just leave like that? Anyone could follow them, you know, and Quincy Market is incredibly crowded and—"

"Everyone has a personal detail," he replied calmly. "They are fine. I promise."

Jane's eyes glistened. She sighed irritably. "I can't believe you just let them go, Eric."

For a moment, he blinked, unsure of himself. She was annoyed now, not scared. That was good. But she was using his given name. That was bad. He never thought he'd actually want to hear that stupid fucking nickname—Petri dish—again, but these days, he'd probably do a fucking cartwheel if she said it.

Instead, he mustered the best smirk he could. "Your mom and cousin are grown women doing what grown women do. They are living their lives. Now it's your turn, Lefferts."

"I'm going back to bed," Jane mumbled, rolling back into the folds of the comforter.

Fucking hell. "No, you're not." This time Eric grabbed her wrist and yanked her back up so that the covers fell away in a pile.

"What the hell!" Jane shrieked as she tucked her arm away. "What's with the gestapo treatment, asshole?"

Mercilessly, Eric flung the covers off the bed entirely. Jane's long, bare legs wobbled in the sudden chill. She really was getting too thin. "Well, first you're going to take a shower and brush your hair. You're starting to look like the creepy girl from *The Ring*."

Jane scowled. "So sorry I couldn't keep up my looks while I slept. And that's mean."

"You're two seconds from climbing out of the television, Lefferts. Do it now, or tomorrow I'm staging an intervention."

"This is draconian," Jane muttered, though she did finally swing her feet to the floor. "Bully."

"Then we're going to Zaftig's for some food," Eric continued as he walked to the closet and started picking out some clothes for her to wear. He'd brought more things last week from their apartment, but only because if he had to see her put on one more pair of fucking yoga pants, he was going to burn them all. "You're getting the banana-stuffed French toast. And maybe some eggs too."

Jane grabbed a bathrobe slung over the chair. "Bossy, aren't you?"

Eric tossed a pair of jeans, a sweater, and Jane's favorite combat boots on the bed. "After that, we're going to run some errands. I want some company, and you need to get out of this room so Skylar's housekeeper can finally change the damn sheets." He surveyed the outfit. Jane would probably pick out something else entirely, but it was a start. "I'll meet you downstairs in thirty minutes. I'll get you a coffee."

Ignoring her grumbled protests, he walked out.

"One more thing," he said, turning at the door. "If you come down without that goddamn lipstick, I'm dragging you back up here and putting it on you myself. And since my handiwork will probably make you look like The Joker, I suggest you do it right the first time, pretty girl."

When her lips—already with more color in them—fell open, Eric only shut the door behind him and hoped he was doing the right thing. But a few seconds later, when he could hear her muttering to herself, Eric finally exhaled and smiled.

TWENTY-THREE

She didn't delay. Within thirty minutes she got right up, showered for the first time in days, and came downstairs for coffee.

That was a good sign.

"Is this respectable enough?" she asked as she entered the kitchen.

Eric turned from the French press to find her toying with the rings on her fingers—two sets of glinting silver bands, plus their wedding rings, including the sharp black diamond he had given her.

She had replaced her boring black frames with one of her favorite vintage pairs, bright red and cat-eyed. With the tight black jeans, a black hoodie, and her favorite combat boots, she looked much like her student days, only missing her old cropped hair.

Another good sign.

But then his gaze had traveled up her body and landed on her face, bereft of its usual makeup, including her characteristic slash of red lips.

Bad sign. Very bad sign.

"Oh, no," Eric said, abandoning the coffee. "You fucking heard me."

Her mouth dropped into a perfect, plump "O," making his pants uncomfortably tight. Shit. It had been a while, hadn't it? Nearly two months since New Year's.

She backed away. "You wouldn't."

"I don't ever go back on my word."

And before she could jump out of reach—Jesus, she was out of practice—he snagged her hand and proceeded to drag her back upstairs, where he pinned her to the en suite bathroom's counter and started drawing the lipstick around her full, kissable mouth.

"Eric!" she crowed, causing him to smear the color across her chin too.

He couldn't help laughing, though he kept her wrists behind her back. "I told you, pretty girl. I warned you what would happen."

And then it happened. She struggled. Twisted. *Grinded* against him. Was it really his fault that the last almost two full months of abstinence decided to take their toll right fucking then and there? Was it his fault that he happened to be poised right between her legs so there was no fucking way she could miss it?

Her mouth dropped again. That perfect shape. And the hell if he didn't want to shove her to her knees right then and there, unzip his pants, and feed her his dick until they both forget where they were, even if just for a few brief minutes.

He almost did it too. Until, of course, she scooted back.

"I, um, I got it," she said, plucking the lipstick from his hand. She swallowed heavily, clearly fighting not to stare at the prominent erection testing his zipper.

Another bad sign.

Eric cleared his throat. She was uncomfortable? Well, he was her fucking husband. She knew exactly what she was getting down there.

But he still turned away. Mostly because he was scared of what he would do if she left her mouth open like that for one more second.

"I'll be downstairs," he said and left before she could answer.

But when she came back down, the lipstick was on. She wouldn't meet his eye, but he could have sworn there was a different spring in her step.

Definitely a good sign.

JANE TOOK EXACTLY five bites of her breakfast at Zaftig's, a restaurant teeming with Brookline families., complete with small children. Lots of babies. Not, Eric realized, the best place to go.

Then she barely spoke on the rest of the drive to the nearby heliport, followed him mutely onto the helicopter, and stared out the window all the way to New York. She hadn't even asked where they were going when they landed.

More bad signs. Fuck, fuck, fuck.

Eric had pretended to work on his phone most of the time. It was hard to hide his relief when she finally said, "Queens?" just as Tony turned onto the Queensboro Bridge.

"Are we going rock climbing again?" she joked.

To be honest, Eric had fantasized more than once about tying Jane into one of the harnesses. The idea of suspending her lithe body like that in midair had a lot of...possibilities.

Instead he watched as she reapplied her lipstick—perhaps in memory of the last time they had been there?—then blinked and shook his head. "No. No, not today. Unless you're interested in a little rope play..."

But she just turned away and watched the river pass beyond the bridge. "Role play. No."

The Manhattan skyscrapers and the riverside buildings of Queens gradually gave way to the more stolid brick apartments and townhouses of Astoria. Jane clearly had no idea where they were. In the not-even-a-year since she had moved to New York, she hadn't really ventured farther than Manhattan, Eric realized, except to visit him at Rikers. God, he had so much more of this city to show her. Things he had forgotten himself.

There would be time for that. They had a lifetime together, right?

Starting now. Eric swallowed. He really hoped this first step would help, because it certainly wouldn't be easy.

"All right," he said as Tony pulled the car to the curb of East Thirty-First Avenue. It was a classic winter day, with wind sweeping harshly off the East River where it curled around the Con Ed plant in the distance, tempered only by the bluebird sky and the bright sun that lit up the squat buildings of Astoria and Ditmars. This was one of the parts of New York that were quiet. Real people lived here, not just rich Wall Street brokers, students, and trust-funded legacies.

The familiar restaurant in the bottom of the walkup met him like an old friend. The Epic Diner's name had always been so incongruous with its humble exterior—the rumbling red brick, the weathered glass door, the blinking neon sign. But for a short period, this had been a natural stop whenever Eric had come home.

"Where are we?" Jane asked as she exited the car to the cracked sidewalk and looked around. "Still Queens?"

Eric pulled at his shirt collar. "Astoria. This is the Epic."

"You took me all the way to Queens to get more mediocre eggs?" Jane peered suspiciously through the smudged glass. "They aren't very busy. We passed a bunch of other places on the way here that looked a lot more crowded."

"The Kostas benefit more from the breakfast rush and the lunch crowd from Con Ed," Eric said automatically, almost defensively. He clapped his mouth shut, but Jane obviously hadn't missed a beat.

"The Kostas?"

Eric nodded, resisting the urge to pull at his collar again. It wasn't even buttoned, but it felt like it was strangling him. "Penny's family."

Jane's eyes widened as she adjusted her glasses and turned back to the restaurant with renewed curiosity. Perhaps she was recalling when Eric had revealed the circumstances surrounding his former fiancée's death. When she had encouraged him to make peace with Penny's parents. But if she was thinking of that, she didn't say it.

"Will you come in with me?" he asked finally when it was clear she wasn't going to respond.

Jane's eyes sharpened, sharper than he had seen them in weeks. "I'm here," she said, and followed him inside.

Nothing had changed. The faded sprigged wallpaper. The cracked vinyl booths. The stained Formica counter, behind which still stood Lazaros Kostas, joking and taking orders on a small pad poised over a growing belly. Behind him, overseeing the cooks and checking the orders clipped to the ticket carousel, was his wife, Antonia. Suddenly, Eric felt like he was seventeen again, skipping polo practice to sit in Penny's section and order too many chocolate milkshakes just to see his girlfriend smile. But other than where her photo hung behind the register amidst the collection of signed head shots of celebrities and local politicians, Penny wasn't here.

Penny wasn't here. But Jane was.

And to his surprise, she took his hand. "Are you all right?" she asked.

Empathy. Definitely a good sign.

Eric nodded. "Yeah. It's just a little surreal."

Jane squeezed his hand in solidarity, then released it as the hostess walked toward them.

"Two?" she asked in that brusque tone characteristic of the New York restaurant industry.

Eric nodded. "At the counter, please."

The hostess gestured that they should sit where they wanted. Jane followed Eric to the counter, where Mr. Kostas had his back turned as he jabbered with his wife in Greek.

"Lazaros," she snipped, then in English: "You have customers."

Lazaros barked something back at her, then turned around. "Hello, what can I—oh!"

It had been almost eleven years since Penny's funeral. Eleven years since Eric had stood behind the rows of Greek relatives wailing their disbelief at his girlfriend's untimely death and whispered behind his back. Eleven years since Eric had informed the Kostas that their only daughter had killed herself in his bathtub and that it was probably his family's fault.

Except it wasn't. Not completely. And the Kostas deserved to know everything.

"Mr. Kostas. It's, ah, been a long time."

Lazaros pressed a thick hand to his chest, then raised it and beckoned behind him. "Toni," he called breathlessly, too low to be heard in the kitchen above the clatter of pans and hissing oil. "Antonia!" he shouted over his shoulder, loud enough that nearly everyone in the diner jumped.

A loud clatter of pans crashed somewhere in the back.

Lazaros turned back to Eric with an uneasy smile. "Take a booth in the corner. We will be right there."

A FEW MINUTES LATER, the Kostases brought over fresh coffee and a platter of dolmades. *Penny's favorites*, Eric thought with a twinge. Mrs. Kostas set mugs on the table in a matter-of-fact way. Lazaros took his seat across from Eric and Jane, then waited for his wife to join him. When at last they were all seated, had each nibbled at one of the stuffed grape leaves and poured the coffee no one would drink, the Kostases faced Eric expectantly.

Eric took a deep breath. "Mr. and Mrs. Kostas. It's been a long time."

"Since the funeral," Lazaros agreed. "And thank you for paying for that, by the way. We never had a chance to say it. You left so quickly."

Eric's tongue felt thick in his throat. He remembered the clouds that had never rained, but threatened it just the same. He had left as soon as it was over. Left New York. Left his family. Everything.

"You didn't even come to the *makaria*," Lazaros was saying. "We held it right here in the restaurant. Toni made very nice salmon.

Everyone came." He pushed his wire-framed aviator glasses up his thick nose. "The whole family. But not you."

It was all Eric could do not to hang his head. "I..."

"Zaro, give the boy a break," Antonia put in with a smack on the man's wrist.

"He's not a boy anymore," Lazaros grumbled. "And it's been more than ten years. It's about time he answered." He turned back to Eric. "What would Penny think?"

Eric opened and closed his mouth a few times before he finally managed to answer. "She'd..." He rubbed his face. "Well, Mr. Kostas, she'd be ashamed of me. She'd wonder where the hell I'd been and why I hadn't checked on her parents sooner."

Lazaros examined Eric for what felt like several minutes, his time-worn face unmoving until, all of a sudden, he burst out laughing and smacked the tabletop. Beside Eric, Jane jumped, but Antonia smiled warmly. Eric relaxed.

"Good for you," Lazaros said. "Better late than never, right? Isn't that what they say, Toni?"

His wife nodded with satisfaction. Eric smiled. This was the warm family he remembered.

"So," he pressed. "How are you?"

"Oh, it's been fine, fine," Lazaros said, still chuckling. "It was hard for a few years there, of course. We miss her so much, but we will see her one day again, God willing."

Beside him, Antonia crossed herself right to left, Orthodox-style. Just like Penny used to.

"Toni's niece came to help with the restaurant a few years ago," Lazaros continued. "That's Steffy over there, from Philadelphia." He gestured towards the hostess, who was wiping down another booth. "She's single, in case you're—"

Jane suddenly cleared her throat, disturbing the entire table. Eric muffled a laugh in his napkin.

"I've been a bit rude, Mr. Kostas," he said. "This is Jane, my wife. Jane, this is Lazaros and Antonia Kostas. Penny's parents."

For a moment, there was a different shine in Jane's eyes when he said the word "wife." "It's lovely to meet you," she said kindly, shaking each of the Kostases' hands.

"We saw you in the papers," Lazaros replied. "But we weren't sure you were still married, I'm sure you understand." He held up his hands, as if to say, "can you blame me?"

Jane chuckled. "I understand. I'm not sure what I was thinking, but I still agreed to marry him."

"You were thinking..." Eric drifted off, trying to find the words to defend himself, but taking too much joy in Jane's sudden playfulness. Would it remain after they left this place? God, he'd be the butt of any joke if she would keep looking at him like that.

"Eric."

Everyone shifted at the sound of Antonia Kostas's direct tone. Eric blinked. Lazaros might have forgiven him for his absence, but Penny's mother was a different beast.

"Why are you here?"

Unlike her husband's, Antonia Kostas's thick Greek accent that wasn't smoothed over by serving the front of the restaurant for forty years. Her dark eyes focused on Eric. It was obvious that she still carried considerable grief over her daughter's death and the role she believed he had in it.

"I came to say..." Eric rubbed a hand over his face again. "Look, Mr. and Mrs. Kostas, I came because I never did apologize. But I also have new information about Penny's death that I believe you have the right to know."

The Kostases glanced at each other, then turned back to Eric and waited.

Eric took a deep breath. Under the table, Jane squeezed his knee lightly.

"She...well, there's a man. A man who hates me and my family. Who seems bent on destroying any good thing that happens to me, for reasons I don't fully comprehend yet."

He took another deep breath, then continued, retelling all of the story as best he could. His father's friendship with Carson. Their business dealings, gone south at some point. His relationship with Jane's mother. And, eventually, his recruitment of Eric to the Janus society.

"I must beg of you," he said quietly, "not to mention the society to anyone. For your own safety."

"Did...did Penelope know about any of this?" Lazaros asked, understandably flabbergasted.

Eric swallowed. "I don't think so. But she was a smart girl, Mr. Kostas, and we were together when I was recruited. It's entirely possible that she figured it out, and I just never knew."

God, he could see her now. The vision of her, the stained bathroom tiles, the cold chill of the room, even on the late spring day. The metallic scent of her blood. The glaze over her open eyes.

He had to tell them.

"Mr. Kostas, Penny didn't kill herself. She was murdered. By a member of the Janus society, probably sent by John Carson. It was only a few days after I was fully initiated and maybe a month after my family cut me off for deciding to marry her. I thought at the time it was my family's ostracization that caused her to do it—the note, which now I see was clearly forged, indicated as much. But Jane and I both heard her killer confess. It was part of a larger scheme to bring me to heel. And for this man, John Carson, to punish me in my father's stead."

For a long time, both of the Kostases sat silently, digesting the revelations. They murmured to each other in Greek. Under the table, Jane reached for Eric's hand.

"That was very brave," she whispered.

Eric darted a look her way. "Thanks, pretty girl."

Jane's cheeks flushed.

"I don't understand." Lazaros pulled their attention back. "What does this man have against you? Why would he...do that...to my daughter?"

"Because the only thing John Carson cares about is power and control," Eric said. "Mr. Kostas, perhaps you remember. When I decided to marry Penny, my family cut me off. I accepted that because I loved your daughter, and I knew we could make a good life without my family's fortune. But I believe now that those terms were unacceptable to John Carson, who needed those resources for his own plans. The fact that it only continued torturing me in my father's place was a bonus."

Lazaros just shook his head, now tearing at one of the napkins on the booth. Antonia's face didn't move at all.

"I don't understand," Lazaros said, over and over again. "I don't understand."

"Mr. Kostas."

Jane's voice surprised everyone, low and unassuming. She placed a hand on Lazaros's wrist, which everyone stared at before she withdrew it.

"You might have known this about Eric, Mr. Kostas," Jane said quietly. "But he's one of the most independent people in the world. When he makes a decision, it's *his* decision."

Next to her husband, Antonia nodded. Respect entered the older woman's dark eyes. "Yes," she murmured. "I remember."

"Unfortunately," Jane continued. "He also was born into a world where, because of his family's expectations, many of those decisions were taken away from him. When he tried to shirk their guidance, people weren't happy about it. Especially my father."

"Your father?" Lazaros seemed even more confused.

"John Carson is Jane's biological father," Eric said quietly. "We didn't know—she never knew—until we were engaged. Until he announced it himself and forbade our marriage, purely out of spite. A decision that we also did not accept. And for which we were also punished."

The Kostases just stared, clearly shocked. Beside him, Jane shuddered.

"Look," Eric continued, more hurried now. "I still can't claim Penny's death wasn't my fault. The truth is that had Penny never known me, she wouldn't have been on John Carson's radar. She would probably still be alive."

Eric's chest felt heavier than ever, but he forced himself to meet Lazaros and Antonia's grief-stricken gazes head-on.

"Yes," Lazaros agreed after a minute. "She would be."

"But she didn't kill herself," Eric said. "That's what I wanted you to know."

"Well, of course she didn't kill herself," Antonia said abruptly. "Penelope was my daughter. I know she would never do something like that."

"Ah, yes," Eric said. "That's right, Mrs. Kostas."

Antonia turned to her husband. "I knew it. Didn't I tell you, Zaro? Penelope would *never* have done that. I *told* you!"

Lazaros was shaking his head in disbelief. "You are sure?"

Eric nodded. "I'm sure."

"And this man? This..." Antonia turned to Jane. "Your father? He is a killer and he is just running free?" She turned back to Eric. "You would marry a murderer's daughter?"

The lump in Eric's throat disappeared, burned away by sudden anger. "Now wait a second, Mrs. Kostas, Jane is not—"

"I get it." Jane's voice cut across the noise with the precision of a knife. "But, Mrs. Kostas, I understand your grief. I truly do. I understand it because I've experienced it for myself, by the hand of the same man."

Mrs. Kostas said nothing. Jane chewed on her lip, staring at the edge of the beaten Formica.

"Jane," Eric said, "you don't have to..."

But Jane shook her head with sudden vehemence, and instead of shrinking into herself yet again, she leaned across the table and took Mrs. Kostas's hand.

"Five weeks ago, I was pregnant. My mother and I were both kidnapped, and by the time Eric found us, I wasn't pregnant anymore. John Carson made sure of it." She sucked in a deep breath. Her body vibrated with contained rage. "I misspoke before, Mrs.

Kostas. John Carson is responsible for my existence because of one night with my mother, thirty years ago. But he is no father to me." She released Antonia's hand and tucked her own back into her lap like a maimed animal. "Just a monster, plain and simple."

A lone tear trailed down Jane's cheek. The hand still in Eric's gripped so hard, he'd see marks from her nails later.

But he wasn't letting go now.

"Oh, my," Antonia breathed. "Oh, my, I'm so..."

"You don't need to feel bad for me," Jane said. "I can't imagine it compares to losing a fully grown daughter."

"A loss is a loss. Just because my husband and I lost our daughter doesn't mean we can't feel your pain as well. We are so sorry." Antonia turned her brown eyes on Eric. "For the both of you."

Jane looked up. That flash. That spark. That fight. He hated that it had taken something like this to bring it out again, it was still there. And he had never been so relieved to see anything in his life.

"John Carson will meet justice for what he's done," Jane said. "Eric and I—we have resources too. No one is going to let that man go for what he has done to so many people. We can promise you that."

IN THE END, after a big lunch and a lot of shared stories about Penny, they had bid the Kostases farewell with promises to visit the restaurant soon ("more than once a decade!" Antonia had demanded). There was something different in the air when they stepped outside. Hope, maybe? Eric certainly felt that way as Jane let him hold her hand again while they waited with their other two detail for Tony to pull up the car.

Eric turned to Jane. "Thank you for doing that with me."

"You're welcome." She stared in the direction of the river, as if she could sense its transitory gleam through the haze of concrete buildings. "But I think we need to make another stop while we're on this redemption tour."

Eric frowned. "What's that?"

"I know what you're doing."

Eric bit back a smile. There it was. That attitude. "What's that, Lefferts?"

But she wasn't joking. "You need to talk to your mom. You need to tell her what you know. There's more there, I'm sure of it. Maybe she can help us keep our promise to Penny's parents."

His smile fell away. "I had another plan, you know. Go back to Boston. Maybe relive a few of our earlier moments. I was going to make you fall in love with me again, Lefferts."

To his surprise, Jane turned to him suddenly, grabbed the lapels on his jacket, and pulled him close enough that when she whispered, he could hear her clearly:

"Don't you know? It was your heart I fell in love with, you idiot. And I've never seen you open it more than you did today."

He cupped her face. He couldn't help it. Another tear slipped from under her glasses, and his thumb wiped it away.

"This hurts," she admitted. "But I think it's okay. It's better than feeling nothing all the time. I don't want to feel numb anymore. It's better than having all these emotions shoved away because feeling them is just too fucking much."

Eric wiped away another tear. "I'll feel them with you, Jane. I wanted her too, you know."

At the mention of the child, a few more tears free-fell. But she didn't break down completely, Eric noted, though maybe she needed to.

Let go, he begged mentally. *Let it all go.*

When she didn't, he sighed. The car pulled up, and after he brushed the last of her tears away, Eric placed a kiss on top of Jane's head.

"All right," he said. "You win. To my mother's we go."

After they got back in the car, Eric watched with concealed triumph as Jane pulled a small cosmetics bag from her bag and removed a pencil, a tube of lipstick, and a compact.

"I'm going to need to change before we go over there," she said as she dabbed the mascara smeared under her eyes. "Your mother won't have a heart-to-heart with me looking like a Cure groupie."

The car pulled into traffic, and she held up the mirror, carefully drawing a path of bright red around the rim of her full lips, then filling it in with the pencil, followed by the brighter, shinier hue of the lipstick. When she was finished, she smacked her lips with satisfaction. Eric was transfixed.

Jane turned, finally noticing his stare with something resembling satisfaction. "Don't say anything," she murmured as she tucked the makeup back into her purse. "Just let it be."

So he did. But it was *definitely* a good sign.

TWENTY-FOUR

"It's going to be emotional enough, right?" Jane called from her room as Eric waited for her to change. "I have a feeling that even seeing combat boots on her Italian marble will make things harder for your mom."

Honestly, Eric didn't really give a good goddamn about what kinds of shoes might ruin Heather's floors. But he did like that for the first time in a month, Jane seemed to care about what she wore. So he waited patiently while she tried on at least a few different outfits before settling on a navy wool dress over a pair of slouching black boots, and then spent another thirty minutes in the bathroom. It was worth it. When she walked out with her sleek black-brown hair hanging in very pullable waves, her lips a deep, kissable scarlet, her black-lined eyes looking sharply at him through her favorite gold-rimmed glasses, Eric felt like he gained another two inches just looking at her.

There she was. *Finally*.

"What are you looking at?" she asked as she put in a pair of diamond studs—the ones he had surprised her with for her birthday.

Eric rose from the couch and approached slowly, taking her in.

"My fucking beautiful wife," he said, and then, before he could help himself, slipped a hand around her waist. He just wanted to feel her again. Touch her. Smell her.

She stilled, but allowed their cheeks to brush together.

"Well, hello to you too." Her hands crept up his chest. She laid her palms flat over his shirt front, pressing one over his heart. It gave a strong thump.

I miss you, Eric wanted to say. *I need you. Will you come back to me completely, or is this just for today?*

He desperately wanted to kiss her, pull her into the bedroom, remind her in much more physical ways what he felt for her.

But. She wasn't ready yet.

"'Who dreams that beauty passes like a dream?'" Eric blurted out, unable to hold back completely.

"What's that?" Jane wondered, still rubbing her cheek to his like a cat marking its territory.

Eric continued, holding her still. "'For these red lips, with all their mournful pride, mournful that no new wonder may betide...'"

"Yeats again?"

Eric nodded into her hair.

Against his cheek, Jane smiled. "Are you back to talking poetry to me, Mr. de Vries?"

God, he loved hearing her call him that again. Eric leaned back and pushed a strand of hair out of her eyes, enjoying the new warmth he saw there. "I'll always talk poetry to you, pretty girl."

Her eyes closed, like it was almost too much. "It helps. It really does."

Fucking hell, a victory. Well, she'd better be ready. He'd be dragging out every volume of poetry he owned if he could get her to call him Mr. de Vries again.

"Thank you for waiting for me," she whispered.

The remaining lines of Yeats's verse echoed through his memory, seeming almost too apt for the moment: *Troy passed away in one high funereal gleam, and Usna's children died.*

In the end, Eric just wrapped his hand around her neck and urged her head to lie on his shoulder. She sighed with something resembling content and allowed her body to mold to his.

"I miss you too," she said in response to his silent thoughts. "We'll get it back, Eric, I promise. We'll get *us* back."

"I know we will," he said, his arms tightening around her. "It's already coming."

THEY ARRIVED at the familiar house on Lexington and Sixty-Sixth just as the clouds in the sky began sprinkling a harsh, cold rain. Eric held an umbrella over them both, providing shelter as they climbed the steps of the brownstone, trailed by Tony while the other two detail waited in the car.

"Is this where you grew up?" Jane asked as Eric rang the doorbell.

He nodded. "Until I was eleven, maybe twelve. Then I moved into my grandmother's penthouse." He didn't mention that memories of the old place had been rushing back more and more. To the point where he wondered if he should dig out some of those old journals he started keeping just after his father's death. Maybe there was something there. Something else he needed to remember.

That is, if his mother couldn't shine her own light on things.

Jane clearly wanted more, but the heavy oak door opened, and Heather appeared. Her large gray eyes, nearly as expressive as her son's, opened wide.

"Oh!" she said. "I—well, this is a surprise."

They stood awkwardly on the stoop while the rain streamed over the umbrella.

"Jane, we are so glad you're back safe, truly."

"Thank you," Jane demurred.

Eric fought the need to take her hand and tuck her into his side. She wouldn't appreciate being diminished, he thought. But at the same time, the awkwardness of this exchange, when his mother and wife had barely interacted much over the last several months, was painful.

"Mom," he said. "We need to talk. Can we come in?"

Heather glanced at them curiously, taking in the umbrella, the rain, the hulking security agent behind them. They made an imposing bunch. "I—well, I did have a lunch, but—yes, yes. Okay, come in."

Eric signaled that Tony could wait in the car, then allowed his mother to usher them inside the house that genuinely hadn't changed much since he was a boy. Same floors. Same tasteful furniture. Same art. The primary differences were things like photos—the ones he remembered of his father were missing completely, replaced by one or two of Heather and her husband.

Heather excused herself to cancel her lunch date, then reappeared having changed out of her tasteful suit into a more comfortable pair of pants, sweater, and rose-printed top. The pattern made Eric pause. How many times had his father swung Heather around in dresses that looked just like that?

He shook his head. "No Horace?" he asked of his stepfather, whom Heather had married over twenty years ago.

Even as an adolescent, Eric had barely known the man. He and Heather had gotten married not even a year after Jacob passed. Horace Keeler was a short, squat, somewhat effeminate man, the polar opposite of the tower of bright Dutch heritage that was Jacob de Vries. Horace had always seemed painfully disinterested in Eric. But by the time he married Heather, Eric had already moved out anyway.

Even so, Eric got the distinct impression that his mother and Horace Keeler lived pretty separate lives and had for some time. Horace hadn't even attended the wedding or his grandmother's funeral.

And no one had said a word.

"He's away on business," Heather said as she took their coats. "At the house in Orlando for the next few weeks. I think."

Separate lives indeed.

Eric just nodded. His stepfather's "business" primarily consisted of commercial real estate developments—strip malls outside of the city, mostly. Small-time operations.

Heather guided them into the sitting room, thanking Jane politely when she complimented the decor. "Well," she said once everyone was settled onto the Georgian chairs and Paul Follot sofa. "To what do I owe this surprise?"

Eric glanced at Jane, who just raised an eyebrow. This might have been her idea, but it was his show.

He cleared his throat. "Ah, Mom. Well, Nina said she kept you apprised of what happened in Korea, right?"

Heather's slim body wilted. "Yes. Such a tragedy, really. Jane, I'm so very sorry. For you both. As for John...there's absolutely no excuse for what he's done."

She didn't, Eric noted, seem surprised. Sad, yes. But surprised by Carson's actions? No.

She glanced between them. "I gather he hasn't been found yet."

Beside him, Jane tensed. This time, Eric did take her hand and wouldn't let her pull it out of his lap.

"Not yet," he said. "But it's only a matter of time. The man has been accused of treason. The second he steps into the United States or a country with an extradition treaty, his bed is made for him."

"Treason?" Now Heather looked genuinely alarmed. "Whatever for?"

"Mom."

She strongly resembled a deer in headlights. "What?"

"Dad's journal is with the FBI now. You wanted me to read it, so I assume you have too."

Heather worried her jaw for a moment, then nodded.

"Then you know what's in it," Eric continued. "Their dealings in Hwaseong and Goseong. Together with the P.I.'s files, the journal makes a strong case for treason. John Carson has been setting up a nuclear weapons operation in conjunction with the North Koreans since the eighties. He's in deep shit."

Heather covered her mouth with a slim hand, as if she could hardly bear the news. "Dear God," she murmured. "I read them, yes, but I never knew...oh, Johnny, what were you thinking?"

Eric frowned. So Johnny *was* Carson. The sweetened version of the bastard's name made him feel sick, and if the way Jane was squeezing his hand was any indication, she didn't like it either.

"Look," he said. "It is horrific. But it's not what Jane and I wanted to talk about today."

Heather dropped her hand. "Eric, I'm not sure what you think I can offer. I don't know anything about treason, honestly. And—"

"Mom, I *remember*," he interrupted. "That day. When Grandmother came to get me. John Carson came and threatened you and me." He leaned across the wide blue ottoman. "Dad's journal had some other interesting things about you. Things I couldn't quite make sense of. The North Korean deal explains why he and Dad fell out, but not his obsession with this family. With me and Jane." He arched a brow. "John Carson has been one step ahead of us for years, and he just cost us our own child." Fucking hell, would his voice *ever* remain still when he said that? "If there is anything else you can offer here, we need to know. Now."

Had she always been this shifty? This skittish? Eric was ashamed to say he didn't really know his own mother that way. But after she had rearranged every goddamn drape of her clothing, she did finally look up. And her deep silvery eyes, the ones she had given him, mirrored his and Jane's sorrow.

"Oh, Eric." Heather's voice was barely above a whisper. "I didn't want to send you away. But it was for your own good. Johnny was... well, I won't say in love, because it was never that. A person doesn't do the things he did out of love. But he thought it was. He was... fixated...on me."

Eric sat back once again, and Jane fell into his side, like she was preparing for a terrible ghost story. Which, Eric thought, it sort of was. He draped his hand over her knee, urging her close.

"Mom," he said carefully, "I think you had better tell me everything that went on between you, Dad, and John Carson back then. Especially if people have lost their lives over it. Especially if others might too."

Heather swallowed, and then she stood up.

"Where are you going?" Eric demanded.

She carefully said, "Eric, you can't possibly think I would be able to do this without a glass of Chardonnay. I'll be back in a moment."

A few minutes later, she returned carrying a tray containing two wine glasses, another drink, and a bottle of wine. She set a glass of vodka in front of Eric, then proceeded to pour the wine into the other two glasses.

"Mom, it's not even one in the afternoon," Eric said.

"Don't be such a square," Jane replied, happily accepting her glass of wine. "I cannot think of a day that better deserves a bit of alcohol. Can you?"

"What in the world do you think we would drink at lunch anyway?" Heather remarked. "Did you forget everything while you were away, my darling?"

Well, he wasn't going to argue with that. Eric took his glass, swirled the liquor around the ice cubes, then took a long sip. Fucking hell, it did taste good.

Eric watched his mother gulp down half her glass. Well, if it would loosen her tongue, he supposed it didn't matter.

"All right," Heather said quietly after she topped off her glass. "I should probably start at the beginning."

TWENTY-FIVE

"We were all friends in college," Heather began once she had topped off her glass again. "I was...well, Eric, you know this, but, Jane, perhaps you don't. I didn't come from a wealthy family. My parents were from a small town in New Jersey."

Jane coughed. *"You're* from the land of Springsteen, Mrs. Keeler?"

Heather offered a wry, satisfied look. "Yes. But Pompton Lakes is better known for cancer than for rock and roll."

"The Stallsmiths," Eric murmured, enjoying Jane's sudden recognition. Clearly she was remembering their first meeting, when he had introduced himself using that name, not de Vries.

"I attended Princeton on a scholarship," Heather continued. "Which was where I met Jacob. And John Carson."

The boys were in the same fraternity, seniors when Heather was a freshman. She had met Carson first at a mixer.

"Johnny was always single-minded, and he was interested in me from the beginning. Because we had similar backgrounds, he said. We were going through the same thing, learning to acclimate to society at an Ivy League school."

THE LOVE TRAP   261

"What do you mean, similar backgrounds?" Jane asked. "I thought he came from wealth. Wasn't his father a big arms manufacturer?"

Heather turned to her. "That's a common misconception, one that Johnny fostered himself. His grandfather owned Chariot, yes, but John Carson grew up in Montana the son of a gun shop owner and a housewife. They were hardly a fountain of wealth. Johnny's grandfather put him through school to become an engineer so he could work for the company. He was quite brilliant, really. Double majored in business and some kind of science. Physics, I think it was."

"Nuclear?" Eric ventured. Jane snorted into his shoulder.

Heather looked uneasy. "Well, yes, come to think of it. He actually started a Ph.D., near the end, but he dropped out of that program."

"What happened?" Jane prodded.

"It was just tragic. First, John's mother died of cancer, just after he graduated, poor thing. Then it was his grandfather, a few months later, and he shocked everyone by leaving Johnny all of Chariot. Then his father died too in a car accident. Johnny went back to Montana, sold the store, and put nearly everything back into Chariot." Heather shook her head. "Can you even fathom that much loss in one year?"

"I can imagine it," Eric said dryly.

Jane didn't move a muscle. She didn't even seem to breathe.

Heather blinked between them, perhaps realizing how tone-deaf her comments were. "Yes. Well. When John came back, he wanted Jake to invest. That was a major disagreement between them, you see. Johnny didn't like rules. He didn't like agreements. He had his own plans and didn't like people asking questions, pulling things apart. Which, of course, Jake always did."

"So he's a cowboy," Jane said. Her voice was toneless, gray somehow. Eric peered at her curiously, but he wouldn't meet his eyes.

"He certainly imagined himself as one. But I'm getting ahead of myself. Their troubles, well, it was about more than just business." Heather sighed. "Before his family essentially disappeared, Johnny took me out a few times. But it didn't last, because on our third date, I met his roommate. Your father."

John Carson didn't stand a chance. From the second they met, Heather and Jacob were inseparable. Heather fell head over heels for the charismatic heir, blissfully unaware of exactly who he was for several months, well after they were far too in love for the white lie to matter.

"Oh, you should have seen him, Eric," Heather said dreamily, the effects of the wine clearly kicking in. "Captain of the crew team, president of the fraternity. A born leader. Tall, handsome, like the sun followed him everywhere. You look so like him, darling, you really do."

"Like the sun," Jane murmured.

Eric turned. "What's a sun without its moon?" he said.

Jane shivered. Good or bad? He honestly couldn't tell. Her mood had shifted again as Heather had started telling this story, but Eric was struggling to read it.

There was a drop of wine on her lip. *Fuck it*, Eric thought as he leaned close. Quickly, he kissed the drop away. Jane started, then inched slightly away.

Fuck, Eric thought. Wrong fucking move.

He turned back to his mother. "So what happened? You jilted Carson for Dad? That seems like ancient history, especially after only a few dates. Not really the stuff of lifelong grudges."

Heather studied the rim of her wine glass. "One would think. But John...did not take it well."

As it turned out, what Heather believed was a dalliance was something much more intense for Carson. It got to the point where he would spontaneously appear when she and Jacob were on a date. He stalked her to and from classes when Jacob wasn't around. Begged her to break it off, and when she didn't, appealed to Jacob's loyalties.

"I honestly never knew if it was me, or if it was because of your father. He seemed to want me more after he learned of Jacob's and my connection. He was always very jealous of Jake, of his family, his resources, his connections. The de Vries name, you know, was very well known on the Princeton campus. They have a hall named for them and several other buildings. Everyone knew who he was." Heather sighed again, perhaps out of nostalgia. "John simply wanted whatever Jake had. And your father, Eric, he had such a big heart. I think he felt guilty about stealing me away."

So although Jacob wasn't willing to end it, his guilt overcame him. He got Carson into the most exclusive fraternity. The best internships. The most exclusive clubs. Things that greased the wheels for the business Carson would eventually build after his father's death.

"Secret societies?" Jane asked tentatively.

Heather looked up with an alarmed expression. "I don't know what you're—"

"She knows, Mom."

Immediately, Heather's alarm transformed into pity. "Oh. Well. That's a shame." She shook her head. "They don't take kindly to their secrets getting out, Jane. They tend to react very...preemptively... toward anyone who discovers them."

Eric could only wonder how exactly his mother knew that. If the society had done something to her. And what it might be. Jane worried her skirt material between her fingers hard enough that her fingertips turned white.

But before Eric could ask, another thought popped into his mind. "In Dad's journals, there was a bunch of stuff about Caesar salads. Were those references to the society?"

Heather nodded. "Yes. Jake was absolutely terrible at keeping secrets. From me, anyway." She shook her head with a curious mix of rue and pleasure. "At any rate, he sacrificed a lot to help John into that ridiculous group. Your grandfather was not at all pleased with him."

"Grandfather?" Eric asked. "What did he have to do with it?"

"Eric." Heather cocked her head. "Did you really read the

journal?"

Eric frowned. "Several times."

"And you must know that despite its Hellenistic references, the Janus society hasn't been democratic since its inception. It's a monarchy. And its leaders have been almost exclusively de Vries." She cocked her head. "You've all been 'making Caesar salads' for generations. Isn't that what Jake wrote?"

Eric's head exploded. Caesar salads. *Caesar*. His grandfather had been the Caesar, and the title had been passed to Jacob upon his death.

"But it didn't work, did it?" Jane's voice, cut through his whir of thoughts with a renewed hopelessness that made Eric very uncomfortable.

Heather turned to her sympathetically and shook her head. "No, dear, it did not. John could not seem to let go of...me. Us. A few years later, he tried to break up our wedding. In nearly the same manner as he did your own."

Eric's eyes flew open. "*What?*"

Jane, however, remained silent. And apparently unsurprised as she stared at her hands.

Heather took a very long drink of her wine, draining the glass completely. "It wasn't quite at the altar. It was on the street. He was waiting for me on the steps of the church when I arrived from the hotel. You can ask your aunt Violet. She was a bridesmaid, after all."

"What did you say?" Jane asked.

"I told him—oh, God, I can't tell you how mortifying it is, but I swear, I would have said *anything* just to get off that street and inside the church. Eric, your father was waiting for me, and all I wanted to do was go to him."

"Mom. What did you say?"

"I had to," she said. "He wouldn't leave otherwise. He kept blocking the doors, and he wouldn't let go of my arm. All I wanted to do was find Jake!"

"Mom!"

"I told him it wasn't our time," Heather whispered. "That I had made a promise, and now I had to keep it. For now."

"For now?" Eric repeated. "For *now*? What in the hell did that mean? Were you planning to stop later?"

"Of course not! It meant I loved your father. But Johnny—he obviously took it differently." She shrank toward her empty wine glass. "He said he would wait for me. As long as it took. But I think... oh, lord, darling, I think he decided at one point that he would stop waiting. It was after he and your father had a serious falling out. Over that business in Korea."

Eric glanced at Jane, whose brow had lifted above the rim of her glasses.

Heather continued. "After Korea, John started coming around the house again, whenever Jacob left. It was worse when he went sailing—you remember how your father would leave on his trips, sometimes for weeks. It got so much worse. John would follow me on the street. On my way to the gym. Outside luncheons. He kept saying things like, it was our time now. It was his turn."

"Didn't you tell Dad?"

Heather shrugged. Her hopelessness, her utter weakness, was heartbreaking. "I did. But Jake wasn't scared of anyone. To his own detriment." With every memory, she seemed to wither even more. As did, Eric realized, the woman beside him.

No, Eric thought. He couldn't. It was too much. Could this really all be about a strange vendetta, about stealing a man's life? But it was all clicking into place.

He had to ask.

"Mom," he said carefully. "Did Carson have anything to do with Dad's death?"

Upon Jacob's death, the heir apparent to the Janus society—Eric —was about eleven. Far too young to be tapped. Which, for the first time in literally two hundred years, freed up the leadership of one of the most powerful secret societies the world had ever known. For John fucking Carson.

"I don't know," Heather said quietly. "Oh, Eric, I really don't. He never said anything. He had an excellent alibi. He was in Hong Kong on business, attending several benefits, seen at nearly all hours of the day. But Celeste...oh, Eric, I do think she suspected some kind of foul play." Heather stared at her nails. "I think she blamed me for his death. The day before he left, Jake and I had a terrible fight about John. And he...well, Celeste once suggested that if he had not been so angry, he might not have been so careless. And perhaps, he might have stayed home." Heather shook her head. "But I checked. John Carson didn't do it."

Neither Eric nor Jane said nothing. Jane seemed to be having a hard time breathing. *Fuck.* This was a bad idea. Even Eric wasn't sure if he could take this revelation on top of everything else. Eric knew they were both thinking the same thing: just because John Carson wasn't present for a death didn't mean he wasn't responsible.

Heather poured another large glass of wine. Eric swallowed.

"But why?" he asked finally. "If by some crazy reason, he did go after Dad, or at least planned to, why would it matter so much to him? The leadership of a stupid secret society? And years later, too."

"Perhaps. But on top of that, he was very angry. Not just with your father. With me."

Jane frowned. "What for?"

"Because," Heather said softly. "Because just before that day, I told him in no uncertain terms that I would never leave Jake. I told Johnny that I would never love him. And that he would never be half the man your father was." She gripped her glass. "He demanded the following week that your father abdicate his position as Caesar with the society. As a show of friendship, or something like that."

"Dad couldn't have done that," Eric argued. "That position is for life."

"I know, dear. I know. And by rights, it should have belonged to you one day. But instead, your father died long before you were ever old enough to be a part of it. Had I known you had been tapped, darling, I would have done everything I could to keep you from it."

Heather sighed with clear regret. "But as it were, staying away from you seemed to be the only thing I could do to keep you safe. Once Jake died, John seemed to think I was available to be his again. He didn't take it kindly when again, I said no."

"After Dad died, he *still* came for you?" Eric shook his head. It was beyond obsessive. It was sick.

It was a sickness, he supposed. Considering the hatred and resentment Carson had nursed against his nemesis, was any wonder that the idea of his own offspring procreating with Jacob's son had sent the man nearly insane?

Heather nodded. "It's the reason I married Horace so quickly. To keep us both safe. John was becoming unhinged. And, of course, incredibly powerful."

"Does Horace know?" Eric asked. "That you used him like this?"

"Horace was a dear friend of mine from high school," Heather replied. "He also happened to be a homosexual at a time where Wall Street wasn't particularly forgiving of his tastes."

At that revelation, Eric's jaw actually fell. "Horace is *gay?*"

He glanced at Jane, expecting to see her eyes spring open. But she was still staring at her dress, ruminating. Unresponsive. Fuck, they needed to finish this up and get out of here.

Unfortunately, they still needed to hear the rest.

"It was Celeste's idea. She thought the only way to keep John Carson at arm's length was to marry someone else. And keep you safe with her. She was right, of course. Horace needed a wife. I needed a barrier." Heather set her glass on the table and looked straight at her son. "Eric, you must remember how it was. I couldn't have loved anyone else the way I loved your father. He was..." Her inhale was shaky. "Jake was *everything* to me."

Eric's chest felt like it was caving in. Memories, so many memories of his parents' tiny moments, all the ways they broke the codes of decorum of the Upper East Side. Secret glances across a cocktail party. Kisses when they thought no one was watching.

Yes, he remembered. He understood exactly what his parents had shared, because he felt it now with the woman sitting beside him, the one looking very much like she needed a life preserver.

Tentatively, he reached into her lap and pried her hand away from her dress, then raised her fingers to o his lips and pressed a long kiss to her knuckles. Jane vibrated, but her hand was limp. Shit. *Shit.*

But something else was missing from the story.

"Mom," Eric said, "I understand why he might nurse a vendetta against you. But why me? Why now? Dad's been gone more than twenty years. You've been long married. Why did Carson care so much that he has been actively trying to ruin my life since all this happened? Coming after me and Jane. Penny, even. Did you know he killed her too, Mom? He sent his fucking henchmen, but he killed her too!"

His emotions got away from him at the end. Jane covered her face with her hands, like she couldn't bear to hear anymore of it. But Heather, for her part, just looked sad as she watched her son fall apart. Sad, but not even one bit surprised.

"Oh, Eric," she said. "I keep telling you. You are your father's son. John Carson doesn't look at you and see a new person. He sees the next version of a man who, in his eyes, stole everything from him that ever mattered. You are the only ghost he can't exorcise, just like I am that last treasure he can't possess. For John Carson, the de Vries family has long represented the only obstacles to happiness. Control. Power. Belonging. Stealing from you and Jane—" She shook her head, as if only now she couldn't believe the lengths this man would come to assert his control and dominance. "It was just an extension of the motivations he has had his entire adult life. He wanted me, Eric. He wanted your father. Our life. Now, I can't even imagine what he thinks of his own DNA mixing with the flesh of his mortal enemy. The son of the man he blamed for ruining his life marries his only daughter?" She she picked up her wine glass and tossed back the rest of its contents. "It tipped him over the edge."

TWENTY-SIX

The sky was darkening when Eric guided Jane to the car, keeping a hand at her back, though she barely seemed to notice him. If she had been quieter as the conversation with Heather had progressed, she was back to being a shadow. She didn't seem to notice the heavy rain or the wind that howled up from the river. Even through his own shock at hearing the story, Eric was worried. Very worried. Something wasn't right.

They fell into the back of the car and just sat as Tony waited for Eric's direction.

"Well?" Eric said at last. "Where to?"

Jane still hadn't looked at him. It took her a moment to realize he was even speaking to her. "What?"

"We did what I came here to do. And then what you thought I needed to do. Where do you want to go? Back to Boston, or—"

"No." Jane's quick gaze darted up to find his. "I want to go home."

Home. There was only one place she could have meant by that. Not her parents' old house in Evanston, or Skylar's compound in Brookline. She glanced in roughly the direction of the west side of the island, where their apartment stood.

Eric's mouth quirked with satisfaction. "Wherever you go, pretty girl," he murmured, then, watching her the entire time, tentatively picked up Jane's hand and pressed a kiss to her knuckles, just like he had done inside the house.

But instead of rolling her eyes and saying something like "God, you're corny," she simply let her hand drop to her lap once he was finished. Then she pressed her nose to the window, and it was like Eric wasn't even there.

Eric sighed, then signaled to Tony, who pulled away from the curb. Heather's townhouse disappeared into the winter gloom. Eric pulled out his phone. He wasn't ready to sink into his own thoughts completely. Not yet.

"Zola, hey," he said when the assistant DA picked up. "It's Eric de Vries. I...look, Jane and I are back in town, and we just had a conversation with my mother that will interest you. If the DA is still building his own case against—"

"We are," Zola interrupted.

That was all he said, probably because that was all he *could* say, depending on who was in the room. Or even the line.

"Well, if you want to come by tomorrow morning, I can tell you what she said," Eric replied. "But I'd like to talk about my father's death too. There's something strange about all of this, put together."

When Eric hung up, Jane was still staring out the window. She hadn't moved an inch.

Eric couldn't take it anymore. "What is it?" He asked. Goddammit. That hopelessness was sucking her back in, like some twisted vortex, and had been doing so since they had gotten to Heather's. What the hell had happened?

Jane sighed and stared down at her hands, then rubbed a thumb slowly over her wrist. Her fingernails were plain and chewed down, missing the sheen of black or red polish. There were a few scabs on her cuticles, places where she had bitten too far or cut too much.

"Sometimes," she said quietly, "I wonder if it's the universe telling us something. I'm honestly not sure if this will ever end."

Eric took her hand again and played with it between his knees, pressing his thumbs into the center of her palm. Jane's hands were so graceful—had he ever thought to tell her that? Her wrists were small enough that his thumb and forefinger could encircle them completely.

And yet, she was the strongest person he knew in so many ways. He had never known anyone so indelibly herself. He wanted more than anything to help her find that again.

He massaged each of her fingertips. "I thought today would help."

"Help what?"

"You know."

She quieted yet again. Then: "It did. At first. I..." She shook her head, like she was clearing cobwebs. "I mean, it's one thing to hear the stories about Penny from you. It's another to see it, witness the relationships. I wish I had been more forgiving of you back then. When we met, I mean."

"Hey." Eric released her hand so he could slip a finger under her chin, asking her to look at him. "That's not why I took you to Queens."

But she pulled her chin away and refused to look at him. "Still. I wish I had been better. You deserved better."

"I thought it would be good to know...I don't know. You're not the only one he's hurt, Jane. You're not alone."

At that, she finally looked up, and the green in her eyes blazed with pain. "Aren't I?" She said it so quietly, he almost couldn't hear her.

"No."

Her eyes watered like she wanted to cry. Eric wished she would. That was the real point of all of this. That by witnessing, talking, getting everything out, she could begin to let go of her own emotions too.

Otherwise she was going to break. And he really had no idea what that would look like.

But instead of crying, she just turned back to the window. And by the time they reached the apartment, she had withdrawn completely.

They exited the car, flanked by the other two security. Their footsteps echoed up the turn-of-the-century stairs. Jane didn't look at him once.

"Thanks," Eric said to the guards after they unlocked the apartment. "There shouldn't be any visitors today, but you have the list."

They nodded and turned back down the stairs to their post. When the door closed, the abyss gaped again. Eric wanted to punch something.

Jane stared around their place like she had never seen it, though she had changed her clothes here only a few hours earlier.

"Do you...would you like another glass of wine?" Eric offered as he hung his coat on the rack. "Mom took care of most of that bottle herself, so I think we earned a few. There might be a few cans of PBR in the fridge. I was thinking about ordering in from Le Zie too, if that sounds good."

He was babbling like an idiot, but goddammit, her silence was unnerving. She was still just standing there, her trench coat dripping onto the hardwoods. The same floors she was always squawking about if he dared not remove his shoes.

Eric approached and helped her coat off. Her arms were noodles. Fucking hell, where had she gone?

"What would you have done if I had died too?" Her voice was a staggered whisper. "Would you have moved on quickly, do you think? Found another woman to help you keep your fortune?"

Eric turned from the coatrack and frowned. "Where is this coming from?"

Jane's eyes were dulled behind clouded, rain-spotted lenses. "I'm sure you could have had your pick."

"Jane, don't be stupid."

I'm not stupid, you asshole. Had he only imagined she had said that? *Yes.* She hadn't spoken at all, was just standing there in the same spot, arms wrapped around her waist while she shivered.

"You're in shock," Eric said, shooting for kindness this time. He reached out to rub her arm, but she stepped out of reach.

"Can you be in shock for over a month?"

Goddammit. This whole day had been a mistake, hadn't it? One step forward at the Kostases', five thousand backward with his mother. Fucking hell.

They stared at each other for a long time. Jane's chin quivered. Finally, she removed her glasses and started to polish them with a bit of her dress fabric. She kept doing it far past the point where they were cleaned.

Eric turned over the mess of negative thoughts running through his mind again and again.

"I'm going to change out of these wet clothes," he said. "You should do the same. Take a hot shower or something. Then we can have a drink or two and just...process."

Jane didn't answer. Eric slumped and turned toward the bedrooms. Five minutes. He just needed to five minutes to reset. And then he could come back to her. Because he wasn't going let her slide into nothingness for another several weeks. Absolutely not.

AS HE RIFLED through the folded shirts in his closet, it struck Eric, not for the first time, that this apartment didn't fit. He hadn't ever said anything, but he'd always hated the way he and Jane had never been able to cohabitate completely. Her things were still mostly kept in the bedroom she had repurposed as a studio. They were both such clothes horses, and the master closet simply couldn't hold everything they owned. Meanwhile, there were two other bedrooms that served as an "office," he never used, a guest room that sat empty.

Even once they had finally come together organically within

these walls, it had still always felt as though she was spending the night at his place, or he at hers. The living room, the kitchen—yes, they were shared spaces. But as units, Jane and he still existed apart. The apartment itself wouldn't allow otherwise.

Eric stripped off his wet clothes and replaced them with a pair of gray joggers. He ran his hands over his stomach, then, out of pure impulse fell to the floor and pumped out twenty pushups, followed by another set of sit-ups. He hadn't been at the gym as much as he wanted, and he was starting to feel it. He didn't want to get soft. He wanted to feel...ready.

When he stood again, the sudden activity cast his muscles in high relief. Eric considered walking out with his shirt off. Jane never could resist the sight of his six-pack, which is why he deployed it sparingly, not wanting to cheapen its hard-won value.

Eric shook his head and pushed back his rain-slick hair. No, now wasn't the time for flirtation. He had managed coaxed her out of her shell a few times today. He could do it again. Compassion. That's what was needed. And then, once she'd softened, maybe another go with her lipstick just to make her smile.

He shoved on an old Harvard t-shirt. It wasn't until he had towel-dried his hair that he realized he hadn't heard the telltale thumps of Jane's boots or rush of running water in the bathroom. The apartment was still silent.

Too silent.

Every hair on the back of his neck stood up.

"Jane?" he called. "Are you in the bath?"

There was no answer.

"Fuck," Eric muttered as he walked out of his room, still barefoot. "Jane?"

He found her standing at the kitchen sink in the kitchen. His heartbeat quieted when he saw her standing there, straight-backed. Just what had he thought had happened? He really was becoming paranoid. Maybe he wasn't the only one struggling with shock or PTSD.

"No, no, no," she was muttering to herself. Her shoulders tensed, like she was working on something, with the same posture people had when they were grating vegetables or scrubbing a pan. "I can't. I c-can't." There was a loud sniff. *"I can't do this anymore."*

Eric approached. "Can't do what?"

"Ah!" Jane shouted as she whirled around.

"Oh, Jesus! Jane!"

She was bleeding. The white shirtsleeves under her wool dress had been hastily pushed up to her elbows. One had come loose, however, and was stained with rows of bright crimson stripes that mirrored those slicing the skin of her other forearm. She held a knife in one hand, and her eyes, were swollen and red-rimmed, like she was just about to start bawling.

For a moment, all Eric could see was Penny. Lying in the bathtub, the long, nasty cuts in her arms raw and cold. Water the color of a dusty red rose.

His heart practically stopped.

"Eric?"

Jane's voice, so weak and threaded with confusion, knocked him out of his stupor.

"Jane." Suddenly, he was all movement, scrambling across the apartment, knocking over one of his barstools in his hurry to reach her. "What happened? Holy shit, I'll call 911."

"Eric, d-don't." Her voice was thick with stifled tears as she held her arms in front of her, like she was preemptively pushing him away. "It's fine, I promise. I'm o-okay."

"What in the fuck?" Eric's mind whirled as he grabbed one of her hands so he could examine her arm. "What the hell is this?"

The cuts on her arm weren't deep, like he'd originally thought. They were horizontal and shallow, neat stripes across porcelain skin. But a violation nonetheless.

"What the fuck are you doing?" he demanded over and over again as he pulled Jane into him, uncaring for the blood staining his clothes. "What in the hell were you thinking?"

"I just—oh, God, I just—" She hiccupped over harsh, dry sobs. She wanted to cry. Maybe she was trying to cry. But she wasn't still. "I just couldn't take it anymore."

"Couldn't take what?" Eric reached around her and yanked a stream of paper towels from the counter and pressed them to the wounds, most which, he realized with relief, had already stopped bleeding.

But they were still wounds. That Jane had given to herself.

He hoisted her easily onto the counter. Fuck, she was so light. Too light. Jane folded over, cradling her wounded arms in her lap while he wet another few towels to clean her up. They didn't speak, both of them entranced with his brisk, careful movements. But that didn't mean the energy in the room had dissipated. Eric vibrated as he worked.

"Why?" he finally asked once he was sure he could speak calmly. "What couldn't you take?"

Jane's arm quivered in his grasp. "The numbness," she said finally. "I—it was back. You couldn't tell?"

He dabbed at her other arm, hating the way the blood seeped easily into the wet paper. "I could tell. At my mother's, you jus started to go somehow. But I thought—shit. Jane, everyone is helping. Things are looking up. Zola, my mother. We're taking care of it. We're coming through."

"Not me," Jane replied with a despondency that scraped his soul. "I—you were pulling me out of for a bit. When you took me to Astoria, showed me that past. I know how hard it was for you to do that. I know. I *know*."

Eric's chest swelled. "I know you know, gorgeous."

"You were willing to do that for me. Show me your grief, your guilt. Accept the responsibility. You're so much stronger than me." Jane fingered his wrist, which was clean and smooth. "You could move through your past to make a better life for yourself. But I—I don't think I can move past mine. Every time I close my eyes, I see her. The baby. What she would have been." She closed her eyes, like she was in the worst kind of pain. "It swallows me up, and so I push it away. I numb myself, because I can't take it otherwise. But I shouldn't be allowed to feel nothing. I should feel every inch of pain that you and I and everyone else feels because of the man who gave me half my DNA. So I..."

She gestured weakly toward the paring knife in the sink. And then, as if out of curiosity, she picked it up again, holding it like she was testing the weight.

"Jane..."

"My dad," she whispered as she held the knife to her thigh, pressing the tip into the white of her skin. "He used to tell me about some of his patients. The veterans. POWs. They would come back from war, and they just couldn't deal with it. With life." She took a heavy, staggered breath and squeezed her eyes shut. A drop of blood appeared under the knife's tip.

"Jane!" Eric took the knife from her and set it on the island behind him, out of her reach.

"Don't!" Jane exploded. "It was going to help!"

"Do you think this is going to bring them back?" Eric demanded. "Penny, my dad? The baby? Do you think that cutting yourself up like a piece of fucking meat is going to make a goddamn thing better?"

"Why don't you blame me? You should. You should punish me any way you know how. Because if you won't, I will!" She bent over, hands clutched at her heart, like its pounding was too much too take.

"I'm not going to punish you, Jane."

"Then who?" Jane whimpered. "If not you, then who? *I* made the decision to go to Korea. *I* left you rotting in that jail. *I* made myself a sitting duck when everyone told me not to go. I didn't know what else to do. But if I hadn't, she would still be here, Eric. *It's my fault!*"

She shrieked the last words at the top of her lungs and buried her face in her hands, her glasses slipping off and to the floor. Eric grabbed her shoulders to keep her from falling off the counter.

"Oh, God," she said over and over again as her sobs shook through her like miniature cyclones, tossing her back and forth in a sea of misery. "I can't, I can't, I can't."

Eric inhaled and exhaled with purpose. "Listen to me. You are not at fault, Jane. The only person who is responsible for anyone's death here is John Carson. That's it. That's all."

"I had a name picked out. You called her a girl, and so in my head, I thought we might name her Jaki Carol. Like—like our dads."

And then, finally, she broke completely, her body, no longer hurt, able to withstand the gusting sobs that nearly forced Eric back. But instead of letting her push him away, he wrapped his arms tightly around her frail body, clutching so hard he thought he might smother her. But the tighter he held her, the tighter she grasped, seeking purchase on his arms, his neck, his chest. She poured every drop of her misery and shame into his shoulder. And he never. Let. Go.

"It's not your fault, Jane," Eric said again and again as he rocked her back and forth. "Do you hear me? Baby, it's *not your fault.*"

At the sound of the common nickname from Eric's mouth—more out of desperation than because it was something he had ever said before—Jane's sobs only worsened, turning into great, choking waves of pain. "Where is it?" she keened. "Oh my God, the knife. I swear to God, I want it right. Here." She pounded on her chest.

Eric reached back and picked up the knife again. He examined its edge. A drop of her blood had dried on the tip.

"Is that really how you feel?" he asked as he stepped out of her grasp.

Jane hiccupped, found the knife in his hand, and stretched out her own.

"Yes," she implored. "Please!"

"Fine." The gravity of Eric's voice echoed around the apartment, a growl from a cave. "But you're going to have to do it to me first."

At that, Jane's mouth opened, but no noise came out. Her body gave one more great, silent, shaking sob.

Eric pulled down the collar of his shirt and pressed the tip of the knife to the base of his neck. "You want penance? Then you're going to have to dispense it too."

"W-what?"

The steel pricked his skin. He genuinely wondered if he would feel that twinge for the rest of his life. Moments like these tended to leave all number of scars.

"You think I don't carry the guilt too, Jane? I was locked up for two fucking weeks because I was too naive to think one step ahead. I should have known what Carson was planning the second Jude suggested I share tips with the society. I should have anticipated everything."

"But, but..." Jane trailed off, shaking her head. "No, it wasn't your fault..." Her words were weak. Her eyes were round, wide pools of pain. And, Eric saw with a gust of relief, love.

"It's all I can think about," he said. "I'm obsessed. Just like you. She was *our* baby, Jane. We both lost her. Just like I lost my fiancée. My father. Everyone else I have ever fucking cared about."

She was right. Sometimes it was too fucking much.

So he did it. He pulled the knife over his skin, allowing the blade to slice through him the way her actions had already done. The way this *life* had already done. Jane stared with horror as blood welled from the cut, gathering in a thick drop that fell over his collarbone and stained the white of his shirt, a blurry rose blooming across the snowy expanse.

"Eric, no," she whispered as he drew the knife down his chest. "Don't."

"You hurt yourself, you hurt me too," he said as he pressed the weapon over the cotton. "You want to stab yourself in the heart? Then you'll do it to me first. Because we're in this together, Jane Lee Lefferts *de Vries*. For richer or poorer. Better or for worse. Until death do us part."

He allowed her to pull him back between her legs. Her hand rose, first to remove the knife from his hand, and then, to his relief, to toss it into the sink—the further one, where neither of them could reach it.

"This is so fucked up," she whispered as she touched the cut on his collarbone. Blood stained her fingertips. "You and I—we are *so* fucked up."

His hand closed over hers, and he kissed her. Not a light peck, or the careful brushes he had allowed himself today. But a real kiss, one that conveyed the intensity of everything they both felt. Not just now. But all the time.

"We are," he agreed. "This shit broke me, Jane, just like it broke you. But I refuse—I *refuse*—to let it break what we are together."

"Eric—" Her voice was cut off by another choked sob, but before he could ask her "what," she was throwing herself at him, pressing her lips to his again in a muffled, stumbling, awkward display of passion, the likes of which he hadn't seen from her in months. Maybe years.

Once upon a time, they had found each other through lifetimes of fury and estrangement from the people they loved. They had healed each other during those strange years, only to ruin each other again and again.

But it was the separations that really broke them. That had been the truth ever since they had met.

This woman might be the death of him. But without her, he was a corpse anyway.

"I love you," he said between kiss after torrid kiss. "You are *essential* to me. Like the air I breathe. The water I drink. I can't fucking exist without you, Jane. Can't. Fucking. Live."

Jane bit his lip, then groaned painfully as he bit hers right back.

"Do you?" she wondered. "Do you really?"

Her doubt nearly broke him all over again.

And so, Eric did the hardest thing he had done all day—which was really saying something, considering.

He pushed her back and stepped away.

"What? Where?" Jane sputtered from lips now swollen from kissing, not crying. "Where are you going?"

Eric held out a hand and helped her down from the counter, then
guided her toward his bedroom. *No*, he thought stubbornly. *Their*
bedroom.

"I have to show you something. And after I do, I *never* want you
to ask that question again."

TWENTY-SEVEN

Eric's heart beat like a drum as he unlocked the safe next to his side of the bed. It was new, purchased just a few weeks ago.

It took him two tries to even get his fingers correctly placed on the fingerprint reader, another to get the stupid door open. He had never been so nervous in his life. Not when he had asked either woman in his life to marry him. Not when he had taken the bar exam. Not when he had officially been voted chairman of the board of his family's company.

Nothing compared to this moment.

He pulled out one of the several Moleskine journals and left the others inside, along with the rest of the safe's contents: his passport and vital documents, the collection of evidence against John Carson, spare cash, and the pistol he had purchased from the Beretta Gallery on Seventy-First and Madison a few days ago. A few well-placed donations had sped up his license applications from three months to two weeks. He really wasn't sure anything could overcome the surreal feeling of walking into a gun shop on the Upper East Side.

He closed the safe and turned around to face Jane, who sat on the bed with her knees pulled into her chest, her glasses back in place over her reddened nose.

"Do you remember when I found you, Skylar, and Brandon snooping in my place?" he asked.

Jane nodded wordlessly.

"Do you remember when I grabbed something out of the safe?" He quirked a brow at her. "The combination is eleven twenty-eight eighty-seven, by the way."

Her full mouth fell. "My birthday?"

He allowed himself a small smile. He'd surprised her. That didn't often happen. "I should probably change it now that we're married. It's too easy to guess." He looked down at the journal, then held it out to her.

Tentatively, she took it. "In Boston, I assumed this had something to do with the society or my father. It looked like you were hiding something more in there."

But Eric just shook his head. "No, gorgeous. It had to do with you. After Carson took me, I needed to remember us, Jane. What we meant."

"But you were so awful to me," she murmured. "You acted like you hated me."

Guilt shot through him. "I was trying to protect you. And I think we both know how long that lasted."

She blinked at him. His guilt grew.

Eric edged toward her and nodded at the journal. "Open it, pretty girl."

After another moment, Jane opened the book. A lock of purple hair fell into her lap. She held it up. "Is this...is this my *hair*?"

Eric smiled bashfully. "It is. You gave it to me, remember?"

"Yes, but...oh my *God*, this is your number! You stalker. You actually *kept* these? Do you have a shoebox full of my nail clippings too?"

This time Eric smirked at the insults. Her face was still tear-streaked, but she was rebounding quickly. Another good sign.

"I told you," he reminded her. "It's a talisman. I wanted to keep your bravado with me."

Jane hiccupped back a laugh, then continued to page through the book, stopping every so often to read the poems, entries, and anything Eric had recorded over the years.

"I wondered if you kept writing after I read that other journal," she said.

"After Penny died, I didn't write anything for a year. I just...didn't care. I traveled, I ignored my friends, my family. I pretended to be anyone but Eric de Vries, family heir. But when I met you, it was like someone jerked me back to reality."

Jane continued scanning the pages. "But you—Eric, I'm not being jealous here, but you dated *so* many women in Boston. How do I know that these are about—"

"Just turn the page, Jane."

To his surprise, she did as he ordered. Out dropped a note written on a coaster, along with a napkin, creased and grayed a bit with time. Jane flattened it against her thigh, whispering the words Eric knew by heart.

"It's our poem. From the bar." She looked up. "You kept it too?"

"I kept everything. Keep reading."

So she did. She lingered over a photo of their first-year study group at the library. Notes passed during Torts and Con-Law. Ticket stubs from that show at Great Scott for her birthday. The receipt from a book of love poems.

Every single remnant of their initial go at it, plus others from the next one, and the one after that.

He watched her page through the intervening years, filled with poetry he'd written, mostly about her. Watching from a distance as she pillaged half of Boston, a mirror image of his own attempts to forget her and move on.

Which, of course, he never could.

The book was separate from his typical journal, something that was dedicated only to her. Sometimes there were months between entries, sometimes a flurry of consecutive days. Eric watched with trepidation as Jane examined the parts that recorded his frustrations with her. The hopes they might get back together. The bitter jealousy. The anger. Disappointment, with her, but more with himself. After all, how many times had they gotten beers with friends in school, and he had chickened out on inviting her home with him? How many times had they seen each other in passing, either at his office when she was visiting Skylar or at the Crosby-Sterlings' house on a few random holidays?

It was all in there. His desperate faith that the woman he was meant to be with would eventually come back to him. If he just had enough patience.

"You made us a scrapbook," she said after she fingered the last page. "You're a midwestern housewife. And I say that as the daughter of a scrapbook-loving midwestern housewife."

"Jane."

She finally looked up, and it was clear that she needed another tissue. Her eyes were wet and reddened. A single tear slipped down her cheek. But her smile lit up the fucking room.

"I'm joking because I don't know what to say," she admitted. "I'm joking because just like always, you overwhelm the fuck out of me. You make me feel all these things, and I don't know what to do with them."

Eric pulled a tissue from the nightstand and gently wiped away the tear streak. She smiled, the curve of her mouth dimpling her full cheek. He kissed it. She hiccupped.

But when she tried to give him the book, he pressed it into her lap.

"It's for you," he said. "I don't need it anymore. It's for whenever you worry. Whenever you're scared. I'm not—look, I know I'm not the best at showing how I feel about you on the outside. So when you're unsure, I want you to read this. I want you to see everything you inspire in me. Because you're fucking everything to me, Jane. You make this life worth living. And if you're not in it...well, the truth is, I don't want to be either."

She stared at the book for a long time. No jokes. No comebacks. Just digesting his confession.

"When I met you," she said finally, "I convinced myself that I was just your plaything. You were so put together, so poised. Everything I wasn't. So I knew I could never be anything more than a lark. An escape. You scared me more than anyone I'd ever known. Sometimes you still do."

She touched each artifact reverentially as she turned the pages again, hovering her hand over the crumpled scraps, the love notes, each tiny piece in the messy mosaic of their history. Then she closed them and cradled the book to her heart.

"When I met *you*," Eric said. "You brought me back to the real world. For over a year, I'd been running away from who I was, what I wanted, everything real. Don't you know why I asked you to marry me, Jane?"

She blinked, her teary eyes shining. "Because you loved me, you said. Don't tell me it's not true after all this."

Eric smiled at the small joke. "Because I loved you, yes. But also because we're real, Jane. More real than anything else. And the second I met you, I knew I'd take any day with you, easy or hard, over the best escape I could manage. You were all I wanted. All I could ever want."

Because he couldn't not, he kissed her, this time letting the tension of the moment feed the charge instead of holding it back. He slipped a hand around her neck so she couldn't escape, fusing her mouth to his almost violently. And then, just as suddenly, he released her, though he kept his hand around her nape. Jane quivered under his touch.

"Do you feel that?" he asked as their breaths mingled. "The way your heart beats faster when I'm here? That sudden rush of blood? That's *us*, gorgeous."

"I feel it," she whispered. "I've always felt it."

"You want a knife, Jane? You've cut me open from day one. Just like I did you. Am I wrong?"

Before she could answer, Eric gently removed her glasses, then took the journal from her hands and set them both on the bedside table. Then he kissed her again, and this time her mouth bruised his right back. Her teeth bit into his lower lip; he thought he tasted blood, bright and metallic.

"Tell me," he ordered, as he pulled her onto his lap. His hands yanked at her skirt, pushing it over her thighs to reveal the milky white of her skin. He attacked her mouth, punishing her, loving her—it was all the same tonight. "Tell me, Jane. Am I wrong?"

His hands wrapped around her sweet, round ass, fingers teasing the damp silk of her panties. The warm, dark place he had dreamed of for weeks. And before that, years. God, he could smell her, that sweet, musky nectar that drove him fucking crazy. A subtle combination of lust, anger, heat, desire. *Home.*

Jane stilled as his fingers breached the silk. They tickled, dipped, dying to enter. But he wouldn't. Not until she said what he needed to hear.

"Am. I. Wrong?"

"No," she whispered, even as her eyelids closed. "No, you're not wrong. But, Eric..." She placed a hand on his chest like she was unsure whether she wanted to push him away or pull him closer. "It scared me so much. It...it still does."

Eric wrapped his other arm around her waist and pulled her even closer, their chests pressed so tightly he couldn't tell if he felt her heartbeat or his. He touched his forehead to hers. She inhaled tightly.

"Let me tell you something," he said as his fingers continued their exploration. "You do not *ever* have to be afraid of me, Jane. Do you know why?"

He pushed in slightly. She arched and bit her lip.

"Why?" she asked, though she was now staring at his mouth.

"Because," he said as he rewarded her with a light, chaste, almost teasing kiss. "You and me, Jane?" His finger dipped deeper, feeling her slippery welcome up to his second knuckle. "We're not just for right now. We're for life, pretty girl. *For life.*"

She squeezed around his hand. He almost came right there.

"Eric," she whispered.

He pushed his fingers in all the way, seeking that spot he knew would undo her completely. When it came to Jane, to finding those dark, secret spaces, it was just instinctual.

"Is that all right?" he asked, though the tension quivering through her limbs seemed like something she was enjoying. He kissed her again, this time biting her lower lip for her. She moaned, and opened to receive his tongue, suckle it lightly in that way that made the rest of him practically die from desire.

"I need..." Her words were gasps as she rocked onto his hand. "Eric, please. I need *more.*"

He didn't need to be told twice. How long had it been? Weeks? Over a month? Two weeks he had been stuck in that cell at Rikers dreaming of holding her just like this, then almost four more between Korea and doing everything he could think of to help her back from the dead.

But.

"Jane, is it okay?" he asked again, hoping she understood what he meant. If she was still healing, he didn't want to mess that up.

She grabbed his t-shirt and wrenched it over his shoulders, then scraped her hands down his chest and abs hard enough that her nails, short as they were, still scraped. And the fuck if it didn't make him that much harder.

"It's fine," she said directly. "I was cleared last week. Eric, *please.* Don't make me beg. You say we're real—I need to feel it. I need to feel *something* more than..." She drifted off as her gaze fell to the shallow cuts on her arms.

Her meaning was clear. She needed him to bring her back to earth? He was more than happy to do it.

"Take this off," he ordered, pulling at her dress. She obeyed, stripped off the wet wool, the black boots, to reveal her simple black undergarments—unfussy, but still sexy as all hell. Had he ever told her what it did to him? That she never felt the need to wear underwear like a costume? She was overflowing with sex, with desire. Anything else would be a parody.

He stripped off his clothes with as much excitement, and when they both returned to the bed, he was too eager for her, pulling her back atop his lap, his cock twitching with anticipation. But before he could pull her down, feel the tight, warm wet of her envelop his needy dick, Jane flattened her hand over his chest.

"Wait," she said, then leaned to the side table and pulled out a condom. Eric frowned at it, then at her.

"Really?" he asked. "I thought..." He couldn't bring himself to say he wanted to try again. That he couldn't eliminate the painful loss of their child, but if she wanted, he could maybe give her another. He could give *them* that future again.

"Not now," she said, her quick glance darting to her maimed arms, to the thin cut that barely stung his collarbone. "Not yet."

Ah. She was right, of course. They weren't ready.

"But you're...you're ready for this?" he asked, carefully brushing back a loose wave of brown-black hair from her cheek. There was still that streak of red in the back, but it was faded, much like the rest of her. Jane's eyes closed to his touch, but she didn't move away.

"Oh, Eric," she whispered. "I don't think you understand. How much I need this. How much I need...you."

When her eyes opened, they weren't faded at all. Instead, they sparked. Eric couldn't wait any longer. With quick, precise movements, he rolled on the condom, then pulled her close again.

"Day one, pretty girl," he murmured as he took her beautiful face between his hands. "I've needed you like the fucking air I breathe since day one."

She shuddered. "Then take me," she said, shifting slightly to adjust to the size of him as he slid deep inside. "Because I really do belong to you."

"No, gorgeous," Eric corrected her. "We belong to each other."

It didn't take long. Not when it had been weeks since they had been together, when before they had rarely been able to go an entire day without joining their bodies. Eric inhaled her, finding any and all surfaces to suck, nip, fucking *feast* on—neck, breast, shoulder, ear. Mouth, oh *God*, that mouth. She opened to him like a flower, welcoming his eager, bruising touch, matching every thrust of his body from below with her own above.

And then, just as he was applying some new, delicious torment to that delicate spot above her pulse, she burst.

"I'm...oh, *God*, Eric, I'm here, I'm...*coming!*"

Her voice, always so brash and brazen, never rose above a whisper, as if her ecstasy threatened to swallow her whole.

"I'm with you," she said, her voice as fluid as a river.

He pressed his forehead to hers, body and soul. "Always."

The sign of her undoing was Eric's own—he fell apart with a loud, hoarse cry, emptying himself completely, totally, into her. Body and soul.

All thoughts of what might have been rushed from his head.

All fears of what they might lose fled the room.

Everything he needed was right here.

And she was all his.

"*SPANAKOPITA*," Jane said sometime later.

Eric shifted lazily. "Have a sudden hankering for Greek food?"

She turned in his arms, and his fingertips brushed over the curve of her shoulder. "I thought of it at the diner, actually. They had a tray of it by the counter. But just now..." She traced a finger over his pectoral muscle. "Do you remember that morning at my apartment, during first year? I offered you spanakopita, and you freaked out. Started babbling about a failed relationship."

He closed his hand over hers, keeping it there, where she could feel the sudden jump of his heartbeat.

"It was because of Penny, wasn't it?" Jane didn't wait for an answer, likely knowing she was right. "The food. It reminded you of her."

"It reminded me of what I'd lost," Eric corrected her gently. He pulled a hand through her hair, wishing for a moment it was bright purple again. Wishing it was that morning after her birthday. When, if he had just taken a second to think before he'd acted, their entire history might have been different. He'd broken down Jane's walls, finally attained her trust, and proceeded to smash it all completely. One shitty morning had cost them, what, eight years together?

He shook his head. Idiot.

And yet, how could he have told her that the last and only other girl he'd loved had died...because of him? Particularly when, at the time, he still thought she had killed herself over his family. Over his very essence?

He had run because at the time, he couldn't handle the risk. He couldn't handle the idea that the magnetic creature that was Jane Lee Lefferts might ever become a shadow of herself because of him.

Eric sighed. It seemed he hadn't been able to avoid that either. Jane had been smashed again, through the complexities he brought into her life.

And yet, as he continued to play with her hair, the streak of defiant red peeked from the back again. She was so much stronger than Penny, than him, than anyone he'd ever known. She brought him back to life countless times over the last almost ten years. He would do it for her if he died trying.

A thought occurred to him as he caught her hand and pressed a kiss to her palm. A few of the cuts on her arm had already started scabbing over. Their bodies would always heal faster than their hearts.

"You have to promise me something," he said as he held her arm still and floated his fingers over the wounds. "That you will *never* hurt yourself like this again."

"I—" Jane cut herself off for a moment as she buried her face into his shoulder. "Okay, yes. I promise."

"Good. Besides, if it's just marks you want..."

He stared at the row of hickeys he'd left on her neck and offered what he hoped was a lascivious smile. Jane just shoved him in the shoulder and made a face.

"Stop that. Normally, devious looks pretty good on you, Petri dish, but right now you look like a Disney caricature."

Eric burst out laughing, hard enough that his belly shook and he had a hard time breathing.

"What?" Jane demanded. "What are you laughing at? It wasn't that good of a burn, you idiot."

"Fucking hell," he wheezed, though like a maniac, he couldn't stop. "Oh, sweet fucking hell, you beautiful thing, you."

"What?!" she shrieked. "Stop laughing at me!"

Her cries, unfortunately, only made him laugh that much harder, until tears were streaming down *his* face this time, and Jane was red with the effort of swatting him with her pillow.

"Uncle!" he cried finally, swallowing back more peals of laughter with everything he had. Chuckles still erupted from his belly like a train tooting its horn. "I give up!"

"Why are you laughing?" Jane demanded, clearly furious. "What the hell was so damn funny?"

"Oh, God," he said as he wiped his eyes. "I just...fuck...I never thought I'd see the day when you could call me that god-awful name again. But it just felt so good...and it hit me in the gut...oh, fuck, here it comes..."

He broke down laughing all over again, feeling giddy like a child. Jane's lips quivered, and all of a sudden, she was laughing too, whispering "Petri dish" and "preppy" and "you goon" over and over until they collapsed into each other, shaking with mirth.

It felt good to be happy again, if just for a moment. Neither of them was in a hurry to let it go.

"I have one more request," Eric said once they had both finally quieted. "I want us both to see a therapist. Starting immediately."

He could feel her scowl against his chest this time, and he hid a smile himself. He knew exactly how much Jane disliked talking about her feelings. It was another thing they had in common. Probably not the best thing, either.

So, yeah, he wasn't going to budge on this one.

"Come on, Lefferts," he said gently. "After all we've been through. It's what your dad would have wanted, don't you think?"

"That's a cheap shot."

"It's not a shot at all. He was a VA psychologist who made his entire career out of helping PTSD victims. So it's the truth, isn't it?"

She finally revealed her face again, which was, predictably, twisted into a scowl. "You say that like I haven't had his voice in my head for the last three weeks telling me exactly that."

Eric shrugged. "Who are we to argue with the dead?" But he still wasn't ready to let it go. "Seriously, though, Jane. You and me, both. We can't keep things bottled up forever. Bad things happen." He hovered his fingers again over her cuts. "Promise me."

She was still for a long minute, and then deflated.

"Okay," she relented, though she pulled him back to her for one more kiss. "I promise."

INTERLUDE III

1990

"What do you think, lovey?"

Heather turned to look at her son, who was perched on the counter of their wide marble sink. Eric re-crossed his little legs and turned toward his mother. Tonight was a fancy night. Rosa was downstairs making his dinner, which would be tacos, one of his favorites. He was looking forward to it. Fancy nights meant Eric could stay up a little later than normal. He and Rosa could watch a movie on the VCR. Tonight was supposed to be The Wizard of Oz.

"I like it," he told her. "You sparkle, Mama. Like Dorothy's shoes."

Heather looked down at the red sequined dress. "Well, aren't you a smart thing? It is like Dorothy's shoes, isn't it?"

She rubbed noses with Eric. He smiled. Mama smelled like roses tonight.

"Say it with me," she said. "There's no place like home. There's no place like home."

"What are you teaching him this time, sunshine?"

Eric's father bounded into the bathroom to check his own reflection, shimmering almost as brightly as his wife. Mama always said he looked like the sun, the way the light seemed to shine off his yellow hair. Eric smiled. He'd missed his dad while he was gone this time.

"Look at us," Jacob said. "That's a damn fine-looking family right there, don't you think?"

"Jake! You have to watch your mouth in front of Eric."

Eric chuckled. Mama was always telling Daddy to watch his mouth, though Eric didn't know how exactly you could watch your own mouth. He'd tried plenty of times, but couldn't manage it without a mirror.

Jacob just darted around Eric and gathered his wife close. "How about I watch your mouth instead?" he asked in that low voice that Eric knew his mother loved. The little boy grinned while his daddy ruined his mother's lipstick.

"Jake." She still protested, but now she was out of breath.

"My turn!" Eric shouted after Jacob finally let Heather go.

Jacob turned from Heather triumphantly. "What's that, buddy? You want a snuggle too?"

"Yes!" Eric cried.

"Well, you asked for it." Jacob swung Eric up from the counter into a giant bear hug.

"Aahhh!" Eric squealed as his father whirled him around the big bathroom, his voice bouncing off the rock walls.

"Jake, you'll wrinkle your jacket!" Heather couldn't stay serious when she was laughing this hard.

"Oh, let the old buzzards see my wrinkles," Jake said as he set his son back on the counter. "They're worth every damn squeeze of this monkey." He pulled Heather next to his son, then wrapped his arms over both their shoulders, tucking his chin between them.

"Can you stay home tonight?" Eric asked. "Please?" Dorothy could wait. He'd rather have more of this.

"Ah, buddy, I promised your mom that when I came back from

Korea, we'd have our own New Year's Eve since I missed it," Jacob said. "Plus, she needs me to protect her from all those stuffed-up penguins at these galas. There's always a few of them after her, you know."

He was joking, but there was something in his voice that made Eric frown. "Like who?" he asked.

"No one," Heather said, standing up to fix her hair. "Your daddy is just being silly."

But Jacob remained crouched around Eric. The two men, one young, one older, gazed at each other solemnly under the lights.

"Little man," Jacob murmured as he stroked his son's hair. "One day, we won't be around anymore, you know."

Eric's eyes widened. "What?"

"Jake!"

Jacob waved away his wife's complaint. "This is important, hen." He squeezed his son. "I hope it's not for a long, long time, bud. But you never know." He blinked, like he had just seen something terrible in the mirror.

Eric stilled. He didn't like this conversation. Now he really wanted his parents to stay.

"But one thing I learned once my dad was gone," Jacob continued, "was that we'll always have moments like these. They'll sit in your mind like a picture if you just try hard enough to keep them."

"How do I keep them?" Eric asked immediately. This was a good one. He didn't want to lose it.

Jacob grabbed Heather by the waist so that she faced the mirror again with them.

"You look at everything for a second, just like this," Jacob told them. "And later, you close your eyes and imagine it all over again. When you're older, you can write it down. Then you can take these memories and look at them like photos in an album. And remember that home's not a place, kid. It's the people you love. And no one, not even death, can take that from you."

Eric gazed into the mirror, memorizing the sleek, shining figures of his parents. Their gleaming hair, their sparkling clothes. Their warm smiles. Their loving eyes.

"I'll always remember this moment," he told them both solemnly. "Will you?"

"I promise," his father assured him. "No matter what. Even after I'm gone."

PART FOUR

QUATRAIN

Didn't you say once,
we were two of a kind,
In spite of our differences,
body and mind?

Yet you argue this joy
Bordered too much on rough,
And that I should know love
Isn't always enough.

What
Utter
Bullshit.
I don't need rhymes to say what's on my mind.
Fuck this meter.
Fuck every rule.
The truth is, I'll always come home to you.

"Broken Rule"
– from the (new) journal of Eric de Vries

TWENTY-EIGHT

Present

I could hear his steps before the door opened. I listened for them every night, the rush of leather soles on granite. They echoed up the brownstone's stairwell, each one ringing with the same chorus:

Home, home, home.

To me.

They were slow today. It must have been a long day, which meant that when Eric walked in, he would probably do three things in this exact order: Strip off his tie. Tie me to the bedpost or maybe the dining table while he had his way with me. Fall asleep by the fire with me wrapped in one arm, a few fingers of vodka in his other hand.

Some people have food on the table for their men. I provided... me, I guess. It wasn't the worst way to start our evenings together.

Unfortunately, tonight I just wasn't available at the moment.

The door opened. Footsteps on parquet. "Jane?"

I didn't even look up from my work. The idea had hit me about two hours ago, and I couldn't stop. I could see the patterns, the colors so clearly. I could see him wearing them too.

I didn't want to lose them.

There was a knock at the door of my studio. "Jane?"

I frowned, then shaded a few more mustard-color stripes. Yes. Yes, that worked exactly.

A few minutes later, I looked up to find Eric watching me, leaning deliciously against the doorframe with his suit jacket tossed over one shoulder and a far too satisfied expression on his face.

I turned from my desk and pushed my leopard-print glasses up my nose. "Hey. You're home early."

He loosened his tie while surveying the sketches littering my desk, then strode into the room. His sleeves were rolled up to his elbows again. Oof. It had been a rough day. But his loss was definitely my gain. My husband filled out a button-down like no one else.

"The board meeting went faster than I thought. Good thing too, because the morning was hell. Hard at work, I see. What's this?"

He reached over my shoulder, giving me a whiff of his Tom Ford cologne as he fingered the sketch. I almost—almost—didn't notice which sketch he was picking up. A suit, as it happened. Drawn on a male figure. Yes, a blond one. Yes, he had gray eyes and biceps for days. Yes, he was not-so-loosely based on my husband.

"Wait!" I snatched the sketch from his hand, unaccountably nervous.

Eric chuckled and sat on the edge of the desk. "What was that?"

"Nothing," I said too quickly. "You know how Dr. Jean said that as part of taking care of myself, I should try to do something every day that gives me pleasure? Besides you, of course."

Eric flinched at the mention of my therapist, the one I'd been seeing regularly since that day. The one with the knives. The one where I'd finally and completely broken down.

It wasn't that I didn't have that ache, of course. The loss of our girl— I couldn't think of our stolen baby as anything else—nearly killed me. I barely remembered January and several weeks of February too, despite Dr. Jean's intention to prevent exactly that. Suppression, she said, was a natural response the brain had to particularly traumatic memories. But it was exactly what fed things like post-traumatic stress disorder. Which was why, she said, I had ended up doing something like slashing at my own skin just to feel again after weeks of existing like a helpless ghost.

"IF IT'S SO natural to suppress trauma, then why is it so bad?" I asked for at least the fourth or fifth time during our daily sessions.

"It's a biological imperative for survival," she answered calmly. "Much like the imperative to eat sugar. We're wired to be attracted to sweets because high-fructose foods provided our ancestors with an evolutionary advantage of higher energy levels. But the world we live in doesn't match our biology anymore. Now we have generations of people fighting diabetes; others suffering from PTSD. Evolution hasn't kept up." Dr. Jean, I had learned, was amiable, but highly unruffled. And she knew exactly how to manage my mood swings with a combination of wit and basic logic.

"I am trying to survive," I said finally, not ready yet to give in. "My psychotic father is still out there, remember?"

The urge to cut still showed up every now and then. It was hard to function when I felt so...useless. I'd start sinking into that abyss I hadn't been able to see my way out of, and the paring knife would spring to mind. Or I'd feel almost too much emotion—anger, frustration, and above all, guilt that I hadn't been able to save her—and the only thing that would feel the slightest bit appropriate was some form of self-flagellation.

That was usually when I would call Eric if Dr. Jean wasn't available. And to the man's credit, he always, always picked up, ready to talk me off the proverbial ledge.

"Still," I said petulantly. "I'm practically a Greek tragedy. And

there's nothing I can do about it? Can you blame me for indulging in a little suppression?"

"Your body wants to let it out, Jane," she said. *"Because, just like it gets sick when you eat too much sugar, it becomes ill when you keep these kinds of experiences locked up and refuse to talk about them. Suppressing trauma is just overloading your body with other toxins. If you don't let it out in a healthy way, you'll just keep cutting it out instead."*

I WAS WASTING AWAY BEFORE, and sometimes I thought I still might. But Eric was unfailing, seeking me out in the dark whenever he felt me faltering. Never to banish that ache, that frightful abyss, but maybe giving us both the strength to endure it.

If you had told me a year ago that Eric de Vries would be my savior, I would have thrown a drink in your face and logged on to Tinder just to prove you wrong. But save me he had, many times over. And I had kept my promise. The knives stayed in the drawers. Together, we kept that terrible numbness at bay.

I did wonder about him, though. Eric had also been seeing a therapist—not Dr. Jean, but another doctor who was apparently trying to help him deal with the decades-long traumas of having his entire life dismantled because of my biological father. When I really thought about it, the fact that he wasn't a walking encyclopedia of neuroses was frankly astonishing.

Then again, maybe he was.

Over the course of a lifetime, Eric had perfected his nonplussed facade, but cracks were now showing. He rarely ever smiled, and it seemed to be only when he caught me watching him. His shoulders were always hunched with tension, and new worry lines had appeared over his forehead along with a streak of gray behind one ear.

I delivered the most impish grin I could, hoping I could distract him into taking his tie the rest of the way off and using it the way he probably wanted to. But the stupid man was too quick. His gray gaze darted back to my drawings, and then just as quickly, he snatched the sketch and backed out of the room.

"Eric!" I shouted as I chased him into the living room.

"Just let me see," he said as he dumped his jacket on the sofa, then wove around the chairs while he peered at the picture. "Is this me?"

"It's not finished!" I reached for him again, but he did some kind of voodoo figure-eight move around one of the Danish chairs, nearly causing me to fall over myself in pursuit. I toppled onto the couch and buried my face in my hands. "You're such a jerk. If I wanted you to see it, I'd have given it to you."

"That's too bad, because I really like this."

I peered through my fingers. "You do?"

He showed me the drawing, like I didn't actually know what it looked like. "I like the vest. Actually, I like the whole suit, even the peak lapels. How hard do you think it would be to have it made up for a benefit or something? We've got a couple coming up this summer."

I dropped my hands. "I might be able to. I haven't done much sewing for men's stuff, though."

"Maceo could probably help."

Eric dropped beside me so we could both look at the drawing. It was one of my better ones. More detailed than usual.

"You really like it?" I wondered. "Even the jacquard vest?"

"Of course I do. Just like you knew I would. That is me, isn't it? Otherwise, I'd sure as hell like to know what other dreamy blonds you're sketching for—ow!"

I took back my elbow, which had found its way into Eric's side. "You're so full of yourself. Maybe I gave the model blond hair because it's a gray tux. They are complementary, you narcissist."

I received a half grin that implied I was definitely going to pay for that later.

"Be honest. You were sketching your dream man, Lefferts." Eric leaned down under the guise of examining the sketch again, but before I could cut back, he captured my mouth in a kiss that left us both breathless.

A terse knock at the door interrupted us.

Eric broke away irritably. "Who the hell is that?"

"Don't answer it," I murmured, licking his earlobe as I snaked a hand between his legs. Holy crap. Someone had certainly brought home the bacon. More like a whole freaking leg of prosciutto.

Eric didn't argue, just set his mouth back to mine with dizzying efficiency. Then came the buzzer. And again.

Reluctantly, I released him. "Goddammit. You'd better answer it."

Eric groaned, dropped a kiss on my head, and went to answer the intercom. "Yeah?"

"Matthew Zola's here, sir," came Tony's deep voice.

He was extra polite these days after taking full responsibility for what had happened in Korea. I honestly didn't blame them—how could they have really avoided being shot with enough tranquilizer to fell a horse after rightfully giving me privacy with my doctor? Eric, however, had only kept Tony and his crew on by my demand. My thought was: we had shared something in Korea. Now they were as motivated to protect me and Eric as we were to bring Carson to justice. Loyalty was a treasured asset these days.

I sat up. "Zola?" We weren't expecting him this week. Not with everything still in limbo.

Eric sighed and pressed the button. "Yeah, let him up, Tony."

A few minutes later, he opened the door for the man we were getting to know very well these days. Eric tolerated him, but I for one liked Zola. He was just a good egg. He checked on me regularly (probably for Skylar's benefit, but I wasn't going to argue) and gave us status updates on the case against John Carson. He didn't have to do that. In fact, he probably shouldn't have, considering he worked a department that had been involved in this mess officially. But it was clear he wanted to give us what peace he could.

"Hey," he greeted Eric and me as he swept inside, shaking rain off his worn trench coat. "I was on my way uptown and thought I would drop in."

No one asked why Zola was here in person instead of calling. Aside from the fact that Zola really couldn't risk leaving any kind of trail to us, we were all acutely aware of the potential for wiretapping. This apartment, as well as Eric's own person, were scanned multiple times per day for bugs. Unfortunately, they couldn't do the same for the DA's office.

I hopped up from the couch and delivered a friendly kiss to Zola's cheek before prancing over to turn on the gas fireplace. Yes, prancing. Eric's dark gaze was way too much fun to fuck with. Jeez, he really had had a terrible day.

I batted my eyes at him as I returned to the couch. Eric's face relaxed as he realized what I was doing. He rolled his eyes and muttered "minx" to himself before going to the kitchen to make cocktails. Vodka for him, red wine for Zola and me.

Zola took his gratefully.

"Thanks," I said when I had mine.

Eric sat closer than was strictly necessary and pulled me into his side so he could toy with my hair while we chatted. Every so often, he yanked on it a little, as if to let me know who was really the boss on this piece of furniture, and what I could expect later.

Um, yes, please.

"This is why I really come here," Zola was saying after taking an appreciative sip of his wine. "What is this, a Margaux?"

I looked at Eric, who nodded.

Zola balked at me. "You don't know?"

I shrugged. "This one has the fancy tastes. I'd probably just bring home Three-Buck Chuck every night, but Eric thinks he's allergic to it."

"Hey, I keep some PBR in the fridge for you," Eric argued. "I just don't see the point of drinking garbage."

"Why, my dear Rockefeller, what a charmingly privileged thing to say. Leave the swill to the slums, is that right?"

For that, Eric yanked at my hair a bit harder and nipped my neck, causing me to stifle a shriek as I narrowly avoided spilling wine all over the couch. I made like I was going to move to the other chair, but my hair was pulled again so I couldn't.

"Just try it," Eric growled. "Seriously. I'm in no fucking mood for that tonight."

I stayed where I was. Zola just drank his wine and looked amused. And maybe envious. He had seen this act before.

"So what's up?" Eric said when he had me appropriately flushed, the bastard. "What's the news?"

At that, Zola's face fell. "Oh, right. Well, I'm afraid it's not very good. I got a call from my friend at the CIA. They, um, they are declining to prosecute. They won't be sending anything to the DOJ."

"What?!" Eric exploded forward, nearly tossing me off his chest.

I, however, was too upset to even protest. Decline. To. Prosecute. The demon from hell who called himself my father. They were letting him go.

TWENTY-NINE

"What the fuck happened?" Eric demanded. "We practically gift-wrapped that indictment for them. The man is conspiring to produce and sell fucking nuclear weapons to an enemy of the state. How in the fuck doesn't that put him away for life? The attorney general should be salivating over this shit."

"The short?" Zola asked. "Look, you know as well as I do that the current administration is basically in Carson's pockets. We've talked about this. A pardon was always a possibility. Now it's just...a reality, I guess."

I stared at my wine, watching the liquid dribble down the side of the bowl. Fucking fuck. Eric was right. John Carson was a monster. We had proved it how many different ways? But no one fucking cared.

"We should take it to the press," Eric was saying. "I'll give an interview to the *Times*. Try his ass in the court of public opinion. Isn't that how they got that campaign manager indicted in 2017? Where's the fucking accountability?"

I winced at the bitterness in his voice. Yeah, I felt that shit too.

"I'd wait on that for a minute," Zola said. "There's another way to go. One that won't give away your hand."

"Like murder?" Eric muttered.

I elbowed him in the ribs. Thankfully, Zola just looked bemused.

"Kidding," Eric said. "Sort of."

"Look, maybe the feds aren't prosecuting, but the Brooklyn DA sure as hell is," Zola continued. "He's interested in the state attorney general position. Booking one of the biggest white-collar criminals of this century will go a long way with voters."

"Ramirez for sure wants to prosecute?" I asked. We'd talked about this before, but Zola's boss had been waiting to see what the DOJ wanted to do. Juan Ramirez was known as an honest DA, as far as they went in New York City. But that didn't mean he would necessarily take on the federal government.

"He's keeping it close to the chest, but yeah, he does," Zola said. "Only one other guy in my bureau is on the case, and we're working in conjunction with the Manhattan DA. No one else knows. But yeah, after the way your arrest embarrassed the Manhattan DA, he's as eager as Ramirez to lock the motherfucker up." Zola took a sip of wine. "It might not surprise you to know that this isn't the first time John Carson has evaded arrest in New York. Juan is pretty keen to put him in his place."

"Because kidnapping, murder, illegal arms dealing, and treason aren't enough, right?" I commented.

"So what needs to happen?" Eric asked. "What are you waiting for?"

"If he's not in the city, they don't have jurisdiction," I said. "And if the feds don't care, there is no way to arrest."

My fingers itched to draw. I really didn't want to talk about this anymore. Talking about my father took me back to Korea, which inevitably took me back to the dark place. As if he knew what I was thinking, Eric captured my hand in his and held it securely in his lap.

"Look," Zola said. "I probably shouldn't tell you this, but we've already presented to a grand jury. The second John Carson enters

NYPD jurisdiction, he'll be indicted. It's just a matter of getting him here."

"I see." I took a long sip of wine. It really was good. "So what you're saying is, you need a trap."

Zola nodded. "I suppose we do."

We sat there, the three of us, ruminating. Eric kept fidgeting, tipping his head back and forth like a bobble head figure and glancing at me again and again.

"Oh my God," I said finally. "Zola can hear you thinking across the damn room. Just say whatever's on your mind."

Eric inhaled uneasily. "You're not going to like this."

I sighed. "Just spit it out, Petri dish."

That dark look reappeared. "Jane."

But I wasn't having it. "Eric."

He glared at me, then exhaled a deep breath. "Janus."

I blinked again, adjusting my glasses while the word sank in. And when it did, it was like a bomb. "Janus? As in the secret society full of members who want to kill you? Are you serious right now?"

"Well, it was just Jude and Carson, but I know. I know. Carson's not just going to saunter into New York and turn himself in, though. He'll only come if he thinks he's safe and for something legitimately important. For instance, if I mounted a challenge."

"A challenge?" Zola asked.

Eric quickly reminded Zola about the de Vries family's history as Caesars. "Theoretically, I have a right to the position. Now, consider this: Carson gets half his power just from being able to manage the members of Janus. He's probably the only one who even knows who they all are. But I can't be the only one he's targeted over the years. I think if I challenge his power, there will be support. People will show up, especially the ones who supported my dad. But Carson will defend his position, considering everything he did to get it. So, he shows up. Bam, arrest the fucker."

"Won't you..." I trailed off, toying with my wine stem. "First of all, won't you get in trouble with the members for staging a meeting just to share it with the cops? Last I checked, secret societies kind of frown on their centuries-old covers being blown. And second of all, don't you have to meet in New Haven? That's still out of jurisdiction."

Eric shrugged. "The Janus society has used different meeting places for decades. *Portas* is hardly the only one. It's just one of the oldest. And Jude liked the bedrooms."

I made a face. Eric had filled me in before about Jude's "contributions."

"That's so gross. Can you have him arrested too for sex trafficking?"

"We're working on it," Zola said dryly. Clearly it wasn't going very well either.

I deflated even more. Eric still wouldn't release my other hand. "There are a few meeting sites in New York. One is even under the St. Mark's Graveyard. Where my family is buried."

I stared at him. "This society is really morbid."

"They usually are," Eric replied.

Zola just waited.

"I don't like it," I said finally. "It seems dangerous. Going to ground like you're warrior bunnies in Watership Down. It'll be you against all of them. What if you're branded a traitor? What if you're stuck in an underground dungeon and you can't communicate with anyone?" I shook my head. "No, no, no. That's not going to work for me. I'm not interested in anyone else in this family being taken prisoner by this draconian nightmare who donated half my genes."

"But—"

"No." My voice shook, but I turned to face Eric. He needed to know I meant what I said. "He'll know what you're doing. He's thought one step ahead of you this whole time. Eric, he will know."

Eric looked like he wanted to argue with me. Well, he could try all he wanted. I was never going to be okay with him setting a trap for a big bad wolf without any way of calling for backup.

Before he could say anything at all, another loud buzz interrupted us. Eric pressed his lips into a thin line, then rose to answer.

"We're not done," he informed me.

I raised my glass to toast the pending clash.

He just rolled his eyes and pressed the intercom button. "Yeah?"

"Mrs. Gardner is here," Tony said.

"Oh?"

Eric and I traded frowns. Nina had been visiting me a lot, but never at this time of night.

"Sure," Eric said. "Send her up."

A FEW MOMENTS LATER, Nina opened the door, shaking rain off her sleek shoulders.

"Hello, hello, I'm so sorry to interrupt your evening," she blustered, tossing a thick binder on the foyer table so she could properly remove her Burberry coat. "I'm a bit desperate, and I needed to see Jane immediately. I—oh!" When she turned around, it was as if Nina had run smack into an imaginary post. "Matthew," she breathed, looking for all the world like she'd seen a ghost.

For his part, Zola looked like he had just been hit across the face. Hard. His pale olive skin was completely flushed.

"Nina," he breathed.

Well, well, well. What did we have here?

Eric glanced between Nina and Zola as he hung Nina's coat. "You two know each other?"

Nina recovered her placid expression, smoothed her tasteful gabardine shift dress, then retrieved the binder from the entry table. "We've met," she said smoothly and made her way across the room. "Calvin made a donation to Juan Ramirez's campaign last year. It was at the fundraiser, wasn't it, Matthew?"

Zola seemed far too interested in her legs to answer.

Eric raised a brow, but went to the kitchen to get Nina a glass of wine. My expression probably mimicked his. I had known Matthew Zola since, well, since he had become friends with Skylar and Brandon, way back when. Not once had I heard a single soul refer to him as Matthew.

Zola cleared his throat. "Oh. Yeah, um, yes. Yes, that was probably it. Good to see you again, doll."

The harmless moniker hung in the air like a bell that had just been rung. Now it was Nina's turn to blush. Well, hell's bells, then. Someone had a bit of a crush on our handsome Italian lawman.

Eric returned with Nina's wine and shot me a curious look as his cousin turned the most peculiar shade of pink from head to toe. I shook my head minutely. It would have to wait.

Nina accepted her wine glass gratefully and took a very long drink. Several seconds later, she cleared her throat. "Ah, yes. Yes, it's nice to see you too, Matthew." She blinked, like she was only just remembering where she was. "Actually, Jane, this isn't purely a social visit. I have a dreadful favor to ask you."

She joined me on the couch and dropped her giant binder in the middle of the coffee table. Eric scowled, clearly unhappy with being usurped. I blew him a kiss. The left side of his lips quirked deliciously before he grabbed the other chair next to Zola.

"What is this?" I asked as Nina opened the binder.

"It's some of the materials that Grandmother put together when she was helping plan the Met Gala," she said. "She was on the board of the Costume Institute. I assumed you knew that."

Now I was the one changing colors: about five different shades of white. "Wait, wait, wait. Hold the phone complete with a Tiffany's dialer. Did you just say Celeste was helping to plan the Met Gala?"

Nina nodded, now paging through the materials. "Yes, that's right. Grandmother worked on the committee every year. She helped plan the theme, the exhibit, all of it. Obviously it's Cora Spring's baby, but Grandmother had her fingers in everything. After all, it wasn't really possible without her money."

I blinked. During her final months, Celeste and I had enjoyed the

Costume Institute plenty of times on our frequent sojourns to the Met, but she had never mentioned that she was involved in it. Now that I thought about it, though, she had been as knowledgeable about that part of the museum as any docent.

"Nina," Eric said. "Look, I get that this is a big deal, but we were kind of in the middle—"

"Shhhhhh, Petri, take a Xanax, all right?" I cut him off immediately. "No one delays the Met Gala."

Both Eric and Zola just stared at me like I'd told them to jump off a cliff.

"The Met Gala," I repeated. When neither of them answered, I started to sputter. "Eric! Come on, I would have expected better from you, at least. *The Met Gala*. First Monday in May. Fashion prom. It's the giant fundraiser of the Costume Institute of the Metropolitan Museum, overseen by the editor-in-chief of *Vogue* magazine. One of the most exclusive tickets on the planet, and something you do *not* say no to. *Ever!*"

By the time I was finished with my rant, Eric at least looked more in the know, although Zola certainly didn't. He peered at Nina, who seemed to be looking at everything else but him.

I threw a pillow at Eric, who calmly batted it to the floor. "Amateurs," I muttered before turning to Nina. "Okay, so what's up?"

"It's awful, just awful. I took over Grandmother's seat on the committee, of course. There wasn't time for them to find someone else. I had intended to give it to you—I think that's what she wanted, since the two of you spent so much time at the institute in her last days, and to be honest, I don't really know much about fashion beyond the houses I like myself. But you and Eric had so many...challenges...over the past few months, I thought it best to do it myself this year. Except I'm absolutely all wrong for it!"

"Wrong for what, Nina?" Eric wondered.

Nina flipped open the binder to a large picture: a black-and-white photo of a man about to break his guitar, over the words

London Calling. "Wrong for this. I can't help organize a party around this theme. I know absolutely nothing about it."

"Oh my merry Mick Jones," I breathed as I stared at the cover of my favorite album of all time. "You have got to be kidding. Have I died and gone to heaven?"

"What?" Eric asked.

"Is that The Clash?" Zola said. "Hey, I like that song."

"It's the theme," I said with a grin. "They choose one every year for the exhibit and the gala itself, and this year it's 'London Calling.' Cora Spring and the Metropolitan Museum are using *The freaking Clash* as their inspiration!"

"Which is why I don't know what I'm doing!" Nina burst out.

Zola reached across the coffee table like he wanted to take her hand, but then, as if he realized they weren't alone, pulled it back again. I watched the moment, then mouthed "wow" at Eric before turning back to the binder. He hid a smile behind his vodka.

"So you see," Nina was saying, "you have to take my spot, Jane."

My head sprang up so fast I was basically a Jack-in-the-Box. "Come again now?"

Nina pushed the binder toward me. "Cora is absolutely sick of me, but if we don't do this, the family loses its seat on the committee. Which we do not want. Grandmother would turn in her grave, believe me. I know you've been busy, but—"

"She hasn't," Eric put in, ignoring my immediate glare. "Not one damn bit. Unless you count the mountains of outfits she's been designing."

"Um, excuse me, Mr. Monopoly. How would you know what I've been doing all day?" I shot back.

"Want me to show them your sketches?"

I flushed. Not that I wasn't proud of my design work, but showing them to someone like Nina was another thing completely.

Nina, however, ignored Eric's and my little spat. "So you'll do it?"

Suddenly every eye in the room was on me. I swallowed thickly. "Just to be clear, you are asking me to help the editor of the world's most prestigious fashion magazine and a bunch of the other most stylish people in the world plan the world's most exclusive fashion event?"

Without a flinch, Nina nodded. "Please, please, please. I look like a fool."

"Well, I only have one question," I said slowly, fingering my wine glass again. "Do I get to go too?"

"Oh, of course! You and Eric are already on the guestlist. Heather and Mother too. Didn't I tell you? The family always has a table."

"Ah, no!" I practically jumped out of my seat. "You most certainly did not!" And then I proceeded to scream with the kind of joy I usually reserved for Skylar.

Nina grinned, maybe a little too widely, but took my frantic hugs good-naturedly. When I finally released her, I found Eric grinning ear to ear as he watched.

"You look way too happy about this for a man who just committed his wife to a massive time commitment for the next three months," I said as I returned to my seat. "First Monday in May is right around the corner."

"So it is," Eric said, "which also gives me an idea." He tapped a pen on the table. "Maybe...we don't need a secret lair to trap the big fish. Maybe we just need a really exclusive event. And the right date to toss out a lure?"

"Uh-oh. Someone is going Scooby-Doo on us," I said to Nina. "Who do you think is under the mask, Fred?"

Nina, unfortunately, just looked confused. Dammit. I was going to have to teach this girl my jokes.

Zola snorted. "Who are you thinking?" he asked, clearly following Eric's logic. "We've tried the Jane card before. Yu-na too. He's not biting."

"No," Eric said. "But we haven't tried my mother."

THIRTY

I awoke that morning like I had every morning for weeks now—as if I had been out for a month, not just a night. Eric and I had fallen asleep in the middle of the alpaca rug in the living room again, a wool blanket thrown over our naked bodies. We'd destroyed at least one pillow the night before, and possibly ruined a throw blanket with candles. Gingerly, I touched a small burn on my wrist. Wax play wasn't for the weak of heart.

Catharsis.

Eric's one-word call to action over the last several months. His mission, for both of us.

The demons that Eric and I had needed to be appeased, and every night that's what we did. For his part, Eric was more, ah, creative than he had ever been, more than willing to indulge those random moments when one of us needed things to be a little harsher than before.

But it wasn't just that bittersweet purging that continued to heal us through the spring. It was also the renewed sense of purpose we both gained as the weeks passed—Eric in finally taking full control over his family's generations-built company. Me, strangely, at the Met, where I had found the people I'd never known I needed.

Cora Spring, editor in chief.

Art Nguyen, head curator.

A whole table full of connoisseurs, donors, designers, planners— all of them people who lived and breathed fashion. They fervently embraced the passion I'd always told myself was just a hobby, despite the fact that it was where my heart had been my entire life. For the first time in years, I went to my "work" with excitement, not just duty. And now, as the big day approached, I was dreading that it was going to end.

I lay on Eric's chest, listening to his heartbeat and watching the skin over his pulse. Tick, tick, tick. Slow. Rhythmic. For now, he was completely relaxed. Peaceful, or closer to a bomb? If it was the latter, when would he go off?

As if he knew I was watching him, Eric stirred, and his heartbeat sped up. "Mmmm, g'morning, gorgeous. Good God, did we really not make it back to the bed last night?"

I smiled into his chest. "It's a good thing the rug is so soft. You're a good pillow too."

Eric rubbed his hands up and down my bare back, fingertips calloused from even more rock climbing these days. "You're in a good mood."

"It's a beautiful day. Spring is here," I murmured, nuzzling that delicious divot between his pecs. Mmmmm, man cleavage. You really can't beat it.

He chuckled, then pulled me fully on top of him, stretching the length of his hardening body under me. "The cherry blossoms popped two weeks ago, Lefferts. Don't you walk by them every day on your way to the museum?"

I shrugged, more interested in the way the muscle rose under his collarbone slightly as it tensed. I kissed it. "I saw them. But today, I appreciate it."

Eric jumped when my teeth closed lightly over his collarbone, but his hands slipped over my back and down my ass. "Don't start something you can't finish."

"Pretty sure finishing is your problem, not mine."

I jerked when his hand found my ass with a loud swat.

"Ah!"

"I think you know I finish us both off just fucking fine, pretty girl. Every single time."

"Prove it." I wriggled over the part of his body that would help him do just that.

Eric hissed with desire. But instead of rolling me over and spreading my legs like I knew he wanted, he flopped back on the floor. "Don't you have the walk-through this morning with the florists? I have a meeting with the CEO at nine."

I groaned. It was true. I hadn't really anticipated all of the work that went into taking Celeste's spot on the gala planning committee for the last two and a half months. Though the rest of the team had been working on it since last summer, it was still legitimately a full-time job.

Now the actual event was nearly upon us, although we were still waiting to hear whether or not Carson had accepted Heather's invitation to act as her escort. Eric was starting to think his original plan of a society coup was the better idea. I was too busy drowning myself in seating arrangements to think about what I would do if my biological father did in fact show up to what was otherwise going to be my version of dream prom.

Repression, kiddo. Ah, there was Dad—my real dad—mimicking Dr. Jean's admonishments as my de facto conscience.

I sighed and mentally pushed them both away. "Cora won't sign off on anything unless she sees it herself, but yeah, I'm supposed to be there. And don't forget, you absolutely have to be here by four for the final fittings today. Take the train if you have to. Traffic is going to be murder at that time."

I rolled reluctantly off Eric and started getting up, holding the blanket around my body. Eric stretched his long, blissfully naked limbs out on the carpet, doing absolutely nothing to hide his still-present erection.

I bit my lip. Damn. There was literally nothing more I'd like to do than ride that particular train right now.

But, no. Duty called. And we had a day ahead of us.

"All right. Shower now. Sex later," I said.

"Who says we can't have both?"

Talk about a change in direction. But before I could argue, I was hoisted over Eric's deceptively broad shoulder and carried upside down toward the bathroom at the end of the hall.

"Well, hello, there," I said as I flopped against his back. "What do we have here?"

What we had was a view of two perfectly formed buttocks, the product of a nightly rock-climbing habit and excellent Scandinavian genetics. So, of course, I did what any sensible, red-blooded person would do in my situation. I took a bite.

"Ow!" Eric hopped the rest of the way into the bathroom and flipped me back onto my feet. He set me on the counter and landed a kiss that was more bitter than sweet. "You little vixen. You're going to pay for that."

I tipped my head up, making my neck available to the delicious scrape of his stubble. "Mmmm, no time like the present, Mr. de Vries. Unless, of course you're out of stamina after last night. Did I wear you out?"

He shoved me against the mirror with a bang, pressing his considerable and now rock-hard cock against my thigh. It slipped between my legs, almost like it had a homing device for exactly where it wanted to be.

But though I rocked toward him, rubbing those dark, eager spaces against him, Eric didn't thrust in the way I knew he wanted to. Instead, he held back, watching me slip over his silky length instead.

"Or maybe," I said as I tilted my hips, deliberately looking for trouble, "you're just finally getting your fill of me."

Immediately, I was pulled off the counter and spun around to face the mirror. Eric delivered a harsh slap to my ass before slipping one hand around my throat to brace my jaw, the other to pin my arms behind my back. I stared at us in the mirror, enthralled with the look of myself completely at the man's mercy.

"You and your smart damn mouth." He twisted my face to his and stamped a thorough kiss on my lips. "One day I'm going to wash it out with soap. Maybe today."

"For swearing too much?"

"For talking about yourself like that."

He kissed me again, and again, and again, until I had no more breath for self-deprecating comments. He turned my body around until I was facing him, then started walking us both toward the shower. Opened the glass door. Turned on the Rainshower. And suddenly I was making out with a god, all soaking wet, six feet two inches of him pressed against me beneath the warm spray.

"Oh!" I cried as his teeth found my neck, and he sucked all over again. The man really was a vampire. "Take it easy, Edward Cullen. I can't have a neck full of hickeys in front of every fashion photographer in the world on Monday."

That, of course, only made him suck harder. "Don't tell me what to do," he growled.

As he lifted me up, I arched against him and wrapped my legs around his trim waist, finally welcoming what I sought. He slid inside, slow enough that I was practically punching his shoulder, begging him to lose control.

Let go, I wanted to cry out. *Please, Eric. Let go of everything*. He may have preached catharsis, but he still bottled up so much.

"Are you still thinking about photographers, pretty girl?" He pulled out, then inched back in again. Considering his size, it took a while.

I squeezed my eyes shut, but I could barely put together a coherent sentence. "Mmphmm."

"That's what I thought."

For a moment, I wanted to see him break. I wanted to see him lose himself in me the way I felt like I was trying not to lose myself all the time.

The muscle under his neck ticked more. "Jane."

I opened my eyes. The shower was full of steam, and in it, with water streaming over his chiseled features, Eric looked like Poseidon, rising from the deep.

"Stop thinking," he ordered. "Let go."

I threaded my hands into his hair and yanked. "You first."

Every muscle he had flexed. Then he thrust forward, and this time, he didn't hold back.

"Eric!" I shouted, my voice echoing off the marble and glass.

"Yesss," he hissed as he pummeled into me, his forehead smacking on the stone right beside the back of my head. We were both going to have headaches later, but I couldn't have cared less.

I reached out, looking for something to help me balance while he ravaged my breasts, while he ravaged me. Even like this, even when we were being relatively tame by our standards, Eric was still savage. I loved it, but I needed something, anything, to hold on to. My hands only found slick walls and shower doors, my feet the sides of the tub. Goddammit, this used to be easier, didn't it?

Suddenly, we were both slipping and sliding, banging to the floor with several painful bumps.

"Ow! Fucking hell!"

"Watch it!" I squawked when I slid into his elbow, my knee smacking his jaw in the process.

After flopping around the tub for more than a minute until we were finally standing again, the moment, as they say, had definitely passed. Eric just glowered at the shower nozzle like it was somehow its fault he hadn't been able to finish.

The muscle under his jaw looked like it was about to split open.

"You...you okay, there?" I ventured.

Just like that, the strange, sullen spell was broken. Eric's face resumed its normal implacability—a new mask, I noted with a bit of resentment.

Instead of answering, he just grabbed a loofah behind me and started furiously washing himself off. As, you know, one does with their sexual partner in whom they were six inches' deep only a few minutes before. Without finishing.

But while he seemed to have moved on, I absolutely had not. As Eric scrubbed, I stared. Water streamed over his rippled abdomen, the clean lines of his chest, the sculpted curves of his buttocks and thighs. He might have been a statue had he not been so...alive.

As was I, I realized. As was I.

"This is bullshit. We barely fit."

His voice echoed abruptly off the marble walls. I was still engrossed by his, ah, equipment, which, though no longer quite up to where it had been, was still considerable.

He stopped scrubbing.

I looked up. Okay, I was caught. "We've made it work before. Like two days ago."

"You had an Easter egg on the back of your head from how hard you slammed into the marble."

My smirk widened into a smile. "I don't remember complaining." I stepped close and reached out to touch those abs. Maybe I could still get a matching bump this time.

But Eric just shook his head and went back to rubbing his stomach raw. "It's too small. This whole place is too fucking small. You don't feel it?"

I wasn't sure what to do with that. This bathroom wasn't exactly small. Enormous, really, by the standards of New York. You could stand in the center, and when you stuck your arms out, you didn't even hit the glass door.

Besides, since when did he care about space when it came to fucking?

"You didn't seem to mind small apartments before," I ventured. "Even your place in Boston now is just a one-bedroom."

"That's because it was just me living there," he said. "What the fuck did I need with space?"

"Space isn't needed exponentially with an additional person."

"Isn't it?"

"And this place isn't exactly tiny. By New York standards, it's a palace. I mean, really, look at our counter. We have two sinks. Two."

"I don't want that," he spat, tossing his arm out with disdain at the sink. "I want a counter so big in every bathroom I can lay you out like a buffet whenever and wherever I want. I want to be able to fuck my wife in the shower without toppling into the bathtub like a couple of drunk college kids. And I really want to stop feeling like half the fucking city is pressing in on me because I live in a goddamn cage I share with fifty other people."

On that bitter note, he appeared to be finished as he practically hurled the loofah at the wall and proceeded to stalk out without another word. I stood there for a moment, taking extra minutes to wash and condition my hair, not to mention let the man cool down.

Well, you wanted him to let go, didn't you? I honestly had no idea if that was Dr. Jean or my dad speaking that time. As subconscious avatars go, they were irritatingly conflated.

When I had deemed the temperature of the room acceptably cooler and my hair acceptably cleaner, I turned off the shower and got out. Eric stood at the far end going about his business with slow, concerted movements, though clearly struggling to see himself in the fogged mirror.

He was waiting for me to get out.

"I like this apartment," I said. "I like this bathroom. I like this marble sink."

A stormy gray gaze found me. "It feels like a cage," he said. "Not all the time. But sometimes. Just like everywhere else."

Ah. Now we were getting somewhere. If I was struggling to let things out, Eric felt like he was trying to get out but couldn't. It made sense, I supposed. He'd lived in one sort of cage from approximately eleven or twelve on, later on, others of his own making. And then, of course, there were the two weeks in January when he was literally in a jail cell. Shit. Why hadn't I thought of this before?

Some people found New York claustrophobic, all these people crowded onto one small island. Eric had grown up here. It had never occurred to me that now, especially, he might feel the same way.

But what did that mean? Would he want to leave the city? The idea made my heart speed up about double its speed. I loved this apartment. I loved this life—well, I'd come to love parts of it, anyway. Mostly, I loved this home, this first home that was really mine, mine. I loved it because I had made it with this man. So, if he wasn't happy... I'd move, of course. But it would break my heart a bit to do it.

Eric turned, holding a razor in his hand. For a split second, I imagined snatching it from him and slicing it across my wrist just to feel the fiery sensation rip through me.

Speak your truth, Jane. That one was Dr. Jean for sure.

But before I could say anything, Eric spoke first. "Do you like this building, Jane?"

I sunk to the edge of the counter, unsure of how to voice everything swimming in my head. "Um, yes. Yes, I do."

"Do you, really? The Upper West Side? Seventy-Sixth Street? Or would you rather move downtown, to somewhere less, I don't know, yuppie or whatever you'd call it? God knows it would be an easier commute for me if you wanted to get a place in Soho or Tribeca or something."

I considered the idea. A few months ago, I might have jumped at the chance. But again, that word home kept coming to mind. Everything that we had made together.

"I like it here," I found myself saying. "But if our place is too small—"

"It is," Eric cut me off. "That's why I bought the rest of the building."

He turned back to the mirror and continued drawing the razor down his other cheek in straight, sure movements, not even bothering to check the reflection for my response.

"What do you mean, you bought it?" I finally managed to croak.

He rinsed the razor matter-of-factly and tipped his chin to scrape underneath it. "Last year. Before I showed you the apartment. I bought the building." He shrugged. "I allowed the current tenants to live out their leases, but you must have noticed the building gradually losing bodies. I let the security team have the unit below us last year when those tenants moved out. I've just been waiting for the leases to run out on the apartments below them while I decided what to do with it all.

I considered the facts. Considered that I'd never really taken the time to get to know our neighbors, so why would I have noticed they were gone. Considered that he had done this without even asking me.

"What if I said I hated it here?" I asked. "What if I said I wanted you to sell the place and that we needed to live in a hovel in Brooklyn? The New York housing version of PBR?"

Eric shook out his razor again and chuckled. "I'd probably take you up on the former, but the closest I'll go for a hovel is Nolita, pretty girl."

"You're such an Upper East snob."

He smirked, but didn't argue. "I want a house, Jane. Like the one I grew up in. Or yours. Not some rat trap we share with five or fifteen other families. I want a real home for anyone we want to be in it."

Children. It was an unspoken promise. We hadn't talked about it yet, but one day we would. One day when our loss wasn't quite so acute.

"Why...why now?" I asked.

Eric finished shaving, and with slow, measured movements, rinsed his razor and laid it carefully on the sink. When he turned to look at me, I didn't notice the blade. Didn't even consider what it would feel like if I scraped it over my forearm or the inside of my thigh. The only metallic gleam I could see was the determination in Eric's steely gray eyes.

"Because we've got to do something, don't we?" he asked. "With any luck, in less than a week, this will all be over. We need to look beyond it, don't you think?"

"I...I guess?" I wasn't quite so sure.

"One way or another, it will be done. That's a promise."

What does that mean? I wanted to ask. *What are you going to do?*

But I found I didn't actually want to know. I was getting stronger, but I didn't want to ruin the beautiful light of the morning with shadows.

"Okay," I said as I wrapped an arm around his neck and pulled his lips to mine. "Let's make this our home for always."

His mouth curved into a smile, the smile I didn't see as much anymore, but which still made my knees weak and my soul tremble.

"Sounds like a plan, pretty girl," he said, his voice a warm hum that vibrated through all of me.

We've got to do something, he'd said. It was a refrain in my mind as he turned us around and placed me back on the counter, ready to finish the job he'd started under the streaming water.

Yeah, I thought as I welcomed him home. *We do.*

THIRTY-ONE

"I think we need to take it in at the ribs, not the waist."

I pointed a few inches higher than where Lake McHugh, the up-and-coming designer from East London, was currently pinning last-minute adjustments to my dress. "It's draping too much, and I look like an empty flour sack. Pull it in there, and let's see what happens."

Lake tapped her lip ring meditatively. "I think you're wrong, but we can try it."

When not spending my time at the Met, I'd been invested in one other thing besides Eric for the past few months: clothes. Specifically, this dress and the matching tuxedo for Eric I'd co-designed with Lake. As a member of the committee and the semi-anointed heiress of Celeste de Vries (not to mention her grandson's wife), I had my pick of designers to work with, even with the extremely short notice. I'd known from the start that I needed a British designer to meet the requirements of the theme. Lake and I had clicked immediately—mostly because she was willing to truly codesign with me instead of allowing me the honor in name-only.

To say I was nervous about the results was like saying the Titanic was just a boat. While I wasn't officially a co-host of the gala—only celebrities got to share that particular honor with Cora—I had already been featured in Page Six twice, and the Times Style section was running another profile on Eric and me. Logically, I understood the appeal. It was good publicity. We were still on the tips of New York society's tongues. Our wedding had only been a few months ago, Eric was only just really getting into the swing of things as the CEO of one of New York's oldest companies, and I still caught the curious looks and whispered gossip when I walked around the east side of Central Park.

I stayed as still as I could while Lake reluctantly pinned the stiff plaid taffeta as I requested. As soon as she saw the effect, though, her face brightened. "Well, what do you know? That certainly did the trick."

I looked at myself in the mirror and nodded. Using a brash black and red tartan plaid, we'd designed the dress as a nod to the high-lo culture of mid-eighties punk, when the anti-establishment aesthetic had snuck into movies like *Pretty in Pink*. The bodice was drop-waisted and strapless, now hugging my torso like a glove until just past my hips where the skirts billowed out. I'd redesigned the suit Eric admired, but with a slightly more mod feel, with tapered pants hemmed just above his shoes and a skinny tie that matched my dress.

"I think that's it," Lake said as she straightened the taffeta. "A few darts will take care of that bodice. Are you happy with the torn ribbon detail, or shall we take it off?"

"No, I think it works, especially with the studs. I don't want this dress to be too polished, you know?"

Lake nodded in agreement. "Was hoping you'd say that." She made a few other adjustments, looking me over critically. "Put on the shoes, will you? I want to see it all together again."

I did as I was told, slipping into the custom Jimmy Choo pumps that had steel spikes attached to each heels like spurs. They gave me about four inches.

"And the hair?" Lake asked as she circled me, assessing the full effect. "Did you decide? You going with a full updo or just the fauxhawk?"

We'd already practiced multiple hairstyles over the last few weeks. It was incredible how much of an event this really was—every designer seemed to plan each client's look right down to their manicures (mine would be black), and Lake was no different.

"Actually, I'm going to go with the bouffant," I said, already imagining the way in which my hair would be gathered over the top of my head and left to flow down my back in a tail of soft waves. "I'm having a bunch of new red stripes put in too. Freddy's coming tomorrow to do the color."

Lake nodded approvingly. "That will look fantastic."

She then helped me out of the heels and dress (I really couldn't remove the thing, which had about a thousand buttons running up my side, without help), and I left her to package it up for transport while I got dressed.

"All right," Lake said as we met in the kitchen, me back in a comfortable black jumpsuit, her carrying the garment bag. "I'll make these changes and bring it back tomorrow for a final fitting. I have to get downtown now if I'm to be on time for Mr. de Vries's fitting."

"Oh, don't worry about him. He's always late. If he gives you shit, just tell him I kept you."

Lake chuckled and delivered a kiss to my cheek. "Laters, Jane."

As she left, a big crash sounded—the demo team tearing down nearly every non-weight-bearing wall in the bottom floor. Eric hadn't been kidding about wanting to build us a home. Literally the day after we had decided to stay here for good, he'd hired an architect and a general contractor. I had a feeling I wouldn't be able to sleep past seven for about a year, but Eric assured me that the final product would be worth it. I trusted him. Finally.

Like he knew I was thinking of him, his face appeared on my phone with a buzz.

"What are you, telepathic?" I answered.

"Daydreaming about me, gorgeous?"

I grinned, though he couldn't see me. "You don't know. Maybe I was planning my escape."

"Do I need to tie you up again? I thought I taught you that lesson the other night with those cables."

I bit my lip at the memory. "I don't know if it totally got through. You might be losing your touch, Mr. de Vries."

He growled. The man actually growled, like a wild animal trapped in a suit, caged in one of the most populous cities in America.

"Bridget," he called. "I think you need to cancel my next appointment."

"No!" I yelped. "No, you can't! Lesson totally got through, one hundred percent."

"Seriously? You really don't want me to come up there?"

His confusion was understandable. I had goaded him into giving me a mid-day lesson in "obedience" more than once—he'd pulled me out of at least two meetings at the Met, had even taken me twice in Central Park because we couldn't make it back to the apartment in time. I was just as bad, having scheduled multiple "appointments" at his office to do unmentionable things under his desk.

"Lake is on her way to Maceo's for your final fitting," I told him. "You cannot blow her off. Not with the gala in three freaking days."

There was a low chuckle. "I should have known. The only thing you love more than sex is fashion."

"That's not true. I also love you. More than both."

Wow. I really had gotten pretty damn mushy as an old married lady. But it was worth it. Eric hummed in recognition, and I could practically feel the warmth exuding clear across Manhattan. Somehow, we had found it again. The world wasn't perfect. We both still ached at night for the people we had lost. Still woke up at night in fear of the man stalking us. But we had found each other, that beautiful place where the world seemed light and full of promise simply because we were together.

"Five o'clock, then," he said with a low note of promise weaving through his voice. The kind that gave me goose bumps with anticipation. "And, Jane?"

"W-what?" I said, just the idea of what he had planned making me stutter.

"I love you too. Like the fucking air I breathe."

"The water I drink," I whispered back.

There was an audible sigh—of relief? Humor? Regret? I couldn't tell.

"Always," he said. "Tonight, gorgeous."

I went back to paging through the binder for twenty minutes or so before I called Cora's assistant and was informed there was nothing to do but wait until this evening to do the final walk-through with Cora and the rest of the committee. And think. About what happened next. After Monday.

The truth was, I still had no idea.

When I'd finally had the wherewithal to do things like go through mail and catch up on bills, I'd discovered that I had in fact been granted a waiver to retake the bar exam. And since I'd passed the NYLE in December, that meant I could now practice law in New York State. If I wanted.

But was that what I wanted? I enjoyed putting bad guys behind bars, but also wasn't sure life as a prosecutor suited me, partly because there were plenty of laws I didn't agree with. I hated being a part of a system, for instance, that practiced mandatory minimums on drug crimes—and New York had some of the worst effects with that. Depending on who I worked for, I could easily be part of a system that continued to enforce unfair incarceration of people of color.

But what was the alternative? Criminal defense? The ACLU? Starting my own shop?

Or, I wondered as I gazed toward my studio, a room packed with fabrics and mannequins and drawings, things I spent progressively more and more of my time these days immersed in, was law even in my future anymore?

I had a bank account that contained fifty million dollars that belonged solely to me—my bequest from Celeste's will, which had been approved in probate. Fifty million dollars I hadn't even touched yet because I had absolutely no idea what to do with it.

Didn't I?

The buzzer rang through the apartment, interrupting my thoughts. I got up to answer it.

"Hey, Tony."

"Mrs. Keeler is here to see you, Mrs. de Vries."

"For the thousandth time, Tony, it's Jane." I rolled my eyes. Our security head never got over his need for incessant formality. Eric seemed to like it, but being called "Mrs. de Vries" made me feel like Celeste's twin. "Send her up."

I returned to the kitchen and went about locating a bottle of white wine in the refrigerator. I didn't spend a lot of time with Eric's mother, but if she was here of her own accord to see me, I had no doubt she'd appreciate a glass of something to take the edge off.

The door opened, and Tony stepped aside for Heather.

"Thanks, Tony," I said.

He tipped his head. "Mrs. de Vries."

"Jane!" I called out just as the door shut. I shook my head at Heather, who was watching me curiously. I shrugged. "It's an ongoing battle, the name thing." I held out a glass of wine. "Would you like one?"

Her shoulders relaxed visibly as she nodded. "Please."

I carried the bottle of pinot grigio into the living room where we both sat.

"Quite a bit of construction downstairs," she remarked as she folded herself into one of the Danish chairs. "I can't imagine it's pleasant."

"Not particularly, no," I replied. "But Eric decided he wants the house ready by the end of the year."

"House?" Heather asked. "I didn't realize you had purchased the building."

I nodded. "Yeah, he did. A while ago, apparently. It was a surprise to me too."

"Hmmm. You know, Jacob did the same thing just after we got married. I was pregnant with Eric at the time, and all Jake could think about was making a house fit for a big family." She smiled to herself. "Everyone says it's women who nest, but in truth, I think the men are just as bad."

I wasn't sure what to say. I wasn't pregnant, of course—just the idea caused a pang of longing. But it was obvious that Eric was, of course, planning a house for more than two. And I hadn't fought it one bit.

"So," I said finally. "It's a surprise to have you here. Everything all right?"

"I suppose it is a bit remiss of me to be such a stranger to my own daughter-in-law," she admitted, visibly ashamed. "I think it's still a surprise to me that I even have one."

"Because I'm such an odd choice?" My voice was tight. Eric had assured me he wanted me and only me, but I doubted I would ever be totally secure with this family's impressions.

"Oh, no," Heather said. She swallowed another sip. "Only because I honestly never thought Eric would move past Penny. It never surprised me that he chose girls outside his upbringing. It's just another thing he has in common with his father." When I didn't reply, she tipped her head. "Jane, you do know that I wasn't exactly Celeste's first choice for Jacob either, don't you?"

My brows rose. "I did not. Does Eric know?"

Heather shrugged. "He must. He's never met any of my family, after all, and this city loves to talk."

I said nothing. The few other times I'd socialized with Heather, I'd discover she was a careful speaker. Someone who usually took a while to measure exactly what she wanted to say. And then she told her story, and I realized why:

"Well, you know a bit about where I grew up in New Jersey. My father worked for the plant there. My mother, well..." She waved a manicured hand. "I haven't seen her since I was very young. And my father, well, he passed when I was still in college. Cancer, of course, like half the town. At any rate, my childhood is less important than the fact that I didn't exactly have the pedigree expected for someone like Jacob de Vries."

I swallowed. Yeah, I knew something about that question of worth with this family.

"I hope you understand," she said softly, "that was not at all why I married Jacob. In fact, I put him off several times. He just...wore me down."

I meditated on that for a bit. Heather had no doubt been subject to many of the gold-digger comments that had been lobbed at me over the past year. She offered a lopsided smile, one that I had come to recognize whenever she mentioned Eric's father. Eric was still skeptical of his mother's motives when it came to helping us, but it was moments like these that had me convinced. This was a woman who would forever be in love with a dead man. It was probably how I would act if something ever happened to Eric.

Like it always did, the thought turned my blood cold.

"I came to tell you," Heather said, "that I received a message from John a few days ago." She pulled a letter out of her purse and handed it to me. "I thought it would be safer to bring it myself instead of calling, given Eric's suspicions about bugs."

"A telegram?" I asked as I opened the envelope. "Seriously? Does he think it's 1945? Why doesn't he just text you?"

Heather shrugged. "Johnny always had a flair for the dramatic."

I rolled my eyes and read the message. It was short and stiff:

Heather,

Received your invite. Pleased to go. Will escort you to the gala myself if the boy is willing.
Glad you are finding your senses. Perhaps peace is possible at last.

My love,
JC

I read it at least three times before my body began to thaw. Carson was coming to the Met Gala. We really hadn't been sure he would. After all, we'd only arranged for Heather to receive her invite a few months ago, and though she had sent Carson her invitation, there had been no reply. Eric had been convinced he was still untouchable. But now we knew: he had taken the bait. He was coming.

But Carson wasn't an idiot. There was no way he didn't know it was a trap—just like he probably knew that I was on the planning committee, that Eric and I were already publicized attendees. So, he was coming into the trap and likely going to turn it into one of his own. The utterly nerve-wracking question was: how?

I frowned at the last line of the message as I read it aloud again: "'Perhaps peace is possible.' What does he mean by that?"

Heather sighed. "Eric may have other thoughts, but I read it as a subtle warning or prediction of sorts. Perhaps it means he thinks his debts have been exacted. Or will be."

"By debts, he means you? As what Jacob stole?" I made a face. "Not like you're a person or anything."

Heather didn't respond. It was sad, really, how acclimated she was to being referred to as an object. The way all the women in this family seemed to be. Eric and I had had way too many conversations about that disturbing pattern, particularly when we were brave enough to talk about the prospect of children again.

We made small talk for a few minutes more, mostly about clothes and what we were both planning to wear to the event. Heather had something fairly basic planned—a dress from a British designer, but nothing out of the ordinary. It soon became clear that she and I didn't have much in common beyond Eric. And after she was finished with her wine, she was just as quick to make her excuses as I was to accept them.

"Jane," she said just before she left. She reached out tentatively and took my wrist, begging me wordlessly to pay attention. Her hand was surprisingly strong.

"Yes?" I asked.

"Please be careful," she said. "I don't like this. I know it's necessary, but I truly don't like it."

"I don't think anyone likes it," I said. "But we can't just ignore him. The NYPD will be waiting. And we'll have security around us the entire time."

She gave me a look that wasn't hard to read—hadn't I had a security detail with me when I was taken before?

I pushed the idea away. This time Eric would be with me. For some reason, that thought was the only thing that calmed my beating heart.

"Still," Heather said. "Take extra care. If something..." She drifted off, looking pained. "Jane, if something happened to you, I don't know that my son would recover."

THIRTY-TWO

It takes literally an entire day to prepare for an event like the Met Gala. I'm not talking about the planning. The entire committee did a full walk-through of the exhibit and party space the night before at about midnight, though the head curator and his installation team were still rearranging the exhibit according to Cora's critiques. Approximately ninety-nine percent of the exhibit, however, was ready to go, including eight different exhibits featuring London-based designers from the seventies and eighties, the AV exhibit doing a room-sized broadcast of Clash concerts all night long (that had been my idea), and the massive reconstruction of the London Bridge in the Met's entrance: made entirely out of flowers.

Lake and I also had a plan for me as a walking fashion exhibit, which required several people to execute. Today, I'd been confined to the apartment while a team of stylists primped every square inch of my body, starting with an exfoliation, scrub, waxing, and mani-pedi, and would eventually end with the smallest details of hair, eyes, even blush color done to perfection. It was like my wedding day, but times ten. We had approximately two hours before Freddy was due to work on my hair, followed by the makeup artist. And then, just before we left, Lake would fully sew me into my dress.

I sat at the kitchen island in leggings and a ripped Brooklyn t-shirt, flipping through the binder, mentally calculating whether all of the details I'd been given had been taken care of. I couldn't find a single thing that needed follow up—and at any rate, I would be unavailable once Freddy began his work.

"Okay," Eric said as he strode out of my studio, followed by Lake. "Jane?"

As Eric had less to do, Lake had wanted to double-check his fit first. She was possibly more nervous than I was about all of this—after all, this was a huge coup for her, dressing us both for fashion's prom.

"What do you think?" Eric asked. He turned from side to side, modeling the tuxedo we'd designed to fit his long, lithe frame. His hair had been combed forward and ruffled in a way that made him look a bit younger than thirty-three, but otherwise he just looked classic, tall, with impossibly long legs—the perfect backdrop to my more dramatic look.

"Oh," I said, not quite able to find my voice. Okay, he was more than a backdrop. The man positively shined.

And then he smiled, and just like it did every time, his entire face transformed. He strode to me and placed a lingering kiss on my cheek. "I'm glad you like it, pretty girl."

At the sound of those words, I shuddered. If I had to be next to him looking like that all night, I had a feeling I was going to have a very hard time focusing on the exhibit.

"Go," I said, waving him away. "You're making my face turn red."

The grin just widened. "I can see that." Eric turned back to Lake and winked. "I think we're a success."

Lake nodded happily. "I agree. Okay, go change. I'll steam this one last time and hang it in the studio for later."

They left me to my binder, though I still couldn't for the life of me register anything I was looking at. Not when every cell in my body was urging me to follow Eric into the bedroom to help him "undress."

"Knock, knock!"

I looked up with surprise to find my best friend entering the apartment behind Tony and followed by...my mother. "Hey! Holy shit! What are you doing here?" I looked over her shoulder. "And Eomma too? Is Brandon coming up?"

"No, he's home with the kids," Skylar said. "We just wanted to come see you on your big day. Yu-na was especially eager to come."

"Wow. Okay." I hopped off my stool to embrace my friend and then exchange an awkward hug with my mother. "Hi, Eomma." A thought occurred to me. "Oh, you guys...you weren't expecting tickets, were you? I'm so sorry, but I really can't—Anna has control over the entire guest list, and it was everything we could do just to—"

"Janey, relax," Skylar cut in with a gentle hand on my shoulder. "We weren't. Your mom just wanted to see you."

"Ah...okay. But why now..." I trailed off as one of the other security team entered with four large suitcases. "Planning to stay a while?" *Please, God, no.* I winced guiltily at the first thought to cross my mind. I mean, I loved my mother. I should want her to be with me, shouldn't I?

"No," Yu-na said as she walked into the apartment. She had seen it before, when we got married, but not for a very long time. Now her interest was renewed. "I am going home. It is time. My flight is in three days from here. I wanted to see you first."

There was really only one place my mother had ever referred to as home. Not that shithole in South Korea she had fled, pregnant with me. Chicago.

As in Illinois.

As in approximately a thousand miles away.

"Wait...what?" I croaked, taken straight back to February, when she had announced the same thing. "You're moving? No. No, no, no, I forbid it."

"Jane, you forget that I am the mother here," she informed me. "Not you. Do you expect me to stay with your friend, this person I barely know, for the rest of my life? It has been three months. Too long."

"But you're there with Ji-yeon, aren't you?" I asked. "I thought you two were having a ball."

"Ji-yeon left a few weeks ago," Skylar said, looking as if she would rather not tell me. "I told them both they are welcome to stay as long as they like, but they were adamant."

I reared back at my mom. "And you didn't think to tell me?"

"Why would I tell you?" my mother demanded. "You never call. You call your friend to check in on me! It's like I don't exist to you, like I don't matter. You stick me in this place to get better, I see that, but now I am better, and I want to go home. So, I go."

"You go?" I parroted her. "You just...go? What the hell is that? After everything we have been through in the last year, you're just going to take off like nothing fucking happened?"

"How do you talk to your mother like that?" she shouted. "Do you see this, Skylar? You see how she treats me?"

Skylar just looked very much like she wanted to leave.

"Lord," I snapped. "You just can't help it, can you? Lay on the guilt, and make everything about you. Well, excuse me for wanting you to be safe!"

Lake came out of the studio looking uneasy at the sudden scene. Eric emerged from the bedroom and handed her the tux, then immediately crossed to me.

"Hey, Crosby," he said with a kiss to Skylar's cheek and another for my mother. "Yu-na. Good to see you." He turned to me. "Jane. Breathe."

"But—she—I—" I sputtered, waving my hands out at my mother. "She's just...leaving! Just like that!"

"Whoa, teapot," he said, gathering me close, rotating me around so I wasn't watching my mother's beady, basilisk eyes staring a baleful hole through me. "Cros, can you..." He gestured at something, and a second later, Skylar brought my shoes and a sweater.

"What—what the hell—" I couldn't get out a full sentence, but somehow allowed Eric to help me into the wool and my ballet flats.

"Let's go for a walk," he said. "It's a nice day. You can clear your head and then come back and talk."

I allowed him to hold me tight until I had stopped spinning like a kitchen appliance. My mother just walked to the living room and chatted with Skylar and Lake as if she hadn't tossed a grenade at me. Eventually, Eric turned us toward the trio.

"We'll be back in a bit," he said, waving at them all.

"Not too long, I hope," Lake called out, looking visibly concerned. After all, we were running out of time.

"Just a few minutes," Eric replied, already towing me toward the door. "We need to walk off our jitters."

The idea of unflappable Eric ever suffering from something as inane as "jitters," much less uttering the stupid word, had me giggling as we left. Much later I realized that he'd probably deployed it just to distract me.

It wasn't until we'd made it into the park, which was basically an impressionist painting with all the mid-spring flowers.

"All right, Lefferts," Eric said as we strode over the Seventh-Seventh Street arch and into the lush greenery. "We don't have time for me to fuck it out of you. Talk. You need to." He kept my hand in his, swinging it lightly as we walked, but his firm grip did not relax. "Why are you and your mother shrieking at each other like chickadees?"

"I..." I inhaled. "I don't like it. Did you know she's moving to Chicago? What the hell is that?"

"She wanted to go home three months ago, gorgeous. And you barely see her as it is. What difference does it make if she's in Chicago instead of Boston?"

"Well, for one, at Skylar's, someone can at least keep an eye on her."

"Is she a five-year-old who might eat too much chocolate?"

I rolled my eyes. "You know what I mean."

Eric sighed. "We can have someone do that in Chicago too. We can afford to hire an entire off-duty police force to follow her around if you want."

I shook my head. "It's not the same."

Eric was quiet as we walked. "Can I be totally honest?"

"Okay, fine. What?"

He stopped. "Has it ever occurred to you that you don't really like your mother, Jane?"

"That's ridiculous. No one likes their mothers."

He frowned. "That's not true."

"Do you like yours?"

"I don't really know her well enough to like her. But when I do see her, we don't fight like the two of you." He shook his head. "I've never seen you and Yu-na exist in the same place without snapping at each other. Why do you think that is?"

I grimaced. "Because she's so impossible?"

"Try again, Lefferts. It's because you're so much alike."

I considered. My mother and I did have some obvious similarities. Both stubborn. Both outspoken. Both maybe too dogmatic about what we thought was right. If we were on the same side of a debate, we got along fine, but the reality was, we usually weren't.

As a result, I had never been able to escape the niggling feeling that I had always been a disappointment to her. Especially this year. Especially with everything I had caused her.

"I know you feel guilty. I know you feel like she should be close. But if the two of you were really supposed to be in each other's lives all the time, you would be. It's as simple as that." He brushed a piece of hair out of my face. "But I also know you feel guilty she's been alone since your father died. And you feel guilty about what happened to her. But it wasn't your fault, Jane. Neither of those things are your fault."

It wasn't until he said so that I knew in my heart of hearts that he was right. She probably knew it true, which was why she kept trying to leave. My mother and I should absolutely not live together.

And yet...how could I let her go?

"How?" I wondered quietly. "How do you know it won't happen again if she is living there alone?"

"Well, to start, she won't be alone. She'll be in her old house, and she'll have her own dedicated security detail until John Carson is caught. They'll stay in the apartment below."

"Her old..." It took me a second to understand what he meant. "You didn't."

Eric shrugged, unwilling to confirm my suspicion directly. The answer, however, was all over his face.

"You bought back my parents' old house? The one in Evanston?"

Another shrug. "I did it a while ago, Jane. I figured you would want it back at some point. Your mother was taken when she was driving by it, wasn't she?"

My jaw dropped. I had considered trying to buy the house a few times, but since it wasn't actually for sale, it had never even occurred to me to make the owners an offer they couldn't refuse. But that, of course, was exactly what Eric must have done. It was something you could do when you had unlimited funds. A whole paradigm of thinking I still hadn't gotten used to.

"Well, you'll definitely be on her good side now," I said, shaking my head. "Jesus Christ, Eric. That's insane."

"I didn't really do it for her." He tipped up my chin, making me look at him, making me see the genuine love shining out of his silver eyes. "Like the air I breathe, right? It was your home, Jane. I see how sad you get whenever you talk about your dad. I know you feel like you lost that home over the last year, and not just because of Carol Lefferts's passing. I figured, if I could do anything to give you some of that back, it would be this."

A warm feeling bloomed in my chest, but I still couldn't quite speak.

Eric rubbed a hand behind his neck. "Tell me I did the right thing."

The warm feeling grew. "It's more than the right thing."

Eric smiled. "Good. Now, let's go tell your mom. I have a feeling she is flying by way of New York because she has a few things to tell you too. You're not the only one who's been healing the past few months, gorgeous. Everyone needs a bit of catharsis, not just us."

THIRTY-THREE

Skylar seemed to have done a good job taming my mother—better than I could. So much that she and I were able to sit together for most of the time I was prepped for the gala. While Freddy styled my hair into the half-up bouffant, Yu-na told me about everything she had done in Boston over the last three months. As the makeup artist worked, I heard about visiting the aquarium and the Freedom Trail, playing mah jongg with Sarah, and entertaining Jenny and Luis. Skylar, it seemed, had lent my mother her own family to help her heal. And apparently it had worked.

"I think we're done," Lake said as she fluffed my skirts one last time after the glam squad had finished. She stood and checked her watch. "And not a minute too soon. You're scheduled as one of the first arrivals, around five thirty. It's four forty-five now. You guys need to get going."

It was hard to imagine that it would really take forty-five minutes to cross Central Park, but she was right. The arrival order for the Met Gala was as carefully curated by Cora as the guest list and the seating chart. I was a major donor and also a recognizable face in the city now—not on par with any of the number of Hollywood celebrities who would be there, but definitely worthy of the red carpet.

Lake wasn't able to attend the actual event, but like many of the other stylists and lower-level designers, she would be available in another part of the museum for touch-ups during the night. Considering every attendee was basically a walking exhibit of each designer's art, we all needed our own personal curators as well. Mine now included my mother on top of the rest of them. I had promised I would sneak them into the exhibit I'd worked so hard on if at all possible.

"All right," I announced as I walked back into the living room where Eric was enjoying a cocktail or two with Skylar and Yu-na. "Are we ready?"

"Oh, wow," Skylar said. "Janey, you look incredible!"

"It's very nice," my mother said, which was the best compliment I was likely to get from her. I wasn't expecting more. After all, this wasn't exactly the Jessica McClintock knockoffs she had tried to talk me into during high school.

"Thanks," I said.

Eric stood, and I looked him over approvingly. "Wow. I know I've seen you in this before, but I'm still stunned. Lake, this is incredible."

"Our work is incredible," Lake agreed as she walked over to brush something off Eric's jacket.

Eric, however, appeared totally awestruck. "Hot damn, Lefferts. You look..."

I twisted back and forth in my finery and touched my hair self-consciously. Freddy had done a fantastic job with the sixties style, piling it high à la Amy Winehouse, with new red streaks shouting "PUNK!" along with the lush tartan, ripped hem, and spiked shoes.

"You don't think it's a little too Tracks?" I asked, referencing the record shop from Pretty in Pink. We had watched it together last night.

He stepped close and pushed a stray fire-engine red lock off my shoulder. "I thought I made it very clear that the record store owner is the hottest one anyway."

I blushed. Beside us, Lake grinned.

"You look perfect," she said. "A perfect match."

Over her shoulder, I caught a glimpse of the two of us in the mirror.

"You hear that, pretty girl?" Eric murmured, his voice rumbling with promise. "A perfect match."

I had to agree.

THE DVS LIMO pulled up in front of the red carpet—which was actually a deep midnight blue—at exactly five thirty. Tony stepped out of the passenger seat and came around to open the back door for the rest of our security detail, and then us.

"Holy shit," I murmured as I took in the walls of reporters and photographers, the bright, tented entrance extending down the famous steps of the Metropolitan Museum of Art, and the swirl of guests already making their way up the entrance. It was clear by the way the photographers already writhed for a shot that we were some of the first "names" to arrive—and our notoriety didn't even approach the lineup behind us.

"It's going to be great," Eric said as he straightened his collar.

His tone was calm, but I could see he was still nervous, likely more about Carson's potential presence than having his photo in the paper. He'd been fussing with his clothes since we'd gotten in the car.

"Stop that." I batted at his hand, which was tugging on his jacket again. "You're going to stretch it out."

"My lapel?"

"It's wool. That's easily distorted."

He opened his mouth like he wanted to argue, then shut it. "Fine, pretty girl. Are you ready?"

I turned back to the cameras, trying not to shiver. "What's that saying?" The shakes in my voice obviously overrode my attempts at bravado. "'You've arrived'?" I turned to Eric. "It doesn't get better than this for me. I did it. I'm here. At this level."

He smiled. "You were already at this level. You just had to wait for the rest of us to catch up with you."

Lake, who had ridden with us, primped my dress and touched up my lipstick, then took a lint brush to Eric one final time. "All right, loves. You're perfect. I'll be in the back with your mother and your friend when you're done with the red carpet. Now go shine."

I grasped her hand, unable to give her the hug I really wanted because:

"'Taffeta, darling,'" Eric murmured.

I grinned at him, then turned back to the designer. "Thank you so much, Lake. For everything."

Tony opened the door with a friendly smile. I took a deep breath, grabbed Eric's hand, and stepped out into a barrage of flashing lights.

"Mr. de Vries!"

"Jane!"

"Over here!"

"Who designed your dress?"

I turned to answer the question. "Lake McHugh."

Several reporters scribbled down the name.

"Why didn't you tell them it's you?" Eric asked as we took a few more steps and paused again for pictures. Lord, how in the hell did celebrities do this all the time without sunglasses? I was already seeing stars.

I shrugged. "I—well, Lake really did most of the work. She should get the credit."

"That's not how I remember it," Eric replied. "You've been working on these clothes nonstop for weeks."

Behind us, there was a roar from the crowd as someone particularly famous must have exited their car. We were losing interest from reporters, and I did want to make an entrance. For Lake's sake as a designer.

And, I realized, I wanted my own recognition.

"Jane! Eric!" called another reporter, beckoning us over. This one wore a clear badge from the *Post*. "Who are you wearing tonight?"

"Do it," Eric urged.

I took a deep breath. "It's codesigned. By Lake McHugh...and me."

THIRTY-FOUR

Approximately two hours later, we had finished mingling and were locating our table along with many other invitees who had slowly made their way through the press corridor, into the museum, and through the exhibit carefully planned for the event.

"That was incredible," Eric congratulated me again. "I can't believe you did all of that. I legitimately feel like I just moved through your brain."

I shook my head. "Most of it was planned before I even came on board. I just...helped where I could."

Truthfully, I was shining with pride. This was one of the most exciting nights of my life. For the first time, I understood what it meant to feel truly passionate about something I had accomplished. I wanted to have that again. I wanted it for the rest of my life too.

"Jane! Eric!" Heather approached us from across the ballroom, where other guests were pouring in from the exhibit and finding their seats for the dinner. It was hard not to be starstruck among all of the celebrities and outlandish costumes—one musician actually had a mohawk that stood nearly two feet tall—but Heather still managed to shine.

I froze, immediately looking for her "date" for the evening, but she quickly grabbed my hand.

"It's okay," she said. "Johnny didn't show. I arrived stag just after you two did." She shrugged. I had a feeling she wasn't terribly disappointed.

My stomach calmed almost immediately. There was no way Carson was getting past all the security surrounding this event without his date. Maybe it was for the best that we couldn't manage to catch him here. Now we could just enjoy the evening.

"It's okay," I agreed, looking up at Eric. "Right?"

He blinked. "Right. Hi, Mom."

Eric greeted his mother with a kiss on the cheek, seemingly unsurprised to find her alone. I frowned. Wasn't the entire point of inviting her that she would be the bait for someone else?

"Hello, darling. My, don't you both look dashing."

Heather's voice was cut with longing, and as she looked us both over, I wondered if she didn't see shades of her dead husband in her son. How many of these sorts of events must they have attended together. I had seen photos of the man who, yes, looked a lot like Eric. Together, Jacob and Heather would have cut quite the figure.

"You look beautiful too," I told her.

She really did. Unsurprisingly, she hadn't really taken up the theme, opting instead for a black dress with a few perfunctory safety pins at the shoulder. It was more Park Avenue than punk, but I supposed that was Heather too.

"Oh, thank you," she said. "Vicki made it up for me last minute. I'm so lucky. She almost always keeps things for me."

I blinked. I was pretty sure she was talking about Victoria Beckham like she was a next-door neighbor who loaned her some sugar, but you never really knew with the de Vrieses.

"Well," I said as equally nonchalantly as I could manage, "that was incredibly nice of...Vicki."

Heather beamed. "It was, wasn't it?" She peered up at Eric again.

"Will you save me a dance?" she asked shyly. "Do you remember your old dance lessons?"

Eric opened his mouth, looking very much like he wanted to say no, but before he could, I cut in.

"Of course he will," I said, earning a sharp look from my husband. I winked at him, and his stolid expression softened.

He sighed. "Yeah, sure, Mom. I'd love to."

"Good," Heather said softly before someone caught her eye over my shoulder. "Oh! That's Helen. I should say hello."

And with that, she darted through the crowd to greet someone who looked a lot like venerated actress Helen Mirren. But again, I couldn't be sure. This was a member of the de Vries family we were talking about. They could be friends with anyone.

Just like me now, I supposed.

"You'd better give me a dance too," Eric murmured as he wrapped an arm around my waist. "Or ten."

I looked up under a sweep of lashes. "You just need to say the words."

"What's that? Pretty girl?"

My belly clenched deliciously at the phrase. "Exactly."

Eric didn't even try to mask the naked hunger on his face. Slowly, he leaned down so that his cheek, slightly stubbled, brushed over mine. "You can count on it," he rumbled in my ear. "And for the record, those shoes are making me want to do a very different dance with you later. You better keep them on when we get home."

I smacked his chest. "You are such a cornball." I was joking, of course. When he looked at me like that, I fucking thrilled.

Eric's mouth just quirked in a slick smirk.

"But first, let's eat," he said. "I'm fucking starving."

We found our table somewhere near the middle of the room. I'd already been briefed on my tablemates: a socialite and her husband, a pair of designers and their dates, and Nina and Calvin Gardner. To my surprise, however, instead of Calvin, I found Nina sitting next to Matthew Zola. He looked particularly rakish in a plain black suit, his dark hair slicked back and a red rose tucked jauntily into his lapel.

They were in very, *very* deep conversation.

"I am not doing this right here," she snapped—well, as much as Nina ever snapped. It was really more like a kitten's mewl.

"Please, doll," Zola said in a low, languid voice that made me almost uncomfortable with its intimacy. "I think you and I both know that under the right circumstances, you would do whatever I told you to do."

"Matthew, please."

"Shit," Eric muttered, and it was clear what he was referring to.

I had to agree. Whatever was going on between Nina and our handsome Italian prosecutor clearly wasn't the result of a casual connection.

"Well, hello!" I was overly jubilant, hoping to cover in case Calvin was returning. I had no lost love for Eric's brother-in-law, but if this was what I thought it was, I wasn't interested in getting Nina into trouble, especially considering how much she had helped us.

Eric, however, wasn't bothered by such considerations.

"What the hell are you doing here?" Eric asked Zola directly.

"This isn't over." Zola eyed Nina once more, then stood to speak to Eric. "I couldn't let the cops have all the fun, could I? Granted, I'll have to watch, but Nina was nice enough to help me in."

"You couldn't just wait with the squad cars? Don't you think being here would give the game away?"

I blinked. "Eric, why does it matter? Carson isn't coming anyway."

"He isn't?" Nina asked. "Oh, I'm so sorry."

Zola met Eric's level gaze, and for a moment, the two of them engaged in a strange little stare-off I couldn't quite read. Nina studied her wedding ring intensely, perhaps looking as if she wanted to rip it off.

Zola cleared his throat. "I...no, you're right. I should probably go." He glanced at Nina. "See you, doll."

Eric and I immediately turned to his cousin.

"Nina, what the hell?" Eric demanded.

She still would not make eye contact. "Calvin didn't want to come, and to be honest, I was fine with that. He's a terrible date at this sort of event anyway. Since Matthew is helping to put John Carson behind bars, isn't he, shouldn't he have come in? I was just helping."

"Matthew? Come on, Nina..."

"I'm going to the ladies' room." She stood up and smoothed her dress, which, I noted with appreciation, was made almost entirely out of something resembling chain mail. She looked absolutely gorgeous as she wove in between the growing crowd, tall and graceful in that way only the de Vrieses could manage. You can't fake that level of aristocratic breeding.

"Should I go with her?" I asked. I wasn't going to lie. I really didn't want to. I liked gossip as much as the next person, but I had absolutely no interest in meddling with the personal affairs of my cousin-in-law.

Eric sighed. "You know what? I don't even care. It's her mess, if there is one at all. Let her clean it up." He swallowed heavily. "I'm going to get a drink. Do you want a cocktail?"

I nodded. "Sure."

He looked me over, and his gaze fell to my lips, which were a particularly vibrant shade of red to match my dress.

"Damn," he murmured regretfully. "I'll be right back."

I blushed under the heat of his gaze. "Soon, I hope."

BUT IT WASN'T SOON. I waited at the table, making chitchat with the other guests for nearly thirty minutes. Waiters started to deliver food, and just as a plate of salmon tartar was set in front of me, I decided to get up to find my errant husband, and then my mother, who was probably torturing all the stylists and celebrities with critiques of their avant-garde wear. We were running out of time to show her the exhibit, and I wanted Eric to come too.

"Did you see him leave?" I asked Emily Beckett, a pregnant socialite at our table with her husband, one of the biggest hedge fund managers in the city. All of our cell phones had been checked upon entrance to maintain then event's exclusivity.

She looked up dreamily, despite having drunk absolutely nothing. Her husband seemed more interested in his cell phone. Then she grimaced and grabbed her belly.

I immediately bent down. "Are you okay?"

She gave me a grim smile. "Oh, sure. Just a little Braxton-Hicks. I had them with the last one." She let out a long breath.

"Hon? Do you need anything?" her husband finally asked.

"Some ice water would be lovely," she told him, and he immediately left to retrieve some from a passing waiter.

"Do you have any kids?" Emily asked, turning to me.

"I..." Oh, God. Would that question ever not hurt? "No. No, we don't." I paused. "We just got married last November, actually."

"Well, it does kind of ruin your figure," she joked. "I'll never get my waist back without some help from a surgeon."

"Here's your water, hon." Her husband returned, and Emily took her drink gratefully. It was sweet, really, the way he hovered over her like that.

"Shit," I muttered, suddenly feeling cold. I pressed a hand over my very flat stomach. Fuck a nice figure. I'd take a baby.

Whoa. I would?

The heart wants what it wants, kiddo.

I warmed. Dad again, imparted his clean logic from the grave. I ached. No, I wasn't ready yet. Not right this second...but maybe...in nine months?

I reached out for Eric's knee, but only found chair instead. Goddammit. Where was he? Suddenly, all I wanted was to find him. To look into his eyes and see his blind faith in our future together. I needed it.

I stood up. "I'm...I'm just going to go find my husband."

It took me a while to spot him at the far side of the exhibition hall. I was stopped by several other guests congratulating me on my work and admiring my dress. But find him I did, just as he had stopped by one of the exits.

He checked his watch. And then he darted away into a darkened hall where tonight's guests really weren't supposed to go.

"What the hell?" I checked the room to make sure none of the museum's security was watching me. And then I followed Eric into the museum proper.

He walked quickly, with obvious purpose, nearly losing me as he twisted and turned through the halls of the Met, directly through several darkened rooms. For a while I lost him, following the sounds of his footsteps on the stone floors. He must have known I was behind him—my stilettos were even louder.

And then his footsteps stopped. I wandered into the darkened wing where the Roman statues loomed like ghosts. "Eric?"

There was a long, audible sigh before he stepped out from behind one of the statues. "Hey, gorgeous."

I crossed the gallery to where he stood next to a large sculpture of Diana towering over an indoor fountain. "What are you doing here?"

He sighed again. "I just needed a break. A bit of quiet."

I frowned. "Already? We barely got here, and you just disappeared." Something in his voice didn't quite sound right.

His gaze sparked in the night.

"Oh." Now I understood. "You're upset that Carson's not here. Look, I get it. But honestly, maybe it's for the best. This night is so special. We can figure something else out tomorrow."

Eric just shook his head. "Jane, it's not that. I..."

His despondency killed me. Suddenly, I felt terrible. He had been doting over me for months, making sure I was healing properly from the traumas we had suffered. He was seeing a therapist, yes, but was I really taking care of him enough? Doubtful.

Well, I could change that.

"Hey," I said. "You're not alone in this."

Eric looked up, a note of warmth brightening his sad gray eyes. "I'm not, huh?"

I walked close, then wrapped my arms around his solid waist. Fuck the taffeta. We needed to be close. I tipped my face up for a kiss. "Well, you do have me."

"And me."

Eric and I both started apart at the sound of the familiar droll voice. My eyes widened in panic, since the last place I had heard that voice, of course, was when I had been held captive.

Eric, however, just rolled his, then stamped a brief, thorough kiss to my still-open lips.

"You're a fucking day late, Hermes," he said before turning toward the voice.

"Since when are you one to follow the rules, Triton?"

And there, the only sign of his discomfort the way he shifted from foot to foot, was Jude Letour. Rich kid. Cocky bastard. And right-hand man to John Carson.

THIRTY-FIVE

"Late?" I asked, turning so fast that my bouffant almost fell out. "What do you mean, 'late'?"

Eric turned to me with a tight jaw. "Jane—"

"Where's my mother?" I hissed. "Tell me she's safe."

"She's got four different security with her plus twenty stylists. I just texted Tony. She's fine."

"All right," I said. "Then what the fuck is this asshole doing here?"

"What's this, you didn't tell your courtesan about our plan?"

Jude approached, looking more like a cartoon devil than ever in a black cashmere sweater and sleek black pants, his irritatingly smug face still lined with a chinstrap beard. What did the man actually do again? Eric had mentioned something about imports and exports, but Jude dressed more like someone walking off a 1970s GQ shoot.

"You don't really want to try me like that, do you?" Eric stepped forward like he wanted to punch the man again, but held back.

Jude touched his nose briefly, then held up his hands in surrender. "Jokes, jokes, Triton. I come in peace, young Skywalker, remember?" He smirked at me. I honestly wondered if he had another expression. "Or maybe that applies more to you, doesn't it, princess? Daughter of the dark father and all. Besides, you need me."

"What in the hell are you doing here?" I spat before Eric could reply.

A hand at my wrist stilled me. "Give it a moment," Eric murmured. "He's right. We need him."

I jerked back. "*What*?"

There was no way he didn't understand my shock. This piece of shit was part of a group that had abducted *both* of us, forcibly aborted our child, and murdered his fiancée. And now he wanted to work with him?

But Jude, too pleased with the spotlight to give it up, continued. "I'm his second, my little dim sum."

"Jude!" Eric snapped.

"What?" he said. "Dim sum is delicious."

"It's also Chinese, you racist prick," I said.

Jude clicked his tongue, but to my surprise, Eric didn't tell him off.

"Jude's here on my request," he said.

Eric's grip on my wrist was iron. *Trust me*, he said wordlessly.

I took a deep breath. And then another. And then, somewhere deep inside me, I found the ability to stifle every nasty comment and threat I had. Because if I couldn't trust Eric, I couldn't trust anyone. Right?

"He's right, tigress," Jude said. "The list of people Carson trusts is shorter than your marriage, Cio-Cio San. And I happen to be on it."

"Does he know you're here?" Eric asked.

Jude nodded. "Of course he does. I'm his 'scout,' after all. He wanted me to watch you to make sure everything was safe."

"Does he make you taste his food too?" I snapped.

Jude rolled his eyes. "Why? Should he?"

"Well, it's convenient, at any rate," Eric cut in. "Gives you a reason to be here."

"That it does. And to that effect, I was sent with a message, which I'm obviously delivering now." Jude's dark eyes sharpened. "You're to meet him right here, in the Greek and Roman Art room." He scoffed visibly.

Eric didn't answer the question. "What does he want?"

"Good God, Triton, what do you think he wants?" Jude snapped. "The same thing he's wanted since before you and I barely existed. Heather, the DVS shipping contracts for the Koreas, and, of course this one." His cold gaze flickered at me with something that approximated sympathy. "I suspect that when you're caught again, princess, you won't get out."

"How would he know where to find me?" I asked, and in answer, Jude pushed up the sleeve of his sweater and shook the small gold bracelet at me—the one bearing a familiar gold coin. Suddenly, the strange nature of the conversation became clear. Both men were well aware of the fact that we were being monitored. Fuck.

"Well, you can pass on my answer," Eric said, perhaps a little too loudly. "My answer is no. More like a fuck no, actually."

Jude didn't look the slightest bit surprised, but spoke as though he were. "You can't possibly think that's a good idea, Triton. Are you looking to repeat your troubles?"

Eric didn't answer—it was clear they were both trying to cultivate a sense of struggle. I was lost.

"Come on, Jane," he said. "We're leaving." But instead of drawing me back through darkened halls, he instead pulled a piece of paper out of his jacket—one with a pre-written message:

Midnight at Portas.

Jude read it, then gave a brief, curt nod before he crumpled the note and shoved it into his pocket.

"You're an idiot," he pronounced clearly for the benefit of his bracelet. "And you'll regret it."

"Tell Carson the feeling his mutual," Eric said.

"Holy shit," I breathed. "You're calling a meeting of Janus?"

Eric just shook his head and held a finger to his lips. I frowned. What was this?

Jude cackled. "This will be fun. I'll give him that much."

I opened my mouth to argue again, but Eric shook his head.

"Hush," Eric said. "He's just trying to get under your skin. It's what he does."

I bit back another complaint. He was right, of course.

Eric released my arm, but his hand still floated around the small of my back, keeping me close. "Jude." He pointed to his wrist, then pulled a pair of small metal cutters from his jacket. To my surprise, Jude willingly stepped forward and allowed Eric to snap the bracelet from his wrist, then dropped it neatly into the fountain. Jude looked relieved.

"That's better," Eric said. "You think he'll buy it?"

I balked. "That was all an act?"

Jude shrugged, like I hadn't spoken. "It's no big secret that you know about these. He'll think it was the price of luring you here."

"And you?" Eric asked. "What's your price for getting Carson to the location?"

Realization dawned. *Portas*. Midnight.

He was staging a coup. And Jude was helping.

I turned to Eric. "This is insanity. We talked about this. You can't just run off to Connecticut in the middle of the night. And definitely not with the Devil's fucking handmaid here!"

Eric just shook his head. "It's the best way. We can't keep doing this, Jane. The feds, even the DA is on the take. We have to deal with this ourselves."

Jude just cackled again.

"Eric," I tried again. "You can't possibly think you can trust him."

"Oh, no?" Jude asked. "Perhaps this might be a bit of a surprise, Chop Sticks, but I don't actually plan to spend my life playing number two to an insane man. The last ten years were normal. A meeting once or twice a year, basic tampering with the Department of the Interior, a solid bit of insider trading, you know the drill. But then the prodigal son here had to show up again, and everything went batshit. It was fun for a bit, but do you know? I don't really have a taste for torture. It's really quite grotesque."

I narrowed my eyes. "You could have fooled me."

Jude's face darkened. "Yes, well. They do say every hero has a fatal flaw. Your family"—he practically spat the word—"happened to be Carson's. And I'm...well, quite bored of it." Then he did spit into the fountain, as if just talking about the whole matter required a palette cleanser. "And I'm not interested in being dragged down with a sinking ship. I've never claimed to be a great champion of scruples, but his little stunt with this one was a bit much, even for me."

I dropped a hand protectively over my stomach. Eric followed the movement before he tore himself away.

"You want to run away and have a whole host of yellow brats, be my guest, Triton," Jude said. "But clean up your house first, please. Carson needs to be disposed of. If you can bring the society back to normal, I'm all for it. Just make me your number two. And, of course, get me full exoneration."

Eric's hands rose with mock innocence. "Hey, Letour, the society I can handle. But I'm not the one writing the indictment."

"No, but you're damn cozy with the one who is." Jude's face twisted into an ugly scowl. "You would end up in league with the first principled DA in the history of New York City." He held out a hand, as if waiting for a handshake. "Immunity from all charges. I assume kidnapping is on the table. Maybe some trafficking? If you tell them I'm innocent, they'll believe you."

Eric blinked. That mask I hated was firmly in place, and I had never been so glad for it. If I couldn't tell what he was thinking, then there was no way Jude could.

"Innocent," he said at last. "By my word."

Jude nodded. "Very well. I'll make sure Carson's at the *Portas*. Midnight." And with that, he disappeared into the dark corridors.

I waited a full ten minutes, until we could no longer hear his foot-steps lingering in the dark. A door opened and closed. He was gone.

Then I turned to Eric. "Tell me you're not going through with this. Meeting John Carson in the middle of the night. Staging a coup well outside the jurisdiction of the NYPD? Letting that scum of the earth go?" With every item on the list, my voice rose an octave and a decibel.

Sorrow crossed Eric's face. "Jane, it's the only way—"

"You cannot possibly believe that!" I cried. "You're going to trust that Jack Sparrow caricature over your own wife? *He is playing you!*"

"It's done," he said. "Jane, some of this is out of your hands. You keep asking me to be the man I was born to be. Well, I was born into this world. Taking back my birthright is going to give me the leverage to keep us safe. Can you fucking get that through your head without ruining things again?"

I stepped back like I'd been slapped. In less than fifteen minutes, I felt like I'd been thrown down Alice's rabbit hole. Who was this person speaking? "Fuck. You."

Eric shook his head ruefully, took a step toward me but stopped when I scrambled backward.

I swallowed, then glared at him. "If that's really what you think, then you are not half the man I thought you were. And if you need the approval of some grown men's treehouse club more than your own wife's...well, then I think you know how this ends."

"Jane—"

"Absolutely not." I shook my head. I knew it. I knew there was another shoe that had to drop before all of this was over. Damn him for making me believe it wouldn't be his. "I think it's safe to say we are going to give John Carson what he wants. This isn't going to work. Maybe it never was."

"Jane!"

I held up a hand. "I need some space. I'm going back to the event I have devoted every waking hour to for the last few months. You can go play your boys' game if that's what you have to do."

Eric stood tall, but not completely without regret. "Jane," he said. "Just trust me. Please."

But I shook my head and turned away. "Trust goes two ways, Eric. I would think that by now, you'd have learned that."

THIRTY-SIX

I moved through the rest of the event like a ghost. Walked my mother through the gallery and vaguely answered her random questions. Listened to Cora and a few other celebrities give perfunctory speeches to a crowd of raucous celebrities. Sat through the musical guest—some pop star who was "co-hosting."

But Eric never reappeared. Clearly he really had gone to New Haven. I began to wonder if he was ever coming back. And guiltily, what that really meant.

Trust me, he'd said. No, pleaded. And I hadn't, instead allowing him to leave in the night.

Somewhere between watching celebrities dance the night away in the crowd and drinking my fourth glass of champagne, I had had enough. I stood up and turned to Nina.

"I'm going home."

She was too busy looking through the crowd. "Really? It's still quite the party in here."

I peered at her, wondering if she was looking for a particular dark-haired someone to part that crowd like the red sea. He, however, had disappeared too. I guessed Eric had updated him on his bullshit plans.

"Didn't Zola leave?" I ventured, just to mess with her.

Nina swiveled back toward me like her head was on a spring. "What?Matthew?" She batted her hand, like she was chasing away a fly. "I don't know what you mean—"

"Nina, Nina, Nina," I joked. "I'm not judging, I promise. It's okay if he's got a thing for you. It's nice, right? Means you still got it."

But the way her cheeks pinked, even under the dim lighting, told me it was a lot more than just a mild crush. Well, shit. That wasn't good.

I set a gentle hand on her shoulder. "Is it...what about Calvin?"

I didn't even like to ask the question—neither Eric nor I could stand the guy. But she was married. And with a child. And messing around with the attorney who was literally the family's only ally in a feud with a crazed autocratic tycoon wasn't the greatest idea either.

Nina swallowed heavily and shook her head. "You don't—you don't have to worry about anything. I promise. He likes me, but I've assured him that I'm not available." Her dove-gray eyes shone in the dancing lights. "Don't worry, Jane. I would never compromise this family."

I examined her a moment. I didn't know Nina extremely well or anything, but she had stayed with me for a bit when Eric was at Rikers. And we had talked enough that I knew there was more than met the eye under that polished, carefully wrought veneer. A lot of unhappiness, in particular. Unhappiness that I doubted she would want to discuss right here. If ever.

So instead of pressing the matter further, I nodded. "Okay, then. Well, it's one in the morning. I know this will go on forever, but I'm exhausted. I need some sleep." I cocked my head. "Will you be all right?"

Nina nodded, and it was suddenly as if the sadness on her face had been wiped away as easily as dust. "Yes, I'll be fine. My car is picking me up at two anyway." She smiled. Like Eric, her quiet beauty transformed with the simple act. "You did a wonderful job, Jane. I'm truly impressed."

She reached out to grasp my hand briefly, then let it go and kissed my cheek. "Good night. Keep my cousin safe, will you?"

The pang of guilt in my stomach returned. Shit.

I swallowed. "I'll do my best."

And with that, I turned and left.

AFTER CLAIMING MY THINGS, I walked down the steps while messaging Tony to come get me. He left earlier to escort my mother back to the apartment, but should have been back by now. I'd check the house first to see if Eric had gone home, I decided. If he wasn't there, we'd hightail it to New Haven. Tony had to know at least where the cemetery was containing the creepy meeting place, and Eric had told me enough about the chamber that maybe I could find it.

"Stupid, stupid, stupid," I told myself as I teetered in my heels. I'd had more than my share of champagne, and I was definitely ready to remove my spikes. But more than that, with every step I felt worse about our fight. I did trust Eric. I should have gone with him rather than forbidding him to go.

Fifth Avenue was jammed, already packed with limo drivers waiting for the gala's guests to leave. Shit, Tony would take absolutely forever to get down this street. I'd be better off walking a few blocks down to the Seventy-Ninth Street Traverse. He could pick me up on the corner, and we'd be home in a few minutes.

As I texted Tony the change of plans, I started down Fifth Avenue. It was warm enough for early May, but too chilly to be standing outside in a strapless dress. The blooming trees above me cast shadows closer to the traverse entrance that weren't exactly comforting either.

"Come on, Tony," I muttered as I looked back up Fifth and then toward the river. "Where are you?" I was so busy looking, I almost didn't realize that I had stumbled right into a woman coming out of the park.

"Oh!" I said. "I'm so sorry!"

Phone still in hand, I reached out to steady her and came face-to-face with my mother-in-law.

I stepped back. "Heather? Are you okay?" I looked around, expecting her driver to pop up. What was she doing in the park?

Her big eyes widened "Oh—oh, Jane. Oh, no."

She looked a far sight from the polished woman I'd originally greeted in the gala. Still beautiful, yes, but her hair was tousled, and a bright red scrape marred her perfect skin.

"Holy crap," I said, reaching out for her. "Oh my God, Heather, are you okay?" I glanced around, looking for help, or perhaps an assailant. "Do we need to call the police?"

"Jane," she said in a voice strung like a rusty violin. "Jane, dear. Run."

Two faces appeared behind her. Faces I knew quite well. One was the haughty, masochistic sneer of the Russian, Anton. The one who had taken such pleasure in waterboarding me with ramen noodles. The other was Jude Letour, black eyes gleaming over that stupid fucking goatee.

"Shit," I whispered.

Jude's smile burned. "Hello, dumpling. Twice in one night. I'm a lucky man."

I looked up and down the street. "Where's Eric?"

Jude's smile widened, and dread lodged itself in my stomach.

But before he could answer, a black sedan pulled up behind us, effectively cornering Heather and me against Jude and Anton. I watched in horror as the back door opened, and the bent, patrician figure who had been haunting my dreams since last November emerged from the depths.

John Carson's deep greenish-brown eyes glinted under the city lights as he peered at me, then Heather. His face was even thinner than before, his salt-and-peppered hair shinier.

But his eyes. Oh, his eyes, they burned.

"Daughter," he said. "I knew it would only be a matter of time."

I couldn't speak. I couldn't even breathe. Wherever Tony was, he obviously wasn't coming now. We'd been bested again, and this time, there would be absolutely no one coming to find me. Eric was two and a half hours away, probably literally being buried in that cemetery, while his mother and I were about to be abducted and taught a lesson.

Which meant, of course, I had nothing to lose.

"I wouldn't run," Carson commented. "Anton isn't very kind to women who do. They usually end up in a ditch somewhere, strangled with their own clothes." He cocked a brow knowingly. "Just ask your mother."

Ditches. Clothes. Holy fuck, Anton was the Hwaseong murderer.

I slipped out of my shoes, ignoring the thrill of revulsion as my bare feet touched the most disgusting of all things: a New York City sidewalk.

"I d-don't think so," I said.

"Anton," Carson said as he examined his watch. "Get them."

Instinct took over.

"No!" I grabbed the only weapons I had—a pair of five-thousand-dollar spiked stilettos, and whirled around, flailing out my arms like a crazy woman until they made contact with something. That some-thing ended up being Anton, who fell back clutching his face. Ha! My spikes had hit pay dirt—he was bleeding like a pig as two gashes appeared in his cheek, another over his eye. He swore loudly in Russ-ian, glaring at me through his hands.

"Jane!"

At the sound of the voice, I froze. Heather. I had been so busy trying to flee, I had forgot about Heather. At the edge of the stone barrier, I turned, and of course found her writhing in the leering grip of Jude Letour. Carson shook his head as he examined at his bleeding Russian goon.

"That wasn't very nice," he remarked. "Anton quite likes his face. And he tends to hold a grudge."

"Jane, go," Heather said.

But all I could think about was Eric. The stories he told me. The last thing his father had ever said to him.

Take care of your mother.

Eric was as good as dead.

You die, I go too, he promised. Well, it went both ways, didn't it? He couldn't save himself. And I couldn't save myself.

But I could save his mother.

"Let her go," I said, full of something other than bravado. "You let her go, I'll come with you. I won't fight, I promise."

Carson's eyes sparked. "Is that so?"

I held up my shoe, like I was planning to throw it. Who knew, maybe I would. I was capable or anything right now.

"Jane," Heather said. "Jane, no!"

"You've already taken Eric," I said. "You might as well take me too, because without him, I'm dead anyway."

"That's very romantic," Carson replied. "And disappointingly melodramatic for a daughter of mine." He tapped his fingers on his chin. "Very well." He turned to Anton. "Take her home. Then meet us at the house."

"Jane!" Heather shouted as Jude practically tossed her into Anton's bloody hands. "Jane, no!"

"Go!" I shouted, even as I dropped my shoe to the ground. As soon as the spiked heel hit the pavement, I was swept up by Jude's deceptively strong arms and hauled toward the car. The door shut on me and Jude, with Carson sitting in the passenger seat beside the driver.

"Go," was all Carson said, and we drove off, leaving Heather floundering with Anton.

"Let me go!" I wriggled my arm out of Jude's grasp. He just

laughed, not seeming to care. And why should he? I had given myself up. I was trapped, yet again, by these men who never seemed to let me or mine go.

"You betrayed him," I snapped. "You sniveling, two-faced, spoiled fucking brat, you betrayed him!"

"Just like you knew I would, my little dog eater," he answered. "But your boy, unfortunately, was too stupid to realize it." Jude cackled. He actually cackled, like some kind of deranged cartoon villain. "Did you really think it would be that easy to overcome a man who has been two steps ahead, every single time?"

"That's enough, Hermes."

"You're an asshole," I snapped at Jude. "Both of you are going down for this. I hope you know that. You can kill me and Eric if that's what you really want, but there are too many people who know what you've done. My mother. Eric's cousin. Our friends. The entire fucking district attorney's office. You think you're going to get away with this kind of thing forever? Everyone's power has limits, you entitled fucking pricks! Even yours!"

A hand flew out from the front of the car and slapped me, open-palmed, across the face. Hard enough that my ears rang and I saw stars. When I could see straight again, I found Carson glaring at me from the front seat like a father who had just given his child a spanking. *Well, fuck you, buddy*, I thought.

"What's wrong, *Dad*?" I snapped, unable to feel anything but nauseous with the use of the term. "Did I get under your skin?"

Carson looked very much like he wanted to slap me again, but instead, he turned around as the car pulled over.

"Right here," he told his driver.

"What in the hell?" I murmured, realizing I knew exactly where we were.

Our little car ride had only taken a few minutes. And here we were parked right outside my under-construction house on West Seventh-Sixth Street.

I turned back to the men. "What are we doing here?"

"What do you think we're doing here?" Jude said. "We're going up."

"The security?" Carson asked.

"Neutralized," Jude said. "Two of them went with Triton to the cemetery, and the others are lying in a heap on the far side of the museum. There's no one here."

My heart sank as I realized that Tony had probably never even retrieved my mother, who, I prayed, was still at the Met with Skylar.

Carson nodded. "Let's go, then."

I was dragged out of the car, stubbing my feet on the sidewalk and then on the construction debris on the first floor as we entered. However they had accosted Tony, they had also taken his key, I realized. They wanted something. But what?

THIRTY-SEVEN

We barged into the apartment with all the grace of a freight train, practically breaking the door down to enter. Just as they had said, the apartment below housing our security was empty. The bottom floors, with their construction debris, were ghost towns. We were completely alone.

"Where is it?" Carson demanded.

Jude shrugged, though his grip on my wrist remained iron. "This would have been easier if we hadn't left Anton bleeding out on Fifth Avenue. He's better at sniffing out hidden goods than I am. Once a thief, always a thief, I say."

"I don't give a damn what you say," Carson snapped. Ha ha! Looks like the Psycho Papa was starting to show his cracks. "We can't stay here. But we need those documents."

Realization dawned. They were here for the journals. The files. The notes. Everything Eric and I had collected over the last several months to trap Carson's conniving ass. He was well aware of the investigations against him, of course. But he must have figured out what was going on down at the Brooklyn DA's office. Just like he had clearly figured out that Zola and his ilk couldn't be bought either.

So, apparently, the evidence had to be found.

"Come on, fellas," I said, not even struggling against Jude's strong grip. "Even if we did have all the goods on you here, don't you think the DA has copies? Just like the CIA? And NIS?" I tipped my head. "I could keep going."

But Carson, to my surprise, didn't look the slightest bit worried. Shit. That meant that somehow he had already tampered with or even stolen the DA's cache. He already knew the Feds were neutralized.

Carson just turned to Jude with a bored expression. "She knows where they are."

I opened my mouth, then closed it. And then smiled. "You'll never get them."

Jude tipped his head. "Try me, princess. We could play hot or cold if you like." He bound my wrists roughly with some kind of plastic tie, then shoved me roughly toward Carson before starting in the direction of Eric's bedroom.

I couldn't help it. I grinned.

Jude, unfortunately, grinned back. "Hot, I see." He pressed a hand against the bedroom door. "Is it in here? Will you be so helpful as to tell me the combination?" He tipped his head. "I wonder if it's your birthday too."

Too? Did that mean they broke into the safe in Boston too? I shook my head as something else occurred to me. "I can't even get to them, you big idiot."

Jude frowned. "Care to clarify that?"

Laughter bubbled up. Because the irony, oh, the fucking irony was too good. Before I could answer, however, a sudden chill of metal slipped against my neck, and I choked.

"I suggest you choose your words carefully." Carson's deep voice hummed like an engine against my ear as he wrapped my hands . Goose bumps sprang up all over my skin. "Otherwise, they may be your last. And I think you know exactly how well I keep my promises in that regard."

I swallowed. "Fuck. You."

The knife tip pierced my skin. I shuddered as a drip of blood slipped down my throat.

"Try again."

Jude stood in front of the bedroom door, arms crossed while he waited.

"I'm laughing because...well, there is a safe. And yes, it's in there. But only one person can open it." I started giggling now, not even caring about the threat of the stupid knife. It would serve him right anyway if he sliced my throat before I was done talking. "You need his fingerprints. Don't you see? If you want that evidence, only one person can get it for you, and you've...oh my God, you killed him!" I was practically choking on laughter now. It was either that or faint. "Because you did, didn't you? Eric is probably bleeding out. You stupid fucking morons, you killed your only chance at getting into the safe that contains literally every piece of evidence against you!"

By the time I finished, I was so delirious with anger and frustration and maybe even some elation that finally this was the end that I started to cackle like a witch. Because even though this certainly wasn't the end I wanted, Eric had still found a way to do exactly what I would have done in his shoes, had I had the chance. Stick it to the man, even on my way down.

"What is she talking about?" Carson demanded. "Hermes, you said his safe was easily opened."

"Well, the one in Boston was a joke," Jude replied, though he didn't look so smug anymore.

My laughter was now full-on hysterical. "You fools. You are the ones who are so, so stupid. He already knew he had no privacy. He *knew* would do this! So he had that stupid thing installed beside our bed that only takes his fingerprints. That thing is state-of-the-art. I—oh God! I can't stop!"

"That's enough!" Carson barked. "Hermes, go find the safe. If we can't open it, we'll just take it with us. We'll dispose of this one on our way out of the country. Daughter or not, she's a liability, and I can't have it." He jerked my hands behind my back and quickly knotted something that felt like silk around them. "I would have liked to finish the job in Korea, you know. It was...cathartic...in a way. You see, I came to terms with the fact that you yourself are tainted, much less worthy of carrying my grandchild. Better we do away with you along with your wretched husband."

I wrenched my head around, and spat in Carson's face as hard as I could. Then, of course, I immediately received another harsh slap.

"That is quite enough!" Carson roared. He turned to Jude, his stupid, hooked-nosed face red with anger. "Jude! Get the safe, and let's go!"

Jude nodded and turned to the bedroom door. I quieted. Fuck. This was really it.

"It's his fault for thinking the society would come to him in the first place, Titan," Jude said as he opened the door. "Not when they've been loyal to you for years."

"No." Eric stepped out of our bedroom. "They've been loyal to the society. It's a very different thing."

"Ahh!" I screamed at the sound of his voice.

"What in the hell!" Jude shouted.

Brandon jumped out from the room as well, and in a sudden rush, Jude was locked in a vicious full-nelson that sounded awfully like it broke something.

"Fuck!" he screamed through a face contorted with pain. "That's my arm!"

Brandon just turned him around, and just as viciously, slammed Jude's head into the doorframe. He immediately crumpled to the floor, unconscious.

"Slimy motherfucker," he muttered, his Boston accent thick and unfettered as he stepped over Jude's body. "You're lucky it was just your arm."

"Eric?" I asked, hardly able to believe what I was seeing. "Brandon? You're...you're here?"

Eric walked further into the room, hands behind his back like he was out for a stroll.

"Hey, gorgeous," he said, his gaze lighting on me warmly. "I'm sorry I had to leave you on your big night. I just...well, I knew this one here wouldn't be able to resist if he thought you and my mother were alone." He narrowed his eyes at Carson. "Where is she, by the way?"

My hands were jerked behind me again, and the knife at my throat found new purchase. Carson practically growled. "Left to her own defenses after my daughter foolishly decided to attempt heroism." He tsked loudly, like I had spilled juice instead of sacrificing myself. Granted, Anton wasn't much of a comfort, but he was hurt, and he *did* have his orders. "Heather was always easy to scare into submission. She's been quiet for more than twenty years. I'm sure tonight will give me twenty more."

Eric just glared at us both. "Let her go, Carson. And maybe you'll get out of here alive."

I could feel the sallow curve of Carson's smile against my temple. He smelled like old men's cologne, far too much bourbon, and something else that was almost medicinal. Pills and plastic.

"I don't think so," he said. "You think I have any scruples when it comes to my so-called 'daughter'? She and her mother have been the stain on my life's work. She's already proven that she'd beyond redemption. If you want to save her life, you'd better run along and get me everything that's in that safe of yours."

To my surprise, Eric just cocked his head. "Oh? And what do you think you'll want from there?"

But Carson was done with the repartee. "Just get it!" he shouted. "Whatever godforsaken things you keep in there are coming with me! Notes. Photographs. Your ridiculous poetry." He sneered. "No true daughter of mine would fall in love with such a whiny little Nancy. It should have been enough to write her off from the start."

"Right," I snapped. "Because you don't have the slightest flair for drama, do you, Pops?"

"Jesus Christ," Brandon muttered to himself, obviously appalled by my terrible self-restraint.

"Jane." Eric's voice was even. "Hush." He was stock-still as he spoke to Carson. "I keep a lot of things in that safe, Carson. Poetry, yes. Documentation, plenty. I also keep protection."

And then, to my combined shock and horror, he raised a gun from behind his back and pointed it straight at Carson.

"Holy shit," I said. "What in the hell is that?"

"It's a gun, Jane," Eric said, like he was speaking to a four-year-old. "A Beretta M-9, the standard issue for the U.S. military. As Carson undoubtedly knows, given how cozy he is with the armed forces."

"You wouldn't, Triton," Carson said. "You're all bluster, just like your good-for-nothing father. Jacob was a joke, and so are you. Do you have any idea how easy it was, pushing him off the boat? How simple? It was him or me, and when it came down to it, he couldn't do it. He had me. He could have just..." " He tipped his head. "So I made the decision for him."

For a half-second, the gun shook. I flinched.

"Eric," I whispered. "Put the gun down." It was fucking unnerving. The saying "looking down the barrel of a gun" carried a whole new meaning.

"Jane," he replied without moving his gaze from Carson. "Please shut up."

I opened my mouth to argue—even then, I was arguing!—but managed to shut it as ordered. After all, I wasn't super interested in being accidentally shot in the face.

"Eric, man," Brandon tried to put in, "maybe you should—"

"Brandon, you too."

"Triton."

"Carson. Titan. Whatever the fuck name you want to go by. I only have one, and it's not the one you gave me after an impotent son of a sea god. My name is Eric Sebastian Franklin Stallsmith de Vries. You killed my fiancée. You murdered my child. You have tormented and kidnapped my mother and my wife. And now you finally admit that yes, you killed my father."

"So prepare to die," I whispered to myself in a fake Spanish accent.

Good one, kiddo. I could practically feel my dad's smile behind me, calling from the dead. He always did like the *Princess Bride.* Jesus, we were inappropriate together, even when one of us was completely imagined. It was like being the person who laughs at a funeral, except it was my own potential execution, and I was giggling with memories of my dead father.

"Shut up!" Carson hissed.

"Go on, Carson," Eric said. "Give me one good reason why I should let you live. Because right now, I can't think of a single one."

The seconds ticked by. My gazed darted between Eric at the door, Brandon beside the wall, Carson's feet, and back to Eric.

"All right," Carson said softly. "How's this? You won't do it. You're a coward, just like your father. Things get hard, and you run away. From the time you were a child, you let people push you around. Tell you where to live. You've fooled yourself into thinking you made a life on your own, but look at you. One call from the great Celeste de Vries, and you came running. You might want to pull that trigger, but you and I both know it's never"—he jerked on my hands —"going"—another jerk—"to happen."

Eric's throat tightened visibly. The muscle in his jaw started to tick.

Like a bomb, I recalled. Ready to explode.

"Aren't I right?" Carson asked one last time. The knife at my throat pressed in further, choking me. "Aren't. I. Right?"

"Eric," I wheezed.

Eric blinked, as if shaken out of a trance by my voice. And then, with the smooth lightning movements of a cat, he raised the gun and shot John Carson directly between the eyes.

I screamed. The hand at my throat fell away along with the body of the man who claimed he was my father. Blood streamed all over the shining floors, so dark it was almost black.

"Holy shit," Brandon whispered as he glanced down at the body, then over to Jude's still-unconscious form.

"Eric." My voice was a ghost as I twisted around, drops of my father slipping down my cheek. My hair, my face, everything was wet. Wet with...him. "Oh, Eric. What did you just do?"

"His reason wasn't good enough.'"

Eric held the gun in the air long after the echo of its shot had faded away. By the time he dropped it, his hand was shaking, and the gun fell to the floor. Then he looked up at me and promptly fell to his knees.

"Eric!" My voice was barely audible. Then I realized that I was falling too, or maybe just tripping in my scramble to reach him. But reach him I did, across the blood-splattered rug, where I launched into him. His arms wrapped around me, and he unbound my wrists, moving as if in a trance.

"Eric," I cupped his face. "Holy shit, babe, what did you do?"

His eyes found mine, dazed, like someone had just landed a punch. "What I had to. I protected us."

He fell back against the doorframe, clutching me to his chest, unwilling to let me look back at the crime scene of our living room. There was a hardness in his voice I had never heard before.

"Jane! Eric!"

We all jerked our heads up at the sudden clamor downstairs. Voices shouting, fists pounding at the door.

"The guards," Eric said. "They've been waiting for us."

"So Tony wasn't accosted at the gala?"

"No, he was," Eric said. "But the others waited with us. I knew..." He sighed. "I knew they would come here. Just like I knew they would take you." He stroked my cheek. "I'm so sorry, pretty girl. I just couldn't see any other way."

"Eric!"

The other two members of our security thundered into the room, followed by, to my surprise, Matthew Zola.

"Oh, fuck," said Clay, one of the guards, as he took in the scene.

"Get Letour secured," Eric ordered. Brandon immediately went to help the two guards do just that. "Where's the Russian?"

"In custody," Zola said. "We found him with Heather two blocks from the museum. You were right. Jane sacrificed herself to save your mom."

Zola looked from us to the crime scene and back again. Then, without hesitation, he pulled out his phone and dialed.

"This is Matthew Zola, Assistant DA for the Brooklyn office," he said as he stared at the crime scene. "There's been an incident at 17 West Seventy-Sixth Street, Apartment 4. Two men wanted by the CIA and the NYPD have been located. We need help."

Eric and I watched, astounded, as Zola continued to rattle off directions to what must have been the police. After Zola put his phone away, he turned to us.

"Boss." Tony stepped inside. "Your mother is safe. We grabbed the Russian outside of the park."

I deflated with even more relief, although I was starting to shake.

Tony gave me a rueful glance. He took one look at the crime scene, walked across the room and, and picked the gun off the ground, stepping over John Carson's bleeding body like it was nothing more than an errant railroad track. Zola, Eric, and I all watched as our head of security meticulously cleaned the weapon with his shirt cuff, then, just as carefully, wrapped his hand around the grip, placing his fingers on the trigger. He pointed it at the body once more and pulled the trigger, though the chamber was empty.

I jerked, though he was essentially only pantomiming. It seemed unnecessary. Eric, also started, like the sound of the gunshots awakened him from some horrid trance.

"Tony," he said. "Don't—"

"I had to shoot him," Tony interrupted. "He was trying to hurt you and Mrs. de Vries. It's my job. I had no choice."

"Christ," Zola muttered.

"Tony," I said weakly. "You're not a cop. You don't have to—"

"It's what I would have done," Tony interrupted evenly. "Please. The DA here called the cops. That's our story, and I'm sticking to it."

"Well, I'm not." Eric held me even tighter, like he was afraid to let me go. In the distance, I could already hear sirens.

But before I could stop him, he gently set me aside, then pushed himself up from the floor. He crossed to Tony and gently removed the gun from the big man's hands.

"I appreciate it, Tony," he said. "But you've helped enough tonight. And it's my weapon. It's my family. It's my right to defend them."

Tony looked like he wanted to argue back, but after perceiving Zola's disapproving expression and my own visible horror, he seemed to relent. He gave a brief, curt nod and stepped back. "Understood."

Eric returned to me. I was stranded in the corner, my father's blood drying on my hair and skin. But Eric's gaze held me fast.

"Jane," he said in a voice that was finally starting to tremble. "Like the air I breathe."

Red and blue lights flashed outside our windows.

I sucked in a deep breath. "Like the water I drink," I whispered back.

Eric's eyes closed when the knocks downstairs sounded.

"All right," he said to Zola, Tony, and the rest of the security team. "Let them up. Let them see everything this man has brought to my doorstep."

THIRTY-EIGHT

It took me months to stop expecting that every knock at the door was the police, there to cart Eric away on murder charges. Or, even worse, some random member of the Janus society, which I found aptly named for a two-faced god.

But after the initial inquiry, which, yes, lasted weeks, John Carson's death was in fact determined self-defense. No charges were brought, except, of course, those against Jude Letour and on Anton Mikhailov for abduction and aggravated assault. The states attorneys of Connecticut and New Hampshire got in on the game too with several counts of murder.

Considering the laissez-faire handling of Eric's case by pretty much all parties involved, I couldn't help but wonder if there were quite a few folks out there happy to be out from under the thumb of that sychophant.

Eric and I, however, weren't quite as easily healed. Surprise! Turns out you can't just have your biological father shot in the head all over you and be magically okay. Nor can you do the shooting, apparently, and walk away unscathed.

Nightmares, flashbacks, anxiety attacks, the increased instinct to self-harm. You name it, I had it, all under the nice big umbrella of PTSD. Just in that first week alone, I scrubbed my skin raw, convinced I still bore the stains of John Carson's blood (and, if we're being totally honest, other parts) imprinted into my skin.

So, it took months of therapy, both the formal kind in a doctor's office, as well as the special sorts we administer to each other, to get to a place where neither of us jumped at every strange sound. Where I didn't need three extra deadbolts on our door. Where Eric didn't sleep with a loaded gun on his nightstand. We left the apartment on the Upper West Side and actually moved in with Heather for a while, citing safety in numbers. Yu-na, who had safely remained with Skylar during that terrible night, put off her return to Chicago and took Heather's basement apartment (the one previously used for staff).

Heather seemed... well, she seemed happy to have us all, like a ghost coming back from the dead. Horace, her jubilant elf of a husband, twittered around us like a hummingbird when he was around at all, and I watched as Eric slowly rebuilt his relationship with his mother. And I, yes, rebuilt the one I had with my own.

Spring turned to summer, then summer turned to fall, and eventually, winter was just around the corner. One day, I woke up without sweat on my brow or Eric shaking beside me. That day turned to several. And eventually, almost all of them.

That's called healing, peanut, Dad would say in the back of my mind whenever I considered what was happening.

Whatever, goofball, I'd think right back before getting out of bed to join Eric and one of our mothers for coffee in the strange new routine.

But routines don't always fit. Nor are they meant to last forever.

One morning at the beginning of November, I entered the kitchen to find two strange things:

Eric, first of all, drinking tea.

And my mother, speaking to him solemnly, with her hand on top of her suitcase.

They both turned. I didn't even have to ask what was going on.

"I suppose I shouldn't be surprised," I said. "She did say she'd get you to drink green tea before she left."

My mother looked entirely too pleased with herself. "It's better for you than coffee," she said, mostly to him, for what was probably the tenth time.

Eric just took a sip of his tea, looking like he was planning to toss it down the drain the second she turned around.

I ignoring the suitcase-shaped elephant in the room, and poured myself a cup of the coffee that, thankfully, had still been put through Eric's science-experiment- looking contraption.

"I'll take a cup of joe, thanks," I said.

"Jane."

I turned around. For the first time in months, I realized my mother looked...normal. Gone were the dark circles under her eyes, the slightly shriveled look about her that must have been rooted in fear. Her hair, short, black, and tamed to a perfect bob, was newly dyed. She wore a full face of makeup and her favorite blue tunic sweater over a comfortable pair of matching indigo pants. She was the solid, coordinated mother I knew, and her sharp, dark gaze ran straight through me.

I sighed. "Want to walk in the park, *Eomma*? Do you have time before your flight?"

She pressed her lips together. She always did hate it when I antic-ipated her announcements. My mother had as much a flair for drama as I did.

I suppose I came by it honestly, after all.

"Yes," she said finally. "Let me get my coat."

WINTER HAD NEARLY ARRIVED in New York, almost a month early. Halloween had felt particularly ghoulish this year when a massive storm swept through the city, knocking every orange- and red-hued leaf from the trees while a wind howled between skyscrapers and brownstones alike.

Much more trick than treat if you asked me.

Today, though still cold, the weather was giving us a bit of reprieve with blue skies and air that was nearly crisp enough to see my breath. New Yorkers were out and about, taking advantage of the sunny skies with the urgency of squirrels getting their last nuts in storage before the heavy snows fell.

My mother and I walked into the park, ambling around the paths. This had become a habit of ours over the last several months, just walking around the park together for a bit of exercise. We didn't talk —actually, it was one of the only times my mother didn't have something to say to me about my life or lack of direction. Again and again, she had continued to pressure me to decide. Decide on a job. Decide on a career. Decide on...something. Anything.

Until now, apparently. Now that she was leaving.

"*Eomma*," I started as we wandered around the back side of the Central Park Zoo.

"I want you to know," she interrupted me. "I think your father would approve."

I blinked. "What?"

She looked at me. She was wearing her favorite puffy coat, the one that made her look like a plum-colored Michelin man. "Of school. The fashion."

I glanced at her, then pushed up my glasses, unsure of how, exactly, to respond to that. She hadn't exactly made her disdain for that particular choice a secret over the last couple of months. She thought I should have taken the job Zola offered me. It didn't matter to her that I—and she, by association—now had more money than I would ever know what to do with. I was supposed to be productive.

So this was certainly a significant about-face.

"Eric showed me some of your drawings," she said. "They were very good. There were many of them. You work hard."

I nodded cautiously. Where in the hell was this going?

To my mother's vocal chagrin, I had decided over the summer to apply for the MFA program at New York's Fashion Institute. Cora had practically insisted on it once I got up the nerve to show her my sketches and some of the clothes I'd made. I still had no idea what I was going to do with it, but it felt like a step in the right direction. Eric was completely occupied with his company these days, even telling Skylar a few weeks ago that he was ready to sell his stake in their small firm. He had sold the apartment in the North End a month before that. We would still always visit Boston, but New York was officially home. It was time for us to grow our roots here.

"Um, thank you?"

"He also took me back to the museum. The one with the exhibit you helped with." She glanced at me. "Will you help again?"

I swallowed. "I...well, I have been. But Nina wanted to help with next year's gala since it's more up her alley. French 18th eighteenth-century styles aren't really my thing." I made a face. Yeah, I wasn't super into helping with that one. "Plus, I'm not really into the whole party- planning thing. I really just wanted to be there for the fashion."

"You like to make the clothes."

I nodded. "I do. I love it, actually. But you always knew that, Eomma."

She was quiet for a minute. "My mother liked to make clothes. Like you."

I blinked. This was something I did not know. My grandmother wasn't someone my mother spoke much about. Her history as a poor farmer's daughter in Hwaseong was known to me only alongside her unfortunate history with World War II. Beyond that...not much.

But my mother didn't say any more than that as we continued to walk.

"I never understood why Americans give thanks in November," she remarked finally as we passed a sign advertising some kind of Thanksgiving event at the ice- skating rink. "In Korea, we do it in September. When we actually have the real harvest."

"Maybe they just wanted to wait until all the food was in," I joked. "If the farmers in Illinois were forced to take three days off in the middle of their harvest, they'd probably picket the governor."

Yu-na didn't reply as we walked through the park. Most of the leaves had fallen and melted into the streets with fall's first hard rain the night before. Today the sky was blue again, but it would probably be the last for a while.

"In Korea, everyone goes home for Chuseok. Not just one day, but three. They leave their cities and go to where their family lives. Make a table for their ancestors. Give thanks as a family."

I didn't reply, though I listened curiously. My mother spoke so infrequently about Korea when I was growing up. And while my only visit to the place was stained with the year's traumas, I was still curious about her life there. How she had become the way she was.

"When I was a girl," my mother continued, "it was our home they would come to, my aunts and uncles and cousins. Ji-yeon too. We would spend a day making the table, all the food, to honor our ancestors. It was not much. We were only farmers. But they were good days."

The wind picked up, whistling around our ears like a ghost calling from days past. Both of us pulled our collars up.

"But then my father died," Yu-na said. "His heart was no good. My mother, she had to sell the farm, and then she died too. I was sixteen. I worked in another house for some time before my friend started working with the airline. She was poor, like me. The job paid very well. I would always take the jobs in September, during Chuseok. I had nowhere to go."

I remained silent. I had never heard this story before. All of the family reminiscing from Yu-na and Ji-yeon were either about games they played as children, or things that happened after they came to Chicago. Korea had always been a bit of a mystery.

My mother stopped as we reached the edge of The Pond. It was a familiar view over the large boulder, the top of the Plaza Hotel peeking through the trees. I had seen it in countless movies, postcards, photographs. And yet, I didn't marvel at it the way I used to. I had been in New York long enough that iconic places like this were becoming, well, commonplace.

"When I think of my home," my mother said, almost like she was reading my mind, "I think of those times. The gathering of family. I didn't have it again until I met your father—your real father, Carol. He brought me to his family, welcomed mine too. We made a family together, with you. We were happy. He gave me a home again."

That, I understood. After all, how many times had I considered our Thanksgivings so fondly? The eccentric mix of food and friends.

She turned to face me. "You have home here in New York. With your husband."

Over the last several months, Eric and my mother had circled each other warily. After all, she had been against the marriage from the start. But even Yu-na, as stubborn as she was, couldn't deny everything he had done for us. His willingness to do whatever it took to protect his own. So while it was odd that she hadn't said his name, it was even odder that I didn't feel the need to argue with her.

"Jane," she said. "I want to go home. I want to go to *my* home. You understand?"

"But—" I interrupted myself. I wanted to argue that she didn't have one anymore. That Dad was gone, and even though she had her house back it wouldn't be the same. That I was her daughter, her only real family. Why couldn't she make her home here with me?

But...did she even want to?

Some families are meant to live with each other all the time. Skylar's was a good example. Her grandmother and her father practically lived with her and Brandon. Her siblings, Brandon's parents. Hell, even me, Eric, Zola. They collected friends and family members like...

"Magpies," I murmured to myself.

My mother looked up sharply. "What?"

"Oh, nothing," I replied. "Just thinking about how some people are like that. They collect family members like magpies." I shrugged. "I guess you and Dad were sort of like that."

She peered at me for a moment more, then smiled. Well, as much as my mother ever smiled.

"You know," she said, "that is the national bird of Korea. Magpie."

I smiled that time. "Really?"

Her eyes, so dark, glinted in the late morning sun. And for a moment, I saw something there I had never seen before. Something I only knew because I was finally reaching some measure of it myself.

Peace. She had stayed here for me. Done what she could because she loved me. And now she was leaving. She needed me to love her too.

There you go, Jane Brain. Dad's voice was warm. Kind. Proud.

Instead of fighting her like I once would have, not necessarily because I truly believed we needed to live together, but more to be right, I hugged her. I wrapped my arms around her small, compact body. She was still for a moment. And then she hugged me back.

When I released her, both of our eyes were shining. But neither of us wanted to argue. Not anymore.

"We'll come for Thanksgiving," I said. "Maybe you can show me how to make a table for the ancestors. Dad too."

She swiped under her eye, the sole evidence of the fact that she really did miss my father terribly. "Yes. He would have liked that."

THIRTY-NINE

Eric and I drove my mother to the airport soon after we returned to the house. Well, our driver did while we sat in the back with her and listened to her jabber about her plans to remodel the house in Evanston. Ji-yeon was going to move in with her there, but she would keep my room for us. It was obvious how happy she was to be going home at last.

"Tell me when you hear back from the school," she told me over and over again as we approached JFK.

I swallowed. "Okay, I will. If I even get in."

"We'll celebrate at Christmas," Eric said as he gave her a brief hug and a kiss on the cheek. "She's a shoo-in."

"Or Thanksgiving, maybe?" she replied.

He glanced at me, and I shrugged.

"We're going," I said. "Get ready to eat a lot of turkey and Korean food."

Eric blinked, then nodded. "I can handle that."

With one last hug, we watched my mother disappear into JFK. Eric shuttled me back into the car and held me securely while he checked his emails, realizing somehow that I wasn't in the mood to talk. We had gotten better at that too, over the last several months. The just being together. No chatter. No repartee. Just...us.

As we drove into Manhattan, Eric put his phone away. "Are you up for another walk through the park? Might be nice before the weather turns again."

I shrugged. "Sure, I guess." There wasn't much to do at the house now that I'd gotten my application in anyway.

Tony dropped us off near the East Seventy-Second Street entrance, and Eric and I strolled easily hand in hand, past the Bethesda Fountain and The Lake, where even in the chilly weather, tourists were taking out rowboats under the blue sky.

"I kind of like the park like this," I said as I swung Eric's arm back and forth. "Is that weird that I prefer it without all the foliage and tourists? A little moodier? A little barren, maybe?"

My choice of words wasn't by design, but we both heard the double entendre. After all, we'd decided to eschew all forms of contraceptives about three months prior. After finding me holding my belly and rocking in my sleep one too many times, Eric had gotten up one night and thrown out every condom we had, then made love to me from four different positions until the sun came up. Both of our therapists cautioned against expanding our family too soon while we were both still recuperating. *Babies aren't Band-Aids*, mine said succinctly.

But neither of us bought anymore condoms, and I refused my doctor's offers of birth control. Every twenty-eight days, however, we were still disappointed.

Eric brought my hand to his lips. "Don't worry," he said, his breath warm against my hand. "When it's meant to happen, it'll happen."

What if it doesn't? I didn't say it, but I wanted to ask. Though my doctor assured me that nothing had been permanently damaged last February, sometimes I wasn't so sure.

Eric shrugged, as nonchalant as ever. But while that imperviousness would have once infuriated me, sometimes I found it comforting.

It's useful being with someone who literally knows he can handle just about anything life throws at him. The little things, somehow, didn't matter so much.

"I have something for you," he said, stopping near Strawberry Fields. Next to us was the famous stone, just across from John Lennon's former building. Imagine, it read, to any passersby who might need it.

And isn't that what we had always done together, when fear and pride didn't get in our way? With Eric, I had found I could imagine almost anything, and he would support me in any way. I had found the one man in the world unafraid of a woman like me. My strengths, my weaknesses, my ambitions, my fears. He embraced them all, and what's more, he genuinely loved me for them.

I turned to face him, noting again just how stupid handsome he was. He was dressed down for the weekend in his favorite navy wool jacket, a tailored wool shirt, and a pair of gray felt pants that somehow made his long legs even longer over leather brogues. Very Swedish Esquire, particularly considering the way the afternoon light was now playing over his cropped blond hair and the light stubble he allowed to grow on the weekends.

But it was never his basic attractiveness that always drew me to him like a moth to a flame. Together we burned, of course. It was a burn I craved. I needed. But aside from sex, aside from looks, aside from charisma. Underneath all of that was a man who was quietly one of the best people I had ever known.

Honest. Pensive. Genuine.

Eric.

"What in the world," I wondered as I traced the line of his jaw with one finger, "did I ever do to deserve you?"

Eric smiled. His full lips spread shyly, then more confidently, with that curious effect of completely transforming his entire face.

"You know," he said as he allowed me to play over his chin, nose, cheekbones, lips, "I think that pretty much every day. As soon as I wake up next to you."

"You are the corniest," I whispered, though there was no joke in my tone.

Eric captured my hand again and pressed a long, slow kiss to my palm. "Come on, Lefferts."

I followed him out of the park and into our old neighborhood, across Central Park West and eventually down West Seventy-Sixth. He stopped in front of our building. We hadn't officially decided we weren't coming back here. But neither of us had voiced a single desire to do so in the last several months.

Eric pulled a key out of his pocket and handed it to me. "Here," he said. "If you want it."

For a long time, I stared at the key. It was different than the old one. Thicker. Brass, not silver. It was attached to a keychain with a mermaid etched onto it.

Ariel, I thought to myself, clutching it for a moment.

"Say the word, and we'll sell it," Eric said, nodding at the building. "But I thought...before we do that...you should see what it looks like...finished."

As his words registered, my mouth fell open. "Finished...you mean, you..."

"Accelerated the remodel?" he finished for me. "Yeah. It's amazing what you can get done with three separate crews and a willingness to pay overtime." He glanced up at the townhouse, which I now realized no longer had the buzzers marking multiple units.

I swallowed. I hadn't been back here since May. Not since we had removed our things and ran away from the bloodshed that occurred there. I didn't know what I would find.

"Okay," I said. "Show me."

THE HEAVY OAK door closed behind us and echoed through the newly emptied space. All the sounds of outside evaporated behind triple-paned windows.

I stared at my brand-new surroundings. The stairs were still here, but nearly every non-bearing wall dividing the old apartments on the first floor had been ripped out, creating a uniquely open-concept living space over shining wood floors. A kitchen gleamed from the back, leading into a general dining area, and a living room that would lend itself to being arranged around a huge stone fireplace near the front. This wasn't a stodgy, traditional home that seemed lifted from an Edith Wharton novel, the way Heather's home felt. Nor was it an icebox, full of chrome and glass, like Eric's old place in Boston. It was spacious, modern, but clean and still comfortable.

Our footsteps echoed across the wood floors.

"There's a bathroom by the kitchen," Eric said, "and a patio out back that also leads to the downstairs. I waited on hiring a landscaper to see what you wanted to do with that."

"What's downstairs?" I wondered. This was what happened when you turned an entire apartment complex into a single house, apparently. Floor upon floor of...what?

Eric took me by the elbow and guided me toward a set of rear stairs that led down to a surprisingly airy basement, which included a small kitchen, a bathroom, and several spare rooms. "Right now, it's a blank slate. A couple of bedrooms if we want live-in accommodations for the help."

"For the help," I repeated. "Does that sound as obnoxious to you as it does to me?"

Eric chuckled. "Maybe a little. To be honest, I was thinking it would be a good space for a startup business. Like a design studio."

I gulped, though anticipation prickled my spine. "Don't you think it's a little early for that? We don't even know if I'm even getting into that program."

Eric turned to me with a spark in his eyes that matched my own. "I think you're unbelievably talented, and so does the editor-in-chief of the biggest fashion magazine in the world. The world is your oyster, Lefferts. You could make this space your pearl. Whatever you want." He tipped his head. "You helped me figure out what I was meant to be. I just want the same for you, gorgeous."

I was quiet for a long time. And, I found, not quite ready to make a decision on that front. But the fact that he was offering this meant the fucking world.

"Show me the rest," I said.

Eric's calm facade betrayed nothing. "All right. Come on."

The rest of the house was an equally beautiful blank slate. Another floor full of empty bedrooms that I could imagine as offices as easily as children's rooms. Eric didn't comment either way, but I was sure he felt the same.

He led me to the floor where our former apartment had been. The living area still had the same hardwoods, the same fireplace, the same windows that looked out toward the park. But that was it. The walls were empty. The furniture was totally gone.

"It's very...white," I said, though I mentally smacked myself for saying something so inane. Yes, it was white. But it was also gorgeous. Clean.

"I told them to make it a canvas," Eric said as he trailed me. He was watching me, of course, not really looking at the apartment.

"Where is all our furniture?"

"Well, some of it wasn't really...usable."

I cringed. It was true. That night had been very...messy. In some of my worse dreams, I remembered just how messy it was to have someone—specifically my biological father—shot at close-range in my living room. There wasn't a whole lot that went unscathed.

Now, everything in it had been removed. And the rest of the apartment was completely different. Nearly all of the bedrooms and the kitchen had been demolished so that now the floor primarily consisted of a single huge bedroom, a walk-in closet that could house about ten hibernating bears (much less the contents of our combined wardrobes), and the biggest bathroom I had ever seen.

"Eric," I said as I explored the new space. "You turned most of our apartment into a single master suite? That's obscene."

I placed my palms on the wide marble countertop that spread from one end of the room to the other, the length of at least two king-sized beds, above which pristine mirrors ran the length of the walls. This bathroom alone was bigger than my old apartment in Chicago.

A pair of hands encircled my waist. Eric's lips touched my collarbone.

"I told you," he said against my pulse. "I need room to spread you out."

Without waiting for me to respond, he turned me swiftly, then lifted me up and set me on the counter. It really was enormous. Solid. Unbreakable.

He set his hands on either side of my hips and looked at me, unflinching. Unwilling to let me look away either. But when he spoke, it wasn't what I expected. Instead, it was poetry, which I hadn't heard him recite in a very long time:

> *Had I the heavens' embroidered clothes,*
> *Enwrought with golden and silver light,*
> *The blue and the dim and the dark clothes*
> *Of night and light and the half light.*

I tipped my head. "Well, that's beautiful. Is that yours or..."

Eric shook his head, a little bashful. I knew he had been writing a lot over the last several months, but he hadn't shared anything with me. Yet.

"No, no, that's Yeats, of course," he said.

"Ah. Your favorite. I should have known."

"That poem...it always reminded me of you. All about the fabric of heaven. His lover makes clothes, just like you. And all he wants to do is give her everything he can if it would make her happy. I thought of it last year, when I bought you all those textiles from Milan."

I tipped my head, a smile playing across my lips. "It is fitting. How does the rest of it go?"

Eric took a deep breath, then stepped closer to me as he recited the rest:

I would spread the clothes under your feet:
But I, being poor, have only my dreams

He stepped between my legs, then unbuttoned my coat.

"I have spread my dreams under your feet," he continued as he pushed it over my shoulders and helped me remove my arms. "Tread softly because you tread on my dreams."

By the time he finished, the room around us had faded. His silvery eyes, as celestial as the heavens evoked in the poem, shone with intensity, lust, and, mostly, love. I couldn't see anything but him as he cupped my cheeks.

"Happy anniversary, pretty girl," he said as he gazed openly at me.

I blinked. "What?"

His mouth quirked again into a sly half smile. "It's November second. One year ago...we got married. Well, the first time, anyway." His thumb hooked lightly on my lower lip and pulled a little before releasing it. "It didn't really go the way I imagined when I met you, but I wouldn't take it back for a second."

"You imagined marrying me when you met me?"

Eric didn't look away. Not even for a second. "Jane," he said softly as he pushed a lock of hair out of my face. "I knew I'd spend the rest of my life with you the second I saw your bright blue hair in the middle of the Harvard lawn. You woke me up, gorgeous. Just like you do every single day."

"Eric," I whispered, searching for a response. Even now, even after all this time, the man simply overwhelmed me in the best possible way.

"What do you say?" Traces of vulnerability crept into his stolid features. "Are you ready to come home, or..."

He was clearly scared to articulate the other option. That we would abandon the house we had worked so hard to make our own once before. Find someplace new, someplace unmarred by the traumas of the past.

But the fact was, those pains would follow us anywhere we went. Life, death, love, hate. They imprinted permanently on your heart, leaving patterns as eternal and terrifying as any actual person or thing. I considered all the years I had done my best to run from this man, whose intensity speared me to the core, but whose love doubled every dimension I knew.

That was when I knew my answer without a single doubt.

"I think," I said, "that we should christen our new-old home. Properly, this time."

Eric grinned. Fully grinned, the kind that made his entire face transform from a staid Upper East Sider, born and bred for poise and comportment, into a walking fucking sunbeam.

"Right fucking now," he agreed.

Before I could reply, he set his mouth on mine, slipped his tongue past my waiting lips, and let our bodies say naturally what I struggled to say with mere language.

Because for all of the hard times we had, this would always be easy. There were so many ways to speak between souls. Words were one. Bodies were another.

"Off," Eric murmured as his hands slipped under my sweater.

"Off," I agreed as I shucked his coat, then yanked at the buttons of his shirt.

It didn't take long until our clothes lay all over the bathroom floor, and I had six feet two inches of glorious, golden god of a man leaning over me, looking at me with a delicious expression that was more devilish than celestial.

"I have one more gift for you," he said as he reached for his jacket.

I leaned back against the mirror, happy to put my own body on display. Mostly because he seemed to take as much joy out of admiring my skinny limbs as I did in his lean, stacked muscle. Lord, he really was a work of art.

He stood up with a small velvet bag in one hand, which he turned over to pour a chain of some sort into his palm.

I sat forward curiously. "What's that? Jewelry, eh?" I winked at him. "First anniversary is paper or clocks, you know. You're going a bit overboard, but I suppose I shouldn't complain considering I didn't even remember."

Eric smirked. "I guess I should correct myself. The house is your present, pretty girl. This one is mine."

"Oh?"

He nodded, and his gaze darkened as he held up the chain. "That's right. Now, place your hands behind you. There's nowhere to restrain you in here...yet. So you'll just have to do what you're told."

That familiar thrum of excitement grew in my belly, but obediently, I moved my hands behind me so my chest was thrust out.

"Beautiful," he murmured as his eyes drew over my body.

I squirmed. "You going to do something about it?"

His hand found my breast in a short, quick slap that made me gasp. Out of pure desire, of course.

"What do you think?" he asked as he pushed my legs apart so he could step between them. He was already hard, the length of him resting against my thigh. I edged forward, but he shook his head. "Not yet, gorgeous. Not yet. First..."

He held up the chain, which was bright gold and extremely delicate. At each end hung something that looked like gold tweezers. I grinned.

"Well, either you're going to play some messed-up version of Operation on me, or those are the prettiest damn nipple clamps I have ever seen, Mr. de Vries."

"Have you ever used any?" he asked. "We haven't."

I shrugged. "Once. A long time ago." I took my chance and leaned forward enough that I could whisper in his ear. "He didn't know what the hell he was doing, though."

Unlike most men, who might get jealous or refuse to hear about previous lovers, Eric just chuckled with satisfaction. "Well, of course he didn't. He wasn't me."

"Someone thinks a lot of himself."

"Am I wrong?" The knowingness all over his face might have been maddening.

"Why don't you get started?" I asked. "Since you've got such a reputation to uphold now?"

Eric's smirk deepened. "You got it."

I watched openly as he fastened one of the tweezer-like parts to my right nipple.

"You know, in some of the French courts, they used to wear dresses cut under their breasts so women could show off jewelry like this." I turned my chest back and forth, admiring the chain as it swung lightly. "Do you think that's the way I should go for the Met Gala next year? It is Marie Antoinette-themed, you know."

Eric's eyes burned, whether at the sight of my pinched nipples or the idea of me parading around society with them looking like this, I wasn't sure. He tugged lightly on the chain, then kissed me slowly, tongue twisting around mine until I was fully out of breath.

"I think for now, the only person who gets to see your nipples is me," he said, giving another swift tug that made me gasp again.

His other hand wrapped around my ass, pulling me to the edge of the counter so that his cock was perfectly aligned with me. He pressed his thumb over my clit, then drifted it down, slipping it in and out of me, then back up.

"Look at that," he murmured as he did it again. "In a hurry, aren't you?"

I couldn't lie. The second he pulled that chain out of the bag, I was turned on. Hell, the second he kissed my neck, I was basically ready to go.

He kissed me then, taking my lower lip between his teeth and worrying it slightly while he tugged on the chain again. And again.

I moaned as his cock slipped between my legs.

"Holy shit." My breath was already choked. "Did you—you didn't, did you?"

Eric pulled back. "Did what, pretty girl?"

I looked down at where we were nearly joined. "It isn't possible that you had the contractors build this counter at exactly this height so you could…"

Eric tugged again on the chain. I hissed at the minor pain and burst of pleasure.

"I think you will find," he said as he just barely slid in, "that nearly every surface in this house"—a few inches more—"is constructed so you"—just one more—"will be perfectly"—kiss —"accessible."

My thighs spread wider as he pushed in completely, finding his seat within my darkest places.

I arched, clamped nipples rubbing against his hard chest while my head dropped back.

His teeth found my neck with a growl. "Fucking hell, you look hot like that."

The sound of him losing a bit of that careful control only made me that much hotter.

"Fuck me," I whispered. "Please, Eric. I need it."

He pulled out slowly, then thrust in, just as slowly. Another pull on the chain. Another suck on my neck.

"Eric…" My voice wheedled. Begged. "Please."

"Shit." Clearly the sound of my begging wasn't helping with that control. "Say it again. Tell me you need it."

Another slow pull. Another equally tortured push. Chain. Mouth. Rinse and repeat.

"Eric!" I shouted as he sucked on my neck. "Oh my God, pleeaaassee!"

"Fuck, yes!" And then, like he couldn't help himself, he pounded into me, those measured movements replaced by forceful thrusts that threatened to undo us both in as much time.

"Say it, Jane," he ordered me. "Tell me what you need."

I was dying to touch him, but I wouldn't dare go against his orders. After all, that was the fun of it. The torture of having to do what I was told for once. The gleam in Eric's eyes as he waited for me to break.

But this time I wouldn't. This time I wanted to be perfect. Just for him.

I stuck my chin out and licked my lips, closing my eyes just to feel the delicious pressure of him as he filled me, again and again.

"You," I cried as I took everything he wanted to give me. "I need you."

"Fuck!" Eric's shout bounced off the stone surfaces, and he pulled on the chain again, this time that much harder.

"Oh!" My eyes flew open. What the hell was happening.

But even as he seemed to get even bigger within me, Eric slowed his movements, clearly conscious of what was happening. He started to focus on a rhythm he was setting with the chain. Short, deft tugs in time with his hips.

"Are you..." He gasped, looking for breath. Clearly he was trying to hold back himself. "Are you close?"

"Am I..." I barely had time to answer him before his thumb brushed over my clit.

"Oh!" I gasped.

Then he pulled off the clamps. The chain dropped to the counter just as sensation flooded my nipples, feeling returning to the slightly distended tips just in time with an orgasm that exploded through the rest of me.

"Eric!" I shouted, grasping for the man since I definitely couldn't keep myself upright.

"Fuck!" he cried as he drove into me for the last and final time.

And then we fell back into the mirror, heaving and driving home, home, home again. Grabbing desperately for each other as we wrung every last solitary sensation out of our bodies. Together.

WE DID IT AGAIN. And again. Once on the counter of the kitchen, just to test Eric's assertion that indeed every surface had been made for us. He was, of course, infuriatingly correct.

After the second time, we collapsed onto the plush carpet of the bedroom, staring at the lone piece of art on the wall: the Gustav Klimt lovers gifted to us from Celeste.

Eric pulled me onto his chest, and I sighed, content to listen to his heartbeat.

"So it's a yes on the apartment?" he wondered as one hand lazily stroked my back. "Do you think we've adequately cleansed it of its ghosts?"

Was that what we were doing? In a way, I supposed he was right. And maybe it had worked. Any trepidation I had had about living here again was long gone by now.

"Do you think," he wondered as he stared up at the box beam ceiling, "do you ever wish you could take it all back? Go back to that day in Chicago when I asked you to go along with this scheme? You could have had a nice life. None of this last year would have happened?"

I set my chin on his chest so I could look up at him. "Are we feeling a mite unsure of ourselves for once, Mr. de Vries?" I won't lie. The petty side of me was a little thrilled by my immovable husband having one of his rare human moments.

Eric rolled onto his side, slipping me off his chest so we were facing each other, then propped his head up with one hand to look at me. "You did hate me an awful lot back then."

"Well, you were kind of a jerk sometimes too. It was like being in love with a brick wall. Totally impervious."

"Come on. I wasn't that bad."

I made a big show of blowing raspberries through my lips, sticking them out like a trumpet.

Eric just stared at me like I was growing horns. "Lefferts, what are you doing?"

"Isn't it obvious?" I asked. "I'm the big bad wolf blowing the house down. Except I can't because it's made of bricks."

"Does that make me one of the three little pigs?"

"No," I replied. "It makes you the brick house. Get it?"

"Ahhh, I see." He laid on his back again, chuckling.

"Okay, okay. Not my best material, I know."

We lapsed into silence, letting my bad jokes and our chuckles filter through the room. I started daydreaming about how I wanted to decorate our mini palace. How I'd shape this room in particular to complement its crown jewel in the Klimt kiss. Our kiss.

"Well?"

I frowned, pulled out of my visions of upholstery and bedrooms sets. "Well, what?"

Eric didn't actually reply. It took me a second to realize that he did actually want me to answer his original question. That even with everything, he still had those moments of uncertainty, just like I did. The thought was incredibly endearing.

All desire to tease abandoned me, and I was left with only the desire to make this man feel as good as he made me feel just about every damn day.

I clasped his cheeks between my hands and brushed his skin with my thumbs.

"Here's the truth," I said. "I don't regret one single solitary fucking thing. Not any of them. Not with you."

Those somber gray eyes sparked with obvious relief. "Yeah?"

I nodded, edging closer. Should I? No, I shouldn't. Now wasn't the time for jokes or the brazenness that tended to get me in trouble.

But then again, it was me we were talking about. And Eric knew that better than anyone. There was no sense in holding back now.

"Well, I might have hated that very first vow," I said honestly as I drew him in for one more kiss. "But, Eric de Vries? I could never hate you."

The End
Or is it?

GRAB AN EXTRA EPILOGUE **to Jane and Eric's story along with a special preview of Nicole's next book here:** www.nicolefrenchromance.com/quicksilverepilogue

YOU CAN ALSO PREORDER *The Other Man*, the first book in Nina and Zola's story here.

WANT SKYLAR **and Brandon's story? Start reading Legally   Yours   FREE   here:** www.nicolefrenchromance.com/spitfire

ACKNOWLEDGMENTS

This might have been one of the hardest books I have ever written. Aside from the rollercoaster of emotion and trauma these characters experienced, I was also dealing with some deeply painful family losses that forced me to delay its release. I could not have finished it without the patience, support, and dedication from the following people:

First of all, my readers. You guys have dealt with my sporadic (at best) presence since June, and your enthusiasm for this story buoyed me. Thank you, thank you, thank you. Words don't even cover my gratitude.

To my alpha and beta readers—Patricia, Danielle, Natalie, Erika, Dawn, and Rebecca. You guys stepped up at the last minute to make this book so, so, so much better. I could NOT have finished it without you.

To my editor and proofreader duo, Emily Hainsworth and Judy Zweifel, thank you for working with the piecemeal nature of the initial manuscript. We did it!

To my other author friends whose ceaseless support means the utter world: Jane, Laura, Kim, Harloe, Claudia, Parker, and

Grahame.and several others. Could NOT do this without you all. Special thanks to Jane for naming the Kostases.

And of course, to my husband, kids, and family. The Dude doesn't always understand what my deadline are, but he sure as hell supports them, and stepped up when life seemed to want to tear me apart. I love you and C to death.

ABOUT THE AUTHOR

Nicole French is a lifelong dreamer, Springsteen fanatic, and total bookworm. When not writing fiction or teaching composition classes, she is hanging out with her family or going on dates with her husband. In her spare time, she likes to go running or practice the piano, but never seems to do either one of these things as much as she should.

For more information about Nicole French and to keep informed about upcoming releases, please:

Visit her website at www.nicolefrenchromance.com/.

Check out Nicole's Goodreads page: www.goodreads.com/authornicolefrench

Want to hook up with other Nicole French readers or interact with the author? Join Nicole's reader group, La Merde.